I0665832

The Ghosts of Benevolence

Mark Randolph Watters

Mark Randolph Watters

The Ghosts of Benevolence

King's Way Press
3721 New Macland Rd.
Suite 200-141
Powder Springs, GA 30157
www.kwp-books.com

ISBN-13: 978-0692717172
ISBN-10: 069271717X

Cover and interior artwork copyright © 2016 by Alex McVey

The Ghosts of Benevolence

For Chris and Kristyn, who chain my ghosts

Mark Randolph Watters

A full moon hung low and mean on the eastern horizon,

 like a wanted poster, its smoky orange stare stoic, stained, fierce, unblinking. Ghostly pockets of fog hovered and expanded over the field, consuming vast stretches of flat farmland and pasture. The chatter and chime of frogs and cicadas signaled the opening movement of the nightly symphony. While day lay down to rest, the haunting of Lance Hawthorne awoke with a rapid blink.

The Ghosts of Benevolence

Ghosts crowd the young child's fragile eggshell mind.

--- Jim Morrison

"Wealthy the spirit
who knows its own flight;

Stealthy the hunter
who slays his own fright;

Blessed the traveler
who journeys the length of the

light."

--- Dan Fogelberg

Mark Randolph Watters

The Ghosts of Benevolence

Mark Randolph Watters

Mark Randolph Watters

The Ghosts of Benevolence

1

"I can't *believe* ..." whispered Lance, stunned, his
warning ignored. *"Now* you've done it!"

Now they would pay.

The boys turned, fleeing, thrusts of thighs launching
their bodies over bushes, fallen trunks, mounds of fire ants,
shadowed obstacles visible only against the grain of dusk.
Legs churned with all their God-given strength. Arms
thrashed aside impediments of vines, branches, thorns.
Broken spider webs wrapped sticky tentacles over their
faces, like traps of nets, pulling. Even the thick air seemed
to push back. The boys burst from a thicket of creekside
scrub, stumbling as they did, and into a clearing of knee-
high grass.

Panting, hands clasped on the tops of their heads,
Lance and Jackson stopped, glanced back, and then scoured
the expanse before them in all directions. They weighed
options, filtered by their panic, mindful their pursuers
thrashed aside the same impediments a few hundred yards
to their rear.

Before them spread a 200-degree arc of remoteness, a
field in the fading light perfect for murder. Jackson bent
over, hands on knees, mouth wide and sucking air.

A full moon hung low and mean on the eastern
horizon, like a wanted poster, its smoky orange stare stoic,

stained, fierce, unblinking. Ghostly pockets of fog hovered and expanded over the field, consuming vast stretches of flat farmland and pasture. The chatter and chime of frogs and cicadas signaled the opening movement of the nightly symphony. While day lay down to rest, the haunting of Lance Hawthorne awoke with a rapid blink.

Streaks of purple and orange sliced across the blood-red backdrop of the western horizon. The familiar stench of sulfur from the stacks of a paper mill upwind drifted through the still air and mixed with the sweetness of petunias in window box gardens; gardenias in full bloom; and the earthy smells of cattle feeding on rye in freshly mown fields, filling the nostrils with an absurd fusion of smells, the scent of the South. Twilight's calm deception cuddled the knolls and fields, knitting another day into the fabric of Sutter County's past.

"You okay, Jackson?"

Jackson wheezed air as hard as his underdeveloped lungs let him. He was in no condition to continue the flight, not at the pace demanded. He could hardly afford not to.

"Gotta ... gotta find a ... place ... place to *hide!*"

Jackson's gasps strangled his words as he glanced rearward, his blood and body begging for oxygen. Neither boy knew the extent of their head start, if any.

Ahead were patches of drought-beaten ferns, honeysuckle, and blackberry, the off-green vegetation weakened and wilted from weeks of moisture deprivation and deadening heat. Realizing the futility of outrunning their pursuers, Lance pointed, thrusting his finger fore and aft, like the connecting rods on the wheels of a steam locomotive, as if to shout without shouting, *"Over there!"*

The boys bent low and scrambled through the field toward one of the thicker patches and took their cover. They camouflaged their bodies as best they could, aware

The Ghosts of Benevolence

each pull of the crackling foliage sounded notice to their pursuers.

Lance Hawthorne and Jackson Willoughby, fingers aquiver, opened slivers between the vines and sandy briars, just enough to afford a view, the obscurity enhanced by the charcoal of twilight. The boys set aside fears of untimely encounters with water moccasins or timber rattlers cooling in the evening air. The present danger overwhelmed all else.

Like pistons, chests heaved from efforts to replenish oxygen expended in the sprint. Their labored breathing may as well have been audio billboards, certain to give them away. Jackson's asthma punctuated their deteriorating situation.

Curses spat from the trio of men chasing the boys, pelting their young minds with the rot of hatred. The voices of their chasers, a drunken cacophony of vengeance and vitriol, drew nearer. Sticks and leaves crunched in the field through which the boys had run. The gray darkness prevented the men from discerning the swaths the boys had beaten through the grass.

The men stopped in the field and listened. Lance stooped low, still as a grass stain. Jackson suppressed the grind of his strained breathing by lying flat on his belly and cupping both hands over his mouth.

"Might as well show yourself, 'cause we're *gonna* git y'all!" one of the men promised, standing not more than twenty feet away. "The more you make us work to find you, the longer we're gonna take to *kill* you."

"*Quiet*, Earl. Listen!" another urged.

The boys, eyes wide, their senses convulsing, lay gripped with an overpowering impulse to spring from their cover and flee. Discovery seemed imminent, a matter of seconds. Jackson and Lance had heard stories of how men such as these dealt with undesirables. The lynching of Raif Toombs two years prior sprang to life in Lance's mind.

Mark Randolph Watters

Lance had become familiar with accounts of the incident while loitering on the steps of Prather's General Store and Dry Goods, chugging Royal Crown Colas and wiling away the lazy mid-days of summer. He feigned disinterest in farmers' porch talk, his straw hat titled over his eyes, but his ears consumed every morsel, the same as his mouth did moon pies. The event grew with embellishment from telling to telling. Still, the images possessed the power of truth and seemed as real to Lance as the burn of summer.

As Lance remembered the tellings, Raif was a penniless field hand, his only possessions the portability of a torn shirt, suspendered denims, a straw hat, a pair of undersized boots, and his name. He had learned neither the skills of persuasion nor had been granted protection of the law. Raif's one true possession, a possession over which he held no sway—his black skin—worked against him like gangrene.

Accused of the offense of 'gazing unseemly' upon the countenance of a white woman, Raif suffered summary backwoods justice. The woman, known fondly as Randy, an affirmed prostitute not averse to the entertainment of men of any race as long as they paid with plentiful, green cash, made her damning accusation.

When word spread that a black man had invaded the space of a white woman, never mind the likes of Randy and from the innocuous, inconclusive point of one hundred yards' distance, certain locals determined to exact a price. Raif soon learned the extent of his debt.

The sun of August, Raif believed, seemed to hover closer over South Georgia than any place on the planet. It gritted its solar teeth and delivered by sheer force of will a heat relentless in its intensity.

Raif had toiled in the peanut fields for better than three hours on that Tuesday morning, chopping weeds around the

The Ghosts of Benevolence

runners that grew in straight rows from horizon to horizon. Sprawling trees along the banks of Pumpkin Creek, along with gray-white clumps of lazy cumulus clouds, provided an occasional oasis of shade. Raif's clothes soaked up his rising sweat and gave him the appearance of a man just stepping from a wash in the creek.

He dropped his hoe to the ground for a moment and removed his hat, to swab his brow, to catch his breath, to minister to blisters bubbling between his thumbs and forefingers christened time and again by the friction of hard work. He swept his forearm across his forehead, stopping rivulets of running sweat.

Like an explosion, a pickup truck burst from the wood line and stormed through the field. Raif turned to run, as if programmed to respond thusly, knowing that no reason was reason enough.

The truck circled Raif one time, two times, three, its tires spinning, spraying dirt, rocks, and uprooted peanuts. Two men jumped from the pickup's bed, grabbed Raif, threw him to the ground, and hog-tied him like a rodeo calf.

The men pulled a burlap seed sack over Raif's thrashing head and secured the sack around his neck with a rope. Tossing him like cordwood into the truck's bed, the men then scrambled into the cab. The driver fishtailed toward Pumpkin Creek, Raif's body rolling and banging from side to side, his screams drowned away by the shouts and laughter, along with which the men intermittently filled the air with empty beer bottles.

Raif's straw hat, dispossessed, rested in the field atop his hoe.

Pumpkin Creek, a winding tributary of the Chagoochee River, flowed wide enough in spots to be a river itself. The men deposited Raif to the ground, creekside. They gave him a beating with bare fists and booted feet, just for fun. A man took chains to Raif, the metal links clanking against

Raif's skull and back, each blow exacted its pound of flesh. Blood soaked the burlap sack like spilled paint.

They dragged him, bleeding and breathing barely, to an ancient oak on the south bank of Pumpkin Creek. Someone flung a hangman's noose over a twisted branch that extended over the water some ten feet above the surface. The rope was looped and tightened around Raif's bloodied neck, his chin touching his chest.

One of the men, in a mockery of judicial formality, spoke.

"Raif Toombs, you have been found *guilty* of havin' your way with a white woman, for which you shall now hang by your neck. Do you wish to address the Almighty before sentence is carried out?"

"Ha, ha. You *funny*, Earl," another man observed, spitting liquid tobacco on Raif's pants, "like he can say *anything*."

Raif, head slumped forward, limp, his body propped up by a man on either side, said nothing. Consciousness had left him, and it was just as well.

"Hang 'im, boys," Earl directed.

The men gripped the rope with a hatred so tight their knuckles whitened.

"Pull!" shouted another.

The men yanked the rope, jerking Raif off the creek bank. Raif's neck snapped like a handful of sticks, his body dangling a few feet above the water's edge. A man tied the pulling end of the rope around the slanted trunk of the oak tree. The men left Raif hanging to rot in the August heat, the rope creaking with the slow rhythm of its swing, emitting the ghostly sound planks of an old house make when walked upon. Maggots and mammals consumed the carrion in a matter of days.

Thus came the porch-talk from the rockers of Prather's General Store and Dry Goods. Lance Hawthorne had little reason to doubt the words echoed by community elders.

The Ghosts of Benevolence

He did not doubt the existence—or the savagery—of the hate exercised in execution of the likes of Raif Toombs.

Lance swung his arm onto Jackson's back, pinning him from flight. *"Shhhhh!"* Lance whispered. "They won't *find* us if we're quiet. An' stop your *fidgetin'!"*

The minutes passed like cold molasses. Lance saw the men, each dressed in the camouflage of hunters, stepping this way and that, heads down. The men whipped the brush with bats and machetes. The low tangle of briars and honeysuckle gave the boys their own camouflage, aided by their dark, soiled jeans and tanned summer skin. Still, Lance knew that one well-placed swing from a bat or machete would exact the same effect as discovery.

A machete blade slashed within inches of Lance's head, tightening a honeysuckle vine across his back, confirming the dead-seriousness of intentions. Providence kept him still.

Lance strained to understand the liquor-fueled conversation spewing from the men. The words were mostly unintelligible, but what struck Lance like indelible jabs of a dagger were the repeated violations of the Third Commandment, hurled his way at home as well by a daddy drunk with homebrew. ·

Ain't it enough, Lance wondered, *that these men're the livin' picture of man's darkest side, like bodies void of souls? Why does God not strike 'em dead, here an' now, simply for their disrespect of His Word, never mind the murder we just seen 'em do?*

Religion and the ways of God bewildered Lance, but he hadn't time now to dwell on it.

Then, as if the torture of bats and machetes were not enough, Lance felt the searing stings of fire ants jabbing his calves and feet. Scores of the insects crawled up and down Lance's legs, inserting their random daggers along their way. The pain burned like the slashes of hickory switches.

Lance could do no less than endure. A single oral acknowledgement of the stings would deliver to the boys a fate far worse. Lance closed his eyes, gritted his teeth and prayed the men would abandon their pursuit, the sooner the better.

"When we *find* y'all," shouted the loudest of the men, a sturdy form lurched forward atop a horse not twenty feet away, "we're gonna cut your heads off, hang 'em from our rear-views!" The leather of his saddle growled as he settled back. "We'll leave your bodies here to *rot!*"

Lance bent lower, his hand pressing Jackson's back, struggling to keep his friend from the suddenness of bolting—or coughing.

"Satchel, bring me your lighter!" the horseman shouted. "Dadgum tooth!"

A lighter delivered, the horseman flicked it bright, touching the flame to his rolled cigarette. The man took a long drag and exhaled.

"Take a look here at this tooth, Satchel," the horseman said, parting his lips and bringing the flame closer to his mouth, smoke spilling forth. "'Bout to fall out, ain't it?"

Lance's eye caught the quick flash of a peculiar gleam coming from the man's mouth.

"You're gonna lose that gold if you ain't careful, boss," Satchel replied.

"*Shaw!* That tooth's fine and'll be there when I die. Find 'em, boys!"

The Ghosts of Benevolence

2

NO PLACE UNDER GOD'S blue sky stirred the surly, sensual passions of humanity like living in the South. Whether the heat begat the fervor or the fervor begat the heat, no one knew with certainty. Ensconced in the heart of that passion, when drawn from its slumber, was the community of Benevolence, Lance Hawthorne's childhood home.

Tradition cut ruts, trenches, as endless as black holes, into the Southern mindset, out of which little escaped and into which little was welcomed. Stagnant within these boundaries and nearly comatose from its rapturous dance with ritual, Benevolence slept. Folks would say that its rusty roads of red dirt and weathered rocks started with nothing and led nowhere.

Benevolence existed as a town fatigued, worn out, but, despite its depletion, proud. Its few sidewalks crumbled under the weight of time, weeds of indifference filling every crack and gap. The wind whistled through shattered windows along its half-abandoned storefront, like spirits free to leave, yet trapped. Fluted, scrolled columns of its once-magnificent antebellum mansions, survivors of the wrath wrought by the Great Unpleasantness of a century and a half prior, gave tacit proof of its strength in the face of recurring adversity.

White oceans of cotton, green and gold fields of soybeans, peanuts, and corn spoke as silent soliloquists to the prowess of the people of Sutter County, testimonies to their ability to tame the land. Purchases of seed, farming implements, clothing, and other necessities were made either with scarce cash, bartered in kind, or earned through the exchange of sharecropping. Pride was plentiful, credit unthinkable.

Maladies, such as malaria, small pox, dysentery, whooping cough, even the heebie-jeebies, were treated with time-honored home remedies by both the unpracticed and professed healers alike. Doctors, a missing commodity in Benevolence, were considered luxuries, as unnecessary as telephones. The citizens of Benevolence and Sutter County lived in this world much the same as they entered it—at their own risk.

Common among the tenets of outsiders was the belief that only mules and black men could face the ire of a midsummer Southern sun. Folks of Benevolence would dispute that assertion, claiming that no July sun could face *them*, blacks or whites, and not be frozen stiff by their resolve to overcome. Generations of ancestral suffering had produced strength, and strength, survival.

Most folks, with the exception of landlord farmers, lived in clapboard cabins slumped by the weight of neglect, sheltered by windows of plastic, walls of tin. Electricity and plumbing were, to most, indulgences of another world. Still, folks survived. They always had. They always would.

"Anybody *smart* enough to get their hands on all that money has got to be *dumb* enough to ever *want* it in the *first* place!" Sara Hawthorne preached as she clutched her dog-eared King James Bible. Money ain't nothin' but the

The Ghosts of Benevolence

prop of complacency, Satan's sedative. You *cain't* serve two masters. You *got to choose* one or the other."

Lance was too young to sort out the nuances of money, but he had no confusion about where his mama planted her feet. Believing it more harmful than helpful, Sara was unyielding in her derision of the device of currency. Not so much its usefulness as a medium of exchange, but the obsession folks had with hoarding it like pocket lint, setting it aside in jars, drawers, under mattresses, forgetting its existence, rendering its usefulness—its value—moot. If nothing else, home was a constant, and Benevolence was home.

Mark Randolph Watters

The Ghosts of Benevolence

3

HOME WAS NOT JUST another buttercup-bordered farmhouse shaded with century-old oaks. Home was a safety net as close-knit as Sara's hand-sewn shirts. Field mice and raccoons found uncontested refuge in these cabinets and closets. Both wandered on occasion into the Hawthorne home with neither the intent of malice nor the courtesy of notice, same as might a drifter seeking cool sips of water or bites of nourishment. No matter. Home served purposes unfailing for all its occupants, like a threadbare blanket that shielded the senses from the indifference of thunder. Home was a sanctuary, its sanctity, Sara.

Home for the Hawthornes was nothing fancy. Absent were the Doric columns of plantation castles; the crystal chandeliers; the engraved silverware and silk napkins; the constrictions of table etiquette; walls adorned with the tapestries of Europe; finely sculpted boxwood gardens; or the trappings of aristocracy. Open doors and open hearts were everyday courtesies-de-jour. Overstatements were few; simplicities plentiful. Home was as predictable and fulfilling as a plate of turnip greens and cornbread. Home was a Rockwell painting.

Mark Randolph Watters

Rusted hinges on screen doors squealed like tortured tigers, the sum of incalculable loops of human traffic. Gaps in the hand-hewn oak floorboards afforded just enough space through which the air of the seasons, along with legged critters, seeped and crept. Experience and wisdom demanded some manner of foot covering, even if only a layer of callused skin, lest one become the recipient of splinters, or worse, a renegade scorpion. Home was a wilderness.

The throbbing chant of tree frogs, katydids, and cicadas filled the evening sway of the green and black reaches of pines and oaks, like hastened hearts, and no one knew with certainty which sound belonged to which, nor did a body care.

Men sat in frayed lawn chairs or propped against pickup tailgates, a Royal Crown in one hand and a Marlboro in the other, speaking of conquests and politics and football. Children without cares beyond the next spanking chased each other, giggly with their patter of innocence. Whippoorwills and bobwhites sang their songs of melancholy and repetition as days slid into nights, reminders that progress was little more than the folly of fools. Home was tradition.

Home was a tin roof over oak planks nailed together above a three-foot crawl space. Home was the tell-tale trail of nail holes and yellowed black-and-whites of family hung in ever-changing locations that suited the whims of Sara Hawthorne and her growing collection of blue ribbons won at the county fair for her sweet pickles. Mélanges of hand-stitched quilts were spread across downy beds and folded over mahogany racks. Home was three bedrooms, more or less, and an open square area containing a wood-burning stove; an icebox; a hutch of hand-me-down dishes; a thirty-gallon iron cauldron for washing; an oak round table with a quartet of ladder-back chairs; and a Stromberg-Carlson floor radio. Home was the mother of simplicity.

The Ghosts of Benevolence

Home was a backyard covered with broom-swept sand and an outhouse plastered with pages of the Benevolence Farm Bulletin. The privy was a sanctuary within a sanctuary, requiring a forty-foot walk, maybe a scamper, depending on the urgency of the moment. Males relieved their bladders out a bedroom window or behind the cover of the ancient cedar, as convenience dictated, a practice Lance loathed, except for its efficiency, and one to which Sara was never witness, lest she castrate the lot of them. Home was a nook of alternatives.

Dirt roads and footpaths surrounded home, each a hint of a world beyond, had one a mind enough to venture so far. Home was breakfasts of pan-fried pork fat; red-eye gravy concocted from coffee grounds and ham drippings; eggs collected at the cost of a rooster-spurring; biscuits smothered in clover honey and the melt of hand-churned butter; and steaming stone-ground grits. Such morning bounty was a daily occurrence, prayed over and eaten before the sun spilled over the horizon, keeping bodies fueled until suppertime. Home was a place of plenty.

Home was a six-day week of plowing and planting and weeding and hoeing and picking and shelling and shucking and cleaning and scrubbing and milking and churning and washing and sweeping and sewing … and anything else that needed doing. Like unnecessary doctors, play occupied the dustbin of luxury, survival being the focus. Home was the Hydra monster, two chores at the wait to replace the chore finished. An observer might cup his hand to his ear and listen with careful intent, only to discern the crackle of burning calories consumed by the furnace of labor. Home was endless routine.

Home was Sweetgum Hollow, a shaded refuge carpeted with vinca and Sweet Williams, to which the family retreated on Sunday afternoons, in search of sprinklings of laughter amid a few moments of stillness, to catch their breath, accompanied by the goodness of

23

watermelons, figs, and tomato sandwiches. Home was escape.

Home was a daily reading at suppertime from verses of the Good Book, something Sara believed as fundamental to the family's well-being as well-water. Sara encouraged her children, whining of the eternal parade of errands, by quoting Psalm 121:1, "I will lift up mine eyes unto the hills, from whence cometh my help." Home seemed hills too few and hence a source of help too little to suit the children. When the light of spiritual exhortation shone dim, Sara resorted to paraphrase by chiding, "Children, obey your mama, for *she* has spoken!" Her inspiration sufficed. Home was the wisdom of the ages, filtered like the trickling of rainwater through sandstone. Unlike husband Peyton, Sara was a devout Scofield-edited, King James Christian. Home was a church.

Home was the lull of kerosene lamps and weekly newspapers and the CBS Mystery Theater. Home was Peyton's cigarette butts smoldering in the ashtray, the bitter, stinging smell of yesterday's smoke clinging to the nostrils. Home was void of pretense. Home was the sweetest word, a trusted companion.

So believed Lance Hawthorne, once upon a time. That was before home turned on Lance, then up and died, like a beloved pet dog stricken with rabies. After its death spiral, home was set aside and forgotten, one plank at a time, until home no longer existed. Home became an apparition, a nightmare, just another four-letter word. A sultry evening along the banks and fields of Pumpkin Creek marked the beginning of the demise of home. Lance was ten years old. Home ... was.

Mired in the pain of stinging ants and staring Death in its glowing eyes, Lance mouthed, "If I get out of this, it will be my *life's mission* to get out of Benevolence. I see nothing—*OWW!*—*benevolent* about it!"

The Ghosts of Benevolence

Benevolence had become a prisoner within barriers of its own making, plank-by-plank and tradition-by-tradition. Lance Hawthorne vowed to be one less plank in its floor and to put Benevolence behind him forever.

That was before the accident, the event that changed everything.

Mark Randolph Watters

The Ghosts of Benevolence

4

BENEVOLENCE CEMETERIES IN SUMMER
were the hottest of places, and in winter, the coldest.
Summer funerals mocked the mourning and misery. Beads
of sweat mingled with drops of tears and became as
indistinguishable as headstones of the unknown. Similarly,
the emptiness of burying loved ones in the dead of a
leafless, lifeless winter turned one's soul, what was left of
it, hard as iron. Cemeteries in spring and autumn, though
not so harsh, were nonetheless indifferent, like a drink of
lukewarm coffee, a bite of a half-ripe peach, or a stone-
laden ground before plowing. The seasons pushed and
pulled in transition, as did life and death. It was the fall of
the year when Sara died, as Lance neared the completion of
his fourteenth year.

He collapsed, like a discarded rag doll, onto the heaped
dirt of his mama's fresh-filled grave, his soul barren, his
grief inconsolable. Try as they might with their well-
intentioned efforts to distract Lance from the irreversible
reality of her death, friends only drove home the bitter
truth.

Godly men attempted in vain to assuage Lance with
their hackneyed reassurances. "She's in a better place

now," they said, their palms resting on Lance's shoulders. "She lived a full life" or "She was loved by so many" or "It was God's will." And so went the assuaging, his heart emptier than a Monday morning collection plate.

All the words notwithstanding, his mama remained six feet down into the lightless red clay, and all the reassurances in the world could neither change that nor how he felt about it.

Her "full life" had ended at the pre-menopausal age of forty-three, young enough still to drop a baby and plow the lower forty, on the same day if need be. How could God, argued Lance, take a woman in the fullness of life, a woman faithful in her worship of God and in commitment to her family? The accident that killed Sara Hawthorne reeked of a god unwilling, perhaps unable, to control fate gone awry. Lance replayed the haunting events leading to her death as he stared with eyes singed by the view of Sara's granite headstone.

Peyton and Lance had returned from the field moments earlier with a cartload of pumpkins, their fattest harvest of such in a decade. Someone made the casual suggestion of pulling the hay wagon out of the shed, hooking up the horses, and taking a joyride down the dirt road that spanned the western border of the family's two hundred acres.

The idea sounded fun, born of a giddy spontaneity common on an autumn afternoon after reaping a harvest plentiful in its yield, beyond all expectations. The wagon, rickety but functional, belonged to Lance's grandfather, and his father before him, used to transport the gathered harvest from field to market, a journey then of ten miles, give or take, on roads laden with potholes carved by usage and dust courtesy of a summer's dryness.

Back in the wagon's heyday, a team of four horses powered the its pull. This day, only two horses were available, and eight years had passed since these last pulled

The Ghosts of Benevolence

anything more than their own sagging bellies through grassy meadows. Lance walked the horses from their pear-tree respites and hooked them to the wagon, despite their growing whinnies of protest. Restless in unfamiliar confinement, the horses bobbed their heads and stepped side to side as Lance, Sara and husband Peyton boarded the wagon for their afternoon reward at Sweetgum Hollow.

While adjusting to accommodate the limited seating space, Lance discovered a coiled object nestled under the seat. Meanwhile, the horses' mouths foamed from their feud with strange bits and bridles. Lance removed the object.

"Wow!" exclaimed Lance as he turned the object in examination. "You make this, Daddy?"

"Yep. Finished it a couple of weeks ago," Peyton replied, taking the item from Lance, "Well, *almost* finished it, but now you've gone and spoiled the surprise."

"Surprise?"

"Still needed to put the cracker on it, but I reckon that can wait. Here you go."

"This is … this is *mine?*" Lance stared at the beautifully crafted leather bullwhip resting coiled in his palms, its polished thong glinting in the sunlight.

"I reckon so, son. Now, why don't you put that thing down for now and take the reins of these here horses. Heck, you're goin' on fourteen years old now. Time you learned how to handle a team."

"Can I give 'er a pop?"

"When we get to Sweetgum Hollow. I'll show you how."

"Peyton, what about them blinders?" Sara asked. "Don't you think you ought to put the blinders on if you're going to let Lance take the reins? It's been a lot of years, and the *slightest* wave from a cluster of Queen Anne's Lace is liable to spook these old nags into a panic," she warned.

Mark Randolph Watters

"These are *pasture* horses, Sara," replied Peyton, slapping the backsides of both animals, "not race horses. I 'spect by now they ought to know Queen Anne's Lace when they see it. Besides, I doubt either of 'em could outrun a pregnant turtle."

Sara knew better than to argue with Peyton once his mind was set.

"Well, then, let's get a move on," Sara said, more to the treetops than to Peyton, certain this trip, while a welcomed break, was a waste of valuable time. "I got to tend to some pickles needin' jars."

"What I'd *like* to learn, Daddy, is how to drive the Ford," pleaded Lance in a near whisper.

"What's that you said, Lance?"

"I'd rather learn to drive the car," repeated Lance more firmly. "That is, if you think it's time."

"Now, we've had this discussion before, Lance," said Peyton. The horses tapped their hooves side to side and whimpered with impatience. "Once me an' your mama pay off the car loan, we'll talk about you learnin' to drive. Until then … well, *here*, take this leather before these damned horses have a spell! Let's scoot on down to the Hollow. Afternoon's a-wastin', an' you an' your mama's done gone to *spittin'* on it!"

Lance had grown weary of the repeated excuse his daddy offered for not taking the time to teach him the nuances of their horseless carriage, a 1959 Ford Fairlane. If the excuse was paying off the loan, the car still had a solid two years left on that. Anything could happen in two years. Might get stolen; might be wrecked; might be repossessed, for all Lance knew, and with it his chances for learning to drive such a four-wheeled jewel. But, pushing his luck by arguing the point made no sense, and he *did* now own a handmade bullwhip. Lance gathered the reins loosely and sighed as all the times before. "Yes, sir."

The Ghosts of Benevolence

"Look here, Lance," Peyton said, trying to deflect Lance's disappointment.

Snap! The crack of the bullwhip cut the air and echoed through the trees like a rifle shot.

"Thought it still needed a cracker!" Lance shouted.

"Does make it louder, but it'll crack a wallop without one!"

Snap!

The startled horses reared in response to the whip's pop. The three riders were tossed back into their seats as they clutched sideboards to prevent tumbling overboard. The horses raced forward, the wagon fishtailing from ditch rim to ditch rim, narrowly avoiding their indifferent depths. Dirt exploded into the air. Pebbles ricocheted off tree trunks.

"Pull back on the leather, son! *Pull back!"* Peyton screamed, as the family jerked and bounced at the discretion of forces capable, it seemed, of unraveling rams' horns.

Peyton strained to grasp from Lance the reins flying up and down like a schoolyard jump rope. Desperately trying to gain some control over the horses, Lance and Peyton failed to observe their headlong approach to a hole with the diameter of a car's tire and deep enough to hide a blue ribbon pumpkin.

Like the dead weight of a body through a gallows' trapdoor, the wagon's front left wheel plunged into the hole. The rear half of the wagon leapt into the air, as if the wagon had smacked an iron wall, scattering the three like buckshot. Sara's chest struck the wagon's left sideboard, her body twisting as would a puppet in a tornado, heels over head, to the road beneath. At that same instant, the wagon's rear left wheel smashed into Sara's forehead, squeezing it between the metal rim and the packed clay, killing her instantly.

Mark Randolph Watters

Lance's mama, alive and vibrant just moments earlier, wanting only to finish putting up her sweet pickles, now lay in the indignity of roadkill, sprawled on the red dirt road like any one of a thousand possums before her. No confetti, no flashing lights, no fanfare, no goodbyes. Just dead. Just like that. And Lance had held the reins.

Thrown into a patch of blackberry bushes thirty feet from the wagon, Lance lay sprawled. Blood poured down his left arm. His vantage point on the high ground across the ditch permitted a blurred view of his mama's motionless body on the road below. He ignored the gash that ran from shoulder to elbow on the back of his arm as he clawed away the thorny vines that snagged his clothing and nicked his flesh.

"Mama!" Lance shouted. *"Mama!"*

The Ghosts of Benevolence

Lance sprang to his adrenalin-fueled feet and hurdled the ditch separating him from Sara. He ignored his daddy, unconscious in the ditch.

Lance dropped to his knees, next to Sara's body. "*Mama!* No!" screamed Lance, seeing her crushed skull. "God, no! Please, *undo* this! Mama, I've *killed* you!"

The wagon rested on its side in the ditch, its left rear wheel spinning and squeaking with the rhythmic click of its slowing cadence. The horses meandered up the road a couple of hundred feet, grazing on morning glories, as if nothing had happened. The bullwhip lay curled over a rock, like a serpent, a few feet from Sara, the echo of its snap ricocheting in Lance's brain.

God had exercised his will in an appalling manner. On the eve of a celebration of his fourteenth birthday in October, 1970, Lance now was of no mind to accept, leave alone understand, god's will. Like a rusted nail, bitterness punctured Lance's spirit, infecting it to its core. The unanswerable questions of life and death pummeled his withering, tender innocence like hailstones in a spring cornfield. Inexperienced in the ways of an unforgiving world, unable to understand its unprovoked assaults on his senses, Lance drew conclusions destined to drive the remainder of his years. Guilt and the poison of cynicism became early, clinging, companions.

Sara Hawthorne, born Sara Wilkes in Sutter County in 1926 to Luther and Mattie Wilkes, was a woman of unshakable faith, despite the agonizing death of a daughter; the indifference of a male-dominated society; and a husband mired in the mediocrity of limited ambition.

She had inherited their two-hundred-acre farm from her daddy upon his death in 1944 from a Nazi bullet in the snowy Ardennes Forest during the initial German thrust at the Battle of the Bulge. Land barons tendered "offers" for

The Ghosts of Benevolence

those two hundred acres, rich in the watered loam deposited in the flood plain along Pumpkin Creek and envied by competing farmers and developers, for pittances of its true worth.

Sara knew enough about the art and science of farming to tuck inside a thimble, with space to spare. Despite this lack of knowledge, as well as other obstacles, Sara never considered surrendering the tradition of farming forged by five generations of Wilkes. She'd figure it out, she vowed.

The community, meanwhile, showed little accommodation for her ignorance, despite her zeal to learn. Men who mattered to the social dynamics of Sutter County seemed unable to accept the fact that, from their point of view, a woman now owned title to an "unearned" tract of real estate, memorialized forever by the blood of Luther Wilkes. They met her with the resistance of turned backs and closed minds when she sought help for the acquisition of such essentials as laborers for plowing and pickers for harvesting, loans for seed or to upgrade equipment. Sara met them with equal resistance and determination.

An event worthy of Irish stubbornness occurred in the autumn of 1951 when Sara was offered, with reluctance, fifty percent of the market rate for the Hawthorne crop of cotton. The month was October, and cotton was rolling to the county ginner by the wagonload. Cotton brokers were eager to fulfill plentiful domestic and overseas orders for the commodity and had little time to waste doing so. These same buyers were well aware of the high quality represented by the Hawthorne crop.

Sara and Peyton managed to harvest all two hundred acres of cotton, paying twenty itinerant pickers double time, plus all the sweet pickles and lady peas they wanted, to get their crop to market.

The excuse given Sara for the proposed lowball rate was that "abundant cotton production" out west, particularly Texas, had "bottomed" the market. A select few farmers, she had learned beforehand, hauled cotton to the ginners and returned armed with full, "unbottomed" offers at true market value. Sara was neither buying the ginner's fabricated excuse nor was she selling her cotton at the artificial rate.

Sara marched out of the buyer's office and mounted her lead wagon. She reached inside a compartment behind the seat and retrieved a small box. Ten of her rented wagons behind her, loaded with the first of several shipments, lined the road awaiting weighing. The wagons held half of her crop ready for market.

"Dump the cotton off the wagons, boys!" Sara instructed. "Drop it anywhere you can, then move those wagons out of here!"

"Ain't we gonna *weigh* it first?" one of the pickers whispered to his companion.

"Ain't no bidness of ours. Do what she say!"

"She still *pay* us?" he pressed.

"She'll pay us! Do what she *say!*"

The mounds of white fluff were shoved and tossed off the wagons onto the road, as instructed. Sara took her small box and walked toward the first triangular mound in the array of cotton hills scattered down the road for a hundred yards. Farmers and pickers watched in transfixed amazement. She opened the box. Sara removed a stick from the box and scraped it along a wheel rim of the first wagon.

One by one, the cotton was fired until a wall of flame and smoke lifted into the morning sky producing clouds blocking the sun but sending a clear message of "buyer beware" to brokers and ginners. Sara preferred to destroy her cotton on the premises of Sutter County Ginning Company, and in the witness of like-minded farmers, than to give the brokers the satisfaction of cheating her. Peyton could only watch as he turned up jugs of homebrew.

The Ghosts of Benevolence

When the smoke cleared, farmers after Sara received market rate plus half again, for which they cheered Sara, becoming instant allies. Sara pocketed the respect and political capital.

But she hadn't earned the respect of all. Vandals destroyed a fifty-acre field of corn three years later, deep in a summer's night, using the crisscross pattern of horse-drawn wagons over the young stalks. All of her milking cows, twelve of them, were poisoned a month after the corn was destroyed. She and Peyton were able to save the life of one, which produced milk no more.

Despite this, her faith remained unmoved. She was Job-like in her resilience, often quoting Psalm 34:1, "I will bless the Lord at all times, and His praise shall continually be in my mouth." Lance remembered the stubbornness of her will and her unwithering faith.

"Don't it make you *mad*, mama, the things they're doin' to you?" Lance would ask. "Why ain't God doin' nothin' about it?"

"Makes me mad, Lance, I have to admit," Sara would reply calmly as she looked out toward her fields and, with eyes squinted, sighed and added, "Real mad."

Then, after a thoughtful pause, she turned to Lance. "God's not ignoring us, son. He's doing plenty. Just not all of it's obvious to us mortals, you and me, that's all. Ever notice how after you kick down an ant mound, they scurry about in what looks like the panic of the great Chicago fire? Then you wake up the next day an' before your eyes the mound's all rebuilt, probably higher and bigger than ever. Point is, Lance, ants don't get mad. Not for long, anyway. They just carry on. Because giving up ain't an option. We've got to carry on, too. These people may get a thrill or two, but they'll never get the final satisfaction; you can *count* on that."

Lance seldom understood the fullness of his mama's words, but he respected them nonetheless and loved her for the softness in her voice as she spoke them and the wisdom born of her ways.

Lance's mama raised him in the shadows and sanctuary of Benevolence Primitive Baptist Church and had insisted on his attendance at every meeting. The family, despite Peyton's objections, always sat in the second pew from the front on the right side of the center aisle, within spitting distance from the pulpit.

Red Hamilton, despite his seventy-eight years, possessed a firebrand-preacher reputation and was as spry as a Doberman. His face folded and creviced like a leather prune; his steel-blue eyes gazed half open in constant back-and-forth movement, suspicious of his every encounter; his black caterpillar-like eyebrows bushed and kinked to the four winds like a hairy Medusa; and his earlobes sagged like the nipples of a worn-out pig. His shoulder-length white hair, unkempt and as tangled as barbed wire, whipped his face as he cast demons from congregants, from Hell itself.

Red, known to folks simply as the Preacher, hated the rigidity of theology but loved the flexibility of religion. Christianity, for Red Hamilton, offered just the flexibility he craved. He invoked God as it suited him and quoted scriptures, preferably out of context, to support his social, political, or prurient leanings. Any excuse, not that there was a short supply in Sutter County, was good enough for Red to declare a revival of the backslidden and the saving of the lost. The most common excuse, it turned out, was Red's ever-diminishing financial means, usually depleted around the end of the third week of the month. Revivals, scriptures, and the name of God were tools Red wielded like a master craftsman to scathe loyal church folk and itinerant attendees alike with a cause-and-effect religiosity designed to convince a body that, with a regularity of once per month, its soul was as *guilty* as hell was hot. Religion

The Ghosts of Benevolence

was Red's means to a self-serving end, a means to a way of life few dared expose.

Indeed, Red loathed the sinner, or pretended to anyway, despite his public claim of hating only the sin. He earned notoriety during a 1955 tent revival by telling a cotton farmer, dying in the misery of a rattler's bite, "I'll pray for your soul, but not for your sin-soaked recovery, you scalliwaggin' *varmint*, because you never did *anything* to make it *worth* saving!" Tact was not his strong suit.

The Preacher engaged in the ritual of tongues, of speaking the Word in the form of languages understood only by an 'interpreter', usually the Preacher himself, and a practice that, even though presented in a scriptural context, only pushed Lance closer to confusion and farther from God.

"What in the world is that old man *saying*?" Lance often asked with arms-folded frustration as Red pranced around the pulpit spewing babblings of consonants and vowels. The garbled syllables of nonsense, observed Lance, correlated with his sermons against the evils of alcohol. "Satan in a bottle!" he'd shout, followed by, "Cradoka frishlond slocacaca blah, blah, blah!" The fire in his message, some of the flock suspected, was fueled by his intake from Satan's bottle. Red preached and staggered, ostensibly under its influence, indistinguishable from church members swaying under the influence of emotion. He'd grab the pulpit's edge for his bracing, to preclude his own disgraceful fall from grace.

The Preacher swore the influence was that of God's, that he was "high on Jesus". But, from the vantage point of the second pew, Lance detected on Red's breath the telltale odor of corn whiskey. Lance translated the confusion of religious hypocrisy into something he might more readily understand, if not appreciate—entertainment. *If I was to light a match now, that old man would literally breathe fire,* Lance thought.

Mark Randolph Watters

It was the same smell with which Lance's father often stumbled through the door, and Lance suspected his daddy and the Preacher transacted business together on those nights Daddy came home smelling of shine and slurring ambiguous excuses.

A healing service came on the fifth night of one of The Preacher's weeklong tent revivals. As it reached its climax, Lance came forward to the altar so Red could lay hands on his scorpion sting.

Why not give this voodoo a try, Lance thought, seeking first the entertainment value rather than the kingdom of God. Though the sting had swollen his hand to painful proportions just shy of a ripe cantaloupe, Lance could not help but spill a chuckle as Red placed one hand on Lance's wound and the other hand on Lance's forehead, and squealed, "Be *hea-a-al-l-ed*, O sting of the *devil-l-l-l!* ... cradoka frishlond slocacaca blah, blah, blah!"

Possessed by his performance muse, Lance fell backwards into the arms of two deacons, as all recipients of healing were expected to do. Except Lance's fall came not from any spontaneous healing of divine origin. The pungency of Red's breath alone was enough to send Lance reeling, tumbling down like the walls of Jericho.

No record existed to prove Red's official ordination as the preacher of Benevolence Primitive Baptist Church. That is to say, no one wrote down the date, time, and details of such an event, though Red insisted it all began in the autumn of 1926 with a sermon entitled "Just One More Last Chance". "Just One More Last *Drink*" might have been more believable.

Townsfolk spoke not of the content of his message, the particulars long forgotten in an endless stream of hellfire sermons that bounced off consciences like bullets off superman. They spoke instead of the veins in his neck that bulged like breathing purple tendrils as the decibel level of a voice possessed rose and fell in an epic battle of ecstasy

The Ghosts of Benevolence

and agony, of good and evil, of sobriety and drunkenness, marked by the distance and spread of saliva spraying from his mouth. The Preacher was *nothing* if not entertainment.

Revered nonetheless by the citizens of Benevolence, Red "The Preacher" Hamilton instead raised the specter of doubt in Lance. Religion was a peculiar thing in these parts. The language itself was perplexing enough, if not tongue-tying, with its 'thees' and 'thous' and 'sayeths' and 'whosoevers'. Like chores that seemed to spawn more chores, Lance's inquisitive mind seethed with far more questions concerning matters spiritual than satisfying answers received.

Lance found himself wondering aloud on occasion why a loving God tolerated, perhaps engineered, poverty and pestilence so persistent and prevalent among the people of Benevolence, alas, the entirety of the South. Were these not the same families that strode through church doors at every opportunity, prayed aloud, shouted "Amen!", read the scriptures, loved their neighbors, raised their children in God's image, and held true as best they could to the commandments? Lance pondered this dilemma and wondered whether God had cast His judgment upon followers of the Preacher, despite their good intentions, punishment perhaps for taking in a contorted version of the Word.

Meanwhile, the high-and-mighty rich of Atlanta seemed rewarded, implicitly by God's favor, allowed to accumulate the wealth of kings, live in the opulence of oversized homes, and drive such cars, any one of which rivaled the worth of Sara Hawthorne's farm. Poor white trash and black folks roamed barefooted like hungry animals, in plain view of God, through the fields and along the dusty red roads of Sutter County without so much as the daily sustenance of a hoecake and sour buttermilk to wash it down. Seemed to Lance the burden demanded of the sweat of the brow had been distributed solely among residents of Benevolence and Sutter County. Seemed to Lance that hard work and faithful service to God meant next to nothing.

"We're storing up treasures in Heaven," Sara assured Lance, but he wanted—needed—the enjoyment of some of these treasures in the here-and-now.

"If God is for us, who can be against us?" consoled Sara, ever armed with scripture.

Lance stared at her, eyes blank with the emptiness of ignorance, like a hog looking at a radio. Matters as these haunted Lance's sense of justice, of mercy, and fueled his rejection of all things spiritual.

Now his mama, the essence of the God-fearing woman and the pillar in Lance's young life, was dead. The wind whistled cold through his tattered soul. God had not only yanked up Lance's anchor, He had ripped out the rudder as well.

Lance turned to Pearl Thomas, a friend dear to Sara. Lance referred to this saint as Aunt Pearl, a moniker Pearl cherished enough to make it so. An aunt by title only, Pearl was the matriarch of Benevolence and was known with affection as Miss Tommie. She was a Godly woman, a widow, and often was asked to share the supper table with the Hawthornes.

Many were the times, Lance recalled fondly, Sara and Aunt Pearl stayed up well past the wee hours rehashing and embellishing last week's gossip, while canning figs and blackberries or stewed tomatoes, perhaps running a stitch or two through quilts, doing those things laughing and carrying on like teenagers at a slumber party. Aunt Pearl concealed the omnipresent pain suffered from swelling caused by her lifelong bout with arthritis that took up in her hand, fingers, and hip. Sara and Miss Pearl were as inseparable as a wall and its paint, each incomplete without the other.

The Ghosts of Benevolence

Aunt Pearl struggled with the physical engagement required by most activities after losing her left arm at the elbow in a 1905 farming accident. She chose the misfortune of succumbing to her curiosities, wondering too close to the workings of her daddy's ginning machine.

She was twenty-two years old at the time and not of the frame of mind to listen to the admonitions of wiser voices. The machine caught hold of the sleeve of a bulky sweater acquired for her by her boyfriend during a trip to Paris. Intended for winter wear, Pearl wore the red wool button-down like a second skin, much to her boyfriend's delight and her daddy's misgivings, despite the early autumn heat and its obvious oversize, finding use for the dangling sleeves as makeshift gloves when picking cotton or cutting okra. The habit stuck. So did the ginner, pulling her arm inside, shredding it to a bloody pulp before her daddy was able to cut power to the machine.

Notwithstanding the severity of limitations imposed upon her, she would say to Sara, a smile curved across her wrinkled face, "God took my left arm so I and my attitude could point only from the *right direction*."

Her uplifting world view in the face of tragic, permanent, personal loss assured all around her there would be no excuse-making from Miss Pearl Thomas.

Sara and Aunt Pearl shared a weekly bible study with five other ladies, the highlight of which was Pearl's recipe for hot sassafras-and-cinnamon tea, with lemon and a splash of brandy. A few of the ladies splashed more of the brandy than others, but all stayed within the boundaries of dignity and sobriety. Sara provided the homemade mayhaw jelly spread onto lard biscuits. The group always ended their study with the first and last verses of "Amazing Grace", Sara's favorite.

After the death of Sara, Aunt Pearl took Lance under her eighty-seven-year-old wings. She made it her mission to reinforce Sara's six sacred values into Lance's being.

Those values, in no specific order, were: fear of God and faith in His Word; respect for fellow human beings; hard work; responsibility; honesty; and self-control.

Sara Hawthorne upheld these values as mainstays of minimum human decency. These values, Sara preached ceaselessly, if planted into the heart and practiced faithfully, would buoy Lance during any storm and deliver to him honor and the grace of God's favor. Abandonment of any of these attributes, Sara warned, was the same as hanging a millstone of shame. Sara Wilkes Hawthorne believed the establishment and preservation of a good name before God superior to all other endeavors.

So began Lance his turbulent journey through adolescence. He needed someone to remind him of Sara's values. Aunt Pearl was there to see to it. But even Aunt Pearl, age overwhelming her endurance, could do only so much.

Saintly Aunt Pearl could not expunge the bitterness coloring and crowding Lance's soul darker than kudzu on a telephone pole. Lance had turned his back on God at his pivotal first crossroads, the untimely death of his mama, such a direction he would learn to regret. He came to reject family and Benevolence and home. Aunt Pearl gave as much as she could, while she could, like the little Dutch boy, fingers plugged into breaches of the dike. But the holes multiplied, widening beyond anyone's ability to control.

The Ghosts of Benevolence

5

LANCE HAWTHORNE STUMBLED through the red-eyed rigors and parties of college, and afterwards a few pointless jobs that extended into his middle thirties, caring little and maturing less. He drifted from employer to employer, like a hitchhiker on a highway to nowhere, leaving a trail of bounced checks and betrayed aspirations. He trekked the backroads of Europe for a year, hoping to find within the tuck of some thatch-roofed village some manifestations of a dream he found impossible to define. "I'll know it when I see it," he would say, with all the certainty of nailing jelly to a wall.

Committed only to taking his next meal, from whomever and wherever he might find it, Lance snubbed responsibility as one might stomp cockroaches. Until he met Jessica.

That she fell in love with Lance—never mind married him—astonished him still. Jessica exuded vibrancy, intelligence, common sense, all things Lance seemed to have left behind in Benevolence or perhaps roadside in a tavern of an Irish village. Jessica saw something in Lance Hawthorne not even Lance knew existed, perhaps because qualities so obvious have uncanny ways as elusive as leprechauns. Lance hoped that by tapping Jessica's fountain of youth, her stream of boundless energy, he might restore *his* vigor, *his* outlook, and mothball a past best left at the bottom of a tavern stein. He thought, with a bit of luck, he might fool others as he fooled himself. For a while he did.

But the anchor of the relationship upon which Lance had hung his hopes of rescue began showing the telltale signs of water intake, the gnawing imbalance of a starboard list. As with a lifebelt in the midnight black of the cold North Atlantic, Lance held fast to the fading promise of a meaningful future.

Like a wide-eyed Vegas novice, cash in one hand and a double whiskey in the other, Lance spun the wheel of his idyllic dreams. His whirlwind romance and marriage to Jessica, twenty years his junior but thrice his maturity, served more to accent their differences, not meld their qualities. He had fallen in love with the fresh spring of transition, not the suffocating summer of inevitability.

Unable to sever the hard-wired haunts of his past, Lance turned to the distractions of his career work. He poured into it a draining investment of energy and hours immersed within a numbing world of numbers, constructing digital tales of budgets and cost reports and analyses and presentations and projects dreamt up to appease the stoic managers of his employer, Standard Paper Industries of Georgia.

His past, tamped down on a tight spring and ready to pounce without notice, could not be altered. But the future, that was different, if managed shrewdly. Lance's canvas hung like a collage of a thousand yet-to-be-painted colors, such splashes, strokes, and renderings ready for his choosing. His future, his clay of choices and attitudes, piled high before him as on a potter's wheel, awaiting his creative shaping. The clay's impurities—the melancholy of

The Ghosts of Benevolence

yesterday and the directionless stupor of today—begged purging.

If given the opening, the ghosts of Benevolence swirled ever present and draped burdensome around his mind like Marley's clinking chains, as irremovable as the tattoo of a curse. Even so, those wrapping chains found ways, from time to time, of digging into the gloom of Lance's morose, connecting within him to certain salient links of pleasurable recollection. Lard biscuits adrip with honey, for instance; carpets of purple-flowered vinca; Sunday afternoons at Sweetgum Hollow or on a cow-pasture baseball field; harvests and hayrides; a handmade bullwhip and …

SNAP!

His mind wandered with fantasies of escape from the rigid grip of the corporate treadmill and the asphyxiation of family responsibilities. He yearned for a return to the simplicities of youth, wagon rides, shucking corn on the porch, fishing in Pumpkin Creek, and spitting watermelon seeds with his first love, Ellen Guthrie.

His mind bubbled with memories of camping under the stars in the backcountry of Yellowstone or the high country of the Grand Tetons, just as he and Jess had done on several occasions before Ginibeth entered the world, his world, a world now cramped for space.

Lifting his hands from the keyboard and forgetting for a moment the spreadsheets and deadlines facing him, his mind's eye peered into the magnificence of the silent, black dome of night pierced from horizon to horizon with countless pinprick holes through which flowed the swift, ancient light of time's beginning. He transformed from the clamor of corporate chaos into the savage comfort of the cold winds howling in concert with Yellowstone's wolves. He felt the reassurance of a crackling white-hot fire warming their wool-wrapped bodies. He smelled the chocolate milk rising to a boil in a dimpled tin pan. He shuddered with anticipation at the notion of being with Jess again, alone in the wilds of nature, umbilical cord cut and away from everything he detested, everything he depended on. His mouth curled with mischief at the thought of him and Jess melting the snow around them, all within the confines of a singular sleeping bag.

Lance closed his eyes and remembered well how he and Jess made the point of making love in the middle of such boundless nights. One would awaken the other with a soft kiss on the mouth, arousing the other from a deep sleep. Nothing quite equaled the blurry, drunken state of Lance's mind upon waking and realizing his lover engaged in the devouring sensuality of touch, even if nothing more than a simple back tickle.

That was before Ginibeth, before fantasy took a turn for the rude awakening.

Papers crashed to the floor, jolting Lance like a carpet shock and scattering budgets and reports and manuals into piles of disorder, followed by the coffee. The malnourished present—the here-and-now—screamed for his attention.

"Crap!" muttered Lance, shaken from his trance. Heads popped up over the tops of cubicle walls, like prairie dogs, to see about the commotion.

The practical side of Lance, a side he had only recently given acknowledgement, considered the pleasant grip of daydreams as little more than folly, the stuff of fools, like walking on rainbows, punctuated *now* by the burn and stain of coffee, unsugared and uncreamed. After all, what really mattered most to Lance Hawthorne, when he got down to taking such seriously, was the "long view" of life, as he termed it.

Lance's 'long view' was more a state of mind, a code he had created and bound himself to follow, same as a computer obeyed the dictates of the ones and zeros programmed to run it. It was an epiphany born in the

The Ghosts of Benevolence

months following Ginibeth's birth, in the blackness of night in which only introspection is visible, under a roof that blocked all those blinking, pinprick stars of fantasy. The straight-and-narrow of the long view demanded that the collage of a thousand flowing, yet-to-be-painted colors become instead a still-life of certainty, that conviction replace whimsy. The present days should be spent in preparation for retirement, the epiphany of the long view demanded, just as the light of the stars had begun its silent journey millions of years ago and had followed its inexorable path earthward.

The correlation between the journey of starlight and the path to retirement was the cockamamie of the romantic, but Lance found logic in its poetry, and it took root in his mind. The long view became the rationalization for his self-absorption. Acquisition of assets, of *things*, required commitment to career, hence less time devoted to the emotional needs of his family. The fewer risks taken with his monetary assets today—always *his* assets—assured the principal would remain intact, that wealth accumulated and tucked safely away in his prime earning years would remain secure from loss of value. Risk aversion, like the unbending flight of starlight through the vacuum of space, assured his eventual arrival and visibility in his later years. Despite the possible cost of irreplaceable time spent with his family, surely they would thank him thirty years hence for not squandering money hard-earned, Lance reasoned. "Then the fun could begin," he would tell himself, hammering another glob of jelly to his wall.

Trouble was, the only gratification deferred was his family's, not his own. He was quick to take care of his comforts and whims first, casting the desires of Jess and Ginibeth into the abyss of the long view.

In one breath, Lance justified buying a new S-Class Mercedes at intervals of two years. "Status, Jess! *We* are the Jones's everyone wants to keep up with."

Mark Randolph Watters

But in another breath, Lance would declare, as if smitten by schizophrenia, "We can't *afford* that, Jess!" whether 'that' was a winter coat for Ginibeth or Chinese for dinner. "We must be responsible *now* more than *ever*," Lance often persisted, pulling one of his mama's sacred values off the shelf and blowing it free of the dust of neglect.

A man of sturdy build and broad shoulders, his health intact as far as he could tell, Lance dreamt of doing something, anything, with his life besides the tainting of balance sheets and the overstatement of income by hiding losses for a company desperate for profits, for Street recognition, and thus the attention of investors. When faced with the choice of security over freedom, Lance chose security, in accordance with the shortfall of any spirit of innovation, a by-product of his long view. He sensed the depletion of clay from his wheel and the fading of his thousand colors.

Lance was paid well to document and disseminate deceit painted with the makeup of truth, and to not look back. He spent his professional life honing these skills, using up his inventory of clay, accumulating financial fruits along the way.

To soothe his distaste for risk and yet feed the monster of avarice, Lance looked for the quick hit, the big strike, and thus often squandered hundreds of dollars on lottery tickets. This was minimal risk, almost no risk at all, he rationalized, versus the potential payoff. Besides, it was leisure, harmless fun, like a game of pickup basketball, with winners and losers but no hard feelings and few regrets. Except Lance became the Los Angeles Clippers; the '62 Mets; a nerd with two left feet, ten thumbs, and Buddy Holly glasses; a white guy who could neither jump nor dance. In a word, a loser.

Maybe investment brokers and financiers and bankers were the real targets of Lance's distaste, people with

The Ghosts of Benevolence

professional mindsets too similar to his own, people who played the Ponzi of deception to a perfection Lance could envy but never replicate. Maybe by funneling his investment capital through convenience store clerks, he enhanced his sense of control over those he deemed his inferiors. Lotteries became, instead, more like bopping himself in the head before someone else beat him to it.

Lance had grown tired of the day-to-day toil of computers and lies, of dogs and ponies, of politics and daggers and such. Ascension to the glory of the 'big picture', that panoramic still-life of market generalities and queries created by Ivory Tower royalty, left to lower forms of life to interpret and explain, seemed the reasonable next step for such a soldier of the corporate realm as Lance Hawthorne.

Short of the grandiose, Lance romanticized retiring altogether to the fallback of the farming life he knew as a child. Some of the embers of home still crackled inside Lance. He craved to breathe life again into that particular segment of his otherwise inglorious past. If only it were that easy. Would that he could, now that spring had come—and gone.

His family in tow, a ceaseless stream of bills remained to be paid for a long time to come, the dark side of the long view that stretched beyond his perceivable horizon.

Lance scooped the fallen papers, stained by the brown of coffee, tilting them to allow any free-standing liquid to drip to the carpet, which only spread the stain.

"Son of a ... *Crap!* What am I *thinking* about?" Lance shouted, cubicle heads bobbing.

Besides, Lance believed—as his eyes roamed the spacious maze of cubes, noticing everyone who had noticed his clumsiness—daydreams were for losers, for the success-challenged. Lance Hawthorne craved the personal achievement as measured in dollars and 'attaboys', no matter how unsavory the means. The sweat of his fingers crunching numbers, though essential to the growth of his net worth, hardly quenched as water for his soul.

No matter. While one hand pounded out analyses like a Marine does pushups, the other reached for the brass ring, the carrot called 'tomorrow'. The restrictions of practicality demanded he stay the course today. Satisfaction would come, eventually, just as starlight strikes the earth … eventually. The reality of today shone in Lance's eyes like the yellow eye of a freight train in a black tunnel. The harder and longer Lance worked for Standard Paper Industries, the less gratifying were the rewards. Games of numbers played for managers incapable of seeing their reflections in mirrors, or uttering the words "thank you", had numbed his spirit and wilted his sense of adventure. His first loves, archaeology and astronomy— and Jess—had been sacrificed at the altar of financial security.

"Can't make money by chasing stars," Lance had concluded with the smugness of drinking buddies crowded around women at a bar.

"Can't live the good life digging rocks. All I'd get would be a stiff neck and dirty fingernails."

Lance felt his lust for life turning to powder, like sandstone in a windstorm. The trappings of materialism had cuddled him in a cloak of conservative comfort. His existence felt as safe as a hot bath on a January night, life's cold truths kept at bay. He yearned to break free from his cocoon, but he had lost his will to give consequences the finger, to take chances and to absorb losses. Daydreams, for now, were his escape.

Like the cold blusters of the northern Rockies on exposed skin, reality had its ways of blasting Lance right between the eyes and sweeping away the dreams. Wearing a threadbare fifty-six years, Lance sensed the doors of mortality swinging wide open.

The Ghosts of Benevolence

He had developed over time the habit of picking callused skin on his hands, evolved from years of field labor, and peeling it away, like old wallpaper. Perhaps Lance was renewing himself, cleansing his body of the visible reminders of death. Perhaps this practice was an assertion in the smallest of ways of some measure of control over the havoc of time. The habit lingered to the present, though his hands had not known the rigors of manual labor for three-plus decades. Life for Lance was now less to be enjoyed than maintained. The calluses always returned like a ubiquitous public service announcement that screamed, ***"You are mortal! Get used to it!"*** Still, denial was Lance's stalwart companion.

Mark Randolph Watters

The Ghosts of Benevolence

6

A CHILD AT HEART, the time had arrived to "act his age", a trite adage that ran counter to Lance's nature. A promotion was at hand. Not a bad thing, he supposed, even if it did mean a requisite honing of his brown-nosed politics. Lance viewed the promotion, the latest step in the winding stairway of the career process, as not only deserved but long overdue. The time had come to cash in some of the chips he had struggled to accrue all these years. But the promotion was anything but a slam dunk.

A micro-managing boss, laden with insecurity and incapable of trusting subordinates beyond making copies and coffee, exacerbated Lance's misery. VP and General Manager of Corporate Administration, Barrett King gave Lance the benefit of his mentoring prowess only in the narrow sense that he hovered over Lance like a thundercloud. Barrett projected an aura of mystery, aloof and secretive, yet stormy and dominant. He branded all meetings as wasted time and communicated via email to his subordinates. Barrett equated knowledge to power. The fewer facts he shared with underlings, the more power Barrett perceived himself amassing.

Mark Randolph Watters

While Barrett had ascended high up the corporate ladder, he had not done so by delegating tasks dependent on the inner workings of political panache. Those responsibilities he kept to himself, like a wolf circling carrion, as he created alcoves of information within a framework of projects and webs of linked spreadsheets, all done in his narcissistic image and under his control. Like a snake oil salesman to the desperately ill, Barrett had managed to finagle a market-sensitive, yet comatose, board of directors into believing he had the touch of Midas.

Barrett King had structured his realm with people he believed to be loyal and unquestioning of his authority, such as Carl Forsch, Director of Internal Audit, and Lance. Barrett had created a new position, the promotion Lance now eyed, in the ongoing expansion of his regime, using the rubber-stamped approval of a senior management team blinded by its own pomposity.

King, riddled with the physical and emotional pockmarks of middle age, enjoyed the life of self-deception. Like Lance, he craved all things material. He drove a candy-apple red 2012 Corvette convertible, gold chains dangling from its mirror like a Vegas pimp, and was never shy to show off its horses. He was not a man who allowed the vows of marriage to interfere with his furtive pursuit of women. He carried a hotel-sized sampler of Scope in his blazer pocket, ready to liquidate germs trapped between teeth and gums before entering sports bars, a favorite haunt. His teeth glowed with a temporary white, a deceptive white, as if he had applied a generous coating of liquid paper. His wore blue contacts, the throwaway kind, and he plucked his nose and ears daily of recurrent hairs.

Lance was not the only one being considered for this promotion, unfortunately, and the thought of another professional setback rendered upon him a burden of anxiety and continuing mediocrity. Dogged by his dependence on the latest and finest of gadgetry, the most recent example

The Ghosts of Benevolence

being the champagne-gold 2012 Mercedes SUV purchased in the mad rush of a Falcons win and a Snickers high, Lance craved this promotion like an addict craved a line of heroin. The equation was simple: better job equaled more money equaled more and better stuff. And so spun the wheels.

Lance had purchased a house a few years ago, at King's urging, all sixty-five hundred gleaming square feet of it, paying half down and carrying a fifteen-year mortgage that beckoned like a baby insatiable with hunger.

All Jessica had wanted was a home cozy enough to hammer a nail any place she damn well pleased. Now she felt guilty leaving a smudge by the kitchen light switch or a dust bunny in the foyer. At least the homeowners' association dues and the covenants and restrictions were costly and suffocating. There could be no *genuine* status without that.

None of Lance's material possessions was corruptive, per se. A bottle of liquor could sit in a cabinet for years unconsumed and do no harm whatsoever. But when the bottle was opened and the genie let out, the possession became the possessor. Lance's love for stuff, his obsession with possessions, dominated his midlife and became the basis for his decision-making. It was this love for tangible personal property that, as a whole, formed a buckling house of cards that drove Lance to dream of escape from forces he felt helpless to satiate.

The real satisfaction, though temporary, came more from the *acquisition* of things, not the ownership. Like orgasm, once achieved nothing was left but to do it again with hopes of greater intensity, or roll over and sleep. He was too restless to sleep, and it was getting tougher to do it again.

Then, of course, there was the baby. Not yet born, but right around the corner, due at the end of September. Unlike the Hawthorne's first, this baby was not planned.

Mark Randolph Watters

Not by Lance. Theories of spousal disloyalty simmered in Lance's brain. The couple had agreed three years ago that one child sufficed. Now Jessica was pregnant with number two. Lance seethed, the ghosts of his immaturity rising, and he wondered if Jess, if not disloyal, had taken advantage of his limited powers of self-control.

The thought of an abortion entered Lance's mind, and he considered insisting Jessica go through with the procedure, but even Lance could not conjure the detachment to commit to such an act of selfish abomination, nor would Jessica have relented. The ultrasound revealed a form entirely human, which was more than one might say for Lance Hawthorne.

The child determined to be a female, Lance believed, as if she had such power of choice. Another female. If Lance was going to accept another child, he wanted a boy, to carry on the Hawthorne name. The roll of the dice, as Lance came to view conception as he did most things, turned another snake eyes. Instead of a symphony of joy, Lance heard only the crescendo of cash registers cha-chinging into perpetuity. The 'long-view' grew longer.

"Snap out of it, Hawthorne!" roared King, an oxymoronic mix of hulking frame and maddening stealth, as he seemed to materialize from thin air. His tone, disruptive and demeaning, sent shards of dread slicing through his intended targets, ripping to shreds any sense of dignity.

The Ghosts of Benevolence

7

BARRETT KING, AT SIX and a half feet, an All-SEC tight end out of the University of Georgia, graduated at the top of his 1988 class from its school of mechanical engineering. He was the New York Giants' first-round pick, destined, thought many, for a place among the greatest of NFL tight ends. That is, until the opposition engineered his rookie-season shoulder separation, an injury which destroyed his potential and chinked his sense of invincibility.

Not one to be caught with his Plan B down, he joined the Marine Corps, spending three years as an ordnance specialist in Iraq and earning several medals of distinction. Returning stateside in early 1992, Barrett earned his Master's in Pulp and Paper Technology two years later.

He enjoyed a rapid rise through the ranks of engineering at Standard Paper Industries of Georgia, gaining clout not only from his technical expertise but from his business vision as well. Charged with the five-year rebuild of SPIG's thirty-five-year-old Raventon mill, its largest, King took a capital budget of four hundred and fifty million dollars and extracted papermill gold out of the strategy of thirty-six bundled projects, using only sixty-one percent of the budget to complete the massive overhaul.

Such savings not only embarrassed project engineers and managers alike, all of whom were certain the original four hundred and fifty million-dollar budget was, at best, understated, it had hoisted Barrett into a realm of industry legend. He achieved unwavering respect from the board and senior management as subsequent paper production and profits exceeded the most favorable of estimates, thanks largely to union/management cooperation, led principally by King, and a burgeoning export market. Barrett achieved untouchability and the plum picking of VP and General Manager of Corporate Administration.

Standard Paper Industries of Georgia, a paper and forest products holding company, operated four paper mills concentrated within the northern third of Georgia, as well as four others scattered along the Tennessee River. SPIG managed papermaking interests in Texas and Kentucky, along with several saw mills and box-making plants in strategic points from Indiana to Louisiana.

Gray hairs achieved conspicuous absence in Barrett's receding hairline. His board-straight posture and rigid gait gave hint of his Marine Corps background, and his trim, muscular build suggested he had lost none of his athleticism, chinks notwithstanding.

Barrett played racquetball twice weekly but only with opponents whom he knew he could defeat, or with opponents whom he knew understood the real game being played. Not that Barrett didn't enjoy a challenge. Lance played Barrett several years ago, losing by two points in a game Lance had in his Spandex pocket until one of Barrett's graceless glances speared Lance between the eyes, serving up a reminder that Barrett hated losing more than he loved winning.

Barrett demanded unquestioning compliance from subordinates in all matters related to SPIG, as well as

The Ghosts of Benevolence

around-the-clock secrecy from colleagues, particularly from those knowledgeable of the inner workings of his projects. If there were a buck to be made, for the company or for himself, Barrett took backseat to no one.

Barrett King had assembled, by way of career incentives dangled like meat before crocodiles, a subservient core of personnel, accountants and engineers and technical support, enough of whom caught King's lures and kept the others hopeful. His lemmings followed wherever his tune led them. Barrett's exploitation of his command began and ended with their undivided loyalty reinforced by a faltering economy and a paycheck-to-paycheck insecurity. The happenstance of subordinates' brainpower or the occasional whiff of independent thought held little value with King except as such served him.

Once in a while wandered the opportunity for advancement within the corporation, an aspect of Barrett's workaday world he controlled with the care of a master gardener. The position of VP of Finance and Analysis opened, and Lance treed it like a coon hound.

"You're in another one of your dazes." King paused for a split, eternal second, studying Lance like a hawk eyeing a field mouse. "You finished the Q2 raw materials and energy variance analyses? And the payables! Don't forget I need you to give me that year-to-date report of vendor payments, with a comparison to the three prior years."

Startled but composed, Lance turned and nodded and tried to maintain the stoicism of a professional, something he knew Barrett respected.

"Gotta have the numbers in Meyers's hands by four-thirty. *Today*, if you don't mind!" King pressed.

"He'll have it," snapped Lance, giving the standard three-word promise.

Though Barrett awarded no one his complete trust, he liked Lance and expressed frequent appreciation of Lance's soldier-like productivity and the accuracy of his work, trademarks of Lance's professional reputation. For different reasons, King also liked Carl Forsch, SPIG's Director of Internal Audit.

A fine golfer, Carl was an able drinker, capable of consuming a couple of six-packs on the front nine, still making par, much to Barrett's cultured amusement. This singular ability was the real source of King's respect for Carl. 'Drive for show, putt for dough', was Carl's hackneyed mantra. He flaunted his golfing skills with the arrogance and annoyance of truth.

Forsch, much like his boss, possessed little in the way of business ethics, an attribute of high value to King. A couple of years earlier, Forsch successfully deflected the external auditors' attention away from booked inventories of raw materials. Barrett and Carl knew that the cost of goods manufactured was understated by eighty million dollars, an amount which had accumulated over the course of three years. This understatement of expense, the direct result of an overstatement of wood and other costly inventories of raw materials, reflected a practice common for SPIG when the company needed earnings to meet Street and investor expectations.

If market conditions happened to result in real earnings in excess of Street estimates, something unlikely to happen in the current economic climate, then an offsetting amount of deferred expenses were absorbed as current. If not, then the masquerade continued. No one was the wiser to the manipulation. Barrett and Carl gave double-entry accounting a whole different twist.

Fortunately for Barrett, Carl exaggerated the quantity of wood "on the ground" when field auditors possessing little experience in the paper industry asked to view the inventories. Carl's material misrepresentations of inventories, as well as other areas related to income, earned him favor in Barrett's eyes. As Barrett said time and again,

The Ghosts of Benevolence

"Perception is reality!" As long as investors perceived
SPIG to be profitable, that perception was just as effective
on shareholder wealth as if the company were indeed in the
black. This was Barrett's approach to managing the
company's scarce resources—manipulate the scarcity.

The company skated through audits unscathed, and
SPIG's reported earnings continued to climb unabated, seen
as the continued result of the King-managed mill rebuild.
Stock prices spiked as the serendipity hit the Street, boosted
further by the negative financial results of other major
forest product companies. A few months later, Barrett and
Carl exercised their options, ditching their company stock
holdings at substantial gain.

Despite his craving for all things material and
comfortable, Lance exercised a shred of decency, refusing
to prostitute himself in hopes of a promotion. Those things
he left to Forsch, who was unfazed by a barrier of ethics.
As a reward for his role as Barrett's good and faithful
servant, Forsch had advanced unopposed to the position of
Director of Internal Audit, a post once coveted by Lance.

Forsch understood the paradoxical world of business,
its complexities and its shallowness, its substance and its
shell. He recognized early in his career that golfing, too,
was one of the official methods of male bonding in the
corporate world. Lance, on the other hand, defied the
politics of good-ol'-boyism and preferred to stand on
magnanimity, even if in pretense, despite his thirst for
wealth.

Noble as appeared the facade of ethics, Forsch pooh-
poohed Lance as any credible measure of a professional
threat. That was the reality of business and competition.

"He's using you like *toilet paper!*" Lance often chided
Forsch in reference to King. Carl just smiled and patted the
wallet in his pants.

"And, Lance, before I forget," Barrett reminded,
"meeting this afternoon. My office, three-thirty. I've got

something I need to run by you and Carl. I think you'll find it worth your while."

King had a way of waving attractive strings void of any reachable carrots, but this time circumstances screamed "Exception!"

"Internal-audit Carl? I'll … I'll be there," Lance replied, eyebrows raised.

Wonder what the god wants this time, Lance thought. *Something worth my while, eh. Anything involving Carl can't possibly be worth my while. Unless ... unless that jerk is stepping down and handing me his card key to the executive bathroom. Ha, ha! Maybe, just maybe, Barrett's floating* **me** *for that VP promotion and he wants Audit's okay. I mean, Carl's got a cushy position; he doesn't need another promotion, not so soon. It'd be more of a lateral move for Carl anyway. Dang! Am I going to have to kiss Forsch's butt to move up in this company? Doesn't matter really; a brown nose is a brown nose. Besides, Barrett just probably wants to review the payables analysis with Carl before we turn it over to the outside auditors.*

Lance pondered the possibilities. Perhaps this meeting was no more than a preliminary discussion of how to deal with the outside auditors. Maybe Barrett needed a fix of ego-stroking. These thoughts faded in the glow and hope for the promotion and its attendant salary increase. After a few minutes of unfettered speculation, Lance filled his coffee cup and returned his attentions to the work at hand. The payables analysis neared completion.

Lance settled into his chair, sighed, and faced his mountain. *Payables analysis. It's come to* **this?**

The Ghosts of Benevolence

8

THE INTERNAL AUDITORS WANTED this analysis a.s.a.p., Lance knew. The year-to-date payment totals, sorted in descending order by amount paid, revealed nothing extraordinary, except for one relatively new vendor, Global Technical Solutions. Eight million, nine hundred and fifty thousand dollars paid to this vendor through the first six calendar months of the year. Not a particularly unusual amount if this vendor were peddling boilers or tanks or kilns or paper-making machinery. But, Global Technical Solutions wasn't such a vendor. They peddled computers and customized software solutions. Lance had noticed over the past couple of years a flow of packages with the Global Technical Solutions logo. Plus, the current-year spike of payments to GTS for technical services—for which Lance had not noticed a single GTS-labeled name tag on site—showed no sign of abatement. Lance's interest piqued.

The grapevine had spread the word of the Board of Directors' verbal authorization for expenditures appropriating ten million dollars of capital funds for mill-wide computer upgrades, a project slated to begin in the following year. Millions of dollars in payments to GTS suggested the timeline had started sooner.

Barrett had not mentioned to Lance the project moving forward. Not a nickel had been invested in a new laptop for Lance, promised him months ago. His desktop was slow by current standards, a mere dual-core processor with six gigabytes of RAM and half a terabyte hard drive. He could use an upgrade for his multitasking. Perhaps part of Barrett's news was that Lance's computer was on its way.

The afternoon passed slowly, painfully, like a kidney stone. Lance completed all the analyses and emailed the files to Barrett and to Meyers. Lance checked his watch. 3:27.

"Lance? Got a minute?" asked his Accounting Assistant, pecking on the opened door.

"Hmm?" Lance replied, his mind elsewhere.

"Yours truly," she sang.

"Oh, Heather! Sure, come in. What's up?"

"Have you noticed this before? These Global invoices?"

"*Noticed* them! I could paper my *house* with 'em!" Lance joked and smiled. "I think that's where all of SPIG's money goes these days. *Somebody's* getting new computers."

"That's just it," Heather said, shifting her weight to her left foot and staring at the ceiling. "Not *me*."

"Or me," Lance said, slapping the side of his flat panel monitor. "My *abacus* is faster than *this* dinosaur."

Heather gazed, arms folded, eyes squinted, trying to convey a tone of urgency.

"Sorry, Heather. I didn't mean ... just not sure where you're going with this," Lance continued.

"You have an *abacus?*"

"Ancient Chinese secret," Lance said, pulling a book-sized abacus from his desk drawer. "Ginibeth gave it to me for Father's Day last year. It's my back-up. And you

The Ghosts of Benevolence

thought us accountants relied on fingers and toes and lightning-speed brains."

"Cute," Heather said. "Take a look at the ship-to's on these invoices."

"Ship-to's?" Lance took a handful of Global invoices from Heather and examined the documents. "What address is this?"

"Don't know," replied Heather, "but it's not SPIG's, unless we've recently acquired an offsite receiving warehouse. Besides, this street doesn't exist in Raventon."

"No offsite warehouse *I'm* aware of," Lance replied. "Is this ship-to address on all of Global's invoices?"

"Not all. I'd say three-quarters, maybe more."

Lance thought for a moment.

"Heather, please make copies of all of Global's invoices for October 2010 through the current month, and then—"

"Already did that, Lance," Heather interrupted. "All two thousand five hundred and thirty-two of them, over twelve million dollars' worth of hardware and technical services purchases during the past year and a half alone. One computer here; two or three there; a server now and again. We've bought over *four thousand* desktops and laptops, Lance, along with printers and flat screens, you name it! *Where are they? NASA* ain't got that many computers, but I bet they *do* know where theirs *are.* Where are Accounting's new computers, *your* new computer? Most importantly, where's *yours-truly's* new computer? The rest of you can go *screw* yourselves."

"Wow. You *are* good! Twenty-five hundred invoices? Twelve *million*?"

"And change."

Thirty years Lance's junior, Heather came to SPIG fresh and wide-eyed from the business incubator known as Yale. She lived her life brash and with confidence, allowing access only to those of her choosing. Lance recalled the exuberance and idealism that accompanied such youth, the feeling that just showing up guaranteed another layer on the pearl. Recalling it was one thing. Living it was now beyond his reach.

"One *would* think a couple of those computers would have made it into our department, now, wouldn't one?" Lance observed, eyes turned toward Barrett's office. "Wonder where they *did* go? Heather, put a trace on this ship-to address."

"Sure, let me just hang my private investigator shingle over my desk, and I'll get right on it," she retorted sarcastically. "I'll send my Boy Friday after it."

Lance opened his mouth to reply, then closed it, unsure how to respond.

"The ones without the bogus street addresses were supposedly shipped to *P.O. boxes*, Lance. Those don't exist either."

"May I have the invoice copies?"

"Got them boxed and ready for you. Shouldn't we be turning these over to Carl?"

"Carl? Yeah, sure, I will, but first I want to take a closer look myself. Thanks, Heather. You're first-class," Lance said with a smile and a wink.

"Darn *tootin'*, buddy boy," Heather said, shaking her index finger, "and don't you forget that fact come annual review time."

Heather brought the boxes of Global invoices, three of them, into Lance's office. "Sorted by invoice date, earliest on top."

"Thanks, Heather." Lance slid the boxes inside his credenza and started for the 3:30 meeting fifteen minutes late.

He approached Barrett's office, the door to which Barrett kept closed as a matter of habit. He knew Carl already had arrived. Clearing his throat, Lance tapped tepidly on the door.

The Ghosts of Benevolence

"Come on in, Hawthorne!" Barrett shouted. Lance opened the door. "You're *late*, as usual. Sit down. Let's chat."

Mark Randolph Watters

The Ghosts of Benevolence

9

LEGS STRETCHED AND FOLDED, body slumped in his chair like a stuffed animal, arms planted confidently on both armrests, Carl smugly occupied one of two pillowed leather chairs facing King's desk. Carl's green-and-white striped tie crumpled on his chest like ribbon candy.

"Shalom, amigo!" said Carl, offering a wave of the arm.

Lance grimaced with a grin slanted and a brow furrowed at the idiocy of Carl's cavalier dual-language greeting, but he reserved vocal comment.

"I thought you *hated* meetings, Barrett," Lance observed, tongue in cheek, lowering himself into the other chair.

"I do; believe me, this is no exception. Sometimes I got no choice, so here goes. Where'd you grow up, Lance?" Barrett queried. "Some little hobo dump in South Georgia, right?"

Lance glanced at Carl. "Maybe. What about it, Barrett?"

"Nothing. Beautiful countryside down there. Reminds me of ... of some little South Georgia hobo dump." Barrett looked Lance in the eyes and smiled. Carl grinned as he rolled up his tie and let it unfurl, avoiding eye contact with either.

Barrett flipped open the top of an engraved gold-plated lighter and touched the yellow flame to the end of a Dunhill Dominican cigar.

"This," he puffed, twirling the tightly wrapped tobacco between his forefinger and thumb "is living." Barrett drew on the cigar and deposited the smoke upward over Lance.

"I understand that South Georgia, mostly the marshy parts," King continued, "is the only place on this green earth you can get a decent jar of mayhaw jelly. Ever tasted mayhaw jelly, Forsch? Sure you have! Your mama probably jarred *gallons* of the stuff."

Carl chuckled. "Ain't never heard of such. Muscadine. Now, *there's* you some jelly!"

"Don't know about muscadine. But mayhaw … mmm, mmm. It's a piece of pure jelly heaven. Spread it thick on a steaming buttermilk biscuit." Barrett paused, eyes closed, and smacked his smiling lips. "*Dadgum*, that's good eatin'! Makes me want to make this trip myself."

Lance looked at King and Forsch, offering each an uneasy smile, unsure of what to make of the conversation's point. *Trip?* he thought.

"If that jelly ain't the pride of South Georgia, somebody ought to go to *jail*. Hell, there ain't a whole lot else to be proud *of* down there, ain't that right, Lance?" Barrett sucked on his Dunhill, depositing rings of obedient smoke and asked, "Sure you don't want one of these?"

"Gimme one of those, Barrett," Carl answered, reaching into the box.

Carl took the cigar and examined it, turning it in his hand, as if evaluating a putter or a new car's leather, then inserted the cigar into his shirt pocket. *He'll probably smoke his pen on his way home,* Lance thought, amused by the image of Carl not discerning the difference.

The Ghosts of Benevolence

"Thanks, no," replied Lance, shifting his weight in the chair, reaching for the cigar box, "but I will take one for later."

"I'll cut the crap and get right to it." Barrett said as he took one final, extended draw, rolling the cigar's gray tip in his pewter ashtray, and extinguishing the stogie. Smoke leaked from Barrett's nostrils and mouth forming a crawling swirl of white and gray smoke, as if he had swallowed the smoldering cigar.

Lance watched his every move, not knowing what to expect next from the mouth of Barrett King. This was just as Barrett wanted it.

King opened the middle drawer of his executive oak desk and withdrew a deck of cards, shuffling them.

"Poker, gentlemen?" Barrett asked, setting the shuffled deck on his desk and reaching for another Dunhill.

Carl and Lance looked at each other.

"You were expecting *blackjack*?" asked Barrett.

"A *card* game, Barrett?" Lance asked. "This is what this meeting is all about—a *card* game?"

"Not just *any* card game, Lance. Look, you both are aware of the position available. I have the unfortunate task of promoting *one* of you, but not both. Therefore, since I despise awarding promotions based on accomplishments alone—work records can be so, how can I put this, so ... *deceiving*," Barrett said, glancing at Carl. "But, poker. Ah, poker. Now that's a *man's* game, where a man's true character and fortitude are revealed! I'll take a man who can veil the disappointment of a pair of deuces over a man who gloats over three aces."

In other words, Barrett will promote the man showing the most talent for deception, Lance thought, mindful of the boxes of Global invoices in his office. *Interesting correlation, if indeed any.*

Mark Randolph Watters

"So, gentlemen, ready for a lesson in this man's game?" King asked, slapping the deck of cards between his palms.

"Lesson?" Carl said, coughing. You mean like the lesson you taught HR? Man, you still owe Rickman $53,000 from your … lesson."

"Those weren't real stakes, Forsch," King replied. "That was only how we kept score, that $53,000, and trust me, they learned the lesson."

"Yeah, never to play *you* again," Forsch replied, chuckling.

King ignored Forsch's borderline insubordination.

"Gentlemen, we are going to play for an opportunity to *earn* this promotion the *unconventional* way." Barrett shuffled the cards; Lance smiled uncomfortably. "Simple game of five-card draw, nothing wild."

"What's the ante?" asked Carl.

"Why, your *careers*, of course," replied Barrett, "and a thousand dollars."

"A thous …? Are you *serious*, Barrett?" Lance asked.

"Serious as a southern lynching, Lance," Barrett replied in his best deadpan, eyebrows furrowed, his cobalt-blue eyes as piercing as those of a snake's. He enjoyed watching his underlings squirm, like salted snails on a tree stump. "And you'll play by *my* rules, which are … well, let's just say my rules are subject to change without notice. Questions?"

Barrett was a gambler by nature, winning baseball card collections in arm-wrestling contests with college buddies, making semi-annual safari treks to the Serengeti, and always managing to pick winning penny stocks with near-spooky success. Barrett had fortitude, if not genius, and he was never one to yield to hesitation. He had developed an ability to level the intellectual playing field, if by no other means than with a convincing flick of flame to the tip of a ten-inch Dunhill accompanied by his stare of ice, thus

The Ghosts of Benevolence

rendering moot a person's accomplishments, degrees, letters, work records, and abilities to focus.

"Minimum bet is a thousand bucks," he added, "but if this promotion means nothing to you, along with its significant raise, then, well, you are free to leave."

Neither flinched, neither wanting to become fodder for the ignominious rumor mill.

Barrett dealt each player five cards. Carl and Lance reached for their cards, picking them up slowly at first, as if each card were a live wire or a dead rat.

"Well?"

"Well what?" Lance asked, the answer known.

"Lay it down."

"A thousand-dollar ante, Barrett? Are you *nuts?* You want a thousand-dollar ante *and* a thousand-dollar minimum bet?" asked Lance, still processing the whole thing.

Barrett placed his cigar in the ashtray. He leaned over to within a half inch of touching his nose to Lance's, and said, "Never, *never* call the dealer nuts, Lance," Barrett warned. "Not within earshot."

Lance paused to let Barrett's admonishment soak in and to recover from the debilitating stench of King's breath.

"Payable in cash, check … or Mercedes," Barrett said, his eyes fixed upon Lance. Barrett relished the revelation of each rule as he made them up. "And no IOUs. This is not a house of credit."

Carl paused.

"Well? You in or what?" pressed Barrett.

Carl gave a quick glance to Lance, and with a slight fidget, declared, "In."

Lance spread his cards and spied at his fate, a slight yet indiscernible frown on his face. *Two eights*, he thought. *Damn!*

Carl looked at his cards, conscious to avoid any facial expression that might reveal a hint of his holdings. One queen, a pair of fives, a nine and a six. Not exactly promotion material.

"What'll it be, gents?" asked Barrett, masquerading his voice with the drawl of a nineteenth century Dodge City saloon dealer.

"Gimme … four, no ... three," said Carl, indecision the rule.

"Three," Lance followed, matching Carl's draw card for card.

Barrett tossed Carl his requested number of cards.

"You know, Barrett," Lance observed, "you didn't ask either of us to *cut* the cards."

Barrett froze and stared at Lance with a scowl of displeasure.

"Just sayin', is all," Lance said. "I'm sure the deck's legit."

Barrett continued the dealing.

Lance offered the first bet, an unusual gesture given his tendency as a follower. But a promotion was at stake here, not to mention bets and pots that might reach the tens of thousands.

"A thousand," Lance blurted with a shrug of nonchalance, quickly scribbling out a personal check for two thousand dollars to cover the bet and the ante but leaving blank the payee. He tossed the check onto the table. "Don't worry; it's good."

Carl spread his cards, shielded and flanked by both palms, as if protecting nuclear secrets. He pondered Lance's bet for a few seconds, then pulled out his checkbook and, without uttering a syllable, began to write a check with his pocketed Dunhill cigar. Lance smiled, having all but predicted such. Barrett snorted. Quickly correcting the mistake, he penned the check for a sum of

The Ghosts of Benevolence

six thousand dollars, covering the ante, Lance's bet, and his own. He tossed it toward the center of the King's desk.

"I'll see your grand and raise you four. Lunch money for a year."

Lance saw the six followed by three zeroes and looked at Carl, shocked by this brazen display of confidence in the face of sheer chance. Barrett smiled as his lips fondled the cigar between his teeth.

"By the way, gentlemen," Barrett said as he issued a smile of the powerful, "for your betting pleasure, and as compensation for services rendered, the loser pays the dealer an additional fee equal to twenty-five percent of the pot."

"What—"

"New rule, said I, the rule maker."

Lance countered. His mouth cotton dry, he smacked, "I'll see your four thousand and raise you … ten thousand. Pocket change."

Jaws and Dunhills dropped. Lance didn't have this kind of cash, unless he tapped his retirement account, but he was not going to allow Carl the satisfaction of intimidation. He ripped to shreds his original two-thousand-dollar check and scratched an almost illegible check for sixteen thousand dollars. In lieu of tossing this check on the table, Lance handed it to Barrett.

Carl stared a moment, then calmly matched the ten thousand, well within his bachelor opulence.

"Call," Carl said, spreading his cards on the desk, a pair of fives and a pair of kings. "Can you beat it?"

Two pair. Nice hand, king high, Lance thought as he took a close look at Carl's cards. He looked first at Barrett, then Carl, showing no sign his hand was better or worse. Then he smiled, revealing his rows of teeth like a slowly rising stage curtain. One at a time, Lance peeled cards from his hand and laid them on the table. First the four of hearts, then the eight of clubs, followed by the eight of spades, then ace of clubs, and lastly, the ace of spades.

Barrett laughed and gasped simultaneously. "That's the dead—!"

"I know, I *know!*" Carl growled. "Aces and eights! The 'dead man's hand'."

Lance stared briefly at the table. He ignored Carl's check and scooped instead the winning cards from the table.

"Keep your money, Carl. That's not what I'm after," Lance said. "Dead man's hand, eh. Sweet!"

Carl groaned and rose to leave.

"Wait a second, Carl," roared Barrett. "Maybe you don't want his sixteen grand, Lance—though, for the life of me, I can't figure why—but remember my rule, twenty-five percent of the pot. Four big ones, baby!"

Carl wrote a check to Barrett for four thousand dollars, expletives gushing under his breath, like water under a bridge.

"Why're you complaining, Forsch? Seems to me you came out twelve thousand to the *good*, thanks to Lance's generosity. Well, well, well, nice going, Lance, my boy!" Barrett added, flush with insincerity. "Keep in mind, being dealt a winning hand doesn't mean necessarily that you ... well, that you *win*. You still have to *earn* it, the promotion, that is. Anyway, congratulations on hurdling this first important step.

"Come back in twenty minutes and we'll discuss your winnings. Oh, *that's* right; you *relinquished* your winnings. We'll talk promotions and such then. First, I need to employ my considerable mentoring skills; you know, talk with Carl, console the loser, assure him he still has *value* ... and make sure his *check* does as well." King laughed.

Lance rose, smoothing wrinkles from his shirt and pants and stepped toward Barrett's office door. He

The Ghosts of Benevolence

wondered if what had just transpired was in truth Barrett's way of deciding the recipient of the promotion, or if perhaps the game was simply Barrett's idea of a boring day's amusement, a way to pass the afternoon before heading to the club and an evening of drinks and schmooze. Lance had witnessed some of Barrett's less rational management style before, so, while not out of Barrett's character, Lance could not help but consider how King might have reacted had he been on the hook for sixteen grand.

"Close the door on your way out, please, Lance," Barrett directed. "Thanks."

Lance closed the door, shook his head, smiled, and made a beeline for the coffee pot. As Lance reached for a cup, he remembered the 'aces and eights' hand he had placed inside his shirt pocket. Taking them out, he turned the cards in his hand and examined them, vaguely familiar with the legend of the tragic combination made infamous by Wild Bill Hickok. Interesting he had received such a hand, such a … random hand. And the cards *weren't* cut. He gave a cynical laugh and an instinctive rearward glance. Then, tossing aside any further thoughts of card-playing, promotion-offering malfeasance, the thought occurred to him that perhaps fate might take the notoriety of the hand and bestow upon Lance a reverse of bad fortune. This *was* about a promotion, after all. VP of Finance and Analysis loomed like just the blessing Lance needed.

Lance took out his wallet and, like adding a token to a charm bracelet, shoved the cards inside.

Mark Randolph Watters

10

"COFFEE'S FRESH, LANCE," Heather noted as she walked past, then stopped. "What's with the smirk? Something good happen behind those ominous doors of secrecy?"

Lance poured the steaming coffee into his cup and took a sip. "Maybe. I'll know for sure in twenty minutes."

"Twenty minutes? The secrecy thickens."

"Carl's still in there," Lance replied, adding more sugar to his cup.

"Okay, Carl, the trap's set," Barrett whispered, head lowered and leaning forward over his desk. "First, let me fill you in on what I've learned so far.

"Heather's asking a lot of questions about Global, why we're relying so heavily on one supplier without the team's input; why we have no requests for bids on computer equipment; why depreciation expense remains flat while capital expenditures for hardware go up; why receiving reports cannot be physically matched to purchased equipment; why there are no *purchase orders*, for God's sake, Forsch, the sort of questions *you,* an auditor, would be asking if you weren't so damned *corrupt!* All of her questions are driven by the fact *she* is upset that *she* has not received a new computer yet. I ought to yank you and put Heather in charge of Internal Audit."

Both men laughed, one more nervously than the other.

Barrett continued. "No doubt she's passed these concerns on to Lance. Those two talk like two college kids on a first date. I think Lance has his eyes on her ... but I digress.

"What's really beginning to bother me are her endless questions about who's getting the hardware. Lance won't leave me alone about *his* hardware upgrade, either. Says he keeps getting bumped off the network by "illegal operations" messages. I tell him to be patient, to clean out the temporary files, to empty his recycle bin, to reconfigure his hard drive, to add more RAM, to upgrade his operating system to Windows 10. Apparently he's upset because he still hasn't received his precious laptop, something he ordered *eight months ago*. Can we just get him a freakin' *laptop*, Carl, and Heather a new desktop, for the love of Pete, just to get their noses out of our business for a while?"

Barrett sighed and whirled a one-eighty in his chair to access his credenza. He punched a couple of keys on his laptop.

"Ah, good, good," he said, hands clasped.

"What?" asked Carl.

"Global's up three. A new fifty-two-week high!"

"Holy Wall Street! Loading up on that penny stock was a great bet, Barrett, especially by making public our contract with them. Doesn't hurt that Global's annual sales have since spiked by fifty percent and their ISO per-share price eight-fold. Investors *love* news like that. I know *I* do! I wonder just *how that* happened," Carl asked, brimming with sarcasm.

"You bet your wireless mouse it was a great bet!" Barrett confirmed. "There's one more small detail, though,

The Ghosts of Benevolence

concerning Lance, I'm afraid. He's also asking questions
about the hardware assets, why they're not showing up on
the fixed asset reports. Told you Heather was talking to
him."

"Direct him to me," Carl said. "I'll tell him Auditing
is on it, that it's just part of the stacks of paperwork in
Fixed Assets' inbox. He'll buy it."

"Not that simple, Carl. The man's a pest, but he ain't
stupid. He knows those computers are supposed to be on
the asset list; heck, he does our cost forecasting, and he's
all about accuracy. If he even *suspects* his cost forecasts
don't reflect the most current reality, he goes hunting like a
hungry wolf. He *knows* our depreciation expense is
supposed to be rising, but it *isn't,* Carl. It isn't, because the
depreciable equipment *ain't listed. Get it listed*, Carl, even
if the stuff's never going to be onsite. You *know* we can't
be undone by *petty* details or an even *pettier* accountant and
his *pettiest* sidekick.

"I worry less about some meaningless auditor—no
offense—inventorying the equipment than I do those high-
and-mighty directors questioning our cost because of a
Lance Hawthorne inquisition!"

"I'm *on* it, Barrett. You, uh … you said something
about the *trap* being set. Tell me more."

"Lance thinks he just won a chance to get promoted."

"Pretty darned convincing, I must say, Barrett. You
had *me* going there for a minute!" Carl noted. "I mean,
poker?"

"I'm going to send him south to negotiate the purchase
of some timberland from Devereaux. The brass has been
advised it's an ambitious quest to acquire a significant
chunk of timber acreage and thus an attempt to shut out our
competition's access to it. Lance will think of it as no more
than a test of his ability, in the wake of his new promotion,
to close a major deal for the company. Lance doesn't

know, of course, about the *arrangements* I've already made with Devereaux."

"What about Global's money?" Carl probed. "For the heroin."

"I'll also direct Lance to deliver the last payment to—"

"Two *million* dollars … *cash?*"

"Why are you *interrupting* me? Sit down, shut up, and *listen!* Yes, *cash*, stupid! No transaction trail, at least none they'll notice while *we're* here. I've sealed the cash tight and tidy inside a FedEx package. Of course Lance won't know that's what he's delivering. I'm telling Lance that it's a single-sourcer contract, fine print and all, issued to Global to cover all future hardware procurement and technical services. When Lance delivers the package, our Global contacts will give Lance the box of powder in exchange."

"Lance will be expecting to pick up this box?" Carl asked.

"Yes. It'll be packed in a Global-labeled desktop computer box ... marked as 'Accounting: Desktop and Printer.'

"Sounds darn risky to me," Carl said, shaking his head. "What if he gets curious, opens the box, thinking it's *his* computer?"

"Let him."

"*Let* him? Are you out of your mind?"

"I'll advise Lance not to risk damaging the new unit, such damage that *might* occur by opening the box and *examining* the machine."

"But we remove computers from cardboard boxes all the time, Barrett," Carl said. Nobody *damages* them."

"I think he'll comply. He's not that impatient; he's familiar with these models. Besides, the packets of H are loaded *inside* the CPU. The guts have been stripped. He'll never suspect he's nothing more than a highly paid computer gopher."

The Ghosts of Benevolence

Carl tapped the end of a cigarette on Barrett's desk. "Okay ... I guess," he said. "Still sounds risky, but you know him better than I do. What about Devereaux?"

"I've *already* secured the board's verbal blessing for acquiring twenty-five thousand acres of prime South Georgia timberland at an outlay not to exceed one hundred and twenty-five million dollars. *Five Gs* per acre, approved."

"That land's pocked with swamps and wetlands, Barrett! It ain't worth more than maybe five *hundred* per acre, if *that*."

"*You* know that; and *I* know that. Hell, even *Heather* knows that. Lance *don't* know that. It's home to him, and home ain't *got* a price."

"So, you're sending Lance to negotiate an already-done deal?"

"I thought I already said that. New *promotion*, remember? Lance has to *prove* his bestowed worth. I will tell Lance that Devereaux is prepared to accept as little as a thousand per acre; that Devereaux will dicker with Lance, play the game. But then Devereaux'll squash Hawthorne's confidence like a little bug. Lance will have no choice but to confirm an agreement well above the ceiling per-acre price I'll be authorizing to him for negotiating purposes."

"What sort of ceiling price?"

"I'm thinking along the lines of three thousand per acre. Sounds reasonable, don't you think? Dev likes it. The Board's approved a max of five thousand per. Our poor, befuddled Lance will think that, because he failed to swerve Devereaux into accepting the pre-arranged lowball price of three thousand—and thus saving the company fifty million dollars—he'll be denied the promotion he thought he'd *earned* in a stupid, *freakin'* card game.

"Hawthorne is an achiever, Carl. But, he's like a crystal goblet in the hands of a toddler. One false move, and his confidence is *shattered*. Shatter his confidence, and we've shattered his ability to achieve, to probe, to *analyze*. Can't have analyzers, nosy ones at that, prying into our business, now, can we?"

"Think this is gonna *work*, Barrett? I mean, it sounds sort of complicated, even risky. I don't know ..."

Barrett picked up a cigar from the ashtray and plugged it into his mouth. He flicked his antique flint-and-wheel lighter, the flame kissing the cigar's tip. Barrett smiled, blowing a line of smoke across the desk toward Carl.

"Relax, Forsch," he said, balancing the cigar between his fingers. "It'll work. Why do you think Lance won the card game, hmm? Short of that, we'll just have to implement our backup."

"Backup?"

"Plan B. We'll just have the fellow fitted with concrete shoes." Barrett laughed, stubs of his grit-worn teeth clutching the cigar, and continued, "SPIG will finally have its South Georgia timber resource, a darn good one at that."

"And us?"

"Devereaux's *willing* to accept fifteen hundred per acre, a grand above its *true* market worth. The SPIG board has authorized me to pay him *thirty-five hundred* per acre *more* than that, which you and I, my friend, will split 70/30 with Devereaux. Sweet or *what*?"

"Seventy/thirty? Why, that's ... that's ..."

"That's thirty percent of eighty-seven point five million dollars for us, or—and you might want to buckle your seatbelt—*twenty-six and a quarter million dollars*, Carl. Of course, your take from *that* amount will be a paltry forty percent."

"Forty percent of twenty-six and a—"

"*Ten and a half million*, Carl! And *you're* in charge of Internal Auditing? On second thought, good thing you *are*!"

The Ghosts of Benevolence

"I rely on *calculators*, Barrett. Wow! Ten and a half *million* dollars? That's why they call you Barrett the Great! Or is it Santa Claus; I forget."

"Yes, the board thinks I can do no wrong. Of course, they're *right*."

"Now I can *retire!*"

"You *could*. But you *won't*," Barrett said, drawing on his cigar and resting his head in his clenched fingers. "You're only forty-three years old. Don't you think retiring *now* might raise a few flags? This is a *cash* transaction, Carl. No depositing it into your account. Can't go leaving trails for … auditors. You can upgrade your lifestyle, but not too extravagantly. Discretion, Carl. And brains. Use yours! Besides, after this deal, we can extend our distribution networks into Atlanta, Mobile, Columbus, Macon, Pensacola, Jacksonville, Orlando and all points in between and beyond. This is only the *beginning*, Carl."

"Sounds good, Barrett, real good, but …what about Lance? Why involve *him* in the first place?"

"Well, as I said, Lance is an achiever; at least he sees the potential. But he also sees himself as an *under*achiever, having accumulated *accomplishments* without *redemption*, without recognition. And he has a tendency to snoop. So, let's let him snoop and achieve under *our* control. Plus, we have an arcane, archaic Board of Directors, Carl, a Board that believes in the *power* and *honor* of the *handshake* over the authority of legal documents and sound corporate procedure. No honor in *paper*, they say."

Barrett paused and chuckled at the irony in what he had said. The humor was lost on Carl.

Barrett continued, "To our esteemed Board, contracts and signatures are like earthen dams—they'll hold back water until it rains too much, until pushed *hard* enough; then they're worthless. Like these earthen dams, a man will eventually *breach* a contract, finding some chink in the fine print around which to build a legal argument to defend the breach. But a man is not likely to breach his *honor*, so thinks the Board. Unless, of course, that man had no honor to begin with.

"As you well know, the handshake of a dishonorable man is meaningless, too, but try telling that to our esteemed Board. Lance is being sent south to satiate the board, to secure the company's largest tract of timber in all its long history, to cut off access to such by our competitors, all with the honorable *shake of a hand*; only then Mr. Hawthorne's going to encounter a bit of … difficulty …. on this trip."

"So you're going to implement the backup *anyway*?"

"Let me just say this, Carl. You ever been a pall bearer?" Barrett asked, grinning, the cigar flame glowing.

11

"THERE'S A TRACT OF twenty-five thousand acres of prime timberland down there, and I want it."

Determination spewed from Barrett's words, an act as practiced—as perfected—as his ability to lie without issuing the slightest hint he was doing so.

"It ain't often a private landowner wants to sell his timberland outright, especially when these people can just about *name* their price for the rights to the trees alone. So much dadgum *recycling* going on that virgin mills making virgin paper are as good as *gold* these days! If *we* don't get this land and its trees, our competition *will*, and the price we pay for a ton of pine wood will only get a lot worse, a lot faster."

Barrett's eyes narrowed as he skillfully rotated the twenty-karat gold cigarette lighter from finger to finger. Lance wondered how *he* fit into this scenario but said nothing, yet.

"This land is owned by a ... by a ... let me see here." Barrett reached across his polished executive desk and pulled a coffee-stained scrap of paper from under several neatly stacked industry publications. "Here it is. By an ... Earl Bentley Devereaux ... the *Third*. Now, doesn't *that* name just *reek* of royalty?" Barrett said, sinking back into the luxury of his leather chair. "Southern aristocracy personified. Brings one to mind of the Old South, of old names, such as Pierre Gustave Toutant Beauregard or Nathan Bedford Forrest or Ambrose Powell Hill."

"Pierre … *who?*"

"Beauregard! Ain't you ever— Anyway, *those* were the glory days. Earl …. Bentley … Devereaux … the Third. Rolls smooth off the tongue, like hundred-year-old cognac."

Earl Bentley Devereaux the Third. Could that be the Earl Bentley Devereaux, the Third? Lance wondered, knowing there could never be *two* of them.

Earl Bentley Devereaux the Third was a childhood neighbor of Lance's in Benevolence. Devereaux, along with his widowed father and three German Shepherds, shared a sprawling two-story brick colonial at the bottom of an escarpment just beyond Sweet Gum Hollow, the narrow, shaded valley that separated the Devereaux and Hawthorne properties, much like the figurative image of railroad tracks divided the poor from the wealthy.

Lance spent many an hour spying on the Devereauxs through a thick boundary of scuppernong vines and pecan trees as the Hawthorne's enjoyed tomato sandwiches and watermelons on Sunday afternoons in the respite of Sweet Gum Hollow. Lance remembered how Devereaux would love his shepherd dogs one moment by petting and hugging and romping with them, the next moment kicking and cursing the dogs, or worse, pelting them with the sting of BBs.

Most Sutter Countians considered Earl Devereaux, twenty-five years Lance's senior, at best reckless and at worst the reincarnation of eighteenth century French royalty, worthy only of beheading.

Devereaux's father, a software pioneer, gained the preponderance of his wealth from having written a business

The Ghosts of Benevolence

software package for which he received the distinction of several patents and the fleeting glitter of notoriety. That a resident of obscure Sutter County had carved fame from the esotericism of computer technology set apart the Devereaux's from the mainstream of Benevolence bourgeois.

An upstart computer maker hastily purchased licensing for the software, paying an obscene sum of six million upfront, venture-capital dollars. The software, initially successful, failed to meet lofty, ever-expanding market expectations and was abandoned after three years in favor of similar business software designed by a Seattle firm.

Devereaux, the elder, blamed the failure on the computer maker's marketing strategy but shed no tears about the wild success of his bank account. Ever the consummate salesman and, when it suited him, quite dexterous with all things legal, he had struck the mother lode despite the product's subsequent bust. Language in the sales agreement entitled Devereaux to a sum certain beyond the upfront money, despite the eventual market obsolescence of the software. In addition to the initial six million earned for anticipated sales, Devereaux pocketed an additional three million in guaranteed royalty money. At the time, he enjoyed something akin to 'super athlete' status in the software industry and was paid in similar fashion.

Earl the Third, thus, was beneficiary of and heir to not only the wealth but the enemies made as well. He enjoyed and flaunted his unearned affluence, all in ways far beyond the abilities and experiences of anyone in Sutter County.

The fact the younger Devereaux never experienced the burden nor learned the lessons of farm work as the means to earning his bountiful pleasures thus fueled much of the community's disdain for the family. Devereaux dismissed such negative sentiment as nothing more than jealousy.

Mark Randolph Watters

Peyton Hawthorne once likened Devereaux the Third to a musician who stumbled upon wealth and fame undeservedly, before his fingers had developed the first callus, before he had spent his first night under an interstate bridge or in a cardboard box, before playing gig after smoke-filled gig until he bled the blues. Devereaux, said Peyton, never paid his dues.

An unapologetic racist, Devereaux maintained connections to suspected Klansmen, though he never spent a day incarcerated for his criminal mischief. Lance knew this all too well, thanks to his childhood friend, Jackson Willoughby and that pig-calling first prize.

The Ghosts of Benevolence

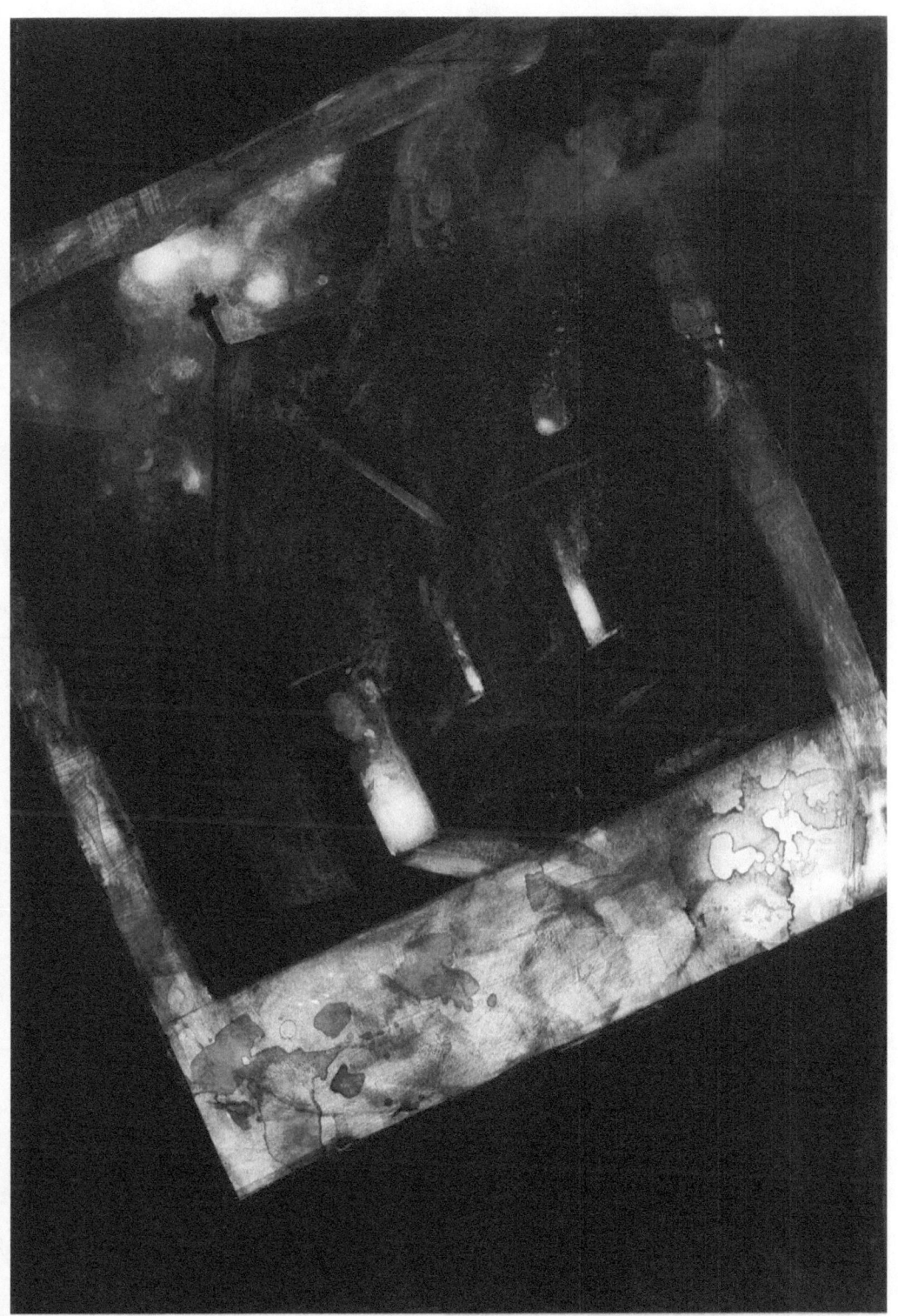

Mark Randolph Watters

12

LANCE AND JACKSON HAD been inseparable during their preteen years, welding a blood bond one foggy morning in one of the Devereaux family's several peanut fields. This field held a certain familiarity for Lance and Jackson, as both from time to time, on mutual double-dog dares, raided its hundreds of rows of peanuts, simultaneously running and ripping the mature plants from of the ground, then retreating unseen to the safety of the foliage along Pumpkin Creek.

This same field yielded many Indian artifacts over the years, artifacts found by the boys during nightly flashlight-aided visits and on other occasions of double-dog dares. Devereaux owned prime Native American-inhabited bottom land, richest in the county, and he collected artifacts as well. Devereaux had discovered burial sites and had begun personal excavations of grave goods, carelessly leaving many prime artifacts exposed. Knowing this, the boys found it impossible to ignore their temptations, slipping in under the cover of night, like cats, and relieving the excavated soil of its ancient bounty.

The five hundred acre field was bound on its southern flank by an African-American church and by Pumpkin

Mark Randolph Watters

Creek on the west and north. Lance recalled the ritual of the blood bond between the two, in this same field, in the aftermath of the horror they had witnessed and the flight from their machete-wielding pursuers.

Jackson brandished the instrument of honor, an antler-handled hunting knife given him on his thirteenth birthday by his grandfather. Jackson removed the blade from its sheath that morning, its six inches of stainless steel reflecting the sun's rising rays like a looking glass. The two boys had borne witness to an act of abomination, an evil requiring, in their minds, the solemn promise of secrecy. Ensuring their knowledge never reached the ears of old man Devereaux, or anyone possessing loose lips, the boys opted for a pact of blood.

Lance remembered clamping his teeth on a leather pouch as Jackson angled the razor-sharp edge against the tender skin of Lance's forearm.

"Here … goes," Jackson whispered, squinting.

Lance, eyes closed, nodded. "Not too deep," he whispered.

Slowly, Jackson slid the blade forward, inflicting an inch-long burn, such flame of a thousand paper cuts. His eyes welled with water, and he desperately needed to scream. Blood streamed forth, pooling in the cup of his bent elbow. Lance instinctively pressed his fingers against the wound to stem the burning and bleeding.

Releasing a sigh, he took the knife from Jackson and repeated the ritual on his friend. Neither boy uttered the slightest whimper, lest such suggest a weakness of commitment, or worse, call attention to their deed. Trails of blood snaked down the boys' forearms, which they pressed together. The blood mixed. The pain diminished. The bond was sealed. That day, in Devereaux's field of peanuts and artifacts, near the banks of Pumpkin Creek and the wreckage of Thankfulness Baptist Church, they became

The Ghosts of Benevolence

as brothers, their secret locked within their consciousness for as long as they lived.

But Lance, to this day, possessed the damning physical evidence in one Polaroid photograph, its colors fading, won by Lance from Jackson in a boyhood game of homerun derby.

Shaken briefly from his reminiscence, Lance's ears received, then discarded, the shaking of Barrett's thundering voice, replaced in Lance's mind by the still-shaking dusk encounter and subsequent event of horror that led to the peanut-field blood bond.

Mark Randolph Watters

The Ghosts of Benevolence

13

THE BOYS WITNESSED THAT night an event that ripped from Lance his sense of innocence and left cracks, gaping chasms, in the foundations of his faith, his heretofore unassailable belief in the fairness, mercy, and love of a just God.

Sutter County and Benevolence differed little from other Georgia counties and communities in a post-World War II era of order and calm—and racism. Farming and fairs and street corner gossip enjoyed light-of-day transparency. Sutter County, too, had its share, its pockets, of underworld meanness, the sort of disregard for humanity as one might find under the thumb of Nazi Germany. As if exchanging smiles for growls, elements of Sutter County transformed under the black of night, practicing a robed malevolence only *they* understood.

Lance and Jackson stumbled one evening upon this world of shadowed contempt. This was more than inanimate signage separating the races in a bus depot or at a restaurant or water fountain. This was an act of depravity by men whose flesh housed only cratered consciences, if that, as dead and cold as Pluto.

Mark Randolph Watters

Lance and Jackson splashed through the cool waters of Pumpkin Creek on their way home from a day's hunt for arrowheads. The fields were filled with the things, certain fields in particular. The boys stopped to take inventory of their finds and to gloat. Lance held in his palm a five-inch Clovis point chipped to symmetric perfection from tan-and-amber chert, sealed with the patina of water and time. Lance found the artifact half buried tip-first, three inches deep, in the base of a fire ant mound smack between two rows of peanuts. Lance bragged to Jackson how he had ignored the hazard of hundreds of maddened fire ants and retrieved the ancient spearhead. The point was perfect, Lance had declared, fluted from its base to its middle on both sides, its edgework the stuff of patient artistry. As the boys marveled at the rare find and wondered if more were about, laughter echoed through the trees. Growling voices of drunken men interrupted the boys' boastful banter.

"Sshhh!" whispered Lance, looking toward the sounds, his hand pressed against Jackson's chest. "Listen."

A group of three men knelt along the tree line of Pumpkin Creek. They formed a crude semicircle facing opposite the boys, maybe seventy-five feet to the left of the boys, maybe closer. Their line of sight pointed towards Thankfulness Baptist Church, a couple hundred yards north. Mournful harmonies of "Tis So Sweet to Trust in Jesus" rippled through the evening air. The oxymoronic mix of melancholy and bliss poured from the soloist's lungs and spilled out the spaces made possible by raised windows, as if the souls of four hundred years wailed in a blend of torment and hope.

The gray-white clapboard structure stood in perpetual disrepair, daring a breeze to knock it over. Several of the walls' planks were broken, some missing, exposing holes through which freely flowed streams of gnats, flies, mosquitoes, and yellow jackets. Paint—what little remained—peeled in long gray curls and shreds. The

The Ghosts of Benevolence

steeple listed like an ancient tower, ready to topple at the next piercing note. The building mattered little, they would explain, for the church was *not* the building. The building sheltered a place *for* the church, the *people*, to congregate for fellowship and to worship God.

Its bell pealed through the evening air. The kneeling men held torches they had just lit, flames licking, black smoke curling over the foliage. Jackson and Lance stood stiffened, fearful, like chameleons on a tree branch. Slowly, with the stealth of ground squirrels, the two boys stooped, shielding their faces behind curtains of scuppernong vines and wisteria. Their hearts pounded like the condemned awaiting the pull of the switch. Lance's stomach grumbled from its indigestion of a snack of under-ripe mayhaw berries. Then, unsettling quiet.

Mark Randolph Watters

14

JACKSON LIFTED HIS RIGHT leg slightly, a practice more instinctive than intentional, and farted, emitting a sound like a high-pitched rip of a canvas bag. Lance turned, eyes as wide as a hoot owl's. The boys, torn between their desperation for silence and reactive eruptions of laughter, held their breaths. They managed to muffle the inevitable laugher, but the creeping stench enveloped them. Lance covered his nose and gave Jackson a penetrating stare. Jackson smiled and shrugged.

One of the men spoke. "Them cotton pickers are goin' *across the creek* tonight, boys!" he declared in cryptic code as he slung an empty Pabst bottle in the direction of Lance and Jackson. The bottle swished through the brush, somersaulted like a runaway wheel, and settled a few feet to Lance's left.

"Cain't you even make it to the *creek*, boy?" another man said. "Don't wanna leave *nothin'* for nobody to find!"

"It's in them bushes, Dev. Ain't nobody gonna see it."

Pumpkin Creek, a stream fifty feet wide in most spots and only a couple of feet deep during rainy season, a trickle any other time, snaked through the fields and woods belonging mostly to the Devereaux family and bordered within twenty feet of the church's west wall.

Lance and Jackson looked at each other, dread in their eyes, prisoners of the choking openness. As far as they could tell, their discovery seemed as imminent as the rising moon. Fear, arid and suffocating, swept over them like a dust storm. They dared not rustle a leaf or utter the slightest sound.

Grayness took its place over the fields and trees until only a concert of crickets and tree frogs, accompanied by the crackling of a few flaming torches and indecipherable whispers, pierced the full-mooned twilight.

Black congregants filled the use-polished oak pews at Thankfulness Baptist Church, as they did every occasion the doors were open. Thursday night prayer service was a special time of the week for worship. Men and women gathered in a setting less formal than on Sundays, as they might at a picnic, placing their covered potluck dishes on wobbly tables.

Churchgoers noticed the flames flickering across the field but could not identify specific individuals from the silhouettes milling about. They reasoned farmers might be inspecting areas of crops stressed by drought, something the Devereaux family did on occasion. Perhaps they were destroying mounds of sleepy fire ants, pests difficult to manage in the best of circumstances. Perhaps a tractor in the creek-bank shadows had run out of gas or had broken down. While nothing seemed extraordinary in strict context, the flames fired in the minds of witnesses worrisome thoughts of pending mischief. They retreated inside for their supper and conversation.

Transfixed by the unfolding spectacle, unsure what to make of its purpose, Lance and Jackson settled in for its climax. White voices, drunk with alcohol, exchanged shouts for shushes, oaths for wordless utterances, all of

The Ghosts of Benevolence

which drowned out any substance their whispered words might otherwise have revealed.

One of the men plunged a shaft into the ground. Snapping in the breeze atop the shaft was a faded flag of the Swastika, as if a line of battle had been established along the Pumpkin Creek front.

"Take this thing, Ripley," another man said, handing off his torch, adding, "They's enough light give off by the church. Won't be needin' this."

He started across the field toward the church, the crunch of peanut plants and dry, sandy soil under foot. Pausing, he assessed the bundle of red sticks he held in his hand. "Hand me another stick 'r two, Jansen. Keep them fuses long, least a foot."

"Fuses?" Lance whispered.

"I ain't likin' this, Lance."

"Just you watch yourself, Dev!" a man whispered, delivering two more sticks. "They catch *you*, they catch us *all!*"

"Stop your worryin'," he replied, resuming his deliberate pace toward the church, eyes fixed upon the door and windows. The moon hung low, an indifferent spectator hugging the horizon. Minutes passed. Lance and Jackson strained to keep the men in view, as well as their own voices in silence. The mesmerizing lull of tree frogs replaced the diminishing sound of the man's footsteps across the peanut field. The building crescendo of events unfolding transfixed Lance's imagination.

"Here he comes, Jansen! Get ready!"

Lance craned his neck upward upon hearing the warning, then shifted his body right, as the man's racing silhouette came into view. Instantly, a blinding blast of fire and thunder split the twilight. Lance and Jackson stood and stared.

"My God!" gasped Lance, "My ... *God!*"

Mark Randolph Watters

Smoke and flames and shapeless debris heaved into the summer air. Shards of boards and glass cut the sky in every direction. The men watched, the dancing light of their burning torches revealing their approving smiles, like children enjoying fireworks on Independence Day. Two of the men removed their caps. The third man sprinted from the charcoal gray of peanut runners.

"You okay, Dev?"

"Finer'n cricket fuzz!" Devereaux said, breathless. "Them extra sticks done the trick, all right. Pretty much blew that church to *kingdom come!* Like to never got one of the fuses lit. Don't reckon I know if I ever *did*, but the job's done!"

"Got a piece of glass in your hat, Dev."

"What? Lemme see that." Devereaux took off his hat and pulled a bloodied three-inch shard of glass lodged in its side. "Well, I'll be dog; dang if it ain't. *Souvenir!*"

"That *your* blood, Dev?" asked a man, pointing to the glass under torch light.

"I don't think—" Devereaux said, feeling his skull. "Ain't got no cut up here," he replied. "Must be from one of *them.*"

"Dang, Dev! Ain't that like a ... a *curse?* Whatchu gonna do with it?"

"Like I said. *Souvenir!"* he repeated, placing the shard back into the hole it made in his hat.

"But that *blood*, Dev. I wouldn't be messin' with no curse. Th'ow that thing away! Come back to hauntchu, it will."

"Shaw! Ain't no truth to it."

Jackson had a clear view of the men through a small gap in the scuppernongs. The ground from the creek's edge to the tree line sloped five degrees, give or take, level enough to afford a clear line of view through the brush. He whispered, "That's *Earl Devereaux the Third!*"

Lance strained to see through the same gap. "Sure is!"

The Ghosts of Benevolence

Jackson pulled an object from his shoulder pouch and raised it to his eye.

"Lance, I got me an idea, but get ready to run like a spooked deer."

The men continued their alcohol-fueled celebration, unaware of the boys.

"Jackson, what the— What are you *doing?*"

"*Pictures*, man!"

Jackson had developed the curious practice of documenting his artifact finds, in situ, as well as in the context of the surrounding terrain, spending his allowance and odd-job earnings on film for his Polaroid camera. Until this moment, Lance was unaware he had brought the device, not one artifact photographed today by Jackson.

"Are you out of your *tiny* mind?" Lance whispered, aghast. "We might as well holler, 'We're right over *here*, you stupid idiots!' *Don't* do this, Jackson!"

"They're so *drunk*, Lance. Look at 'em, fallin' over each other like bowlin' pins. They won't be able to catch us, even if they *do* chase us, which they *won't* because it's gettin' too dark!"

"Oh, they'll *chase* us, all right, you dimwit! Killers don't take kindly to witnesses! Don't *do* this!"

"Evidence, Lance! We've got 'em dead to rights!"

"Yeah, and they'll just have us *dead!*"

"Lance, if I don't get this shot, who's gonna know *Devereaux* did this? *Who?* I bet there're *twenty coloreds* in that church. Maybe more! Thursday night prayer meeting, for God's sake! I *have* to do this! Otherwise, ain't nobody gonna know."

"An' you reckon we ought to be the ones tellin folks?"

Jackson framed the view and held the camera steady, same as he held his asthma.

"Who else will, Lance?" Jackson answered. "Put your deer legs on, 'cause here goes."

Mark Randolph Watters

Jackson pressed the button. The camera's flash ignited like a ground flare, a counterpoint to the earlier explosion, brightening the darkness for an instant and revealing their presence. Jackson grabbed the picture as it exited the camera.

"Let's get the heck *out of here!*" Jackson shouted, as if he needed to.

The boys turned and sprinted along Pumpkin Creek's bank, tearing through thorns and leaping over small trees, mud and water splashing their clothing as if they were dodging bursts from geysers. The astonished killers paused with breathless silence, a vacuum of unexpected events sucking away their secrecy. Invaluable seconds passed.

The men extinguished with dirt the flames from their torches and began their chase after the boys, following the zigzagging sounds of crunching leaves, snapping sticks, and panting lungs. Sprinting after the boys, they were slowed only by the nuisance of beating aside brush with their machetes and sawed-off shotguns.

"What was that *light*, Dev?" shouted a man, pausing to get a bead on the sounds of the fleeing boys.

"Beats the fire outa me. Firecracker, maybe. A flashlight. All I know is its owner ain't long for this earth!"

"Sounds like more'n one of 'em."

"*Owners*, then!"

The men had not considered the use of a camera, much less that they had been its target. Such a context seemed as senseless here as bouncers at a child's birthday party.

"You don't reckon it was just lightnin', do you?"

"Not unless it was a fireball that just happened to fall a few yards from us, which it wasn't. B'sides, moon's fuller'n a slopped pig!"

"Maybe it was one of them UFO things," another suggested.

"Yeah, an' it landed, and the green men're runnin' that way! Don't be *stupid!*"

The Ghosts of Benevolence

"Well, reckon who knew we was out here?"

Only one logical conclusion could be drawn, they agreed. Someone, somehow, had witnessed the killing.

"Don't care who knew, long as we find 'em."

The men stopped their pursuit, catching their breath.

"Shhh! *Listen*," Devereaux said.

Hearing nothing, Devereaux shouted into the darkness. "I know y'all can hear me, so listen *good!* Y'all *best* keep this *quiet!* Unless we find y'all first, which, if we *do*, we'll help you keep quiet. But, even if y'all manage to survive this night; tomorrow; next week; next month, it ain't over! It won't *ever* be over! Word gets out an' we find out who's *spreadin'* the word," Devereaux continued, "your lives and the lives of your loved ones ain't worth the dirt to cover your graves! From now on, you belong to *us!"* Devereaux held out one hand, gesturing for his companions to be still. He listened for movement. He heard crickets, a whippoorwill, and the crackle of distant flames. "We *will* find you!"

The boys kept their flinch in check despite the stench of another of Jackson's lingering farts. But that wasn't the worst. The boys had settled atop a mound of dirt. Scores of fire ants crawled up and down their legs, stinging like tiny branding irons.

Calm columns of smoke curled into the air, colored silver by the moonlight. The church was a church no more, flattened, smoldering, the singing silenced. Splintered boards of walls and roof, shards of glass, and fragmented sheets of twisted tin roofing covered the ground within a radius of a hundred yards. Supper dishes and pieces of clothed bodies lay scattered over the killing ground. Except for the eighteen-inch brass cross once affixed to the pulpit and found a week later blackened and embedded into the Homecoming live oak, not a trace remained that might suggest holy ground. No bibles, no hymnals, not a recognizable smidgen of a pew survived the blast and the brief, consuming inferno. The lives of thirteen human beings, five children among them, snuffed like candles in a hurricane.

Investigations of the incident, conducted only by local authorities, yielded little substantive information. Few physical clues survived. Those that did, charred torches and such, raised more questions than answers. The locals remained in quiet speculation, despite an unspoken unanimity as with whom the guilt belonged.

Given the nature and targets of the crime, speculation pointed to Jedidiah Ramsey, Supreme Master of the Sutter County chapter of White Aryan Rebels, who was as well the county's incumbent sheriff.

A member of Thankfulness Baptist church, Tibor Johnston, gave public voice to the private scuttlebutt and accused Ramsey outright of the crime. Johnston was not a man to yield to anyone's claim of supremacy, the least of which a white man's. He and fellow church member, Rufus Stephens, were the first blacks since the latter days of slavery to openly challenge white authority in the county. Someone found Johnston's body some three weeks later tied to a cedar tree in his backyard, disemboweled and his throat cut from ear to ear. Stephens was not seen in public again, until that fateful day.

The Ghosts of Benevolence

15

JACKSON WILLOUGHBY AND LANCE
Hawthorne, while possessing key evidence of the identities
of the bombers—and itching to tell someone, anyone—
knew firsthand that relinquishing such evidence was
pointless and would result only in a similar fate handed
themselves and their families. The boys reasoned it best to
let the matter itself die, not the lives of more innocent
people.

Bigotry was omnipotent in these parts, not because of
any robe-wearing, sign-toting conspicuousness. The public
display of physical symbols had all but disappeared from
Sutter County. Images of hatred and memories of violence,
seared into a collective recollection, spawned specters of
fear, haunting the minds of many, paralyzing their wills to
defy the underlying hatred. Folks relied on the salve of
out-of-sight-out-of-mind. Look the other way, and it will
go away. The bombing blew away that mindset of artificial
bliss, becoming instead a harsh reminder that too many
hearts remained unchanged.

Lance viewed twentieth-century racism as peculiar as
the practice of the slavery that had once embodied it.
Racism, justified by religion when need be, befuddled

Mark Randolph Watters

Lance's sense of right and wrong and thus brought into question the validity of religion itself. How, Lance questioned, could God love mankind and send His son to *save* mankind, while, through His silence, vindicate the atrocities one race of mankind inflicted upon another race? For Lance, the first action, the love of God given mankind, contradicted the second.

16

"EARTH TO LANCE! *Earth to Lance!*" Barrett thundered.

"Sorry, Barrett." Lance cleared his throat and squirmed in his chair. "Reeks royal, man. *Too* royal, like southern aristocracy! Just … who is this *Devereaux* fellow anyway?"

Barrett shook his head.

"As you are aware, Mr. Hawthorne, we are in need of timber, pulpwood, and this *fellow* just happens to be the largest landowner in all of South Georgia. He's floated the word that he wants to *sell* this tract to the fattest wallet. Problem is, our competitor, Consolidated Papers, wants this timber too, and they—"

"Consolidated's not going to let that resource get away," Lance interrupted. "Besides, that timber would be far too cost-prohibitive to transport three hundred miles *upstate*. And I thought we sold off most of our timberlands. So … why do *we* want it?"

Barrett sighed with impatience, not only at the interruption but also at Lance's ostensible lapse in basic economics.

"Consolidated's operations are smack in the middle of the vast timber basket of South Georgia. This gives them a comparative strategic advantage over us. Our resources are drying up all around us, what with all the suburbanization in the counties surrounding Atlanta and folks retiring to the mountains. Developers are paying top money for tracts of countryside to build upscale neighborhoods and all the shopping centers and infrastructure to supply those neighborhoods. We might get local wood as that wood's cut down to clear the land, but we've lost our capacity to replace in sufficient, timely quantities what's harvested. We're losing our *leased* timberlands, too. Private landowners in this part of the state, all of whom see the gold their real estate represents, aren't giving papermakers the time of day anymore.

"If you ask me, the sell-off of our timberlands—which generated cash for stock buy-backs and debt reduction—was still as boneheaded and shortsighted a move as our seniors have ever made. I mean, how can we expect to maintain a going concern, never mind achieve a return on investment and declare stockholder dividends, if we lose access to our *basic* raw material, our *core business* of making paper? I screamed my opposition to the sell-off until my voice was but a whisper, but nobody listened. The board was convinced that the region contained enough wood resources for our long-term use without locking up cash in land ownership. 'We'll build chip mills in those remote locations and save money on local woodyard assets. Lease the land or purchase the rights!' they argued. Fools, *all of them*!"

Barrett leaned back in his executive chair, its cracked, padded leather creaking like the pomposity of academia. He paused, basking in the glow of his self-perceived managerial genius. He clasped his hands on back of his balding head and stared at the ceiling, as if beckoning the gods of capitalism to shed enlightenment upon the ignorant masses.

The Ghosts of Benevolence

"Let this be a lesson to you, Hawthorne. Once upon a time, opinions and a quarter wouldn't buy you more than a newspaper. Let me put it this way. Our Directors are waking up. They're pulling the wax from their ears and are listening to what I have to say. We have a chance to *save* this company. We have to clear the fog created from the board's long-held view that we abandon timberland assets. If we have no reliable, long-term raw material base, a base that *we* own and that *we* control, then we might as well hang our 'gone fishing' signs. The board, I think, gets it now.

"So, that said, our ten-year business plan cannot stop merely at acquiring and maintaining more timber rights within our *historical* economic radius," Barrett said, his fist slamming the desk. "We've got to replenish our raw material base by putting the crunch on our *competitors'* access to raw materials. If we don't slow down Consolidated *now*, our cost of wood will ramp up far higher than theirs over the next decade. Our competitive advantage, thanks to our reputation for quality products, not to mention our better roads, will erode correspondingly, if not erased entirely. You *get it* now? Think of it as preservation of that … that *mansion* you live in and that second *kid* you're about to have."

Lance listened with respect, even giving perfunctory pause before responding.

"I understand the economics of competition, Barrett, as well as the realities of maintaining this going concern. But how does my *promotion* help that?" Lance asked.

"*Chance* for promotion, Lance," Barrett clarified. "It ain't a done deal, not *yet*. Mr. Devereaux is a lifelong resident of Benevolence. That's *your* neck of the woods, right? Or *somewhere* down in that abyss of trees, cotton, and red dirt you people call home. I want you, *personally*, to contact Mr. Devereaux and *negotiate* with him for the sale of his twenty-five thousand acres. Don't email him, and don't put a stamp on anything. *Call him* and make a real-time, voice-to-voice appointment. He likes to *hear* the voices and *see* the faces of the people he deals with.

"Mr. Devereaux is not going to be thrilled with *any* offer coming from a forest products company closer to *Atlanta* than to Benevolence. The man has taken it upon himself to alter geography and history by *lowering* the Mason-Dixon Line to the north side of Macon. He hates Yankees; hates Atlanta, too, and all points north; one and the same to him. That makes any one of *us* as good as a direct *descendant* of one William Tecumseh Sherman. Except *you*.

"I'd dust off your South Georgia accent, too, if I were you. Not only does the man hate Yankees, but like your granddaddy's bird dog after a covey of quail, he can sniff out phonies. Drink his liquor like any good ol' boy, if he offers you any, and assure him Standard Paper Industries of Georgia wants this land. Tell him we're looking for wilderness areas host VIP deer hunts or to conduct motivational retreats for management. Tell him he has a lifetime invitation for such, with free accommodations. Tell him it's more land than we need for timber harvests and that any harvesting of timber will be limited to half the acreage purchased. I don't want him to feel like he has betrayed his Consolidated cash cow. Not that the man's capable of *any* feelings at all. Aw, hell, go ahead and tell him we're thinking of *green-fielding* another mill down there, and that, after all, money's money. Money is the *one* language a man like Devereaux understands without regard to geography. The price we pay, I think, will mitigate his sense of ... betrayal." Barrett issued a knowing smile.

"How much does he want for it?" asked Lance.

"Our people tell us that he wants twenty-five hundred per acre, and we're not talking timber rights alone. Consolidated wants *only* the timber rights. We do know he's anxious to rid himself of any major taxable real estate, so maybe we have some foothold here. That's about fifteen hundred dollars per acre higher than if the land were valued for tax purposes as cleared, fallow acreage. Devereaux doesn't want *any* taxable base, much less a taxable base of twenty-five million dollars, after timber rights are factored out of the equation. He's an old man ready to enjoy the fruits of his business acumen. So, maybe he'll take fifteen hundred per acre, lock, stock and barrel. It ain't twenty-five hundred per acre, but it ain't a fallow thousand, either.

Lance crunched numbers on his handheld calculator, as King rattled off the scenarios.

"Wow!" Lance said, his head reeling. "Thirty-seven point five million dollars. *Some fruits!*

"While I don't want to risk losing this tract to a higher bidder, I think we can likely get it for *less* than fifteen hundred per acre. Tell him you'll beat any *documented* offer, but open with a firm offer of eight hundred per acre, which is what Consolidated pays for those timber rights."

"How'd you find that out that bit of intelligence?"

"Barrett the Great has his ways, my friend."

"Why doesn't Devereaux just raise his timber rights price to Consolidated, in lieu of selling outright?" Lance asked.

"Do I have to repeat myself? He doesn't want this huge tax base hanging over him. Now, you can negotiate in fifty-dollar increments, or whatever your subject-to-be-promoted gut tells you, but *do not exceed* fifteen hundred per acre. This is where we get a look at your skills for the art of negotiation and problem management. You did read The Art of the Deal, did you not?"

Barrett paused, taking the half-smoked cigar to his lips and lighting it. He sucked and smacked his lips to stoke the fire, exhaled, and leaned forward slowly in the brown leather chair until his forearms were at rest on the desk.

"That's about seventeen and a half million dollars more than anybody else is going to give him, even

Consolidated." Barrett sucked and blew. "I want this land without a fight, Lance. Bottom line, use your South Georgia origins and get me this land at *my* price and the promotion's yours. Plus a *thirty percent* signing bonus calculated on any difference between the seventeen point five million-dollar premium we're willing to pay and the lesser actual premium you negotiate. How's *that* for a crunchy carrot?"

Lance's attention focused like the Hubble telescope. He crunched more numbers.

If I can whittle old Dev down to, say, a price of twelve hundred, that's a ... seven million, five hundred thousand dollar differential. Times thirty percent ... two and a quarter million! That's what I call a signing bonus, all right.

"I see your wheels turning," Barrett noted, grinning. "Schmooze him all you have to."

I'll schmooze him, all right!

"Play on your common backgrounds."

Hmph! Common killing grounds!

"Share a biscuit. Smear on some mayhaw jelly. I think he likes NASCAR. Dale Earnhardt, maybe? Or is it Petty? Anyway, kiss his feather-plumed hat if it comes to that! Just *get* me that land, and do it for *no more than* fifteen hundred per acre."

Lance struggled to understand Barrett's reasoning for wanting *him* to spearhead such a sensitive purchase. This was a job better suited, Lance believed, for senior management, Procurement perhaps, or Legal, notwithstanding his Benevolence ties.

Maybe, Lance speculated, this indeed was as Barrett had intended, a way for the company to evaluate his skills as a negotiator and manager before officially rewarding him with the promotion. Perhaps the company had long-term plans for Lance after all. He rested his chin in the cup of his forefinger and thumb, his eyes darting with thoughts

The Ghosts of Benevolence

of that schmooze-laden signing bonus. Carrots did not come any crunchier.

Who needs a promotion when I can pocket two and a quarter million, he thought.

Warming to the challenge, he preferred to view this whole matter as a ticket *out* of SPIG, not as digging a deeper hole *within* it. Besides, thirty-eight years had melted away since he last visited his hometown, and hot buttered biscuits smothered with mayhaw jelly were pretty darn good.

Mark Randolph Watters

17

THE NO-MAN'S-LAND OF PREDAWN hours gave Lance the sort of frustration that lingered like the burn of indigestion. He awakened almost every morning at the unconscionable hour of four, sometimes three-thirty, this morning no exception. His eyes popped open, as if his brain were responding to a renegade electrical impulse from an insomniac neighbor's TV remote.

The clock radio displayed a blinding red three, colon, zero, zero. Lance yawned, rolled onto his stomach, and swished his legs across the cool sheets, seeking a solution to his discomfort. Pain from a neck twinge caused by pillows too firm, perhaps pillows too many, shot down his back.

"Son of a—!" he whispered loudly.

His inability to sleep this particular predawn morning correlated more likely to the plan brewing in his brain. The plan was simple, really. He knew the players and had the evidence. He believed Barrett would offer no resistance, once confronted, but Devereaux … He was another matter.

The paperboy tossed the morning anachronism to neighboring driveways. Lance had years ago made the leap to online news sources, and, with the possible exception of the comic pages, he could not imagine anyone, anymore, dropping six bits a day, a couple of bucks on Sunday, for the privilege of accumulating stacks of newsprint and annoying department store advertisements, along with grocery store coupons for everything except what anybody actually bought. For those who had to have their daily dose of Dilbert or Doonesbury, there were websites for that, for God's sake! Lance Hawthorne found the burn of indigestion in the most inane things.

The rusted Civic's booming bass echoed throughout the neighborhood, interrupting the sacred intervals between hits on Lance's snooze button. Newspapers flew with indifference out the car's window, falling onto driveways and flower beds.

These paperboys have it made, Lance thought, envious of the freedom he perceived. *Their only concerns are food, techno gadgetry, and more food. Makes me long for the life again.*

Lance rolled onto his back, finding solace in the beams of moonlight sliding through the slats of the bedroom window's plantation shutters. He stared at the silhouettes of the dogwood and pine trees in the backyard and smiled at the thought of being as free as the neighborhood dogs barking and scurrying after squirrels. He heard the distant wail of sirens and gave thanks that he was neither their destination nor their cargo.

He turned to Jessica. She curled onto her left side and breathed the soft, steady sound of sleep, unconcerned with the realities of consciousness. Lance was going back to Benevolence, his birthplace, his hometown. Despite his plan, or perhaps because of it, he did not look forward to the trip. Not really.

He slid his legs across the mattress and onto the floor. He slouched forward, hands braced on the bed, searching for the strength to rise. The fast-fading life of dreams adrift found passage to his mouth as he uttered a mixture of

The Ghosts of Benevolence

contemporary sense and long-ago fog. Slogging his way to the bathroom, he whispered aloud, "I didn't *want* to take those reins, but that so-and-so *made* me ... he *made* me! And ... and I *killed* her! I let those horses get away from me because I was too wrapped up in my own desires. I pouted instead of paying attention. What's more, God could have *stopped* it all!"

The whole thing, Lance had convinced himself, locked in the mental mirages of the dead of night, was God's fault. "He could have prevented *all of that* from happening. He could have *stopped* it!"

"Lance? Lance, are you okay, sweetie?" Jessica asked, awakened by the chatter.

"Fine, Jess. Go back to sleep."

"Bring me water?"

"Water? Sure. Let me get *rid* of some water first."

Water shed and water delivered, they did go back to sleep for a couple of hours, Lance drifting off under the influence of Jessica's sedative touch.

A flock of a dozen Canada geese, their squeaking bellows announcing their arrival, glided through a shroud of fog to a landing in the Hawthorne's backyard. The geese touched down in unison and immediately began feeding on insects and earthworms washed out of the ground during the night's rainfall. Lance checked the contents of his suitcase one last time making certain it contained plenty of socks and underwear.

"Don't you trust me, sweetie?" Jessica asked, smiling. "It's all there, and then some. Go eat your breakfast. Ooommf!"

"Babe, you okay?" Lance asked, feigning full sincerity, his eyes fixed upon his fidget with the suitcase's contents.

"I'm fine; just that nagging twitch in my middle back. Guess I'm just getting too big now, front-heavy." Jessica reached around Lance's waist and snapped the suitcase closed. She sat on the bed's edge. "Your little girl is moving around a lot lately. Want to feel?"

Lance, having perfected his daily appearance of caring, placed his hand, warmed by a cup of hot coffee, squarely on the zenith of Jessica's abdomen, which seemed to roll from side to side like a special effect.

"See? Jerri's telling her daddy that she loves him and to hurry home!"

Lance gazed into Jessica's eyes, rubbed her tummy, and kissed her forehead.

"I love you," he whispered, the words dripping with a seduction that once upon a time rendered Jessica faint and full of anticipation.

"Go eat your eggs, you silly goose," Jessica replied, unaccustomed lately to such acts of affection from her husband. Slowly, she slid forward off the bed, pushing herself to a standing position. Lance gave Jessica a moving massage as she lumbered toward the kitchen. Jessica cooed her approval.

"I want to check on Gini first," Jessica said.

Three-year-old Ginibeth slept snug under her flowered covers, oblivious to the complexities and posturing of the swirling world of adults.

Lance had managed during Ginibeth's infancy to bob and weave his way out of a father's more personal responsibilities. Diaper changes, story readings, stroller pushings and other intimate moments of father-daughter bonding was as foreign to Lance's sense of manhood as water off a waxed car. He had not failed in his provision of the daily recommended allowances of food, shelter, and clothing. For Lance, these 'DRAs' fulfilled his responsibilities, as if marriage and child-rearing were a form of contract, a purchase agreement, and thus a superior substitute for a weak-kneed expression of hands-on love. Twelve-hour days in the office, along with monthly feedings of a college fund, served as Lance's justification

The Ghosts of Benevolence

for after-work inertia. Thus, he showered Jess and Ginibeth with the power of his credit score, and left himself comfortably wondering what more to fathering could there be.

Private moments found Lance lamenting the passing of the intimacy he and Jessica shared prior to Ginibeth, and now Jerri. Looking for the convenient scapegoat, the easy answer, he blamed the children for the "loss" of his wife and for his inability to adapt to the strange new world of parenting. He feared an ugly manifestation of his resentment should the delicate silk of circumstances tatter. He guarded these raw truths from Jessica, whom he fiercely loved as much as any of his other possessions, despite his growing complacency toward her.

Lance peered over Jessica's shoulder through the narrow opening into Ginibeth's bedroom door. Ever the cruncher of numbers and spinner of estimates, Lance calculated in his mind the total monetary cost of raising a child from birth to the age of eighteen.

"*Three hundred and ninety-six thousand legal tender American greenbacks*," he mouthed, each syllable flipping off his tongue like coffee grounds. "Times two! A lot of stuff could be *had* for eight hundred grand."

"What's that you said, honey?" Jessica asked, her mind focused on her sleeping daughter and her shifting unborn.

"Nothing, Jess. Just … just thinking out loud."

"Penny for your thoughts," Jessica replied, wrapping her arm around Lance's waist and resting her head against his shoulder.

You don't want to know! Lance thought.

"I was … just thinking about … about what we should name our baby."

"*Name* our baby? Lance, her name's *Jerri*. You named her yourself." Jessica touched her palm to Lance's forehead. "Are you feeling okay?"

"*Jerri*. Right! I'm a ... a bit distracted today, Jess, trip and all. I'll be fine. Breakfast?"

Not fine! he thought. *I'm going to blow this Devereaux deal, and I'll be the one going to jail, if for nothing else, withholding evidence!*

Ginibeth slept soundly, like a fawn in a meadow, shrouded with innocence and utterly unaware of the menace evolving in her midst.

"Speaking of geese, have you—"

"Shhh, Lance!" Jessica interrupted. "You'll wake her! What *geese*?"

"A few minutes ago," Lance whispered. "You called me a silly goose. Speaking of which, have you ever *seen* such a crowd of 'em in our yard?" Lance turned and made his way towards the kitchen. "She sleeps too long, anyway."

Jessica sighed, again dismissing Lance's indifference, and followed behind.

"That rain last night emptied the ground of earthworms and other yucky stuff only feathered animals could eat. The geese are reaping the harvest." Jessica pulled back the kitchen window curtain, careful not to startle the dining geese. "They could have landed anyplace. I love seeing them pick *our* yard for a meal. It's such a peaceful sight."

"Yeah, peaceful, until we have to find our way around all the goose crud. Not good for Ginibeth to play in a goose-crudded backyard," Lance observed, as if he cared, sipping his coffee, immediately chasing it with a swallow of water. *"Ow!* You have to make it so damn *hot?*

"I'm *sorry*, honey. I didn't mean to ... I mean, it's no hotter than usual. Please keep your voice down," Jessica chided with a smile, patting her tummy. "Jerri will *hear* you!"

Lance rolled his eyes and sprinkled salt and pepper on his scrambled eggs. He took his fork and mixed the seasonings.

The Ghosts of Benevolence

"Eggs feel a bit rubbery, Jess. Cold, too."

"I made them a half hour ago, when I thought you were ready for them."

"I wasn't out of bed a half hour ago."

"You're *always* out of bed a half hour ago, usually no later than five o'clock."

"Whatever."

Lance shoveled the eggs into his mouth while scanning his to-do list. Gas up Mercedes. Call Earl Bentley Devereaux, the Third. Lance mouthed with contempt "the Third", tilting his head right and left, emphasizing the snobbery he perceived to exude from the generational appendage affixed to Devereaux's name, as if, indeed, the Devereauxs had presumed royalty upon themselves.

"Why do some parents give their sons the same full name?"

"What do you mean, Lance?"

"You know, a dad gives his newborn son the same name but adds on 'the second' or 'the third', 'the *sixteenth*', as if the boy were the latest in a long line of kings, trying somehow to clone himself."

"It *is* sort of lazy, now that you mention it."

"It's freaking *narcissistic*, at best unoriginal! You'd think these people could come up with a fresh name for their kid. How hard can it be? Don't matter anyway. I got Mr. Earl Bentley Devereaux, *the Third* by the short ones, and when I'm through with him, I won't need this stinkin' job."

"Are you okay, honey?" Jessica asked.

"You can stop with feeling my forehead, Jess. I'm fine."

"What's this about not needing your job? Maybe *you* don't need it, but the rest of us do!"

Lance sighed and took another clump of rubbery eggs to his mouth. "Nothing, Jess. Just some frustration with Barrett, is all. Eggs are fine, really."

Lance looked up from his list for a few ponderous moments and out the kitchen bay window toward the geese, dining contently on their slithery bounty.

"Ah, to be a child. Or a goose." Lance smiled, continuing with his to-do list. "Let's see, deliver package to Global Technical Solutions."

The name Global Technical Solutions chimed in Lance's brain like the bells of Big Ben. The name should have been just another of the hundreds of like-sounding company names competing for attention in the information technology industry. Lance awaited the results of Heather's investigation into incorrect—perhaps improper—ship-to addresses on most of Global's invoices to Standard Paper Industries of Georgia.

"Don't forget this package," Jessica said. "Heavy. What's inside this thing, Lance?"

"Contracts. Purchase agreements. Maybe a check for payment of thirty laptops and an upgraded PowerSystem7 server, supposedly delivered two weeks earlier. Who knows?"

"Supposedly?"

"Nobody's seen them, those servers and laptops" Lance replied. "Barrett signed the invoice approving payment, all one hundred and fifty thousand dollars of it, not including installation charges, so I guess *he's* seen 'em."

Lance examined the large, bubble-padded FedEx envelope, filled to a thickness of three inches, tightly packed. Barrett had given Lance the package the day before, exhorting him to handle it with utmost care, as if Lance needed such an admonition.

Lance brought to mind one of Barrett's hated meetings from a few weeks ago. The subject was the single-sourcing of computer hardware and outside IT services suppliers. Seemed strange to Lance that any payments and contracts, if indeed that's what the envelope contained, were not

The Ghosts of Benevolence

being channeled through normal corporate mailings. Hand-deliveries seemed so … paperboy-like. Maybe it was part of SPIG's latest management epiphany: 'Vendor Relationship Enhancement' or some other mumbo-jumbo initiative doomed, as were all the others, for the pits of obsolescence.

"Jess, I'm not sure how long this is going to take. Could take half a day or a couple of days, maybe longer. I'll be as quick about it as I can. Barrett wants that land, and, well, you know what's at stake for us. You *do* want me to get that promotion, don't you?"

"What I want is for you to be *careful*. Those people don't like to be rushed down there. They follow a certain … *protocol* when conducting matters of business, and—"

"*Those* people? *Protocol?* Since when do you know anything about protocol? Or *those* people?"

"You know what I mean, Lance. All I'm saying is that folks down there live in accordance to a strict, shall we say, 'code of conduct' and are not given to our Yankee ways."

"*Yankee* ways? Now, what does *that* mean?" Lance pressed, a bit annoyed by Jessica's affinity for labeling.

Jessica sighed. "Lance, you know as well as I that those people consider anyone living north of Macon a Yankee equivalent, just another in a stream of endless northern transplants."

Lance stared at Jessica's balloon-like belly and muttered, "Lee referred to Yankees as 'those people'."

"What? Lee *who*?" Jessica asked.

"Robert E, the one and only. He hardly ever referred to Yankees as 'the enemy', though he meant 'those people' as a more denigrating equivalent. Is that what you mean?"

"Of course not!" Jessica paused. "Not really."

"Could it be your *Pennsylvania* upbringing showing?" Lance teased.

"You might be surprised to learn I once heard one of those people—"

Mark Randolph Watters

"There you go with 'those people' again."

"—say that the only thing worse than a Northern Yankee was a Southern nig—" Again, Jessica paused. "I can't even *repeat* it, the words were so *repulsive!* We're not 'Northern Yankees', like such New Yorkers or Ohioans, but we might as well be."

"Oh, so we're more like *Pennsylvanians*."

"Hush, Lance. Stop teasing me; I'm trying to be serious. Doesn't matter to them that we're Georgians, is what I'm saying. To them, we're the functional equivalent of Yankees. What matters in *their* minds is that we've all but *abandoned* our southern dialect, maybe our southern heritage. We drive foreign luxury cars; we cavort with transplants; we sip lattes at Starbucks; and we don't pay homage to the Confederate flag. That, my dear husband, is akin to treason in their world. They're farmers, and we're … well, we're *city folks*."

"Why do you box those people in, Jess?"

"You said it, too."

"Said what, too?"

"Those people." Jessica enjoyed her return of tease to Lance.

"Look, *you're* as bad as you claim *them* to be, Jess, *worse* maybe. What, exactly, are our 'Yankee ways,' pray tell? We live in a 21st-century America, not 1861. By the way, I happen to *love* the Confederate flag, for its history, not its stereotypes."

"You know what I'm saying," Jessica replied, fumbling to put the proper context to her prejudices, "get things done *now*; removing all obstacles at any cost; accumulation of material wealth; indifference to emotion; no time for basic respect. Those sorts of things. Maybe they have a *point* about our having Yankee ways. We're a lot *like* that, you know. I'm beginning to understand how they might *not* be too fond of us, how they might *not* trust us."

The Ghosts of Benevolence

"Do *you* trust *you*?" Lance asked.

"Come to think of it," Jessica replied in a moment of self-indictment, "I'm not so sure."

Lance dodged an array of Ginibeth's toys on his way to the coffee pot to pour a second cup. Stirring the mixture of cream and sugar, he peered with growing annoyance at Jessica.

"Yankee ways," Lance mumbled, his back turned. "Should *I* trust you? And can we get these *stupid toys* out of the floor?" Lance shoved aside a stuffed animal. "We don't have a house; we have an indoor playground!"

Lance set his coffee mug on the counter.

"Look, Jess, I'm going to my hometown to deliver an invoice and to strike an honest deal with an old acquaintance and hopefully, by doing so, win a promotion for me and you and little Ginibeth." Lance paused in afterthought. "And Jerri. Okay, so maybe I'll have to resort to some good old fashioned arm twisting, but no one'll be the worse for wear. That's *business*."

"*Bad* business, if you ask me." Jessica sipped her milk. "You're taking the photo, aren't you?"

Lance tapped the left breast pocket of his jacket. "Got it right here, babe, a copy anyway."

"You sound glad of it. Lance, *no one* can know about that photograph. I thought you *understood* that. It's evidence withheld, for one thing. But mainly, if Devereaux finds out about it ... well, I go back to that good ol' Southern code of justice. *Do not take the picture!*"

"Jess, it's my *trump* card. I intend to get that land, and for a lot cheaper than Barrett thinks I'm capable. I'm the middleman, a go-between. Besides, Mr. Earl Bentley Devereaux, the *Third* is in no position to refuse any offer of mine. He just doesn't know that yet. You think he wouldn't do the same thing if the tables were turned? You think he amassed his empire on good looks and a Southern drawl? The man's *cunning*. Why, I'll be lucky if he

131

Mark Randolph Watters

doesn't see right through my 'Yankee ways', exposing me for all my corrupt *carpetbagging* ways."

Lance grinned but could see in Jessica's frown she did not share his humor.

"You've got that look in your eye, Lance."

"What *look*?"

"That far-off look; that ulterior-motives look."

"Don't worry, Jess. I'll be *fine*; really, I *will*. It'll *all* work out. I'll call you soon as I as get down there and check in." Lance poured the remaining coffee into the sink and reached for the car keys hanging on a wall hook. "Owww. My back is *killing* me. All that leaning over and pulling weeds last evening has really fouled up my lower back. You know, Jess, you're *really* going to have a time with me when I get old."

"I *am*?" Jessica said, grinning.

"*Aren't* you?"

Jessica pushed the garage door button. The door screeched of metal on metal and rose slowly.

"Need to have that looked at, too," Jessica noted. "Sounds awful, and the door's moving slower and slower."

"Take care of it when I get home."

The foggy air spilled in. Geese fluttered and winged westward, startled by the sudden sounds and movement. Jessica waved to her husband and mouthed "I love you" as he pulled out of the garage and down the driveway.

She stood watching Lance disappear through the fog. Silence flooded into the early-morning void. She listened for approaching flocks of geese. Hearing none, she returned to the comfort of her bed.

The crud, alas, lingered.

The Ghosts of Benevolence

18

THE DRIVE SOUTH HAD a numbing effect on Lance, like watching paint dry. Lance set the cruise control at seventy in a sixty-five-mile-per-hour zone and strained to avoid a head-flop onto his steering wheel along the straight, featureless stretches of roadway. The roads from Atlanta to Columbus to Benevolence had improved during Lance's thirty-eight-year absence from the region, but the terrain and its pines still were little more inspiring than carpet stains.

Lance reached under the seat, taking the first CD case he touched, and removed the disc. He inserted it into the player, avoiding a peek at the title so as to preserve the surprise. He waited for the music to begin. The comforting strains "Elmer's Tune" filled the car's cabin, much to Lance's delight, striking every string of his ideal of a romanticized past.

Ah, Glenn Miller. Perfect! Lance thought, settling snugly into the soft leather holds of his Mercedes.

"What makes a lady ... of eighty ... go out on the loose?" he sang along. "Why does a gander ... meander ... in search of a goose? What puts the kick in ... a chicken ... the magic in June? It's just Elmer's Tune."

Mark Randolph Watters

Exposed in childhood to the music of Glenn Miller, Fletcher Henderson, Benny Goodman and the like, Lance had adopted as his own such big-band swing tunes. He remembered fondly the New Year's Eves spent listening to the innocuity of Guy Lombardo and Lawrence Welk.

Music of the Beatles, the Stones, any band with an electric guitar—"spawn of Satan himself," Peyton drilled into Lance—was forbidden in the Hawthorne household, not that Peyton Hawthorne spoke eloquently for God regarding any subject. But Peyton cursed this electrified music of a changing America, as if it were the growling fangs of rabid dogs, not the velvety licks of submissive pups. Throbbing bass lines and searing guitars gave emphasis to music's suggestive spirit, a universal articulation of immorality and irresponsibility, an in-your-face mindset of anything-goes thinking.

Maybe Daddy was right, thought Lance, as the music played on.

> 'The hurdy-gurdies, the birdies, the cop on the beat;
> The candy maker, the baker, the man on the street;
> The city charmer, the farmer, the man in the moon;
> All sing Elmer's Tune.'

Not just *some*. *All* sing Elmer's tune, old and young alike.

Didn't they?

Shouldn't they?

The more Lance listened to the "golden oldies" of the decades of the rock-and-roll era, the more obvious it became to his mind that the values of his parents and generations prior were not simply trashed. No, they had been recipients of musical kicks to the head, thrown to the curb as impertinent to the new cultural progression.

The music played on.

The Ghosts of Benevolence

'A, B, C, D, E, F, G, H … I've got a gal-l-l-l … in Kalamazoo.'

Maybe something as simple and complex as music rooted Peyton's bitterness, his torturous isolation he had long ago adopted as the foundation for raising his family. Farm life embodied the art of preservation. If it took isolation from a changing culture to preserve a bygone world, a world reveled still by farmers—and the man in the moon—then Peyton obliged.

Peyton Hawthorne became just another of countless pre-boomers rendered irrelevant in the decades following World War II, upon the advent of the pelvic swivel and cereal-bowl haircuts.

Daddy was not rejecting me, per se, Lance thought, *not so much as he was a world he couldn't intimidate into submission.*

Rationalization served Lance well, almost as numbing as the landscape zipping by him. He blasted through an intersection, unaware of the stop sign's octagonal shout or the T-boning he had narrowly missed or the blaring horns and squalling tires of reactive cars.

Peyton had rejected, instead, an America infected with the rot of apathy, so the rationalization went, a disease without a cure, spreading across the land with the contagious, contiguous fervor of yellow fever.

'Pardon me boy, is that the Chattanooga Choo-Choo? (Yes, yes!) Track 29! Boy you can give me a shine …'

Peyton had wanted only to protect his family from the contagion, from a railroading of disrespect upon a generation who had more than earned the world's eternal respect.

Still, for Lance, the memories lingered and burned, notwithstanding the rationalization. He drove the baron, black ribbon … and remembered.

Mark Randolph Watters

The anger in his voice, vengeful as a Hitler oration, sliced through the soggy air like an April bolt of lightning. The verbal assaults began in earnest after Sara's death. Peyton reasoned his rantings as necessary for his family's nurturing as water for an arid soil. He believed Sara's brand of nurturing too soft, too lenient on the children, and thus in need of rectification.

"You don't know *crap* about nothin', boy, and the passage of time ain't makin' you no smarter!" screamed Peyton, his arms waving like a whirligig. "Look at you! Cain't you dig a simple *posthole*, for God's sake? Plunge. Squeeze. Pull! You hardly know *warts* from *watermelons*; you can't tack up a simple line of barbed wire, much less clean sparkplugs or plow a straight row. I reckon you'll need direction shovelin' that horse dung.

"Homework? Oh, you know your *'rithmetic* all right, spellin', too. You can rattle off the answer for twelve times nine or eighty-four divided by seven and such nonsense as that in less time than it takes me to burp in my beer. You can even tell ever'body what the capital of Egypt is, bragging as you go, wherever the heck Egypt is—as if anybody gives a rip—and even spell it right, but you cain't so much as clean a paintbrush without spillin' the turpentine all over you. Have you got around to knockin' the mud off them plow tines yet? *Shaw*, no! What good's all that book learnin' when I got me a *family* to feed? Tell me how these multiplication facts is gonna keep my corn green and my livestock in milk. You think knowin' the capital of Timbuktu or what Lincoln said at Gettysburg is gonna pay a *dime* of my mortgage? Of course it ain't. I need your *hands*, boy, not your brain. My *God*, boy, what's got *hold* of you anyhow? You want *homework?* I'll *give* you homework.

"The sooner you realize you ain't nothin' more'n spawn of a South Georgia farmer, and *accept* it, the sooner you'll understand what I'm *sayin'* to you, boy. Bein' *field*

The Ghosts of Benevolence

smart, bein' *field* productive, *not* memorizin' gibberish
from books, least not *here*, which is where you'll still be
forty years from now, is what you're meant for, boy.
Books're for yankees an' niggers an' politicians and folks
like Devereaux, folks who never did, never will *do*, this
country any good anyhow. It's folks like me that's kept
this country from speakin' the tongue of the Nazis. Them
Yankees, them bookworms an' such, might *think* we're
trash, dadburn 'em all, but at least we *know* how to survive,
boy, *survive!"*

Young Lance was as captive to his daddy's rants as a
convict was to a prison cell.

"You think that while ol' man Devereaux counts his
millions, he gives a hobo's pile about me, about us?"
Peyton asked rhetorically, gesturing in the direction of the
Devereaux house, his teeth pressed together with mounting
resentment. Peyton stopped. Taking a breath, he softened
the harshness in his tone.

"You got to look *around* you, boy, keep your ears
open; pay attention to what God put in your *bones!"* he
said, as if he'd ever done anything of the sort. This *land'll*
tell you all you'll *ever* need to know," he said, pointing to
fields filled with sustenance borne of sweat and callouses.
Truth be told, Peyton Hawthorne feared the dishonor of
failure more than he craved the glow of success. "But you
got to pay close attention.

"Now go get them gloves. I don't wanna hear another
word about your homework. *This* is your homework! You
wouldn't even *go* to school if it wasn't against the law to
keep you home. The only real homework you got is in
them fields. The seasons and *me* are the only teachers
you'll *ever* need! We got us a month's worth of work to do
in a week's time. This land and its harvest, boy, it's our
lives, our *survival*, yours and mine and ..."

Peyton paused, his thoughts catching up to his words.

Mark Randolph Watters

"Sara's an' mine, yours an' Aunt Pearl's," he whispered, "An' Becca's. Go on, now!" He hadn't yet burned through his grief over Becca's passing.

And so it was in the young life of Lance Peyton Hawthorne. He struggled without end to satiate the insatiable, to impress the unimpressible, to break through the symbolic stacks of suppressive hay that surrounded him, to pave a road over the red clay of ignorance keeping him penned. As an oyster converts into a pearl the irritant of a grain of sand, Lance wanted to 'pearlize' his life before the irritant encased him.

Peyton Henry Hawthorne meant well, Lance believed, but Lance dared not cross his daddy, a hulking broad-shouldered man who referred to Lance as "boy" and had sculpted a living out of the red earth during the days when book-educated men wielded pencils but were penniless nonetheless.

Lance raced to the shed to retrieve his gloves, more from fear of his daddy's ire than a desire to conform to his wishes. Lance's teal-blue eyes welled with tears at the thought of opportunity lost, of his future dying before his eyes, of never seeing a beckoning world through the windows of enlightenment. But he was careful not to let one drop of those tears emote from their holds. If nothing else, Lance still had his pride. *It ain't really crying if the tears don't fall,* Lance believed.

Besides, Peyton *never* cried, even when Lance's older sister by three years died in the fall of 1960 from a tetanus infection. The tender flesh of her bare foot found a rusted nail down near the cedar swing tree in the front yard. The nail protruded from a discarded plank, several of which had been deemed unsalvageable after a tornado destroyed the barn in the spring of 1953. The planks lay long forgotten in high rye and low blackberry.

Becca never had a chance. She preferred enduring the pain, the blood, even the ravages of infection, rather than admitting to her daddy the carelessness of her accident, rather than face his heartless judgment of such folly.

"A fallow field is fraught with danger," Peyton would say, index finger pointed skyward like some heartless tinman. "You should have *watched your step*," he would chide, dismissing the episode with a swallow of homebrew as another in a stream of life's lessons, their unfortunate effects thus deserved, regardless of the cruelty of the cause.

"The wound looks *shallow*," reasoned Becca as she squeezed the hole to relieve its deep burn. "It ain't hardly bleedin' none."

Her flawed reasoning took her beyond the point of no return, the infection coursing through her bloodstream, overwhelming her system's ability to fight, developing quickly into facial cramps, each in hopeful dismissal assigned to nervous twitches. The spasms soon spread to other areas, locking her jaw and sending her back contracting into a relentless pull of pain. She lingered another three days writhing and contracting in semi-consciousness, unable to speak, to eat, or to drink.

"Them spasms is just *fever* spells, Precious; they'll peter out, you'll see." Peyton insisted, unable to meet Becca's eyes with his own. He stroked her contorted cheeks, swabbed away her rising perspiration, as he struggled to divert focus from his own folly.

Peyton's world pushed and pulled, like tectonic plates in their inexorable grind for position, a mighty struggle between the acceptance of rural realities and the remedy of personal denials. Peyton stubbornly refused to deliver Becca to Doc Porter. Matters of life and death deserved treatment at home, always at home. Pride was a powerful force.

Becca Hawthorne died of suffocation, her painful form unable to embrace Sara at her side. At her moment of death Peyton finished his frenzied plowing of the southeast corner of Mr. Godfrey's cotton field, a job taken just that morning, after having denied for days the need to earn a few extra dollars for Becca's visit to Doc Porter, who would have treated her for nothing. Peyton relented finally, his denial awakened by the sight of his bent Becca and her pitiful, muted screaming.

But it was too little, too late. Peyton burst through the half-closed door, clenching in his fist a crumpled twenty-dollar bill.

"I got the money!" he shouted. "Let's get her to Doc Porter's!"

The Godfrey field completed and his work compensated, Peyton's wildly ecstatic eyes narrowed, then closed, upon the realization his beloved Becca had passed. Sara's quivering cries drowned out the five o'clock peal of the distant church bells. Peyton dropped the worthless twenty to the floor and retreated to the kitchen, where he stood motionless for what seemed to Lance hours into the night, as if he were one of Sara's ceramic ducks, eyes hollow, cold, refusing to allow again any image of his dead daughter to enter his mind.

Daddy changed that day, Lance remembered. Despite all that suggested the contrary, Peyton saw in Becca innocence in its purest form, an antidote to all he loathed about the new American attitude. He refused to accept her mortality, until backed into a corner like a wounded coyote, until acceptance became the only option.

Becca's death shattered any hope Peyton harbored that his world might be salvaged. Lance was Peyton's boy, but Becca was his jewel. What little lived within Peyton, up until the moment of Becca's death, fell stone dead that day.

19

ANGRY FROM HIS DADDY'S scathing rebuke, and embarrassed with the apparent vanity of the wasted hours of study and dreams of learning, Lance reached for his gloves atop the splintered, spider-webbed shelf. An appreciation of the farm's unforgiving ways would have served Lance well this day.

Lance pulled the stiff, mud-crusted glove over the skin of fingers thickened by the drudgery of endless farm labor. He repeated with the other glove. Immediately, he felt the stab, followed by a radiating sting of a point thrust inside his palm. Lance shrieked. He seized his gut and shook free the glove. Pain pulsated through his body like the ripples of a mighty splash. This time the tears tumbled.

Peyton heard the commotion. He thought at first his boy had met up with the fangs of a snake. More from the inconvenience of losing a tolerable work hand than from a father's compassion, he stormed through the rows of head-high corn, gaining speed from the gentle downward slope of the field.

Lance saw through the distorted vision of his watered eyes the path of mangled stalks swaying in the wake of his daddy's charge. Resolved to be dry-eyed by the time his daddy reached the shed, Lance looked skyward and breathed deeply. Peyton had a couple dozen rows yet to trample, plus the leap of a shallow creek; time remained for Lance to absorb the electric pain, to free himself of emotions shaken loose, to become a man.

Peyton skidded to a halt. He doubled over, hands on knees, nostrils flaring like a maddened bull.

"What *happened*, boy? What you screamin' for? You … you *snakebit?*" Peyton queried breathlessly, his heartbeat vibrating his overalls.

"Don't rightly know!" Lance responded, shaking his hand. "Something's done gone and taken a bite of me. Right here. Hurts like a *bitch!*"

Peyton smiled, eyes widened in surprise at his son's choice of words. He took the boy's hand.

"Sho nuff," Peyton confirmed. "But it ain't no snake."

Indeed, something had stung the center of Lance's right palm. The purple-red point of penetration topped an expanding swell, consuming the hand to just above the wrist.

"Scorpion, son," Peyton mumbled, shaking the glove to reveal the guilty dirt-brown creature.

Lance pressed his teeth, squinted his watered eyes, and suppressed the expressions pain demanded.

"There's what gotcha. See it?" Peyton observed, pointing to the dirt floor.

Lance looked down at the scorpion, its defiant tail curved upwards, tipped by its ready stinger and poised to strike again any unfortunate who dared dabble within its range. As it began its spidery crawl away, Peyton slammed the sole of his mud-caked leather boot down onto the doomed arachnid. He gave his boot several rapid twists, until the scorpion became indiscernible from the soil.

The place was crawling with the things, Peyton knew, but this sort of thing was common knowledge among country folk. This was as much the scorpion's domain,

The Ghosts of Benevolence

more so, as it was the Hawthorne's. The boy should have known. Peyton's thoughts turned to Becca.

"Daddy?"

"Becca," Peyton mouthed. Shaking loose his thoughts, Peyton turned his attention to his boy. Tearless, Lance clutched his wrist and grimaced.

"Why didn't you check the gloves first, boy?" Peyton demanded.

Never did before, thought Lance.

"Don't you know 'bout scorpions and black widders an' such, boy?"

Always his 'boy'. *Only* his 'boy'.

Once upon a time, Peyton would have stopped after issuing his admonitions, his loveless lessons of life on the farm, turning his focus to the endless beckoning of chores. Not this time.

"Let's get you up to the house and rub some tomato leaves on that thing, get that swellin' down. Corn shucks'll do it good, too."

The bulge of redness had extended beyond the wrist, halfway up Lance's right arm, and appeared tight enough to pop with a pin. The home remedy of tomato leaves applied to a sting was Peyton's way of preparing his son for what really needed doing.

Peyton understood the power of the South Georgia scorpion sting. Thunderheads, he called them. Lightning waiting to strike. Hawthornes had a history of sensitivity to its venom, as if bitten by a diamondback. Peyton had come within a gnat's whisker of dying as a child from a similar encounter and believed the necessary preparatory act was to apply a tourniquet just above the swelling's boundary, to slow the march of poison-laden blood to the heart and brain, before cutting the puncture of the sting and sucking out whatever poison could be removed. Such was the method applied to field-treating the bites of vipers or black widows, even fiddlebacks, experiences as common to farmers as birthing babies were to midwives. The concern now was the extent to which the venom had invaded the bloodstream. Peyton yanked open the kitchen screen door, its hinges screeching with years of neglect.

"Sit down right here, boy," he said, pointing.

With his right hand, Peyton unbuckled his belt and stripped it free of his pants in a single whipping motion, like cracking bullwhips, a move he had perfected over years of inflicting his brand of justice upon the boy.

He cradled Lance's deformed hand in his left palm. Deftly, with his free hand, he twisted his 36-inch leather belt around Lance's taut, sinewy upper arm, using his teeth as effectively as he would his other hand, had he its use.

Lance closed his eyes. He knew what was coming. No baseball for at least a week, maybe the rest of the summer. Lance pondered this emerging truth, tallying his losses. And his gains. Thunderheads, after all, had their silver linings. More time for books. No weeding, plowing or digging postholes; no fence-tacking, either. *Maybe all this pain's worth it*, he concluded.

Just then, he squinted to see the tip of the blade of his daddy's bone-handled pocketknife as it entered ground zero, cutting an opening for Peyton to apply sufficient sucking. At that moment, the balance of loss and gain was tipped decidedly in the favor of loss.

Lance recovered physically from the scorpion's sting, but the same recovery could not be said of the sting of his daddy's indifference. The chores continued, the hours longer to compensate for the loss of Lance's agility. More than to possess all the gold of Fort Knox, Lance wanted to please his daddy, to feel the warmth of his approval.

Apathy had overtaken Peyton, rendering him unpleasable. After the loss of Becca, then Sara, Peyton's life devolved into a merciless journey of torturous awareness, accelerating his way to an inevitably premature death. Peyton had died already, long ago, and nothing

The Ghosts of Benevolence

Lance did, nothing he aspired to do, could unring the bell. How Peyton died, or when, mattered little anymore. His was the death of a thousand cuts, the cumulative effects of experiences that had spiraled beyond his control. That one physically died was the universal certainty. Not knowing when became enough to polarize Peyton from the pleasures of living. He entertained time and again thoughts of suicide, but prurient pleasures visited upon his eroding character, like demons toying with him, pulling him time and again from the merciful brink.

As time passed, Hawthorne became a name of dishonorable renown undeserving of others' sympathies. Peyton slipping back into the sins of a reputation he had inherited and honed, then exploited. "Sins of the fathers", he'd often heard, and he played the prophecy well. The citizens of Benevolence knew too well his reputation, as permanent as a deformity and just as repulsive.

A child of a self-sacrificing mother and an itinerant father, Peyton grew up during the lean, long years of the Great Depression. The services provided to men by Peyton's mother, services meant for the purposes of filling her family's plates and clothing her children's backs, were rendered in exchange for such promises often unfulfilled and IOUs seldom redeemed. Survival was a great motivator and teacher, even when the means lacked the appearance of decency. People independent of desperation took notice, people whose opinions ordinarily would not have mattered.

As a child, Peyton spent days drifting where his imagination dictated, often out of the house and into nearby fields, finding refuge from the volatility of his parents' vitriolic engagements. He developed a taste for the entrepreneurial spirit somewhere along the way by resorting to the peculiar, yet resourceful, practice of digging earthworms and collecting crickets, offering them for sale to the ready market of fishermen engaged in their

145

own refuge along the banks of Pumpkin Creek, most of whom otherwise settled for pieces of pine bark or homemade lures as bait.

He learned the craft of farming by means of the indifference of trial and error, relying mostly on the kindness of neighboring sharecroppers for his field education and his sustenance.

Peyton's mother, when not soliciting the seamy side of a man's nature, would lay motionless on her bed for the better part of the days, as if to induce by sheer force of will the fortunes of her depleted hopes to somehow materialize and fall from the sky. None did.

Peyton, thus, raised himself. Stumbling through childhood as best he could, Peyton hoped for someone, *anyone*, to click off the switch of darkness. The click never came.

Lance stared at the spot of his scorpion sting, the swelling nearly gone but its memory seared. He watched as the shackles of ignorance and loneliness tightened their grip on Peyton, as if his every breath made the grip tighter. The harshness of the years had rendered Peyton Hawthorne's view of the value of life as blind as the fish of cave rivers.

20

THE MEMORIES OF LANCE'S childhood spewed forth, a sudden regurgitation, blocking his attention on the present. In a moment of breathless surprise, Lance whipped the wheels of his Mercedes back onto the highway, narrowly avoiding the steep, guardrail-less embankment. Lines of sweat drooled down Lance's flush face, his reminiscences exorcising a cerebral fever.

Benevolence, one hundred forty-six miles. Every mile nearer bubbled faster the stew of Lance's memories. The haunting of Lance Hawthorne beckoned beyond the point of no return, and he could no more escape it than hold back the ocean's tide.

Lance pulled dead skin off calluses he maintained through years of such pulling, calluses once earned from the honesty of hard work. He smiled, the stew smelling sweeter. Each strip removed heightened his memory of the blisters of baseball games and the honor of competition among the boys of Benevolence. He remembered, too, the dishonor of the choice of indifference.

The strains of Glenn Miller played on.

"Summer ... you old, Indian summer ..." crooned Ray Eberle through the crinkle and pop of the monotone recording. Lance smiled. His Mercedes hummed. The newsreel rolled, memories wafting.

Moments of leisure were savored like cold water in a desert. Lance recalled skipping the precious calm of Saturday lunches, such time better spent in pick-up baseball games played under a ruthless summer sun in the middle of a treeless South Georgia pasture, usually on ground belonging to the Devereauxs.

Kids played baseball as hard as they worked, until they wore each other out, whether it took four innings or *forty-four*. The essence of play, its breath of freedom, gave release from the strenuous routine of living. The games stroked dreams had by each of the boys, dreams of someday becoming professional ballplayers, wealthy, worshipped, and unencumbered by the rigors of less lucrative sweat equity.

Each fearless player displayed to a greater or lesser extent the badges of honor earned from games hard-fought. Bloodied knees; torn jeans; clay-stained tee shirts; blistered hands; grass-grimed butts; lost teeth. The more badges, the better.

The count was three balls and two strikes, in the bottom of an inning somewhere at the end of a long string of innings, the known quantity long lost to the blur of competitive spirit and the heat of the afternoon sun. Boys from the team they called Sweetgum Hollow stood atop each of three cowpie bases, now no more than brown smears on yellow grass. Some kid had the audacity to suggest the game end now, in the interest of preserving the ball.

"Not 'til we get *all* of our time at bat," shouted Lance, spitting into his palms and rubbing them together, bat between his legs. "Not 'til I show Jackson Willoughby what for."

The Ghosts of Benevolence

"Keep dreamin', Hawthorne," Jackson shouted back. "I done struck you out four times today already. Ainchu had enough?"

"Homered off you, too," Lance replied. "Gonna do it again, right now, an' send you boys home cryin' to your mamas."

"We been playin' all day, Lance," shouted the kid in left field. "Finish him off, Jackson!"

"Intend to!" Jackson shouted back.

Lance took his stance at home plate, ready to receive Jackson's finest. Tempers swarmed on both teams like the hornets in the loft of old man Powell's barn. The score was four to three in favor of Jackson Willoughby's team, the Sutter Swatters, which had taken the lead on the strength of a Willoughby three-run homer the previous inning.

Though best of friends off the field, Jackson Willoughby and Lance Hawthorne treated each other like two bull elks in rutting season when in competition. Neither gave quarter to the other, not if such could be helped.

A hit would score the tying and winning runs. *No way,* thought Lance, *is Jackson Willoughby going to beat my team!*

Just thirteen years old, Jackson possessed, in addition to his withering fastball, a prodigious knuckleball, which, when properly thrown, was liable to drop sharply, resulting in a batter's over-swing, or worse, cause a batter expecting his fastball to lunge like a blindfolded kid after a piñata. Left-handed hitters were especially vulnerable. Lance was left-handed.

Lance did not expect the humbling Willoughby knuckleball. Not now. Not with the bases loaded and pride on the line. This was not the time for finesse. This was the time for nose-to-nose, here-it-comes-see-if-you-can-hit-it baseball. Lance knew the pitch of choice would be the feared Willoughby fastball, the very pitch that had struck out Lance four times today. The likelihood of his fastball was as certain as the day was hot.

Lance pushed the count to three balls and two strikes after fouling off the first eight pitches. Jackson bent forward, sweat dripping off his forehead like water from a spring, his fingers twirling the brown and green stained baseball resting in his right palm set against the base of his spine. Glancing over his left shoulder toward first base, Jackson spat. The mound was splotched with darkened globs, coagulations of mud formed from these saliva meteorites. Jackson waved off sign after sign, knowing exactly what pitch he wanted, and brushed aside dangling drops of sweat from his brow.

Lance awaited the heater he knew was coming. Just as Jackson began his windup, his knuckles pressed against the stitches, the sound of squalling tires rolled over the field like a sonic boom. Lance rested the Louisville Slugger on his shoulder and stood up straight from his batter's crouch. All eyes turned toward right field in the direction of the county's only paved highway to see the black sedan leave the road, airborne, and disappear in the low brush and trees behind the embankment opposite the ballfield's centerfield boundary. The car plunged hood first into a swamp stagnant and dotted with thriving cypress trees, their countless knees rising like periscopes from the water, which sprayed in all directions like the geysers of Yellowstone.

The Haint, they called it. The depths of the swamp's black waters reached the status of legend over the fermentation of decades of front porch conversations. Campfire ghost stories aided its reputation. Now, the Haint had claimed another. The boys stood staring, stunned and stiff.

21

LANCE WAS THE FIRST to break the grip of stunned disbelief and race toward the scene. Followed closely by seventeen other boys and a couple of itinerant hitchhikers, Lance charged through centerfield. Instinct in control, he hurdled the five-foot barbed-wire fence that separated the field from the road. Lance reached the edge of the highway's shoulder at precisely the location the car's tread marks left the asphalt. Blackberry bushes and three-year-old loblolly pines lay snapped and scattered in the wake of the vehicle's plunge into the swamp.

The bobbing car, water bubbling around it, was sinking at a slight rear-down angle, its doors submerged to halfway up the closed windows. The driver appeared lifeless with the head slumped forward over the top of the steering wheel.

The boys gazed first at the car, then at each other. Lance turned toward the adults, expecting leadership from an older, more experienced source. They, too, stood mesmerized by the gurgle of the slowly disappearing car, resigned that the Haint possessed powers beyond the response of mortals.

Mark Randolph Watters

The water had reached the roofline. It was now or never. Acting with the spontaneity of youth, Lance ripped off his tee shirt and rushed for the snake-occupied water. His arms stretched forward and his body prone, Lance hit the water stomach first. Sunday skinny-dips in Pumpkin Creek had taught Lance ways to coexist with water vipers and had blessed him with the ability to hold his breath upwards of three minutes, sometimes four, depending on the girl watching, such skills demanded this very moment.

Lance speared his lean body through the dark waters, blurred by the slime of the stirred depths and the bubbles of air rising from the car. The car pitched forward and back, like a four-wheeled pendulum, in its slow descent to the swamp's bottom, not nearly as bottomless, Lance discovered, as old-timers' stories insisted.

Finally, the car settled. Silt and beer bottles were displaced all around the vehicle. Lance managed to shatter the driver's window with one thrust of his metal cleats. Clutching the occupant's shirt, he wriggled the body through the narrow opening.

A crowd of a few dozen persons assembled along the roadside to witness the rescue attempt. Four minutes passed.

The distorted sound of a distant siren could be heard bouncing off the waves of heat carried by a soft breeze.

Five minutes.

The density of air bubbles popping on the surface diminished. The crowd chattered among themselves, full of speculation.

Truth be told, folks relished the prospect of witnessing an event upon which they could embellish, like candy sprinkles on an ice cream sundae, if further tragedy did not embellish it for them.

"It's a *fact!*" they would insist.

"Two boys—or was it three—yeah, I do b'lieve it *was* three—disappeared into the darkness of the Haint that day.

The Ghosts of Benevolence

Seen it myself!" they would say. "Never did recover their bodies."

"Their spirits *still haunt* that ol' swamp," they would agree. "I have *seen* on some of these moonlit nights them air bubbles risin' to the surface. Like drops of oil above the Arizona, them bubbles, always there! As them air bubbles pop, those poor souls—I s'pect their ghosts—*rise* out of the depths and *glide* across the swamp, a *glow* about 'em."

And so it would go, had it gone.

Grandchildren and tourists would eat it up like buttered popcorn. Had it gone.

The Haint Swamp cottage industry would have received from the death of this day an infusion of new life. A circus-like atmosphere would have emerged, the entrepreneurial wheels turning with frenetic energy, like clowns juggling bowling pins on a high-wire unicycle. Visions of tee shirts and hand-painted barnwood signs boasting, "I Witnessed The Haint Claim Another!" or "I Survived Haint Swamp!" danced unseen behind the darting eyes of most onlookers. Tragedy had ways in these parts of spinning itself into opportunity.

Had it gone.

As sure as roadkill rots, had it gone, someone was bound to realize the value of the death car itself and extract it from the swamp, piece by opportunistic piece, branding it with the mystery that was the Haint, inviting the wide-eyed to invest in the legend. But even death cars are finite. After the last slice of tire rubber or piece of windshield glass, they would then turn to the abandoned vehicles curtained in honeysuckle behind their shacks and sell those, too. No one would be the wiser.

Nothing so ripe with capitalistic potential had come this way since the tarring and feathering of Mose Fortenberry, a destitute sharecropper accused of snatching a five-dollar bill from the fingers of an elderly woman paying her electric bill.

Mark Randolph Watters

Lance burst through the water's surface, desperation gushing from his eyes, his mouth wide and lungs heaving for lifesaving air. Lance held tight the forearm of the driver pulled from the depths. Jackson Willoughby lay flat on his stomach and extended a baseball bat toward Lance. Lance reached for the bat, struggling to keep his and the driver's mouths above the water. He missed. Slapping the water, he missed again. And again. His hand splashed the water in a frantic search for the wooden lifeline.

The crowd shouted directions, none of which was discernable to Lance amid the watery fray. Finally, Lance found his grip on the bat, his pull almost taking Jackson into the water. Jackson and a bystander pulled the bat and its cargo toward shore. Lance alternated between gasps for air and retching expulsions of water. Flat on his back and motionless, the victim made no sound.

"That there's *Rufus Stephens!*" several of the onlookers whispered among themselves.

"Ain't he that no-good moonshinin' trash Devereaux's been tryin' to shoo off his land?" asked another, imbibed, as most here were, with the habit of gossip.

"Ol' man Devereaux's a moonshiner hisself," declared a voice in response, as if to justify the practice. "This ol' boy was one of his *runners*. Check the trunk of that car sittin' on the bottom of the Haint an' I bet you'll find some of Dev's shine. Looks like Devereaux's done took out some competition."

"Devereaux ain't no moonshiner!" shouted a female wearing a white tank top and blue-jean shorts, a cigarette in one hand and an infant squirming in the other. Just who Devereaux was seemed more a matter of opinion than fact, at least in terms of who was doing the opining.

"Not anymore, anyhow," she continued. "He's a lot of things, one of 'em bein' … well, let's just say he's a *whole* lot of things, most of 'em bad, but I reckon y'all don't want to hear *that* story. Anyway, they ain't enough money in

The Ghosts of Benevolence

liquor these days to suit this batch of Devereauxs. This ol'
boy's a small fish, liquor-speakin'. But, drugs, prostitutin'.
Now, *that* might be a whole nother story, if you got an ear
for it."

The speculations, most of which were laced with
kernels of truth, buzzed like spring hives of honeybees.

A Fort Gaines ambulance arrived. Paramedics
scrambled to the body. His breath caught, Lance pulled
himself to his knees. No one tended to him. He sat on the
road's shoulder for the next hour, exhausted, wet, alone in
his thoughts. Not even a Jackson Willoughby knuckler had
this much bite. A black halo of buzzards circled the Haint.

Lance rested but could not help overhearing a
conversation between the Sheriff, a detective, and a scuba
diver.

"Shot?" asked the Sheriff, surprised. "You sure about
that?"

"Through the head," affirmed the detective.

"Self-inflicted?"

"Don't think so," offered the diver. "Didn't find a gun
in the car or anywhere near the car. Position of the wound
suggests otherwise, too."

"Appears to be a small caliber wound, .22 probably,
clean, about the diameter of a dime," the detective added.
"Shot at close range, base of the skull; no exit wound.
Looks as if somebody was in the car with him, shot him,
and bailed out."

"Bailed out? From a moving vehicle? Get some men
and dogs in those woods back there," the Sheriff said to his
deputies. "What about a sniper shot?"

"No holes in the rear glass," replied the detective.
"Only place such a shot could have come from was *inside*
the vehicle. But, we can't be sure, not yet, because nobody
saw it happen.

"Keep me posted, detective," the Sheriff said.

"One other thing, minor probably," the detective said in afterthought. "Divers found this on the front seat." The detective handed the Sheriff a bible, its cover and pages torn.

The Sheriff peeled through the soggy pages. "Can't make out this signature. Water's smeared it."

"Doctor Williams, sir."

"Williams? *Frank* Williams?"

"Yes sir. Killed in that bombing back in the sixties, with the rest of his family."

"This car belong to this ol' boy?" the Sheriff asked, pointing to the sheet-covered body of Rufus Stephens.

"It did."

"What was *he* doing with Williams' bible?"

Feigning disinterest, Lance wiped his hair with a towel given him by an officer. He thought about the photograph Jackson had taken in the field that unforgettable evening. If this murder happened as he had just heard the officers describe, indeed Devereaux had made his point. Again.

The sedative of Glenn Miller's music pushed Lance onto the shoulder of the highway. The car rattled on the rippled asphalt, shaking his focus upon the present emergency. Encased with dried saliva, his tongue scratched the roof of his mouth with the roughness of sandpaper. Attempts to swallow felt like tiny fingernails tickling his throat. The time was ripe for a drink and a snack. Time to give the haunting a break.

He turned his Mercedes onto the lot of one of several new convenience stores dotting the three hundred miles of rural emptiness between Raventon and Benevolence.

Gone, perhaps, were such establishments as Prather General Store, but it was comforting to see that at least the time-honored Southern tradition of Royal Crowns and moon pies had not gone the way of the "See Rock City" barn roof.

The Ghosts of Benevolence

He purchased four of the pies and a couple of colas and walked the premises. He stretched his stiffened legs as he tore the wrapper off a pie. As he raised the pie to take a bite, he sniffed a familiar air filled with the perfumes of fertilizers, insecticides, and sulfur, like musty reminders in a long-dormant scrapbook. Lance felt the grip of home tighten around his senses. His surroundings whispered to him he was already sitting on home's front porch.

Mark Randolph Watters

The Ghosts of Benevolence

22

LIFE'S CHOREOGRAPHY, ITS COURSE, was supposed to be a steady waltz of the senses, augmented by the perpetual fulfillment of the desires of the heart, as fresh as the dawning of each day and filled with as much anticipation. These were ideals embraced by the tongs of innocence, forged in the fires of youthful abstraction.

Instead, these ideals had flamed out, as did Peyton's, casualties on a blood-soaked dirt road under an auburn Georgia sky on a Sunday vivid still in Lance's mind.

SNAP!

Life for Lance had contorted into relentless frontal assaults. Survival seemed no better than a series of surges to the next lines of earthworks, a force of will, a battle of attrition, efforts laden with one unsavory choice after another. Since that fateful Sunday, life had evolved into the quagmire of trench warfare, a stalemate of misery fought from the moment the bullwhip cracked.

Lance had not lived, not really *lived*, for forty-two years. He *existed*, his head down, a soldier caught in a blizzard of bullets.

He had stumbled into a career handed him by a friend of a friend. Perks, relative market stability, and above-average compensation made the tap dance—the choreography—easier to endure.

Regardless, the job came arid of professional challenge, lacking in the psychological rewards of meaningful work, void of the satisfaction of accomplishment. His tasks could be handled by any clever accounting software package, several of such available if Barrett so chose, and the work itself served little useful purpose other than the pay deposited each month into Lance's bank account. The money alone, while ample, was not enough. Far from it.

But Lance knew no other way. Money was the quantifiable metric of the only success his mind had known. Money represented a departure, a U-turn, from the poverty and struggle that destroyed his daddy. The path of least resistance demanded he pursue more of that measure, no matter how superfluous the means, like an alcoholic who promised to stop drinking after one last drink.

Lacking the stimuli of roadside distractions that might redirect his thoughts, Lance pondered these and other personal philosophical truths that smacked him like countless flying insects, millions of them, hovering in the stagnant twilight air of South Georgia. Air forces of dragonflies, miller bugs, gnats, mosquitoes pummeled the windshield like tiny Kamikaze planes, as if sheer strength of numbers would overwhelm the enemy. The bugs, now a gooey smear of gray and green, covered the Mercedes' grill and glass, their sacrifice total, if not futile.

Guess I better stop and clean this crap off, Lance decided. *These wipers are worthless.*

Lance steered his Mercedes to a stop on the sand-covered pullover.

Benevolence.

Home.

The Ghosts of Benevolence

23

TURNING RIGHT, LANCE DROVE a few hundred feet and parked, his gaze shifting right and left as he took in the view of physical reminders and remnants of his childhood home.

Time had worn ragged the welcome mat. Lance preferred to remember Benevolence as an innocuous contradiction, an island of simplicity surrounded by, but shielded from, an ocean of complexity. He knew better. Evil whispered its warning here, even now, like the muffled rattle of a hiding snake.

Lance retrieved a cloth and glass cleaner from the glove compartment. He sprayed in a sweeping motion across the windshield. He scrubbed. He scrubbed harder. The bugs smeared like oatmeal. Retaliatory gnats buzzed about his face and into his ears. Lance cursed the smear and slapped the gnats, then cursed the gnats and slapped the smear, neither action producing anything but compounded frustration. The mosquitoes swarmed in omnipresent clouds, Pandora's demons. Despite determined wiping, vestiges of the smear remained, like indelible fragments of his haunting. He slapped the slime-covered rag over his face and shouted a muffled expletive, his will to fight drained.

"Let them have it," he whispered conceding the issue, and turned to confront the present manifestations of his past.

Prather's General Store occupied the southeast corner of the crosshair, as it had since its founding in 1856. The family-owned store, the proprietors of which once claimed in printed advertisements to sell anything from horse collars to hairpins, breathed life no more. Blackberry bushes, poison ivy, and honeysuckle consumed the planks of its boarded windows and splintered flanks. Wasps hovered near the roof's overhang. Bees entered and exited a hive inside. Chipmunks scampered into and out of tiny spaces.

The last of the Prather family, Ambrose, murdered twenty years ago this June, had fallen victim to a Jack-the-Ripper-style knife attack, to this day unsolved. Accounts of the incident stated that Ambrose's body was found on a bench in the public square of downtown Colter in east Sutter County. He had been relieved of two kidneys and one hand. The store was bequeathed to a family friend, who continued its operation until opportunity called him to more prosperous ventures.

Lance removed the ignition key and scanned the full circle. Not another vehicle disturbed the shaded serenity provided by elms and oaks. The occasional rustling of the leaves in the trees and along the shoulder of the road gave Lance the impression of a ghost town. The lowering sun cast long shadows extending beyond the crossroads and across the community cemetery in which was buried Becca and Sara. He stretched his arms high, his six-foot, tiptoed frame touching the sky, giving relief to tired muscles.

"*Damn* these gnats!" Lance cursed, swatting in vain at the elusive irritants. "Don't know which I hate more: gnats, skeeters, or fire ants!"

The Ghosts of Benevolence

Same ancient cemetery; same church; same mediocrity. Just older. Crushed cans of Coca-Cola and broken bottles of Budweiser littered the weedy ditches. The sounds of tree frogs, a throb of rhythm that could turn a mind claustrophobic, filled the salty air of dusk. Though in the warm arms of home again, Lance felt an uneasy chill course through his body, as if he were being scrutinized, studied like a microbe.

Lance walked to the rear of the car and opened the trunk. He removed a gray concrete urn and a plastic bag with an arrangement of silk and plastic day lilies and Sweet Williams.

"Mama sure loved these flowers," he whispered in third person, closing the trunk. "Wish I had some real ones, Mama, but I reckon they'd end up same as you before too long," Lance said with a respectful smile, aware he had slipped into his Deep South dialect, the same he had tried for years to discard. The reason was lost on him now.

He made his way across the road, reflexively checking for oncoming vehicles, and into the cemetery surrounded by an iron fence, its rails and arrow-pointed posts pocked with the rust of time. Lance knew the way and in a few minutes stood at the foot of the grave of Sara Hawthorne, flanked by Becca's and Peyton's. The weathered headstones tilted slightly, yielding to the bulge of a magnolia root, its flower her favorite.

Lance cleared his throat, glancing to make sure no one was near.

"Hey, mama. It's me …it's Lance," he whispered, discerning himself from any confusion another visitor might present. "Just wanted to bring these flowers to you. Sweet Williams and day lilies." Lance's voice rose with excitement as if she were standing before him, arms extended to accept his gift. He balanced the urn and flowers against a clump of chickweed. It leaned anyway.

Mark Randolph Watters

An old man, standing as motionless as a palace guard, stared in Lance's direction from the front steps of the town's only surviving church, Benevolence Primitive Baptist, cattycornered in relationship to Prather's store and a stone's throw from the cemetery. The pristine clapboard structure, a century and a half old and recently whitewashed, gleamed like a sun-drenched iceberg. A bell tower extended twenty feet above the roofline and housed an iron bell, as big as the Liberty Bell and still functional as a community fire alarm. Lance remembered the bell and wondered if the old man were its keeper.

The Ghosts of Benevolence

24

THE APPEARANCE OF THE old man put Lance to mind of Red Hamilton. He smiled. *Perhaps the old man is no old man at all*, Lance thought, his smile broadening, *but Red's spirit come to haunt me for all my years absent from the pews.*

An owl screeched from the innards of Benevolence Betty, startling Lance. The church's stalwart companion, a stately live oak anchored in the front lawn by tentacles of roots that folks insisted kept the world from spinning off into the reaches of deep space, kept the grassless yard company. Its branches hooked and twisted with the torture of time and had provided ample shade to nomadic churchgoers and occasional sightseers longer than history could remember. Streamers of Spanish moss shrouded the tree with the wisdom of a million beards. The oak, christened Benevolence Betty by church members and sworn as truth to predate God Himself, bore the evidence of lightning strikes, carvings of juvenile love long forgotten, and the scars of disease. Still, high and strong it reached, a living monument to perseverance.

The tire swing swung no more, but vestiges of its rhythmic incisions remained, fore and aft grooves carved

Mark Randolph Watters

by the swing's chain, like the coming and going of the
days. Lance thought of the picnics and semi-annual
homecomings held under the protection of the branches of
Benevolence Betty, named for Betty Stegall, a Christian
stalwart and tree in her own right.

A tolerant license for mischief was conferred upon all
who entered the realm of the great oak. Teenagers stole
kisses behind the shield of the tree's expansive trunk.
Children spat watermelon seeds at one another, despite
admonitions against it, and sought refuge behind the trunk
and out of their mamas' sights. Adults struck matches to
Pall Malls and Chesterfields and took long draws on the
cigarettes, despite the un-Christian example this practice
cast before the children. Benevolence Betty offered a
temporal balance for the warring forces of morality and
tomfoolery.

Lance stared at the old man and listened for the ageless
echoes of fiddles and hammered dulcimers playing "Simple
Gifts" or "Be Thou My Vision". No memory soothed his
soul like the satisfying strains of these serene tunes played
in his mind this summer evening in Benevolence.

Aunt Pearl's favorite hymns, remembered Lance.
Sweet Miss Tommie. She hummed one hymn or the other
in the church kitchen while mixing apples, brown sugar,
butter, and cinnamon for one of her prize-winning apple
pies. Miss Tommie's not-so-secret ingredient was her
ability to draw smiles from the faces of even the crustiest of
souls. Lance welcomed some of her pie now.

The old man stared blankly in return, giving silent
notice to Lance that his presence was not without notice.
Lance raised his arm and waved with a casual salute,
acknowledging the old man. The man offered no return
wave. Just stared. Gray-white smoke curled and drifted
from a filterless cigarette tilting from the old man's lips.

Lance spotted the empty left sleeve tucked into the
jeans pocket and at once felt a twinge of guilt for having

The Ghosts of Benevolence

solicited a wave from a one-armed old man. Lance gave a respectful smile and nod, which too went unacknowledged.

Never mind, old man, thought Lance, turning his gaze back towards the gray wood of the general store.

In its day, Prather's General Store served also as a stop for a stagecoach line. Ambrose Prather regaled his customers for eighty years with his stories of folks brought into sleepy Benevolence by the stage. He shared tales of brazen robberies and shootouts, no doubt embellished for a paying clientele who sat sucking colas and chomping crackers, riveted by the weathered old words he spoke. Rickety Prather, folks called him. His death, after a life of one hundred and one years, hammered the final nail into a bygone era.

Ambrose was the son of founder Pinkney. Born in 1878, Ambrose succeeded Pinkney in 1910. Pinkney remained vibrant of mind until the point of his death a few years later. The store's one hiccup in its one hundred and twenty-three years of operations, a lightning strike that burned the store to the ground in 1894, despite the call to buckets from the church bell, afforded Pinkney his life's lone vacation, which he spent rebuilding the store.

Prather's was the center of social and political life in Benevolence, a point where the lines of racial boundaries were ignored, where whites and blacks interacted as equals. A white man might engage a black man in a game of checkers atop a pickle barrel, while in the relative sanctuary of Prather's General Store, sharing jokes and family stories and farming tips. When folks managed to get to it, distance and roads being as they were, Prather's served as an oasis for social contact in the midst of racial isolation. The stench of prejudice seemed as distant from the walls of Prather's as the two arctic poles.

Lance thought about the childhood pleasure of pouring salted peanuts into five-cent bottles of "co-colas", savoring sips of the concoction while he lounged on the store's steps, half-attentive to the talk of the glories of wars past and rumors of wars to come. The salt gave the beverage a tolerable counterpoint, Lance remembered, like sucking a sugar-coated lemon. The peanuts completed the enhancement of flavor, like Sara's touch of bacon grease mixed with her pan-fried corn.

Lance stooped to retrieve a plastic coke bottle from the ditch.

Who'd want peanuts in this? Lance thought, examining the faded label on the crushed plastic. *Glass bottles were so much better!*

The cheapening of America, he figured, tossing the bottle into the weeds. Paths of least resistance.

A tremor then shook Lance's Mercedes. The rush of air that followed shoved him like a schoolyard bully. Every manner of debris, pebbles and acorns; leaves and dirt; cigarette butts and candy wrappers, pelted Lance. As Lance rubbed the red dust and grit from his face and eyes, he saw vaguely the long, scraggly-barked logs atop the pulpwood truck racing down the crumbling blacktop, the drone of the truck's overworked engine receding with distance. The truck carried the essential raw material for making paper. Lance thought of Consolidated Paper and his upcoming meeting with Devereaux.

"Devereaux trees," said Lance, flicking bits of leaves from his shirt.

A red bandana adorned with the Confederate Southern Cross flapped affixed to a log's end impaled with a screwdriver. Lance had seen it a million times before and still it amused him. The red handkerchief, required by law, gave trailing drivers a contrast to the dullness of colors, a perspective of depth alerting them to the dangers of protruding logs in the event of a sudden stop or sharp turn. The Confederate battle emblem, on the other hand, was a personal sentiment of the driver's, as sacred to certain segments of the South as grits, football, and auto racing,

The Ghosts of Benevolence

sure to be ridiculed, if not feared, by the streams of Yankees flowing southward.

Consolidated Paper owned near Benevolence one of the largest and most technically advanced paper mills in the industry. Lance had known the mill in his childhood as Southland Linerboard, a mill of two paper machines capable of producing two thousand dry tons of 42-lb linerboard per day when operating at full capacity. The mill limped for years with under-capitalization and had been maintained with band-aid fixes and shortsighted management, its conversion process outdated. Production dropped to a paltry four hundred tons of linerboard per day, hardly justifying its operations. The mill sank into the undertow of overhead and shrinking sales.

Complicating matters, Earl Bentley Devereaux III threatened, as he was now doing, to sever Consolidated's access to his plentiful supply of pinewood, long-term rights to vast tracts of woodlands available within a few miles of the raw material-starved mill.

Employee apathy accumulated at Southland over the years like plaque in the carotid. Management neglect of equipment and indifference toward matters of labor lead to poor quality-control measures and an inevitable decline in demand for the company's products. Operations stayed afloat by means of accounting shell games. Expenses were deferred, even capitalized, hidden for absorption in the apparitions of more lucrative periods, if absorbed at all. The delusion was rationalized year after year until the snowball became an avalanche.

The purchase of the dilapidated Southland Linerboard by Consolidated Paper in 1991, followed by a five-year capital infusion of an unprecedented sum of one billion dollars, had assured Benevolence and surrounding communities that the region's dominant employer, outside of farming, was safe for perhaps another generation.

Mark Randolph Watters

Midway through the project, management reviewed the mill's capital strategy, stripping funds originally earmarked for the acquisition of the timberlands Southland relied upon for its raw material sourcing. The new strategy called for a transition to the total leasing of timber rights, away from land ownership, mirroring SPIG's strategy, along with the construction of remote-site chipping mills in lieu of capital expenditures for woodyard equipment and mill-site chipping of delivered trees.

In the project's planning stages, Devereaux had been promised, and thus had relied upon, the sale of his land to Consolidated. Last-minute changes in capital strategy, including the method of raw material sourcing, diverted funds away from purchased timberland—Devereaux's land—for sourcing of raw materials and towards a focus on stockpiles of repair materials necessary to support millions of dollars spent on new paper machines and other conversion-process equipment.

Lance realized his success as SPIG's VP of Finance and Analysis rested on his ability to not only satisfy Devereaux's need for revenge but also to slice the jugular of Consolidated's Benevolence mill once and for all. Padding his bank account, the bonus King promised Lance, provided the serendipity he had not expected. Lance's success might very well destroy the promise of Benevolence's economic recovery. He stared at Benevolence Betty, wondering when a sense of treason might hit him. The thought, like acts of tomfoolery, was fleeting.

The Ghosts of Benevolence

25

LIGHT FROM THE AMBER full moon touched the rising darkness and pushed the day to its brink. Bats darted in directions defying physics. Lance thought it best to find a place to stay. He saw that the widening of the highway, completed two years ago, had resulted in a flurry of small motels.

Admiring the red and purple bands of color cutting low across the western sky, Lance felt a tap on his right shoulder. Turning, he faced the old man, indeed absent a left arm. The man, a head shorter than Lance, offered a slight smile. A cigarette clung to the old man's lower lip. He spoke with the rattle of a whisper.

"You're new around here," he said.

Lance resisted a rising chuckle. The old man and his cigarette, its smoke curling like gray hair, only stared.

"Well, yeah ... you might say that," Lance admitted, turning away from the man and toward the sunset. "This was my boyhood home, but I've been away for over thirty-five years."

"Ah, your boyhood home. You're a Benevolence lad, are you?" the old man asked, each raspy syllable annunciated free of southern dialect, the first point of value Lance noticed about the man.

"Yes, sir, I am," Lance replied, scanning the landscape. "Doesn't look like things have changed much."

The old man laughed and coughed. "Fact is, things haven't changed one iota," he said, patting his pants pocket. "No, sir, not ... one iota, save the addition of years. Excuse me, sir, but I seem to be short a match."

"Sorry. I don't smoke."

"Mmm," the man acknowledged. "When did you give it up?"

"Gave it up years ago." Lance paused, turning toward the old man. "How did you know—?"

"Lucky guess, I suppose," the old man interrupted. "Too bad, really. I believe it's the *relinquishment* of the pleasures we love that kills us. What's your business in these parts, young man?"

Lance cleared his throat. "Well, like I said, I haven't been here in quite some time. Thought I'd look around a bit. Reacquaint myself." Lance tapped his shoes free of their layer of sand. "Maybe go by the old home place and—"

"It's gone."

"What's gone?"

"Your home place. The structure, that is. Gone. Been gone for twenty years, plus or minus. Ever since Consolidated Paper bought all the long-term timber rights around here that they could get their sap-covered hands on. Except for Devereaux's place, of course."

"Devereaux's place? Something wrong with *his* timber?" Lance asked. "And how do know about *my* place?"

"You are ... Lance P. Hawthorne?" the man asked, looking down to a card he held.

"Why, yes, but how'd you—"

The Ghosts of Benevolence

"You dropped it when you got out of your car," he replied, holding up Lance's business card. "I knew your folks. Too bad about them. Anyway, they tore down your place and everybody else's place, for that matter; clear-cut the timber, and replaced the trees with saplings. Only thing, those saplings never developed. Pine beetles." The old man peeled the cigarette off his lip. "Destroyed every last tree. Oh, they're coming back now, some of those trees, but the land's cursed, so say the timber buyers. Can't say I disagree with 'em.

"Nobody goes to this church anymore, either," the old man added, pointing to Benevolence Primitive Baptist Church. "Practically nobody, anyway. Somebody had the heart and presence of mind to give her a facelift a year or so back. Beautiful building, but emptier than King Tut's tomb. Crying shame, it is. People ought to *be* in church. If Red Hamilton were alive, he'd drown in his own spit worrying about where and when his next meal would come. You go to church, young man?"

The question caught Lance unprepared. "I don't discuss ... that is, I haven't been in ... no, I don't go to church," Lance conceded, facing again the setting sun. "But, sir, as surely you know, that really isn't any of your—"

Lance stopped his admonishment of the old man, replacing it with empathy, and turned back to face him, saying, "Look, if you *must* know—"

But the old man had vanished, as if he had never existed. Lance looked left, then right.

"Where'd you go? Where did that old cuss *go?*" Lance mouthed, aghast with the disappearing act. Hands on hips, Lance continued to scan the area, certain he would locate the old man.

"Guess I should call Jess." Lance took a peek around Benevolence Betty, just to be sure, and shook his head as

173

he pressed '1' for Jess's cell phone number. "Who *was* that guy?"

"La … Lance?" answered Jessica, four rings later and groggy from sleep.

"Jess?"

"Hey, babe, how was your drive down?" Jessica whispered.

"Did I wake you, Jess? I am so sorry! I didn't realize—"

"No, no, Lance. I had only dozed a bit," Jessica interrupted, yawning.

"The drive down was fine. Boring, but fine; not a lot about it to remember, and *nothing* about it worth discussing. How was your day?"

"Good. Except my back seems to be hurting more. You know, that same spot in the middle, just to the right of my spine? It needs your tender touch. Do you want to say something to Jerri?"

"What?" Lance said, rolling his eyes. He sighed. "Yeah, sure, let me talk to the little rascal."

Jessica placed the receiver on her abdomen.

"Hey, sweetness!" Lance whispered with the sincerity of a mall Santa. "Go easy on mommy, now. I can't wait to hold you and read you stories and sing to you. I love you, Jerri," Lance said, aware Jessica's ear was in range.

"Jess?" Lance said. Jessica brought the phone back to her ear.

"I'm back."

"Any messages for me today?"

"Yeah, you got a call from Doctor Harper. He said he had the results of your checkup. Nothing serious, he said, but he does want you to call him. Probably just to set up your next appointment. He didn't sound concerned, so I guess things are okay. Here's his number."

"I'll call him when I get home."

"Call him in the morning, Lance. Here's the number."

The Ghosts of Benevolence

Lance sighed and pretended to write down the number. "Got it. Thanks, Jess."

"Promise me, Lance."

"I'll call him first thing tomorrow morning. I promise."

"What about that Devereaux fellow? You going to call him first thing, too?" Jessica asked, toying with Lance.

"Just as soon as the Doc gives me the all-clear," Lance replied, chuckling.

"Lance, you ought to swing by your home place while you're down there, check it out."

"I may drive by it, but I'm sure it's overrun with weeds. Heck, it's probably blocked out completely by a forest of pines. Been too many years, Jess. I think Consolidated owns that land anyway. Maybe I'll swing by, take a look, just in case. Want me to dig up a couple of cedar seedlings for you while I'm here?"

"Of course. And stop at one of those roadsides and get us some mayhaw jelly! And pecan divinity logs! That's logs-*s-s*," Jessica said, hissing, "Plural."

Lance laughed. "You got it, babe! Oooooff!"

"What is it, Lance?"

"Nothing. Just my head. That drive has given me a doozie of a headache, a crick in my neck. Think I'll take a couple of aspirin and hit the sack. Wanna come down and hit it with me?"

"You're funny. Be easier if I just reached through the ether and massaged your neck. Call me tomorrow sometime during your busy South Georgia day?"

"I've got you booked third right after Mister Devereaux and Doctor Harper. Wait, make that fourth, after I call Barrett and update him. Got to get all the *important* stuff taken care of first, you know."

Jessica was silent.

"*Kidding*, babe! I'll call you *first* thing, and you *know* that," Lance assured his wife.

"I knew you would. Just wanted you to remember who's in *charge* here, is all," Jessica said musically, her voice rising and falling.

"I'd never forget. I'm a puppet on your strings, sweetie. I love you. Now, you and Jerri get some rest. Tell Ginibeth I love her."

"I love you, too, Lance. One more thing."

"What might that be?" Lance asked, knowing what was coming.

"The photograph."

"Night, night, Jess."

"Lance, please. What are you going to do with that picture?"

"Don't worry, Jess. It's just a *conversation* piece."

"What, for people to talk about at your *funeral*?"

"Calm down, Jess. I promise to be careful."

"But what are you going to—"

"Night, night, Jess."

Lance ended the call and tossed the cell phone onto the passenger seat. He pulled the photograph from his jacket pocket. Lance wondered why he had not considered the picture's value, a gold mine in waiting, until this trip. He had thought about it, the fact that he might someday revive interest in the Thankfulness Baptist Church explosion, but not so much its financial potential.

The time had come to unleash that potential, for Devereaux to pay.

The Ghosts of Benevolence

26

THE NEXT MORNING, LANCE had a craving.

He steered the Mercedes into the crowded parking lot of the blue-roofed restaurant, a sort of modern-day Prather's, folks milling about exchanging greetings and snippets of gossip.

Not just *any* craving.

Inside these glass doors, smudged by the coming-and-going remnants of fingerprints over a span of seven decades, lived the sort of food Lance pined for but had abandoned reluctantly—Doc Harper's orders—after his heart attack and triple bypass six years ago.

A country-crossroads craving.

His dangling hopes of immortality long dashed, replaced by the realities of aging, entropy, and his gradual physical descent courtesy of the second law of thermodynamics, Lance watched as others engaged in the south's second favorite sport—clogging arteries. He added his fingerprints to the door's glass and stared, like a child through the windows of a toy shop. A customer exiting gave Lance all the excuse he needed, the doors now wide open.

Mark Randolph Watters

Lance hoped to carve out *some* moments of relaxation during his visit home. The world spun slowly here, if at all. No better time, he reasoned, to shed the worries of the workaday world and enjoy a few forbidden pleasures of indulgence. His heart forewarned, Lance entered the shrine of Belle's Diner.

Waffles it would be, he decided, and eggs with bacon, biscuits drowned in sawmill gravy. To *hell* with sensibility! Mortality, too. If such a breakfast of "cholesterfat" (a term given him by Doctor Harper) did not kill him outright, he might reconsider once again *challenging* the notion of mortality.

The day's plans were taking shape. First, deliver a certain package to Global Technical Solutions. That diversion would allow him time to tour some of the back roads of Sutter County, many of which to this day remained little more than pioneer-era wagon cuts through the wilderness.

"Mornin'!" shot a shout through the buzz, voices intermingling and colliding amid the ant-like frenzy of employees and patrons. "Welcome to Belle's! Seat yourself, honey."

Morning paper secure under his left armpit, Lance approached the only unoccupied booth. He dropped the paper onto the table as he gave the restaurant a scan of reminiscence. He sat.

"Be with you directly, honey!" another shouted. Voices of customer contentment buzzed.

Before him, against a wall, like a gleaming altar to the gods of remembrance, stood a Rockola, *the* Rockola, on which he spent many a nickel wooing teen love, Ellen Guthrie. Lance stared at it, it staring back, and he wondered if it still worked, wondering if it sounded as magical today as it did in '71. He reached into his pocket and pulled out a quarter. The crowd, Lance decided, needed a blast of wake-up.

The Ghosts of Benevolence

The air filled with the acrid-sweet blend of frying bacon, cigarette smoke, burning waffle batter, and the hum of chatter. The morning regulars greeted each other as they came and went, individual days beginning and ending.

"Hey, Baxter!" the banter might go. "How you doin'? Peanuts comin' in yet?"

"Hurtin' for rain!"

"I heard that!"

"Lookin' like a perty day out yonder."

"Sure could use some rain!"

"I heard that!"

"Don't let them gnats 'n' chiggers eat you up!"

"They already *done* that!"

"I heard that!"

"Have a good'n!"

Lance deposited his quarter and pushed G-26. Heads turned as the thumps of an unwanted bass shot from the speakers, slamming ears and vibrating water from glasses and eggs from forks. Lance scanned the diner. He analyzed reactions, when his line of sight intersected with a woman sitting at the counter on the opposite side of the restaurant.

Her shaking head and defensive gestures gave proof of an argument in progress. Her head bobbed side to side, eyes wide and hair dancing, as she pushed away the reaching hands of her companion. Unable to discern their words above the music, Lance listened instead to the music of her beauty. Others ignored them as if their argument were standard fare in Belle's.

Spellbound, Lance saw something familiar about this woman. High cheekbones; full lips; large almond-shaped, blue eyes. Hair like silk, thick and flowing, like curling black water over mountain boulders. For a moment, Lance imagined touching it, running his fingers through its coolness, lifting the curls and letting them fall onto his arms. He imagined his hands sliding down her soft back,

179

lifting and falling over each curve. The pounding bass gave accent to his thoughts.

Lance removed his bifocals, a habit he had developed when in the vicinity of a beautiful woman, believing the absence of glasses somehow shaved a few years off his appearance, giving back Lance youth long departed. His wedding band, ignored like a mile-marker, put all those ravages of time back into place. He squinted, crows' feet flanking his out-of-focus eyes.

She looks a lot like Gwen, thought Lance, thinking back to the marvels of the first woman he had ever lusted, Gwen Summers. Lance, then seventeen, thought, as do most seventeen-year-olds, he had found love. Infatuation, certainly, but his memory was clear about the power Gwen once possessed over his hormones. *A whole lot like Gwen*, he thought, bifocal-less. *Could it be?*

The song finished.

"Shut up an' eat!" bellowed the woman's dining companion into the relative void of sound, in a fit of fantasitis interruptus.

The mustachioed man donned a black Stetson cowboy hat adorned with multi-hued peacock feathers in the center-front, much as one might expect of Richard Petty. He was a large man, muscular, ranging near six foot six. The veins of his arms bulged, his muscles taut. An oil-stained white tee shirt, like a second skin, clung to his chiseled chest. No man seemed inclined to interfere, certainly not Lance.

"Take your order, honey?" interrupted the server.

"Hmm?" Lance muttered in half reply. "Oh ... sorry, yes ... I'll have ... bring me a waffle and ... biscuits and gravy ... a couple of eggs, scrambled ... bacon, a slice of ... toast—"

Lance paused, now concerned less with the cravings of a country breakfast, his eyes fixed upon a craving of a different sort.

The Ghosts of Benevolence

Irritated with Lance's distraction, the waitress slid a step to her left and bent down, filling Lance's view. She looked at him squarely in his eyes.

"I ain't got all *day*, honey," she said with drawling impatience, pen at the ready. "That be all?"

Lance said nothing.

"Hey, *mister!* Piece of advice. If I was you, I'd keep my rovin' eyes on the *menu*."

"Sorry," Lance said, embarrassed. He cleared his throat. "And bacon, please. Did I say toast?"

"You said bacon *and* toast."

"So I did. Okay, bacon, toast … and coffee. Cream, please."

"You still want that waffle and them two scrambled eggs and biscuits and gravy?" the server asked.

"Yes. Please." Lance blushed with the realization the stringy-haired server was on to him.

"Just want to be sure," she said. "You sounded like you was just readin' a menu pasted on that woman's body."

She reached behind, a pivot of her waist, and grabbed a half-empty coffee pot. Pouring the beverage into a chipped brown mug, she peered over the glasses perched midway on her nose bridge, down toward Lance.

"You ain't from around here, are you?" she asked as she handed the coffee pot to a co-worker.

Lance pulled the business section from his USA Today and offered no reply.

"Look, mister, it ain't *none* of my business. Fact is, I'll probably lose my tip for sayin' what I'm about to say. Hell, nobody tips nothin' anyway," she said, shaking her head in disgust. "So let me give *you* a tip. You'd be wise to *stay clear* of that, in case you're gettin' ideas," she offered, tilting her head in the direction of the arguing couple. "If you know what's good for you, that is. Not sayin' that *you* have any designs on the leggy one, mind you. But if you happened to notice, the lady has a man, a rather *large* man, sittin' with her. Just sayin'."

Lance sighed as he turned back the front page of his paper.

"An' while I'm at it, let me tell you somethin' about him. He possesses women like Midas possessed gold. He has the touch, and he don't let go of 'em to *nobody*, that is until the glitter fades."

Lance snapped the wrinkles from his newspaper and licked his index finger in preparation to turn the page.

"Midas?" Lance mouthed out of view of his server. "You're right, of course," Lance said, pretending to scrutinize Wednesday's market closings. "You probably *will* lose your tip." He resumed his read.

"Figures," she mumbled. "Your funeral."

The server shoved her order pad into her pocket and wiped her hands on her apron. She shrugged with the acknowledgement that Lance was no different than most of her customers, and shuffled toward the next.

Curious diners, careful not to lock eyes with either of the pair, snuck occasional glances of the warring couple over the rims of their raised coffee mugs. The pair ended their public argument, one neither looking nor speaking to the other. Lance peered over the top of his paper. The man and woman exited the diner, shooting unheard shouts at one another. Lance made no attempt to conceal the slow 180-degree turn of his head, his eyes glued to the woman's rear and tight-jeaned legs as the pair walked through the parking lot. As if her shadow, Lance's eyes followed her to the truck.

Tires squealed as the late model black Dodge Ram fishtailed out of the parking lot.

"Here you go," the waitress said, placing on the table the waffle and another plate containing one fried egg and two strips of bacon. She wheeled around and whisked a

The Ghosts of Benevolence

coffee pot from the hands of a passing server. Her adroit display of athleticism impressed Lance.

"Need cream, hon?" the waitress asked stoically, as if Lance were her millionth customer of a day already too long.

"I hope you realize I was just kidding about your tip. You'll *get* one, don't worry. You been doing this a while, haven't you?" Lance asked, smiling. "Waiting on tables."

"Don't *need* your tip," she answered defiantly, her toes tapping. "You needin' cream or what?"

"Yes. Thanks." Lance gazed upon the fare and realized he was short one rubbery egg and a slice of burnt toast.

"What is it *now?*" she asked.

"Well, I … I ordered *two* eggs. Scrambled. And toast. And this bacon, well—"

"Mister," she interrupted, "you may be a tourist an' all—not that I care—but you're *doggone lucky* I don't open your shirt and pour this coffee right down it. You see how many folks're in here right now, not to mention all those *tippin'* folks waitin' on a seat, *your* seat? And I'll *give* it to 'em, too, if you ain't careful. You want your eggs *scrambled?* Mash 'em with your fork, or get yourself a job here an' scramble 'em *yourself.*"

So much for Southern hospitality, though Lance.

The crowd noise hushed, the silence countered with the pounding beat of "Achy Breaky Heart". Lance sensed many sets of blazing eyes frozen upon him, eyes he dared not confirm. He didn't need to. He felt their pierce. And he longed for the soothing strains of "Moonlight Serenade". He fixed his gaze upon the food.

"Ma'am, it's fine, really. This'll do just fine. Thank you."

Lance smelled the hostility, like bubbling tar. He took a fork to his egg, shuffled his newspaper to the sports section, and kept his profile low. While still hungry, crippled now was the craving.

The Ghosts of Benevolence

27

AN OLD MAN APPROACHED and set his palm on Lance's table. His yellowed, unclipped fingernails, thick as quarters, held the soils of ancient Babylon, so it seemed to Lance. A half-consumed cigarette smoldered stuck to his lower lip, the tilt of its ash threatening to drop.

"Morning, sir," the old man said, removing the cigarette and speaking with calm desperation. "Mind … mind if I sit with you a few moments?" The old man glanced in several directions. "All the tables and stools appear full, and I would appreciate your indulgence, as I have a *considerable* need to take a load off."

His mouth full of waffle and a coffee cup at his lips, Lance's eyes lifted in surprise. "I … beg your pardon? Take a load off?"

The old man stared, motionless, unblinking, showing no signs of abandoning his request. Lance believed it best under the circumstances not to refuse. *What harm can he do?* Lance thought.

The man carried a black bible, its rough use evident from the diagonal gash across its leather cover. Church bulletins, sticky notes, and other torn pieces of scrap paper, protruded from dog-eared pages, like a disorganized

collection of leaves. Certain any hope of relaxation had
now vanished, Lance did not dare stoke further trouble. He
urged the man to take his seat.

"Sure," Lance said, "why not?" offering with the
extension of his hand. "Sit."

The man had no sooner sat when his odor shoved
Lance against the back of his seat. Smells of smoke, sweat,
breath, and those sickly sorts of the outdoor scents one
brings home from camping trips exchanged places with the
relatively appetizing smells rising from Lance's food.
Mindful not to offend the offender—and to perchance save
his breakfast—Lance inched his plate toward the table's
farthest point in a daring move of conspicuous subtlety.
His appetite for country vittles, alas, his *craving*, vanished.
His mortal challenge, minutes ago the simple intake of fatty
foods, had now taken a human form.

The man appeared to be in his late seventies, perhaps
older, and he wore the stubble of a beard that covered his
face like thorns of a cactus. A slight mustache framed his
mouth, giving accent to his bottom lip, a chapped and
cracked line of flesh pocked with festering sores.

His breath, which sent forth a stench like the
decomposition of roadkill, possessed a power to derail the
likes of freight trains and probably had, Lance concluded,
noting a string of lifeless boxcars resting at angles off the
tracks a few hundred feet downwind from the diner. His
teeth, what few remained, donned an alternating plaid of
brown and yellow, several of which were cratered by
decay.

The left-arm sleeve of his tattered gray blazer briefly
distracted Lance's attention from the man's hygienic
shortcomings. The sleeve, perhaps the most organized
piece of clothing covering his frail body, tucked neatly into
his pants pocket, and only until after the man had sat, and
Lance had taken time to consider his unusual guest, was it

The Ghosts of Benevolence

clear the sleeve was armless. Lance *recognized* this
gentleman.

Mark Randolph Watters

The Ghosts of Benevolence

He's the man I saw on the church steps yesterday,
Lance recalled. *The magician! What could he want with
me, other than the obvious—a free breakfast!*

"Do you know what this is?" he asked, pointing to his
ragged bible. The man spoke with the vocal clarity of an
on-air reporter, belying the effects one might expect from a
smoker. He then reached into his shirt pocket and retrieved
another cigarette, bent slightly in its middle, a few strands
of tobacco kinking out its end. "You don't mind, do you?
I have to keep them going, else I'll lose the ease of lighting
them. You understand, I'm sure."

"Looks like a bible, sir," Lance replied with the respect
due his elders, one of few attributes retained from the
manners taught him by Sara and reinforced with the
persuasive powers of Aunt Pearl.

"Not just *a* bible, son. It's *the* bible, the *Holy* Bible,
the sanctified and inspired word of God Almighty. I'm
here to ask you about your salvation. Are you?"

The man's gray-green eyes, like the rotating clouds of
a thunderhead, fixed firmly upon Lance's. White-dagger
eyebrows accented the man's piercing gaze, and Lance
wondered if God Himself had joined him for breakfast.
Each word the man uttered seemed to carve deeper into the
crevices of his forehead.

Oh, God, not again, Lance thought. "My *what? Am I
what?*"

Lance understood clearly what the old man said, what
he meant, but he had not yet brought himself to accept this
might happen. Not to *him*. Not in Belle's Diner. Not
during breakfast.

"My ... *salvation?*"

The old man nodded. "I've come, sir, to ask you about
your relationship with Jesus."

Lance stared. *Jesus,* he thought, *pinch me!*

Mark Randolph Watters

"Sir, my salvation is *right here*," Lance asserted, smiling, referring to the photograph, patting his jacket pocket. "I have a little something here that will *salvate* me for quite a while." Lance smiled. He inserted a forkful of eggs into his mouth and looked down at his newspaper, hoping the old man would receive the cue and go away.

He gazed upon Lance's plate, like an obedient dog awaiting permission, but he didn't go away.

"What concern of *yours* is my salvation, old man?" Lance restated.

"My concern is for *everyone's* salvation," the man replied. Son, don't you realize that Jesus Christ suffered the weight of your sins, *all* our sins, and died for you on the cross at Calvary and sits now at the right hand of God making intercessions on your behalf?"

Lance jiggled his fork, lifting and dropping pieces of egg, feigning inattentiveness and staring again in disbelief.

Is this guy serious, or is he just panhandling? Lance wondered, realizing that regardless of the reason, the old man had made himself a fixture at Lance's booth, the 'kook de jour'. *Might as well humor the old bastard*, Lance conceded.

"In-ter-ces-sions!" Lance mocked, his head tilted upward, fingers stroking his chin. *"You*, sir, must be the ghost of Red Hamilton, because I sure as hell can't imagine anybody *else* wanting to *intercede* on my behalf, on my breakfast, at least not in the manner *you* have chosen."

The old man cleared his throat. "Not so much *Red Hamilton*, my boy, but … you're on the right track. Allow me to continue?"

Lance dropped his fork, placed his head in his hands and prepared his surrender. Short of nuclear annihilation, Lance realized, the old man *would* continue.

"If you confess your sins before God and profess your faith in Jesus Christ," he continued, leaning forward as he spoke, roadkill breath spilling, tapping his skeletal fist on

The Ghosts of Benevolence

the Bible with the cadence of a drummer, "He is faithful *and just* to forgive you your sins. But you must *confess*, verbally confess. You must not be *ashamed* to confess before a Holy God ... and before Man. Have you confessed, my son?"

Not sure whether to laugh or to cry, Lance leaned back and sank into the booth.

Who is this guy? thought Lance, on the brink of intolerance.

Lance's waffle, once basking in the soggy warmth of its syrup, took on a chill. The toast limped in its buttery baptism. Not a patron had turned, yet, to witness the witnessing. Just as city streets and sidewalk corners served as soapboxes for lunatics proclaiming the end of time, Belle's Diner provided a pulpit, an audience, and an occasional meal for religious and ideological drifters. Diners, regulars in particular, had learned to ignore the likes of these zealots, preferring gravy-bathed biscuits over the indigestion of spiritual food.

"I'm talking about *your* eternity, son," the old man stressed, his determination growing. "Where are you going to spend *your* eternity?"

"Go talk to somebody else about *their* eternity," Lance said, dismissing the old man. "I have a feeling this breakfast will provide eternity enough for me."

"Narrow is the gate through–"

"Matthew 9. Verse 37," Lance said, tearing a bite from his bread, engaging the old man in biblical gamesmanship, hoping to surprise him with his familiarity of scriptures.

"You know this truth?"

"*Know* it? I *lived* it. It was one of Aunt Pearl's most quoted verses."

"*Was?*" pried the old man.

"Still is, maybe," Lance said, sipping his coffee. "Don't know whether she's alive or dead. I *assume* she's dead. If she were alive, she'd be well over a *hundred* years old. That's a pretty *darn old* age, wouldn't you agree, for such ham-hocked Southerners as we." Lance laughed, speckling his newspaper with coffee.

The old man sat stone-faced.

"Warm-up, hon?" a passing server asked Lance.

"Please. And bring a cup for my guest."

"Black, hon?"

"Yes, please," the old man answered. "Thank you."

"Comin' up."

"Let's just say," continued Lance, "she had *lots* of favorites. That, and the ubiquitous John 3:16, among others." Lance again chuckled softly, looking out a window.

"You find it humorous?" the old man asked.

"Not the verse so much. The whole Bible thing. It put me to mind of how she'd tell folks—and I quote—'You just need to read this here Bible. It'll scare *Hell* out of you!'"

Lance waited for the old man's reaction to the subtle turn of phrase.

"Not '*the* hell'," Lance explained, "as I might casually say. Just 'Hell'. As in Hell itself, with a capital **H**."

"Ah, a *wise* woman, your aunt. May I ask … what I mean is, is she still … with you?" the old man asked, not so much in the context of the physical, but rather of the effects of her influence on Lance. Lance did not discern the distinction.

"Are you not *listening*, sir? Maybe she *is* alive; I doubt it. But if she is, then she's older than the dirt under your fingernails, no offense."

"None taken."

His mind straying briefly to an earlier time, an Aunt Pearl time. Lance toyed with his waffle, tearing apart the walls and squares softened to vulnerability by syrup.

The Ghosts of Benevolence

"Anyway, Aunt Pearl's not actually my aunt, if you *must* know. It's a long story, but rest assured, Aunt Pearl—some knew her as Miss Tommie—was a one-of-a-freakin'-kind. She could make a tornado look like a spring zephyr."

"She, being the genuine tornado, I presume?" the old man asked with a smile, seeking clarification.

"Absolutely! She memorized scriptures so *thoroughly*, she could recite passages, whole chapters even, backwards, while in the next breath, if so provoked, cuss you out like Patton had she a mind to. You would have had no better a friend, nor worse an enemy." Lance looked down, poking his waffle.

"Where did Aunt Pearl call home, sir? Her roots, that is," asked the old man.

"Roots? Your guess is as good as mine. Wherever life put her. Benevolence was her home, I suppose," Lance answered, awash in a moment of private lament, "having spent most of her life here, but she never mentioned her birthplace. The *world* was her playground, her home."

Lance spoke fondly of Aunt Pearl, bragging of her resilience and the diversity of her enduring nature.

"Not that she traveled the world, mind you. She scantly ventured beyond the Alabama line. But Aunt Pearl paid attention to world events, things that other folks just ignored or refused to acknowledge or otherwise thought boring. She was as tough as an old hardwood and as wise as Solomon," smiled Lance. "She'd seen it all, so she said; heard it all, too. God rest her soul."

"*God* rest her soul? I thought you didn't believe—"

"I never said ... When did I say that?"

"And what would *she* say about salvation and eternity?" pressed the old man.

"You're not going to let it go, are you? I thought you wanted to know more about Aunt Pearl."

"Oh, I *do*. I just asked you what she … Believe me, I *do*," the old man replied. "That's why I asked about her thoughts on salvation and eternity."

"Sir, I have no doubt my … 'eternity', as you term it, will be spent in *restful, blissful non-existence*, rotting to dust in a coffin costing *far* more than it's worth, after an overpriced funeral *filled* with phony sentiment, flowery speeches, and hackneyed hymns, attended by people fulfilling their notion of social obligation, satisfying their daily yearning for Facebook yakkity-yak, afterwards rewarding themselves with free food, spicy gossip, and phone numbers, all the while sipping their green tea, club sodas and mint juleps, stealing coy glances at folks they don't know, discussing yesterday's ballgames or their dear daughters' debutant balls, never mind their exaggerated golf handicaps or equally fictional stock portfolios.

"Eternity is endless *nothingness*, man," Lance declared, extending his empty palms, "no more, no less. Besides, you Christians are too *exclusionary,* and a lot of you are just, well … *outré!"* Lance said as he poked his waffle.

"Outré? Got me on *that* one."

"O-u-t-r-e. French. Look it up. You denounce other faiths, condemning those non-Christian faithful. Muslims, for example, and Jews. As far as you're concerned, these equally devout believers are destined to *eternal* damnation if they do not turn to your Christ."

"So you *don't* believe."

"Don't put words in my mouth! How is it that Christians' claims to truth are more bona fide than any other faith's claims? In one fell swoop, you eradicate the hopes of *millions* of people, of whole *races*, whole cultures. Are Hindus or Buddhists nothing more than chopped liver to you people? God's *chosen*, the Israelites, are doomed in the minds of Christians to an *eternity* of hell because they haven't accepted Jesus as their so-called savior? Isn't that

The Ghosts of Benevolence

a bit *presumptuous?* What about Native American Indians who lived *thousands* of years ago, hundreds of years ago, even *today* ... those who never *heard about* Jesus Christ but instead worshipped the sun or a snake? I suppose as far as you're concerned, these people occupy special pits in hell or are hell-*bound?* Give me a break!"

Patiently, the old man listened. He'd touched a nerve. Lance continued, determined to fill his uninvited guest with his long-latent anger.

"In fact, sir, Christianity *itself* is fraught with division. How many denominations exist, each with its own set of rituals, its own interpretations of the scriptures, each *competing* for souls, and, if I may be so blunt, congregants' dollars? How can *anyone* be certain *any* set of interpretations are correct or God-endorsed? What if they're *wrong*? What if *you're* wrong? And just how much tolerance for error is your god willing to accept? Sounds to me like religion's pretty much a roll of the dice, a freakin' lotto game! Heck, even the lottery has winners, winners from all walks of life. The only winners I see in Christianity are the big-church preachers and televangelists."

"Endless *nothingness?* Candler responded, as Lance took a breath. "No doubt you make good points, each worthy of its own conversation," the old man acknowledged, "but whether or not you agree or are willing to admit, God has a plan for *you*, Lance P. Hawthorne. All you have to do is accept Christ as your personal savior and seek His perfect will. I can't say how God will judge practitioners of other faiths and other deities. As for denominations, God, I believe, has a sense of humor. He *invented* the sense of humor. While differences do exist, those differences are inconsequential and take nothing away from the substance that matters."

"But those denominational differences are so divisive. You people *judge* all the time! You're *always* doing that!"

"You're right, some of us do, unfortunately, but Jesus said to *judge not*, lest ye be judged. He also said, 'those with ears let them hear.' I believe that when a person has been *exposed* to the Christian faith, to Christ and His teachings, then the choice is unavoidable whether or not to believe and accept Christ's free gift of eternal life, along with the *consequences* of either choice."

"Consequences, you say?"

Lance had not attended church since the days shortly before Aunt Pearl sent him away to college, and he was in no mood for church attending him, especially during the middle of a country breakfast craving.

He remembered the rantings of Red Hamilton, a man for whom God was no more than another tool in his box of deception, a means to his selfish ends. This, coupled with his daddy's cavalier use of the word, affixed often to the word, 'damn', spoken in the rage of the slightest provocation, long ago shattered the black and white of Lance's perception of religion and God. The hypocrisy about which so-called 'OMG' Christians bandied God's name left Lance cold and colored gray his sense of the Truth. Devereaux's consequences of wealth and power, for example, appeared to Lance to be a reward hardly deserving of so vile a human.

"Appears to me," Lance continued, "that a body would be better off *never going* to church in the *first* place and never being exposed to the teachings and knowledge of Jesus Christ. Am I right? Why would God present man with such a paradox? The *consequences* of such knowledge seem dire to me, especially to us doubters, who, by the way, would not *engage* in doubt if we never had received the knowledge, or if answers to our questions were clearer."

The man sat silent. He slid another cigarette from its pack resting on the table and held it tip-to-tip with the burning one. He took long draws, transferring the fire.

The Ghosts of Benevolence

"Have I stumped you, old man? Look, I'm not sure why you chose to assault *me* with your religious drivel. Do I look a more *dastardly sinner* than any of the rest of these folks?" Lance asked, gesturing with the spread of his arms. "Does my skin look more *devilish* to you than *theirs?* Are my eyes more bloodshot, *beadier* perhaps? Oh, *I* know! I have a *pentagram* burned into my forehead! Look at my palms. See any sixes? No, and you *won't*. Go peddle your piety to someone else, for the love of—"

"God?" Candler finished.

"First of all, I don't believe in *your* god—"

"Ah, I thought as much."

"That's not to say I don't believe *in* God. But even if your god were real, he'd have some *explaining* to do about how his 'perfect will' has resulted in so much tragedy for so many, not to mention why he allows *loons* like you to ruin the breakfast of folks like *me* who want only to be left alone, thank you very much! What say you, sir?"

Lance now abandoned all pretensions of his respect for the old man. Discussions such as this never failed to push Lance's emotional buttons. Best, he believed, to avoid these conversations altogether, as well as the people whence such came, but the old man's persistent, calm brevity had thrust Lance out of, and far to the rear of, his primary defenses.

Mark Randolph Watters

28

LIKE A MAN SLAPPED with the gauntlet, Lance sat firm, resolved to return the gesture. He preferred the old man take his Bible and, without a word, move on. Instead, the armless old man drew his spiritual sword and planted his gaze upon Lance. Thus notified, Lance resigned to let loose the Hawthorne ire.

"What say *I*? I say that God loves *you*, young man," replied the old man," in *spite* of yourself!"

Young? Lance thought. *That's one point in the old man's favor.*

"He did not make the ills and injuries that have plagued ours and other cultures throughout history," the man said. "God gave mankind intelligence and the gifts of *cognizance* and *conscience*. He allows a person, using those gifts, to *choose* his own destiny. What better gifts than free will and life eternal? These are gifts of *freedom!*

"Dogs can't exercise free will. Deer can't. All animals can do is respond to their instincts, their needs to eat, drink, sleep, and reproduce. To survive. But man is *aware*, aware of powers far superior to his own! Man can learn and apply that knowledge, in concert with, or in the face of, his instincts. That a man has *chosen* the path of sin is not *God's* doing. It is *man's* doing. Some lessons, I am sorry to say, are not so well-learned."

"So," Lance argued, "you're telling me that when a virus kills millions of defenseless men, women and children; or when children worldwide starve; or when planes are guided into buildings; or when drive-by gangbangers take the lives of innocent bystanders; or when drunk drivers kill mothers and their babies and destroy families; or when women abort babies; or when someone snaps and murders anyone within sight, a la Columbine and Newtown—you're saying to me this is *ignored* by your god in *deference* to man's *choice,* his *free will?* If your god were truly an omnipotent, loving god, then *none* of this evil would ever happen!" Lance shouted.

"Seems to me, old man, that your god, who 'so loved the world', too often checks his love at the door of that world. Either that, or he's simply an absentee god. He sounds like an *enabler of* sin, not a savior *from* sin. How much *choice* does one have when thrown to the ground and crushed between runaway wagons and potholes? I *reject* that god! What sort of god *spectates*, like a Roman emperor projecting his thumb up or down in accordance to his *amusement?* Is god himself not guilty of the sin of *omission?* Where is the mercy in *this?*"

Lance was breathless, his face flush. He drew strength from agnostic convictions built over years of skepticism fueled by disdain for fraudulent television evangelists, many of whom sold God's favor for thousand-dollar 'seed offerings', thus fleecing their flocks. He held no concern for the judgmental nature of the breakfast crowd now attentive to the debate. *Let them look*, he resolved, and he continued.

"Religion, in all its sordid and colorful mutations, is designed simply to keep the masses at bay," Lance observed, "to keep an otherwise anarchic society in check. Without the morals ostensibly originating from religion,

The Ghosts of Benevolence

anarchy would reign, and indeed we would have *hell* to pay. I concede that religions can provide moral compasses, direct people in paths of decent conduct and self-control. But, religions also lead to the outright cockamamie, not to mention its history for the justification of wars and inquisitions.

"Religion. Salvation. Jesus. These are little more than *commodities*, sir, commodities sold to the highest bidders. It's all a monumental con game."

The old man sat in his silence, content to let Lance exorcise himself.

"Furthermore, what kind of a religion, what manner of superior being, justifies the murder of innocent women and children by means of evil persons exercising *their* wills?" Lance lowered his head. "My God," he whispered, "those poor, poor children.

"What god *compels* parents to keep their children *away* from doctors so that some *faith healer* can *lay hands* on the kid? Seems god gets his kicks watching a pitiful human being handle a *rattlesnake* in the name of *faith.* Didn't this same god also create man with intellectual abilities— common sense—screaming at him to leave that rattlesnake *alone?* What are these fanatics *thinking*, for God's sake?

"Didn't God create the cognitive skills and intellects that have *produced* scientists, researchers, doctors, folks who, through painstaking study and experimentation, unlock God's secrets, *helping* the sick and injured?

"I think that people turn to God because of the one thing in life they are genuinely *afraid* of and have no control over—death, the very *real* fear and the mother of all unknowns, the last word in final frontiers. People want to believe, to cling to the notion, that *surely* there is *something* beyond this mortal coil, a Utopia *somewhere* over the rainbow.

"People *long* for the security of the womb whence they came. 'What if the devil *does* exist?' they ask, frozen by their fear of the possibility. People want the security, it turns out, of something they can neither prove nor disprove. We're like children looking over our shoulders for the looming school bully; though while not always seen, those bullies are nonetheless visible lurking in the psychological shadows they cast. So, we say, 'best be on board with God; can't hurt.' A belief in God and an afterlife gives people an *assurance* of a sort of divine *insurance*.

"In other words, sir, I assert that most people who profess religion are hypocrites. They "worship" god because of what they've been preached is in it for them, a heavenly *reward*, a personal *gain*. *Not* because such a god himself is worthy of our worship simply given the fact he is *God*."

Lance noticed the old man's eyes drift toward the plate of food to his front. He felt a sudden twinge of empathy for the old man. "By the way, are you … are you hungry?"

"Hungry? As a matter of fact, yes, I *am* hungry. Same as you, I suppose, and here I am keeping you from your breakfast."

Lance glared at his cooled plate of food. "Hmm. Such as it is. Waitress!" Lance said, waving a server to his table.

"Give this gentleman the desires of his belly."

"Thank you, sir," the old man said with a bow of his head. He opened a menu. The server stood ready to receive his order. "Hmm, shouldn't have to think very long about this. I'd like … two eggs, sunny-side ablaze; biscuits, light as clouds; bacon, crispy and stiff; grits, heaven's food; and water, holy and clean; oh, and a warm-up."

"That all?" the server mumbled.

"And a glass of *sunshine!*"

"Whatchu mean, glass of sunshine?" the server asked, aggravated.

"You know. *Orange juice*. The same brand *Bing Crosby* drinks."

The Ghosts of Benevolence

"Bing Crosby don't *drink* no brand o' orange juice no mo'e, mister. He *dead!*"

"Dead, you say?" the man asked, tilting his head downward. "So sorry to hear that. I should have *known*, I suppose, but I haven't *seen* him. Do you suppose he's in Heaven?"

"How the hell would *I* know?"

"Point taken. Okay, then, the same kind he *drank*."

"We ain't got no Minute Maid," the server answered.

"Well, what *do* you have?" the old man asked.

"We got Tropicana, Sunny D, or Joe's Orange Squeezins."

"Well, then ... give me some of Joe's Orange Squeezins."

"Make it so," Lance said with a wink to the server.

"You gettin' his bill?" the server asked, suspecting the old man's wherewithal.

"Yes, I'm paying." Lance turned to the old man. "Now then, Mister ..."

"Candler. Horace Candler."

"Now then, Mr. Candler—"

"Friends call me Horace. Misters are for strangers."

"Now then ... Mr. Candler, if God *does* exist, why is heaven the carrot on a string? Isn't the creator of the universe carrot *enough*? If one's soul is so blessed to find its way to heaven and live eternally, then has God not granted us his serendipity? God, if he exists, deserves our unmitigated worship, even our fear just because he *is* God, no? Instead, the emphasis is on my-faith-in-exchange-for-eternal-life-and-heavenly-rewards quid pro quo. You give me *this*, says God, and I'll give you *that*."

"This is nothing more than a game to you, isn't it, Mr. Hawthorne? Waitress? More coffee, please. Black. And a refill for Mr. Hawthorne." Candler settled back into the booth, prepared for the brimstone storm. "He's going to need that refill."

"How ... how do you know my name?"

"Your card, remember? But I think this might be of greater importance to you," Candler stated calmly, reaching into his pocket and removing a black bifold wallet. "Yours?"

"What?" Lance patted his back right pocket, and then snatched the wallet from the old man's fingers. "Where did you *get* this?"

"Polished Italian leather, satin smooth. Very nice, indeed. Seems it fell from your pocket as you reached into the newspaper box for your USA Today. You do have a way of ... losing things, don't you?"

Lance took the wallet, opened it, and quickly thumbed through the currency and credit cards.

"Don't worry; it's all there. I may be many things, Mr. Hawthorne, but a thief is not among them; if I *were*, I would not be sitting here handing you your wallet."

Lance paused, absorbing the logic. "Right. I suppose you wouldn't. Thanks. I appreciate your honesty."

"Shall we continue our discussion on ... 'religious drivel'."

Lance took in the collage of contradictions presented by his breakfast guest. Unkempt and filthy as a freight train hobo, yet as articulate and intelligent as a man of letters, this wizened country gentleman did not impress Lance as ordinary. If nothing more, perhaps their conversation would unravel the mystery surrounding him.

"No offense, Candler, but you ... *do* need a bath."

Candler smiled, sipping his coffee. "And *you*, sir, need a *cleansing*."

"We'll just see about that," Lance replied, privately impressed with Candler's retort.

"So, you *don't* believe in God, Mr. Hawthorne."

Lance grinned, tilted his head, and spread his arms across the back of the booth, confident that the heart of the debate had now been breached and that he would prevail.

The Ghosts of Benevolence

"I'm amazed that you, and those like you, *do* believe. Tell me *why*, sir. Tell me why you *insist* on believing in something you cannot prove, something you cannot touch, smell, see, hear, or taste. Would a loving god grant us these senses and then *deny* us their ultimate use?"

"*Ultimate* use? What do you mean?"

Lance shifted position, irritated with having to explain what seemed to him an obvious shortcoming of God.

"Candler, I can't *touch* your god; I can't *smell* your god; I can't *see*, *hear*, or *taste* your god. If he's among us, as you unflinchingly claim, then why doesn't he make himself known to at least *one* of our five senses? Why does God seem like a roulette wheel in an Atlantic City casino? I've known folks who have *sworn* God had a direct hand in their "miracle" recovery. I've known other folks, *good* folks, who have prayed *ceaselessly* for his intervention, to *no avail.*"

Horace Candler pondered Lance's challenge a moment. He leaned forward, arm rested on the table. He sighed and spoke with a whisper.

"God has given each of us a *sixth* sense, Lance, and if the other five senses fail to reveal to you His existence, it's through that *sixth* sense He makes His presence and His glory known, sort of a *bonus* sense to jumpstart your other five."

"A *sixth* sense? And what might *that* be?"

The server returned with Candler's breakfast, setting the plates on the table.

Candler drew a long sniff. "Ah! Smells delicious! Thank you."

"The only sixth sense—"

Lance stopped. The old man bowed his head in silent prayer. Lance sighed, slurped his coffee, and waited.

"The only sixth sense I know of is the sense of *appreciation* for the *glory* that is *Southern cookin'!*" Lance proclaimed, as he praised the warm aromas drifting his way.

"Faith, Lance. Faith is your *sixth* sense. Only you refuse to acknowledge it, to let it work for you. The sixth sense of faith enables you to grasp God with all five of your other senses. You *can see, smell, taste, hear, and touch God*, all around you, everywhere you are. I hate to sound so trite, sir, as I am neither a lover nor a user of platitudes. But you are the *perfect* example of one who cannot see the forest for the trees. Lance—may I call you Lance—you are among a rapidly growing apostasy. I wholly support legitimate doubters who ask the valid question, 'what if?' *'What if* God *does* exist? What if He *doesn't* exist?' they ask over and over, haunted by either prospect.

"And, why *not* ask these questions and others, if such propels one toward an ultimate acknowledgment and a purer understanding of God? The answers to these questions are *pivotal* for such people. I do not think that their subsequent acceptance of Jesus Christ renders them holders of 'afterlife insurance'. God is not the lottery, Lance, and one's set of beliefs cannot be equated to a set of winning—or losing—numbers. God is *truth*. God is *real*. Such doubters—and I tend to believe you are firmly among such—merely seek truth; doubting is part of that process, and God grants us that privilege."

"But, Candler—"

"Ah, ah, ah. I let you speak. Now let me."

"Go ahead." Lance took his coffee cup and slumped into a posture Sara would have scolded him for.

"Granted, there are those who would don the cloth for personal gain, and I abhor them. But, you, and 'those like you'," Candler said, pointing out and mocking Lance's own words, "have come to worship your own self-importance, your own self-sufficiency, your own ... *self*.

"You have no *fear* of God because for you there *is* no God to fear. Instead, in your privacy you fear your *shadow*,

The Ghosts of Benevolence

afraid of your fellow agnostics' desire to *consume* your sixth sense, to suffocate your need to acknowledge something *greater* than yourself. You scratch and claw all day to gain more and more in a world of *your* creation, a world doomed to crumble in its finiteness, and yet still you walk away at the end of the day, dissatisfied and exhausted. Never *will be* satisfied; nor rested.

"And the world grows more violent and indifferent, the *real* cause of your angst and unbelief, dare I suggest, because of people like *you*, Mr. Hawthorne. The anarchy you alluded to earlier is upon us. Your apathy for spiritual fulfillment, as well as your resentment of Christians, gives legs to the permissiveness that pervades our society. Your answer—and I use the term in its loosest sense—is moral relativism. That is to say, for you *nothing* is moral and yet *everything* is moral, depending on the circumstance. Your emotions dictate for you what is 'right' and what is 'wrong' according to the *moment* and your state of mind, to how you *feel*. Kids are growing up without dignity, honor, self-control, respect for others, self-respect, for *anything*. Anything but *themselves*, and even *that* is unclear.

"I believe in God, Mr. Hawthorne, because I cannot accept the notion that, despite our human failings, we are without hope, that our society is beyond redemption, that *this,*" Candler said, arm raised, "is *all* there is. It is *because* of our cognizance, our awareness of self, of others, of things we could never ourselves create, that I look to a higher being. Look around you, Lance."

Candler sighed, his eyes filled with tears, and he turned facing the window.

"Look at the simplicity, the complexity, of the sprawling, twisted branches of that oak across the street. Look at the sea of white in that cotton field yonder. Look at the *simple life-sustaining elegance* of the water in your glass. Consider the countless number of people who have come before us. Consider the *magnificence,* the infinite *complexity*, of the human body and mind. Even scientists, *Darwinists*, wrestle with explaining the mystery of life's beginnings. What, for instance, differentiates the animate from the inanimate?

"Mankind can do most *anything*, Lance. He can create the most marvelous of machines and comforts to enhance our everyday lives, as well as the most horrid of weaponry to destroy it, but … but, mankind certainly *cannot* create *life from scratch,* except through God-given *reproductive* means, and, of course, that's not really from scratch.

"Do you *honestly* believe life and its attendant complexities just … appeared, just *happened?* Did *you* just appear on this earth? Did *Sara* just appear? Did I … did *Aunt Pearl* just … appear? What about Gini and Jerri? Cognizant, but soulless, creatures, here for a while, here for us to know and love, then gone? I cannot accept that."

"You knew my mama, my *family*?"

"Let's just say Sara and I were friends. Saw your kid's picture in your wallet."

"Friends? How so?"

"That's not important now, Lance. What *is* important is that you realize there *is* a God, a God who so loved the world. And He loves you as a *part* of that world. My belief is driven by my sixth sense, Lance. I'm troubled by the same things you mentioned earlier; drunk drivers killing babies; planes flown into buildings; disease; famine; indiscriminate death; hypocrites, all that stuff. But it doesn't shake my faith. I cannot *let* Man's inhumanity shake my faith, because I know beyond *all my doubts* that God controls, that God lives, and that God *is*. I leave to *Him* the sorting out of consequences."

"Okay, *okay*. I think I was looking for the *short* answer, but I get your point."

"That *was* my *short* answer," Candler said, reaching for his Bible. "Here's your *complete* answer, Lance."

The Ghosts of Benevolence

Lance turned his eyes toward the short-order cook flipping fried eggs and hash-browns. He thought about shortcuts and Doc Harper's admonitions against them. Both men paused to take some coffee. Horace opened his bible, upon which Lance winced, like Dracula at dawn's light.

Oh brother, thought Lance, *weapon drawn; going for the kill.*

"You *do* agree, Mr. Candler, that your god is omniscient and omnipotent?"

"I do," Candler replied without hesitation.

Not more than five feet away, a server heard Lance's question and, without turning her back, stopped to eavesdrop. Others were tuning in as well.

"If indeed your god is omniscient, all-knowing, then he *must* have known you, me, *us*, before we were born, before he created all this … this *world*, this *life*," Lance said, waving his hands in gesture. "True?"

"True," acknowledged Candler, flipping the pages of his bible toward a response in anticipation of Lance's query.

"You say it is God's will that every man shall be saved. This implies the converse, that it is *not* God's will that any man be lost, or *unsaved*, or whatever is the proper nomenclature. Am I right so far?"

"Continue, Lance."

"You believe that souls, because of their lack of faith—their unsaved condition—now dwell in hell, a so-called lake of fire for the lost."

Lance paused, expecting some response to his set-up. Horace Candler sat silent, chewing his crispy bacon, a slight smile and an unwavering gaze telling Lance his breakfast guest was attentive.

"How, Mr. Candler," Lance continued, "can a *benevolent* god—you *would* classify god as *benevolent*— knowing that millions of his creations will not only be *born* into a sinful world, but will march through life *unrepentant*, and will *die and go to hell* … how, sir, can such a god, knowing their ultimate, unalterable fate, *allow* their existence in the *first* place?

"Nobody *asks* to be born, Candler. My four-year-old daughter had *nothing* to do with what has gone before. My unborn child has *no clue* of the world she is about to enter. Their existence is not of *their* choosing. *We*, their parents, made that choice. Yet, the choices people make in life, whether made with full knowledge of the consequences, or out of simple immaturity, or some genetic flaw in their reasoning capabilities, determine their *eternal* destiny. Given the enormity of life's temptations—and the contrast of humanity's weaknesses—the simplest choice becomes an awesome responsibility. Where is the justice and mercy in that? God knew of Hitler and the evil he would release. I think you'll agree Hitler dwells in hell, if there *is* a hell. If that were Hitler's destiny, and god *knew* it before time began, *why* would God create him? Or Stalin? Or any of the entities of evil, past and present and to come? Why allow such horror to befall man when, by God's foreknowledge, he could have *avoided* it all? Why send a soul on a one-way trip to hell, with a wake of misery cast upon humanity, knowing the journey and destination were *unalterable?*"

Folks gathered near the table as word spread of the topic of conversation. Religion in these parts was as sensitive and rooted an issue as states' rights and the war it generated generations ago. Tenets carved deeply into the psyche of a Sutter Countian forbade his belief in, even tolerance of, notions contradictory to tradition. Lance became aware of the gathering audience, and he knew his position lacked popularity. Still, he did not waver.

"Trust in the Lord with all thine heart and lean not on thine own understanding," Candler replied.

The Ghosts of Benevolence

"Yeah, yeah, and god's ways are not our ways. Isaiah 55:8," Lance said, dismissing Candler's references to scripture. "More coffee, please, ma'am. You've hardly touched your food, Candler. Strange ... it still steams with warmth, as if it were just brought to you."

"Your cynicism dominates your thoughts and your ways, Lance. You have slammed the doors on all of God's attempts to influence you, to dwell within you. You see this world as sets of obstacles to be hurdled or cast aside, as enemies to be destroyed. You see Christianity as an *impediment* to your independence rather than the *fulfillment of* your independence, as a part of that *enemy* that must be destroyed.

"Yes, the bible seems filled with contradictions, and not all of God's mysteries come with footnotes of explanation or convenient answers. God's ways are supernatural and, as such, are not subject to scientific method and confirmation. His ways and His Words were not *meant* for our testing or our approval. We are His creations and He desires—*demands*—our humble faith. Faith comes by hearing and hearing by the Word of God. Don't you see it's His intention that we come to Him through that sixth sense of faith? He doesn't care that you come to Him filled with sin. He's already taken care of that through His Son, Jesus."

"Romans 10:17."

"Correct. Aside from your impressive memory of scriptural references, you've closed your ears and eyes to God. Do you think Sara and Aunt Pearl are pleased with that? You're as a blind man in a dark room looking for a black cat that does not exist. The evil of the world is Satan-made and man-embraced. God did not—"

"Wait a minute, old man. You're telling me this so-called loving god had nothing to do with the evil and sin in the world? Take that bible of yours and turn to Genesis, chapter 2, starting with verse ... 7, I think."

Candler's gaze fixed upon Lance while shuffling the pages to Genesis 2:7. He read silently.

"Let me know when you get to the part about the tree of the knowledge of good and evil." Lance waited.

"Okay, I read it. So?" Candler tilted his head slightly and lifted his eyebrows, in full defiance of Lance's efforts to humiliate him or repudiate God.

"So?" Lance said, chuckling at Candler's nonchalance. "It says god formed man from the dust and he made every tree in the Garden of Eden, including—and I emphasize *including*—the tree of the knowledge of good and evil. Seems god can't even get past the second chapter of the first book of his own bible without admitting he is the source, the catalyst, of all that is evil. If you read on, you'll find that Eve ate the fruit of this tree and gave the same to Adam, and *voila*, man has suffered wretchedly ever since. Why would God make such a tree available to man as a tool of *temptation*? Why was evil allowed *parity* with good? Why did god not *destroy* the fallen angel instead of casting him into hell? Why give man a *choice between good and evil?* Why not limit man to choosing between *good* choice 'A' and good choice 'B' instead of between *good* choice 'A' and *bad* choice 'B'? Was your god so *weak* he was unable to *prevent* evil?

"And another thing. Turn over to Romans 5:18. Never mind; let me just read it to you. 'Therefore, as by the offence of one, judgment came upon all men to condemnation; even so by the righteousness of one, the free gift came unto all men unto justification of life.' This verse tells me that because Adam committed the original sin, all men are born with the sin nature. Don't you see, Candler? God *allowed* man, all men, to be *predisposed* to sin rather than to *righteousness*. At least, that's how *I* see it. Our nature from birth is to commit sin, to commit evil. That's pretty tough baggage for mortal man to lug around. Why didn't God give man a predisposition to righteousness

The Ghosts of Benevolence

instead? That way, it would be man's nature to commit *good*, not evil, and the temptation to commit evil would not be prevalent, and—"

Candler grinned.

"I see your wheels turning," Lance observed. "What are you thinking, Candler?"

"Don't you hear yourself?" Candler asked.

"Hear my— What are you talking about?"

"Your argument is laced with examples of the *actions of God*. For a man who does not believe in God's existence, you argue rather *vehemently* in *favor* of His existence. I find that amusing, even *hopeful*, that's all."

"My argument, Candler, is *hypothetical* in the context of the *possibility* of God's existence. Just answer my question."

"Okay. Adam had a predisposition to righteousness, yet he yielded to temptation anyway," Candler said.

"What?" Lance responded, surprised by Candler's succinct reply.

"Adam wasn't *born* with the sin nature," replied Candler. "Still, he *sinned* against God. Satan is a powerful tempter, especially when one turns one's back on God. It's like spitting in the wind, Lance. God just wants our *faith*, not our *flawlessness*."

The gathering crowd buzzed rancorous of Lance.

"Who is that jerk?" someone asked.

"Came in a while ago."

"Played the Rockola, just as I was enjoyin' a quiet breakfast."

"Sounds like a *Yankee*."

"More like the *devil!*"

"What's the difference?"

"Ain't got *no* respect!"

Candler drew a breath, smiled slightly and motioned the people to channel their disgust into forgiveness. Lance gawked at the gesture but knew his hometown now reviled him as the outsider he had shown himself to be. A quiet breakfast in a small town, his hometown, had become the setting for a theological firestorm. The conversation continued.

"Look, Lance, I don't have all the answers, and neither do you, nor neither *will* we. God did not mean for us to *have* all the answers. I *am* sure of this, that without faith, it is *impossible* to please Him. If we had all the answers to all the mysteries, there would be no *need* for the *very thing* that pleases Him most. God made the rules; not I. And not you.

"Faith is the common thread throughout the Scriptures. Daniel needed it in the den of lions, as did Noah in the great flood, as did Jonah in the whale. Job would have been putty in Satan's hands had he not exercised his absolute faith in God. David, a man after God's own heart—and not the *saintliest* of God's instruments, by the way—could not have slain Goliath without it.

"Faith is the manna of man's existence, the substance of things hoped for. God does not promise us a smooth flight, Lance. Only a safe landing. Faith does *not* require God to cast aside all the physical ills and hard times we confront in the natural world; instead, it ensures our favor, our *eternal* favor, not the sort of televangelists' miracle-for-your-seed favor you so rightfully loathe. What could be more reassuring?"

Lance stared at Chandler.

"Who *are* you anyway? The official spokesman for Jesus Journeys Airlines?" Lance asked, an uncharacteristic glow in his smile.

Candler chuckled. "You might say that. Can I ... book you a flight?"

"That sounds a bit like a threat, old man."

"A *threat?* Oh, no, no, no," Candler said, shaking his head smiling. "Do I look like such a man who would threaten you? It's not a threat, Lance. All I am saying is

The Ghosts of Benevolence

that God has given man free will to make his own choices. Many choices are inherently good or bad, loving or hate-filled. God does not want a hoard of mindless robots following Him. So, He allows people choices. If you choose not to accept His Son, Jesus Christ, as your savior, that's *your* choice. Simple as that. God makes choices, too. I believe that God chooses *not to know* the outcome of your choices, even when He knew of your existence long before the world was formed. He gives you life, and He wants your love and obedience without undue influence. He uses folks like me to spread His message. That's all. I don't think God ever intended the faith thing to be so difficult for man to grasp. You take Him or leave Him, believe in Him or not."

Silenced for a moment, Lance could only focus on the sparkle in the old man's eyes.

"Don't you think the threat of hell tilts a bit toward the side of ... *undue influence?*"

"Don't think of hell as a *threat*. Instead, think of *heaven* as a *gift*," replied Candler. "The choice is rather clear and simple when you get right down to it."

"You're the old man I saw on the steps of Benevolence Primitive Baptist Church yesterday, aren't you? I was talking to you one minute, and the next minute you were gone. Not a trace, not even a cloud of dust. How'd you do that? Where did you *go?* Where did you come *from?*"

Candler did not answer, and Lance did not persist. Lance pulled a crinkled five-dollar note from his pocket and tossed the tip onto the table.

"Do you mind my asking a ... personal question?"

"Not at all, Lance. Ask away."

"How did you ... lose your arm?"

"Ginning machine," Candler replied, smiling. "Took it clean off one morning, back on the farm, back when I was young. I was *too* curious about things then. I liked asking lots of questions about things I didn't understand, as would any kid, I suppose, except I didn't pay a lot of *attention to the answers* ... or the *wisdom* behind the answers. Such is youth, I suppose. Guess I need only *one* hand to carry this," he said, gripping his bible. "I've managed, but I do regret my stubbornness. Do take care, Mr. Lance Hawthorne."

"Hope your day goes well, Candler, and ... thanks for the wallet." Lance paused, patting his back pocket and feeling a twinge of pity for the one-armed man. Extending his hand in a gesture of truce, a fifty-dollar bill between its fingers, Lance said, "You're a blunt, confident old man. You've got my mama's blend of guts and respect, as well as her love for all things spiritual. I appreciate that and your willingness to consider the thoughts of another man adrift. If there *is* a god, he is alive in you. Here's a fifty. Eat hearty."

"Keep your money, Mr. Hawthorne. My breakfast companionship and conversational services are free. I've planted the seeds. Up to you to supply the water. Good day to you, sir; thanks for the breakfast. God bless and keep you." Horace Candler walked out of the restaurant, his bible under his right arm.

Lance sighed as he made his way to the cashier, paying her. He pushed open the glass doors and stepped into sunshine, shielding his eyes from its unexpected brightness. He felt the stare of a couple dozen sets of eyes piercing his back. Lance fumbled in his pockets for his keys and looked around for Candler in hopes of offering him a ride to his destination, had he such. The old man, again, was nowhere in sight.

Where did he disappear to this time? Lance wondered. *He's too darn old to move that fast!* Lance re-entered the restaurant and approached the cashier.

"Just who was that old man I was talking with? I assume he lives in Benevolence and comes in here from

The Ghosts of Benevolence

time to time. I mean, *where* does he live; where does he *go?*"

"Just who're you referring to, sir?" the cashier asked.

"Who am I refer— That old man, the one talking to me about the existence of God and salvation and such. Didn't you witness our little discussion? Everybody *else* seemed to!"

"Sir, you wanna table or what?"

"No thanks; just ate. But, surely you saw—" Lance stammered, his hands simultaneously pointing out the window and at the booth. Frustration pulsed in his veins.

"Look, mister, I don't know *who*, or *what*, you're talkin' about, but either you have a seat or you get *out* of here. Ain't got *no time* for crazies."

"But … you *waited* on us." Confused, Lance stared at the cashier. Finally, he turned and walked out.

Then it struck Lance like an epiphany. He stopped, mouth open. The old man stated, Lance recalled, that he lost his arm—his *left* arm—in a *ginning* machine accident.

So had Aunt Pearl.

Mark Randolph Watters

29

LANCE UNLOCKED AND OPENED the car's door, tossing the USA Today onto the passenger seat. He turned back toward Belle's Diner and shook his head, thinking about the strange conversation with the one-armed Horace Candler and the cashier's inexplicable ignorance of the whole animated thing. Lance himself wondered if the old man, let alone the conversation, existed only in his sleep-deprived imagination.

Shrugging, he noticed the assortment of newspaper boxes in their tilted alignment against an outside wall of Belle's Diner. The box containing copies of *The Benevolence Connoisseur*, its headline screaming, **"FEDERALLY MANDATED DISASTER TO STRIKE REGION"** caught Lance's attention.

A copy purchased, for which he grudgingly inserted six quarters, Lance leaned against the Mercedes and read aloud:

> "Government officials announced yesterday a program to divert immediately the use of all water taken from the Chagoochee Reservoir Agricultural Basin, water promised two months

ago to beleaguered area farmers for emergency irrigation of crops withering from the ongoing drought. The diversion, termed "temporary" by officials, will now channel this water to the habitats of the flatwoods salamander, an endangered species discovered recently in near-parched Sutter County wetlands.

"Officials had no additional comment on the abrupt reversal of policy, except to say the habitat had been discovered in Sutter County and neighboring JaNell County and was exclusive to these counties.

"Local farmers expressed outrage by the decision, saying that the government's priority is misplaced and that the feared worsening of an agricultural and economic disaster for the already-impoverished community is now made imminent by this decision.

"In a separate but related development, it was learned yesterday that area farmers are being encouraged to sell parched farmland to an 'interested' buyer. The buyer's identity is not known, and it is unclear whether the buyer is an individual, a partnership, or a corporation.

"Sources indicate a blanket offer of $800 per acre is on the table. Interest appears high, as some farmers have stated that the offer is better than losing their life's savings to the effects of an uncontrollable drought and the discretions of an indifferent government. One land owner cited the 'bird-in-the-hand' adage as his reasoning for selling. Others agreed and are expected to follow suit.

"Still others, however, have expressed skepticism and wonder who would want the land

The Ghosts of Benevolence

all at once, estimated to be as much as forty
thousand acres, and for what purpose."

"Wow. Because of some stinkin' *salamander?"* Lance
asked, tossing aside the newspaper. "What *else* is new?"

While maybe not new from any historical perspective,
a conspicuous lack of farming activity during this peak-
planting season did give Lance pause. He turned, scanning
full circle. No tractors mingled with cars. No clouds of
rising dust in adjacent fields or rumbles of farm machinery.
The cotton field across the street from Belle's appeared
covered with snow, thanks to the long links of irrigators
distributing sprays of water pulled from the field's
advantaged point along Pumpkin Creek.

Tally's Seed and Feed was dormant, its commerce
stilled, despite a few milling about its porch like zombies.
The drought, in its fourth year, had limited rainfall amounts
to a devastating thirty percent of annual averages. Aside
from a singular oasis of cotton, the county wilted as brown
as a winter leaf.

*Guess I better get over to Colter and deliver this
package*, thought Lance, *and then to Mr. Devereaux's.*

Colter was six crow miles west of Benevolence, but
Lance hadn't the luxury of wings. He drove the twisting
dirt roads typical of those connecting all communities in
Sutter County, adding another five miles to the trip.

Periodically scraped and widened since Lance's
boyhood, other improvements to the roads included the
removal of embedded stones that once projected like
spikes, potholes that swallowed like sink holes. Still, the
roads were packed Georgia clay, and though as resilient as
asphalt, the orange dust swirled like a Rockies blizzard.

"Some things never change," Lance observed,
depressing the button lowering his window. Dust, and a
certain aroma, sailed inside, smacking Lance right between
the nostrils.

Mark Randolph Watters

A Benevolence constant widely regarded as producing the finest barbecue east of the Pacific, This Little Piggie had dished up delectable dining since 1950. Lance often walked the five miles from home to a boxlike shack not much more spacious than his daddy's tool shed, its only sign of life a black smokestack, out of which wafted a hypnotic stream of smoke, the blends of hickory mixed with the roasting flesh of pigs and chickens.

A walk of any distance in pursuit of this slice of barbeque heaven gave a body no reason for complaints. It was the walk home *from* This Little Piggie that produced all the complaining, for such only prolonged the suffering of the hungry.

Abel Ratliff, the proprietor of This Little Piggie, procured most of his pigs from Peyton Hawthorne. Lance thought nothing of making the trek for the lure of the smell alone, but he did so mostly to collect payment for the pigs in the form of barter for barbequed meat, Brunswick stew, and Abel's incomparable sauce.

No one quite figured out how Abel concocted the delicious magic of his sauce, though many in vain tried. Abel catered countless socials in Sutter County, not the least of which was the annual homecoming for Thankfulness Baptist Church, an event he catered free of charge. Folks assumed Abel, his barbeque, and his sauce would outlast infinity, as timeless as Benevolence Betty itself. But, something happened.

The apparent victim of a stroke while plucking feathers off chickens, Abel carried his secrets to his grave in April of 1965. As he collapsed unconscious, according to the final opinion issued by the medical examiner, a butcher knife fell with him, his body and the knife seemingly falling in such precise timing as to penetrate his throat, severing the spine at the base of his skull.

Until the autopsy results were obtained, police suspected Abel had been murdered, a more plausible

The Ghosts of Benevolence

scenario given the circumstances preceding and the brutality surrounding his death. The butcher knife belonged to a set of pearl-handled knives given him by Earl Bentley Devereaux, Sr. in partial consideration of a catering job performed for Devereaux, the younger's, birthday. The remainder of the catering payment, sixteen hundred and fifty dollars, was never paid. Some folks maintained he *had* been murdered, the stroke a result of the shock of the knife wound. Lance, convinced then and unmoved in his opinion today, believed that Abel Ratliff, indeed, was another Devereaux victim, the medical examiner just another of his cronies of cover-up.

Lance stared as he drove slowly past in respectful remembrance. A few surviving planks, shreds of pink paint clinging still, leaned against the oak that once shaded Abel's barbeque shack. The tattered green-and-pink oval sign of 'This Little Piggie', rusted around its perimeter and pocked with bullet holes, rested against the planks. Lance sniffed. The aroma was that of wishful thinking, of the workings of Lance's vibrant memory. The home place was just a few miles ahead, on the east side of Sutter County.

Similar to other quiet southern towns, Benevolence was built around a town square in the middle of which stood a proud, anachronistic statue of gray marble, a European-American on horseback, bearing the colors of an era belonging now to ghosts. The town's population had ebbed and surged through the years in direct correlation to the success of its agriculture-based economy. Benevolence stood fast in the face of all that nature and man could sling its way. Like a punch-drunk fighter determined to avoid knockdowns and go the full fifteen rounds, the community took its punishment year after year, round after round, and held its ground. Despite this strength of character, or perhaps because of it, Benevolence swooned in a perpetual state of semi-consciousness.

Mark Randolph Watters

Lance recalled fondly another tire swing, its chains attached to the thickest branch of his front yard pecan tree. He thought of the dizzying heights attained with his father's determined pushing, the rush of air roaring past his ears and through his hair, the speed, the altitude. Lance pressed the accelerator softly, unaware he'd done so. The wind whipped his hair, kissed his face.

Daddy was pushing me, perhaps only in a figurative sense, but to new heights, beyond Benevolence, Lance realized from the left side of his brain, while the right side insisted, *though I'm sure he was not conscious of the symbolism.*

Lance thought about how sheltered he had been from the misfortune that had befallen the region. Never a day passed that his table lacked food. Payton and Sara did the best they could.

Yet, parents were *supposed* to do the best they could, for their children. It was the things parents were *not* supposed to do—the rampages of his father—that stayed with Lance, like carvings in marble statues.

The curse of drink had infested Peyton like lice. One particular day stood out in Lance's memory.

The Ghosts of Benevolence

30

THE JANUARY DAY HAD developed atypically harsh for a Benevolence winter, the midday temperature hovering no higher than the low thirties. Peyton stumbled through the front door, his arms around half a dozen sticks of firewood. The task, usually handled by Lance, had taken longer than normal.

Peyton's secret, the most dangerous of his volatile vices, lay hushed within his addiction to a whiskey he brewed from a still pieced together in the woods along Pumpkin Creek, opposite Devereaux's peanuts. He paid Devereaux two hundred dollars a month for the privilege of isolation and secrecy, plus a five-gallon surtax, a stash of which he concealed behind a shield of saws, pickaxes, and hoes in the woodshed.

Angry that foraging coyotes had killed two of his four milking cows the night before, Peyton exploded in fury when he dropped a two-foot hunk of hickory on his foot. Enraged, Peyton unleashed a stream of curses, some of which Lance had not heard before, words followed simultaneously by his retaliation against the nearest animate object.

Mark Randolph Watters

That object, Sara, met face-first with the wedge-shaped end of a fire log. The blow sent her crashing to the kitchen floor, blood spilling from cuts to her mouth and cheek. Lance always accepted without question his daddy's love for mama ...until *that* moment. Worse, Peyton never apologized for the incident, as far as Lance recalled.

Lance winced and fixed his eyes upon the blue air as if he were gazing through a portal to his past. The old home place was along the road to Global Technical Solutions. Another diversion wouldn't hurt.

The Ghosts of Benevolence

31

THE FARM ON WHICH Lance was raised consisted of two hundred acres, split more or less between undulating meadows, fields for plowing, and stands of pine and hardwood, the latter used in the Hawthorne ancestry for producing lumber. Peyton's motivation to continue the toils of a working farm died with Sara. He executed long-term leases on all but fifty acres the following year, which earned enough money to keep him and Lance fed and clothed. The rest of the acreage supported a small vegetable garden and a buffer space in Sweetgum Hollow. 'My piece of peace,' Peyton called it. Sadness overwhelmed it, and, before a half-year's passing, the tradition of Sunday excursions ceased. Alas, in turn, soon Sweetgum Hollow ceased, succumbing to pine saplings and sassafras trees, to kudzu and wisteria, to time and indifference.

Peyton died sometime in the mid-nineties; Lance couldn't remember the exact year or date. Lance did not attend his father's funeral. He left Lance title to the farm, as Sara had wished.

Shortly thereafter, Lance hired an agent to sell the two hundred acres to parties unknown, for the lump sum of one million, five hundred and forty thousand dollars. This windfall enabled Lance the purchase of his current home, cars, country club membership, and other amenities and investments, as well as to live the life of unearned opulence.

But, the years passed, and the well of Lance's unchecked spending dried up. He had sunk a half million cash into his million-dollar home and another quarter million into shares of Medico and American Century. The subsequent accounting scandal at Medico and the bankruptcy of American, followed by their collapse, wiped out the bulk of Lance's capital investments, soaking up most of his liquidity. He carried a thirty-year, half-million-dollar, 6.5% fixed-rate mortgage. Though the floor for rates had collapsed since, he found refis as off-putting as office parties.

His position with Standard Paper Industries of Georgia, well-paying considering he did not occupy a rung within the corporate pecking order, until perhaps now, lacked the compensation necessary to sustain his furnace of consumption.

Lance wanted more. Lance needed more. The boxes of invoices and shipping documents handed him by Heather, as well as the simmering photograph of the long-ago Devereaux church-bombing, represented luxury-car tickets on the gravy train. The beauty of good timing had brought Lance to Benevolence to redeem those tickets.

The dirt road wound through the woods like a slithering snake. Lance left a wake of red dust that colored roadside foliage and left his Mercedes begging for excavation.

An occasional opening through the elms and oaks revealed open expanses of farmland dotted with rolls of hay. Little but the date and, in some cases, the sophistication of the farm equipment, had changed since childhood. Crumbled sharecropper shacks, reminders of a

The Ghosts of Benevolence

world not too far removed, were a bit less visible now, shrouded with blankets of poison ivy and kudzu.

Turkey buzzards, awaiting their next carrion, perched atop the stems of bleached, dead cypress trees. The occasion of abandoned homesteads gave clues of their former existence by the remnants of stacked-stone chimneys, clusters of oak shade trees, and the skeletal remains of tractors and wagons scattered like the dead of battle.

Dust devils, whirlwind mixtures of soil and leaves, frolicked directionless, as if they were the ghosts of children playing around picnic tables at family reunions. Rusted Coca-Cola signs, holed with bullets and dented by BBs, hung by single nails to porch posts. Haunting images, filtered by years of rationalizations, swirled through Lance's mind as he visited a past as much a part of his present as the steering wheel he clutched.

Ahead, Lance spotted the towering top of the landmark cedar tree that bordered the earth-bare pathway cut from the road ditch to the front porch of his childhood home.

"There it is," he whispered, as his throat tightened.

The view toward his home left much to his imagination. Little tangible evidence remained of anyone having lived here. The front yard, a yard no more, had surrendered to wilderness. Lance discerned shallow ruts in the driveway, possibly made by logging trucks and cars of the curious. Day lilies and daffodils planted by Sara mixed amid honeysuckle and blackberries.

Lance parked the car on the vestige of the driveway, crushing stands of wilted Queen Anne's lace and discarded beer cans. Old habits took over as Lance picked at callused skin on his hands. He stared at the intermingled growth of honeysuckle and blackberry, out of which loomed mimosa trees that now occupied the area inside the perimeter of the house's foundation. A lulling hum whisked from place to place as bees plundered the few remaining pollen-rich blossoms.

Lance approached the site and strained for perspective. He could see through the thick vegetation the mossy stone steps of the front porch. Ah, the steps. The steps gave Lance a point of reference in an otherwise nondescript setting. How Lance had leaped these stony obstacles, running from one chore to the next, from house to outhouse, from memory to memory and back again!

Snippets poured over Lance like rain. The tree house in the cedar tree; hours spent in the fields removing weeds and gathering the yield; the rattlesnake bite; the mysterious cemetery in the woods behind the house; the swimming hole at the gully; pick-up baseball games; broom-sweeping the yards; the pleasures of canned vegetables in the dead of winter; visits to the outhouse, always wary of the lurk of black widows and scorpions; heating bath water over the kitchen woodstove; fireside chats; Guy Lombardo and radio serials; each an enduring memory from an era itself now overrun by a contemporary wilderness of progress and melancholy.

Lance noticed signs tacked to trees. They read, "No Trespassing, By Order of Earl Bentley Devereaux, III. Violators Will Be Dealt With."

"Dealt with? So *Devereaux* owns this land now," Lance said. "Knowing him, he probably has cameras mounted in the trees." Lance gave cursory glances to the tops of trees and wondered how close to the truth he had stumbled.

As Lance started back to his car, he stopped to ponder the view down the dirt road. Cicadas chirped their dispassionate chorus. Lance felt the urge to find a bucket and head for the butterbean patch. Distant thunderheads, clouds darkened to near black by the contrast of sunlight, sent muted rumbles.

The Ghosts of Benevolence

"Well, I'll be!" Lance said. "It's raining on *somebody*. Maybe here soon."

He took a few steps toward the car. He turned facing the distant clouds webbed with tentacles of cloud-to-cloud lightning and whispered, "Lilies could *use* a few drops."

Another few steps.

"If there *is* a heaven," he said, looking skyward, "mama's there."

Mark Randolph Watters

32

LANCE STARED. THE BUILDING occupied by Global Technical Solutions looked inversely proportionate to the enormity of its billings to SPIG. He expected a vast manufacturing facility, much as one might expect to see from an automaker. Global, instead, seemed embarrassingly meek, a David shadowed in a world of Goliaths.

Package in hand, Lance pulled open the double-glass door and approached the receptionist's desk, unoccupied. He adjusted his tie and glanced at the package's addressee, a Mr. Billy Ruben.

The store's interior struck Lance as remarkably uncluttered and ordered, like an exhibition booth at a trade show. The walls displayed a few motivational posters flanked by ten-point deer heads and award-winning fish catches. Lance could not help but notice the conspicuous absence of customers, given the world's frenzy with all things digital. No, GTS wasn't located in the sprawl of an Atlanta suburb, but still. Aware of the volume of business SPIG alone conducted with Global, surely other, larger industrial customers existed. None was apparent.

Shelves of monitors, keyboards, CPUs and accessories, along with scanners, printers, storage media, video games, and application software collected dust in rows of undisturbed display.

"Can I help you, sir?" a man asked, swishing aside strands of plastic colored beads hung to serve as a curtain separating the lighted front from the darkness of the unknown.

"Yes. Hello," Lance replied, surprised by the sudden interruption. He extended his hand, which the man ignored. "I'm looking for Mr. Ruben ... Billy Ruben. I'm from Standard Paper Industries of Georgia, and I have a package, *this* package, for him."

Lance noticed the name label sewn in white cursive on the left pocket of the man's gray shirt. Ruben.

"You can give that to me. I'll see that he gets it," replied the man, anxious to complete the transaction. "Now, if you'll excuse me. Have a nice day."

As the man turned away, Lance asked, "A receipt?"

"What?" the man replied, peering over his left shoulder.

"A *receipt*. You know ... for the *package*? May I get a receipt for proof of its delivery? My boss will want it."

The man paused, unsure how to handle this unexpected request.

"A receipt. Yeah," the man said, patting his pockets for a pen. "Sure, a receipt. Let me just write up one for you here." The man pulled a pencil wedged between his right ear and coarse black hair and scribbled out basic information on a scrap of cardboard. He handed it to Lance.

"Now if you'll excuse me."

Lance studied the crudely scripted receipt.

"Needs to be dated and signed, sir," Lance noted.

Agitated by Lance's persistence, the man mumbled something and jerked the receipt from Lance's fingers. As

The Ghosts of Benevolence

if expecting someone, the man glanced repeatedly at the glass doors. He jotted a date and signed the scrap in an illegible whorl of curves and loops. He handed it back to Lance.

"What's this name?" Lance asked. "And it's twenty *sixteen*."

"What? Twenty—"

"Don't worry about it," Lance interrupted, "this'll do. I'll correct it later. Have a good day … Mr. Ruben."

Lance gave the man a wink and turned to leave. Ruben fingered the name label on his shirt.

"Wait!" the man shouted. "I have something for you to take to King."

Ruben bent over behind the counter top and lifted a brown cardboard box, about two feet cubed, heavily taped along each seam. Lance took the box, nearly losing his grip from its unexpected weight.

"Thanks; almost forgot this. What's in it?" Lance inquired. "Kind of heavy."

"What do you think's in it? Computer equipment, that sort of thing. Just make … just you make *sure* King *gets* this, understand?" stressed Ruben, anxiety lacing his words as he again glanced beyond Lance's left shoulder toward the door. "Uh … take *your* package, too. Won't be needing it after all."

Two men walked in, their hands buried inside the pockets of their black leather jackets. Red toboggans covered their heads to mid-ear. Neither removed his sunglasses.

Ruben leaned closer to Lance, his eyes still upon the two men, and whispered, "Leave through the beads behind me. Go right. There's an exit door at the end of the corridor. You must *hurry*."

"What are you talk—?"

"No questions! Just *do* it! *Now!*"

Mark Randolph Watters

Lance noticed Ruben's distracted glances as he spoke the instructions. Turning to satisfy his curiosity, Lance saw both men approaching slowly. The taller man had a Confederate battleflag tattoo on the left side base of his neck. The other man's hair was tied into a ponytail, its frizz bobbing like a hitchhiking porcupine. Judging from Ruben's reaction to the pair, unlikely were they here to purchase the newest iterations of iPhones or MacBook's.

The Ghosts of Benevolence

33

LANCE TOOK THE BOX from Ruben, the other package stacked atop, and disappeared like a carnival magician behind the curtain of beads, curving his way down the corridor. He raced for the exit, forcing his way through and around the clutter of empty brown boxes blocking his path. As Lance reached for the door's handle, he heard a sound, like someone beating a dusty rug—***thuk, thuk, thuk, thuk***—coming from Ruben's side of the curtain of beads.

Lance listened, unaware his curiosity was stepping him back toward the curtain.

"Where's the package?" one of the men demanded of Ruben. Silence followed, interrupted by broken breaths.

"Dude, you *gave* it to that man, didn't you?" The man shook Ruben by the shirt collar. "We'll get it back, Ruben, make no mistake. By the way, your skimming days are *done*." The man pointed his pistol toward the curtain and to his partner ordered, "Check it out. *There!*"

Hearing this, Lance turned and scrambled over boxes, tripping and falling to the concrete floor, dropping his own. He heard the man kicking aside boxes on his approach. Lance shoved open the exit door. Out of the building, he pushed the door closed and hurried under the cover of a debris field of crushed boxes and discarded, broken furniture.

What in the name of God is happening? thought Lance.

The man reached the door's handle and, just as he lifted his foot to kick open the door, he stopped. Mindful not to arouse the attention of passersby, the man opened the door slowly. He looked left, then right, then left again, as one might before crossing the street. Buildings, streets, sidewalks, trees slumbered like piles of autumn leaves. Nobody seemed aware of the mayhem unfolding.

Lance huddled still as stone under his pile, taking in as little air as possible. He waited. The scene struck Lance like déjà vu, like a church-bombing. Boxes seemed to vibrate with the pounding of his heart.

"See 'im?"

"Nah. Looks like the SOB got away!" replied the tattooed man, kicking a trash can end over end, landing it next to the stack of crushed boxes under which Lance hid. Lance's stomach turned inside out.

The frizzed man kicked aside stray boxes. "Maybe he's hidin' under all this trash. Think I'll fire a few rounds into 'em."

"Out here, in the broad open? *Think*, man! Did I finish off Ruben?"

"Crap, yeah! You shot him *four* times. If he ain't dead yet, he'll bleed out soon enough."

"Well, go check! And lock the freakin' front doors! We got to get *out* of here!" shouted the tattooed man.

Ruben lay sprawled on the blood-pooled floor, four bullet holes in his body, two of which penetrated either side of his navel, another through his right shoulder, and the fourth into his chest above the sternum. A stream of blood meandered out of a corner of his mouth. Clinging to life, each of Ruben's labored breaths gurgled.

The Ghosts of Benevolence

"Well, well, well," said the frizzed man, tapping the barrel of his handgun on the side of his head. "I thought I aerated you pretty good, but I see I underestimated your sheer drive to live. Want to know what I'm guessin'? I'm guessin' you ain't got the blood left to make it through this next bullet," whispered the man into Ruben's ear as he pulled back the hammer of the nine millimeter. "But, then, why hurry? I think I'll let your life pass before your eyes a few minutes more, time enough for you to give your mistakes some thought. On second thought, you don't deserve those few minutes, and well, turns out I *am* in a bit of a hurry. Skimming the earnings was a *no-no*, Rubie; *big* mistake! You ought to have *known* better. I think you did know better, but you got greedy. Devereaux paid you *well*, and *still*, you got greedy. Tell me who you gave the box to. The *money* too, and well, I just might spare you this last bullet."

Ruben's eyes narrowed with his furrowed brows, his final measure of defiance.

"Well, it don't matter. We'll find him. I have to tell you, Rubie ... you're just another *dog* I got to put to sleep."

The man raised the pistol and parted Ruben's lips with the silencer.

"Give it some tongue, Rubie. Last kiss you'll ever give."

Ruben curled his fingers into fists, accepting his fate, and stared his killer in the eyes.

"Bye, bye, Mr. Billy Ruben."

Thuk.

Ruben's skull and brain exploded, splattering pieces of each against the floor, wall, and the shooter's face. He reeled from the shot's effects.

"Let's get the hell out of here!" shouted the frizzed man. Good thing business here's as dead as Ruben."

"Yeah. We'd have to kill *them*, too.

"You find any cash in Ruben's office? We got to make this thing worth our while, now that that other fellow done made off with the packages."

The tattooed man pulled a wallet from Ruben's back pocket. "I found some in the office, all right. And I found *this*, too. *Whooee!* Won't you just *looky* here!"

The frizzed man dropped his nine and reached for the wallet. "My *God!*" he said, thumbing through the cash. "There must *ten thousand dollars* in this wallet, maybe more! Think we ought to take the money to Devereaux, since we don't have the package?"

"Are you out of your meth-fried *mind*, boy? Must be a *couple hundred thousand* skimmed dollars in his office safe. I say we take that cash and leave Devereaux in our dust. Anybody comin' this way?"

Lance figured covered ground was safe ground and had re-entered Global through the opened exit door. He hid behind stacked boxes in a darkened space near the beaded curtain, within earshot of the men's conversation. "So this is Devereaux's doing."

"Ain't nobody comin'," said the frizzed one, peeking out the front door glass. "I'll just flip this 'Closed' sign and lock up."

"Good. Let's go out the back."

Hearing those words, Lance scrunched down, perfectly concealed, and waited for the men to pass. He rested one arm on the box given him by Ruben and cuddled the package in his other arm. The men hurried past, spitting expletives, kicking and throwing boxes helter-skelter in their haste. Lance heard the click of the closing exit door but sat motionless for several minutes.

Alone, Lance felt the tension of quietness grip him. His mind spun like a top as he struggled to take hold of a thought.

Somehow Barrett, Global, and Devereaux are linked. Dev's men just killed a man, a man with hundreds of

The Ghosts of Benevolence

thousands of dollars, and I'm thinking those dollars came courtesy of Barrett King. But for what? Computer equipment?

Lance looked at his box and package. *Can't open these here, but I've got to know what Barrett had me deliver to Ruben. And what's coming back to him.*

Standing, Lance stacked the package on top of the box and carried both to the exit door.

12:56, Lance noticed.

He pushed open the door in a manner he hoped attracted as little attention as possible, giving peripheral glances to his left and right, keeping his head faced forward. Lance whistled 'Elmer's Tune' and walked deliberately, as if he had purchased, and was carrying, his overdue desktop.

Finally, he thought, grinning at the levity. *My new computer!*

He placed the package and box on the backseat of his Mercedes and got inside. Issuing a sigh, he grabbed the SPIG package and stared at it. Then, he had an epiphany.

As far as Barrett knows, Lance thought, *the package has been delivered.* Lance had a signed receipt, albeit from a dead man, as proof.

I can't be held responsible for the package's disposition once delivered. That I now possess the package is beyond my control and King's knowledge. Perfect.

Convinced by his own rationale, Lance ripped the package open. Out spilled banded stacks of Federal Reserve notes, hundreds and fifties. Lance's sighs turned into gasps.

Mark Randolph Watters

34

REFLEXIVELY, HE REACHED TO gather up the scattered bounty, as if he were hastening to clean his room before Sara walked in and discovered the clutter of pornography spread about.

He wondered which of the silent streetside vehicles might contain the killers waiting to follow him, or worse, kill him on the spot. Ruben's involvement, his murder, had now become Lance's burden.

"Did they *see* me? Would they *recognize* me?" Lance asked. These questions plagued him as he tried to reconstruct the minutes just after the men entered Global.

He remembered turning away from Ruben to give the men a brief look.

"Sunglasses! *Damn!* Maybe they got a look; maybe they didn't."

Lance turned and fixed his eyes upon the box resting on the backseat. It beckoned as innocently as an unwrapped gift. A crude label addressed to Barrett adorned its top, taped securely, but no return address.

Lance pulled out of Global's parking lot and maintained a steady thirty-five miles per hour down Cotton

Street, a speed his vibrating right foot maintained with shock-inspired precision.

"Barrett's in this neck-deep. But *why?* Where'd all this cash come from, and the cash in Ruben's office?"

Lance's mind danced from question to begging question, groping for the answers he feared would be revealed to him all too soon.

"Need to play it cool for now, get more info from Barrett. Time to give him a call, let him know the package ... has been delivered."

Then he remembered, as if in afterthought, his appointment with Earl Bentley Devereaux, the Third. He retrieved his cell phone from the console and punched '2' for King's office number, swerving to avoid head-ons with a couple of horn-blowing vehicles. Lance winced, expecting bursts of gunfire from any of those vehicles. He noted the time.

1:16 p.m.

"I bet he's still at lunch, or flirting with the secretaries," Lance noted, truth on his side. "Answer the phone!" Lance rapped the phone against the dashboard as if to alert an inattentive King. Barrett answered.

"King here!"

"Barrett! Hawthorne. Just calling to give you an update. I've delivered the package to Ruben and am on my way to Devereaux's. Anything more I need to know at this point?"

"Delivered? Good. Devereaux's expecting you. Might want to give him a heads-up anyway, that you're in the neighborhood."

"Ruben gave me a box, addressed to you, filled with who knows what. Pretty heavy, too. At least thirty pounds. Should I be concerned?"

"Never mind that. Just bring it back to me. I'll get it to the IT guys. It's probably those ... *memory chips* I asked Ruben for. You need to forget about this and focus on Devereaux."

Memory chips? thought Lance. *There must be a million memory chips in that box. That, or they're packed with lead peanuts.*

Lance wasn't buying Barrett's answer, but he kept his doubts silent.

"Will do. Call you later."

"Text me, man. Ain't got the time to chit-chat."

"Who's chit-chatting? Just updating you. Later, then."

"One more thing, Lance. SPIG's got a considerable investment in that box, those chips. You might want to put the box in the trunk, you know, away from sunlight, heat, such as that."

And curious eyes, such as that, thought Lance.

"Got your pitch ready for Devereaux? You've had three hundred miles and an overnight to get it right. Your promotion's on the line, remember."

"As if I could *forget*! Barrett, this is sure sounding a lot like chit-chat."

"You're right. *Go!* Do well. Call me."

"No texting?"

"Wise guy. Call me, text me, shout it from the mountain tops; just let me know what happens."

Lance said nothing more and pushed the button ending the call.

"Got to find me an RC and a moon pie. Heck, what I need is a shot of daddy's homebrew! *Memory* chips?"

Lance pushed '3' on his cell phone.

"This is Heather."

"Hi, Heather. Lance here. Thought you might be taking an extended lunch break, what with the cat away." Lance chuckled, hoping to avert offense.

"Lance! How's it going? How do you know I'm *not* still lunching, hmm? Got your promotion yet?"

"Maybe."

Mark Randolph Watters

"When you're all high-and-mighty, don't forget who held your hand all these years, buddy boy."

"I'm sure you won't let me forget. Meanwhile, I need your help, Heather."

"Anything. What's up?"

"When did we last purchase memory chips, from whom, and how many did we buy?"

"Hold on a sec ..."

"I'll wait. Got any elevator music you can regale me with?"

"I can hum you something; make a request."

"Elmer's Tune."

"Whose tune? You mean Elmer's glue, right? Okay, here it is. We bought some memory *modules*; you know, printed circuit boards and such, along with some SOJs."

"What the heck are ... what'd you call 'em ... SOJs?"

"Ah, the burdens of the unlearned," Heather said with a sarcastic sigh, "and those who must *teach* the unlearned."

"Heather, I'm not blessed with a techie's intellect."

"I'll say! Just kidding you, Lance! SOJs are Small Outline J-lead chips. Clear now?"

"As Mississippi mud!"

"They're just memory chips that connect to the circuit board. Their mounting pins are shaped like Js. Anyway, we purchased a couple of boxes containing twenty-four each. Received 'em a few days ago, from Circuitry Inc."

"Nothing from Global?"

"Not that I can see."

"How much do those SOJ things weigh, individually, that is?"

"If you dropped an SOJ and a feather at the same time, the *feather'd* hit the ground first. They weigh *nothing,* maybe as much as a dime."

"So, is there any way we'd need *thirty pounds* of SOJ chips?"

"Thirty pounds?"

The Ghosts of Benevolence

"Thirty pounds, give or take."

"Not unless we're buying 'em wholesale and are stocking up for the next twenty years!"

"Thanks, Heather. This is very helpful."

"It is? We'll ... glad to help, mister VP. When'll you be back in the office, so I'll know when to stop lunching?"

"Love your sense of humor, Heather. Let's hope I *make* it back. Talk to you later. I hear a moon pie calling me."

"You're *weird*. Have fun."

A short distance ahead, Lance spotted a PikThis sign, its blue circle screaming like a beer vendor at a baseball game. He turned the Mercedes onto the store's lot and slowed to maneuver the car around gas pumps and one Dodge Ram pickup, black, with customized off-road tires, tinted windows, and red and yellow flames painted along its mud-splattered sides. A Confederate battle flag covered the rear glass.

Lance remembered this truck. It belonged to the couple he saw arguing in the restaurant earlier that morning. He exited the car, keeping a peripheral view of the truck but avoiding anything that might be construed as direct eye contact with its occupants.

Inside the store, Lance made a beeline for the soft drink coolers. He opened the door to grab the Royal Crown and felt a tap on his shoulder.

Mark Randolph Watters

35

"LANCE? LANCE *HAWTHORNE?*" asked the female voice.

Lance turned. He opened his mouth to answer but managed only an unintelligible stutter. The beauty of the woman paralyzed Lance into brief silence.

"*Gwen* ... Gwen Summers?" Lance whispered.

"Mmm Hmm. How you been, sugar?" she asked, a showcase of unblemished white teeth smiling at Lance. "Ain't seen you in thirty, thirty-five years."

"Thirty-six. I mean, yes ... thirty-something, at least. So, how are *you*, Gwen?" The open cooler's door covered over with condensation.

"Makin' it," Gwen replied, shrugging her shoulders. "So ... can't a gal get a hug from an old friend?"

"Oh, yeah! Sure, but ... but what about—?" Lance asked, nudging his head in the direction of the truck.

"Oh, *him?* Don't worry about him; he's—"

"Don't *worry* about him?" Lance asked, his voice rising in disbelief. "The man's a *mountain*, Gwen, an *Everest!* He'd rip my head off and hang it from his rearview mirror, *just for fun!*"

"A *hug*, Lance," pressed Gwen. "It's just a *hug*, not *sex* ... not yet."

Lance blushed. He put the RC back inside the cooler and turned to give Gwen half of a hug, out of a sense of social courtesy, he told himself.

Gwen moved her arms slowly upward around Lance's back until they encircled his neck, her hands probing his hair. Hers was no half-hug. She smelled fresh, like a patch of lilacs, and her hair glided over Lance's face like satin.

"You look *good*, Lance," Gwen whispered, seduction falling from her lips. Gwen squeezed tighter. "Still got that night at Sweetgum Hollow on my mind, like it was yesterday." Lance's sense of social courtesy turned abruptly to lust, the same infatuation he felt for her all those years ago, particularly that night at Sweetgum Hollow.

"You, too, Gwen. Really good. I mean, the years have treated you quite well—"

"Quite ... *well*, Lance?" Gwen asked, stepping back, hands on her hips, head tilted. "If we were in a bar, that'd be the lamest pickup line in the history of male piggery, except for maybe 'come here often?'"

Lance cleared his throat and grinned. "What about Mister Everest out there?"

"Like I said, sugar, don't worry. He can't see us anyway. Besides, he thinks I've gone to take a piss. Are you ... are you *married*, Lance?"

Lance limply lifted his left hand to reveal the gold wedding band. He shrugged.

"Figures. All the *good* ones are taken. Wife with you?"

"No, I'm alone, on business," Lance said, stumbling over the head-on collision between his raw attraction to Gwen and his vows as a husband and father. "She's home with the kid."

"How long are you *here*, Lance?" Gwen chirped with the melody of a songbird as she stroked Lance's back.

The Ghosts of Benevolence

"Couple of ... days, maybe one. But ... but I'm meeting a *very important* client today, and ... and the work's liable to go *nonstop* ... for the duration, you know, and—"

"*All* clients are important, Lance," Gwen interrupted. She reached into her pocket and pulled out a pen and a piece of wadded paper. "Tell you what," she said, scribbling. "Here's where I'm staying. Bama ... Mister Everest ... doesn't *live* here and won't be around tonight, if you know what I mean. Call me, Lance? We have some ... catching up to do, don't you think?"

Gwen winked and flashed that same sumptuous smile that launched a thousand silent sins. She turned and headed for the door. Peering over her shoulder, thumb at her ear and pinkie finger at her lips, she mouthed, "Call me."

Mark Randolph Watters

36

LANCE DEVOURED THE MOON pie and wanted another, but the cola did nothing to satisfy his thirst. He took the last cold swallow, which served no other purpose than to push the crumbs of moon pie to his belly. His mind ricocheted from the events of the day and those to come, not to mention his possession of the tainted fortune. His trip down Benevolence's Memory Lane had drained him dry as dust. The RC chilled his throat, but some thirsts defied quenching, no matter what. He tossed the pie wrapper onto the sloppily piled packets of cash.

Resisting the urge to expend valuable time counting it, Lance took his suit bag from the trunk and stuffed the cash inside.

Another tempter, the one tapping him on his shoulder, tugged at Lance's resistance. "Okay, buddy boy," it said, "you got your cash and lots of it. What say you keep this vehicle heading south, into Florida; catch a plane to Bermuda, and *budda-bing, budda-bang*, your life is *yours* again!"

He resisted that urge, too, for now. Lance popped the trunk and placed the suit bag inside.

Devereaux's residence was a few miles ahead. Driving, Lance decided to rehearse his skills for improvised salesmanship.

"Mr. Devereaux," Lance said to his rearview mirror, "I am Lance Hawthorne, Vice President of Finance and Corporate Analysis for Standard Paper Industries of Georgia, Northwest Georgia Division. My card. (*Oops. Ain't got a new card yet.*) Barrett King sends his compliments. I believe you know Mr. King?

"As you are aware, SPIG has expressed interest in acquiring some twenty-five thousand acres of your timber-rich land holdings. I've come prepared to tender our offer, if you'll allow me. I believe you'll find it most satisfactory."

Lance sighed.

"Oh, *brother*. It'll be *okay,* Lance. *Relax.* What the—"

"YOU ARE ENTERING THE KINGDOM of EBD3! PROCEED WITH CAUTION"

The digital billboard bellowed its message in alternating flashes of red and blue as Lance drove down U.S. Highway twenty-seven towards the residence of Earl Bentley Devereaux, the Third.

Images of peaches, pecans, cotton, magnolia blossoms, corn stalks, and other such southern icons one might find stenciled along the perimeter of a kitchen wall, flashed along the message's border, as if the place were a theme park.

The Kingdom? Lance thought. *He really admires himself. And I suppose he has the money to do so.*

A mile down the road Lance came upon another billboard flashing the same words, this with unsettling graphics. The image of a grinning gray-white skull inside an inverted red triangle, the skull's forehead emblazoned with a flaming dragon, moved from left to right, shimmering on a background of black. Two swords

The Ghosts of Benevolence

hovered point down over the triangle. The word 'DAMOCLES', spelled out in the font of old-English, one white capital letter at a time, shimmered against the contrast of black.

Lance imagined the power Devereaux possessed over his kingdom. Either side of the highway, row upon row of pecan trees, straight as headstones, stretched to the horizon. Workers scurried, some mowing grass around the trees, others leaf-blowing, and still others using pecan pickers to collect fallen nuts. Pick-up trucks contained scores of baskets of pecans. Lance observed the red triangle-skull-sword signs posted on every tree and fence, even on the doors of trucks, reminders of the "Kingdom".

Another billboard, larger than the first, loomed ahead, inescapable, like Mount Rushmore.

Lance stopped the car dead still and lipped the words as they scrolled right to left.

"To sit back hoping that someday, some way, someone will make things right for you, is to go on feeding the dragon, hoping that he will consume you last—but consume you he will."

Lance read the sentence thrice, each time stressing a different clause, a different word, each reading adding layers of clarity to an essence of the Devereaux he had long known.

Mark Randolph Watters

The Ghosts of Benevolence

37

DESPITE PECAN ORCHARDS AND an occasional hill pushing against the horizon, the land was flat enough to see several miles in any direction. In the distance to the right, perhaps a half mile off the highway, appeared a structure rising from a low ridge like a range of white volcanoes. Along the highway, cameras mounted atop metal poles every hundred yards followed Lance's approach.

Giant azaleas, beds of pansies, clusters of hydrangeas, and sculpted boxwoods flanked the last mile of highway approaching the entrance to the mansion grounds. An expanse a hundred feet deep, with three rows of thirty-foot-tall magnolias, bordered behind and parallel to the flowers and shrubs, giving an ominous backdrop to the stereotype of pure Southern Aristocracy. Like a tourist, Lance slowed the car to a crawl, taking in the grandeur of the spectacular landscape.

Black-painted cast iron bars, rising to a height of twenty feet and topped by gray foot-long iron Romanesque spearheads, gated the mouth of the estate's driveway. The double gate hinged on either side to thirty-foot stucco-and-brick pillars positioned at inward angles of forty-five degrees. The pillars sported mottled marble sculptures of the skull and swords, each angling downward and appearing to cast its omniscient gaze upon those entering Devereaux's realm.

Atop each pillar, dragons of marble squatted and faced each other, mouths open and wings spread. Each dragon grasped in its talons a polished bronze shield. The letter **D** dominated the center of the each shield.

Several life-sized crocodiles, carved from jade, perched on blocks of pink granite, sat scattered about in no obvious array of order, guarding the plush grounds. The phrase, ***"Power — the Ultimate Aphrodisiac"***, chiseled into each block, gave Lance pause and a smile.

Twin ribbons of cobblestone, each wide enough to accommodate a vehicle's tires, formed the driveway. Kentucky fescue, uniformly hunter-green, grew between and on either side of the cobblestone strips. The grass was mown to a level an inch higher than the cobblestones, giving the driveway a slight sunken appearance. Sprinklers delivered sweeping arcs of spray, casting rainbows.

Overhead, like perched vultures, more cameras kept their quiet vigil. Lance noticed the domed cameras and their piercing stares. Clearing his throat, he pushed the button closing his sunroof, as if such would conceal his presence. He wondered with uneasy laughter what the consequences might be should his wheels stray off the cobblestones or if he stopped to pick a wildflower.

The length of the bending drive was interrupted at intervals of thirty feet by the sprawl of two-hundred-year-old live oaks. Patterns of azaleas, tulips, and marigolds connected the ground between the oaks. The trees' limbs mingled and gnarled overhead forming a canopy of shade, a Southern rainforest, until it became impossible to determine which side of the driveway the limbs originated. The venerable branches, thick with the nurturing of time, curved and bent at excruciating angles. Spanish moss, kinky and

The Ghosts of Benevolence

gray, twisted from branches and swayed in the gentle breeze like remnants of spiders' webs.

The cobblestone ribbons hooked left ahead. Lance anticipated the sight about to greet him around the bend. As he completed the wide curve, the view unfolded, like heaven itself. Before Lance's gaping eyes emerged the very manifestation of Southern mythology, as if being pulled deliberately onto stage from the depths of the wing.

White paint shimmered on walls and columns, bright as a pasture of snow under a midday sun. Lance's lips parted with awe, and his lungs lost a breath or two. A deception of welcome spilled from the rows of green magnolia towers hugging the flanks of the structure.

Behind the mansion, farming machinery hummed and maneuvered in the fields. Lance offered a smile upon the realization of Old South architecture sharing the same scene with the modernity of twenty-first century farming.

The three-story Greek revival hulked inside a perimeter of twenty-eight fluted Corinthian columns, each crowned with ivory carvings of scrolls and leaves, which curled downward in their reveal, like the strata of the ancients. The columns bulged in their middles, these living, heaving behemoths, giving Lance the impression the pillars held up the weight of the world, Devereaux's world.

A sweeping double flight of marble steps flowed obliquely to either side of the portico, then swooned outward to greet visitors. Lance visualized Samuel Clemons sitting in one of several oversized maple rockers that lined the length of the porch, puffing a cigar, his legs crossed as he busily penned rewrites to The Adventures of Tom Sawyer, the monotone of a distant paddleboat whistle announcing its arrival and the ripple of river waves lapping the banks.

Mourning doves cooed. Tall fescue, cut in a crisscross pattern, producing alternating shades of green, surrounded the mansion. Beyond the house and lawn, the expanse

opened like a panorama, fields of peanuts, cotton, and corn
extending to the horizon. Earl Bentley Devereaux, the
Third occupied a plantation oasis glowing like a mirage in
the economic desert of a parched South Georgia.

Lance pulled the handle of his car door and moved
each leg slowly out, eyes never straying from the view. He
made his way up the gardenia-lined, bricked walkway to
the foot of the porch steps. The aroma of gardenias tickled
his nostrils with the sweet smells of his past, of treasures
tucked away like roses pressed in the pages of a long-
forgotten text.

The mid-afternoon sun's lengthening shadows
suggested evening's approach. Lance listened to the distant
drone of tractors. The hypnotic calls of bobwhites and
crickets, sounds usually reserved for the transition of
afternoon to evening, coursed through the branches, giving
Lance an ever-heightening sense of home.

The wet air and high sun produced perspiration that
saturated Lance's shirt, but he hardly noticed. Cicada
exoskeletons, shells of the departed desperate to live again,
clung to trees. Squirrels scampered from limb to limb
chasing each other, thinking nothing of mansions or
memories.

"So *this* was the old Wyndham place," Lance
remembered. "Devereaux's got *style*; I'll give him that.
Wonder how many cameras he has trained on me *right
now*. Probably should have put the box in the trunk before
I got here." Lance paused, giving the matter more thought.
"It'll be fine."

Lance took a long breath at the thought of facing a
murderer, the very man who had brazenly taken the lives of
innocent men, women, and children and had managed
somehow all these years to avoid justice. Lance vowed to
change that, even if justice took on the stench of greed.

He stepped toward the front door, across the hardwood
porch, taking all his care not to deposit dew-covered blades

The Ghosts of Benevolence

of grass, all the futility of walking clean on washed dishes. Seeing damp grass stuck to the bottoms of his shoes, some of which peeled off and onto the polished planks of oak, he reached into his jacket-pocket and retrieved a white handkerchief. He knelt and wiped the soles of his shoes clean and squeezed clumps of grass from the planks into the cloth.

Watching a pair of doves waddle across the lawn, Lance reached for the gargoyle-faced brass knocker. Startled by its grotesqueness, he flinched with the pullback of his hand.

"Mister Lance Hawthorne!" grizzled Devereaux, his drawl spilling from overhead.

Looking up, Lance could see only the balustrade of the balcony.

"Give me a minute, please," Devereaux begged, his words dripping with the grease and grandeur of a South Georgia dialect. "I'll be right there!"

Lance managed a half smile and a quick shake of his head. He felt transported into the middle of a scene from Tara and expected at any moment to witness a Southern horseman galloping through the magnolias, announcing the call to arms. Lance had long ago abandoned the dialect, as he had Benevolence, fearing both would handicap his career. Neither had handicapped Devereaux's.

The doors, tall and heavy with the thickness of three-inch mahogany, opened slowly, producing a rising creak, as if they harbored remnants of all the souls who had passed through these premises over the past two hundred and fifty years.

"Mister Hawthorne, sir! So delighted to see you. I'm Earl Bentley Devereaux, the Third. Won't you come in, please?"

Lance extended his hand still holding the grass-covered handkerchief. Realizing his faux pas, he smiled and gasped, withdrawing the palm and handkerchief to his pants pocket.

"Excuse me, sir! Nice to … a *pleasure* to meet you, sir … uh … Mr. Devereaux. Indeed, a pleasure. I hope you are doing well."

"Finer'n cricket fuzz!" Devereaux said, pressing his palm of leathery flesh with Lance's, his furrowed eyes measuring his guest's social clumsiness. The skin of Devereaux's hands crinkled like a well-worn roadmap, his squeeze pushing outward the branches of veins. Fingernails, yellowed and cracked with the residue of a lifetime of cigarettes, capped three fingers and a thumb, the middle finger a nub.

Finer'n cricket fuzz? Where have I heard that before? thought Lance.

Devereaux caught Lance's eyes fixed upon the space once occupied by the middle finger. "Guess you might say I gave the finger … one too many times, hmmm?"

Lance smiled, embarrassed that Devereaux had discerned his gaze. As they shook hands, Lance felt the strength in the old man's grip, as if Devereaux discerned something else as well.

"Step into my parlor," said Devereaux, eyeing the briefcase held in Lance's left hand.

The Ghosts of Benevolence

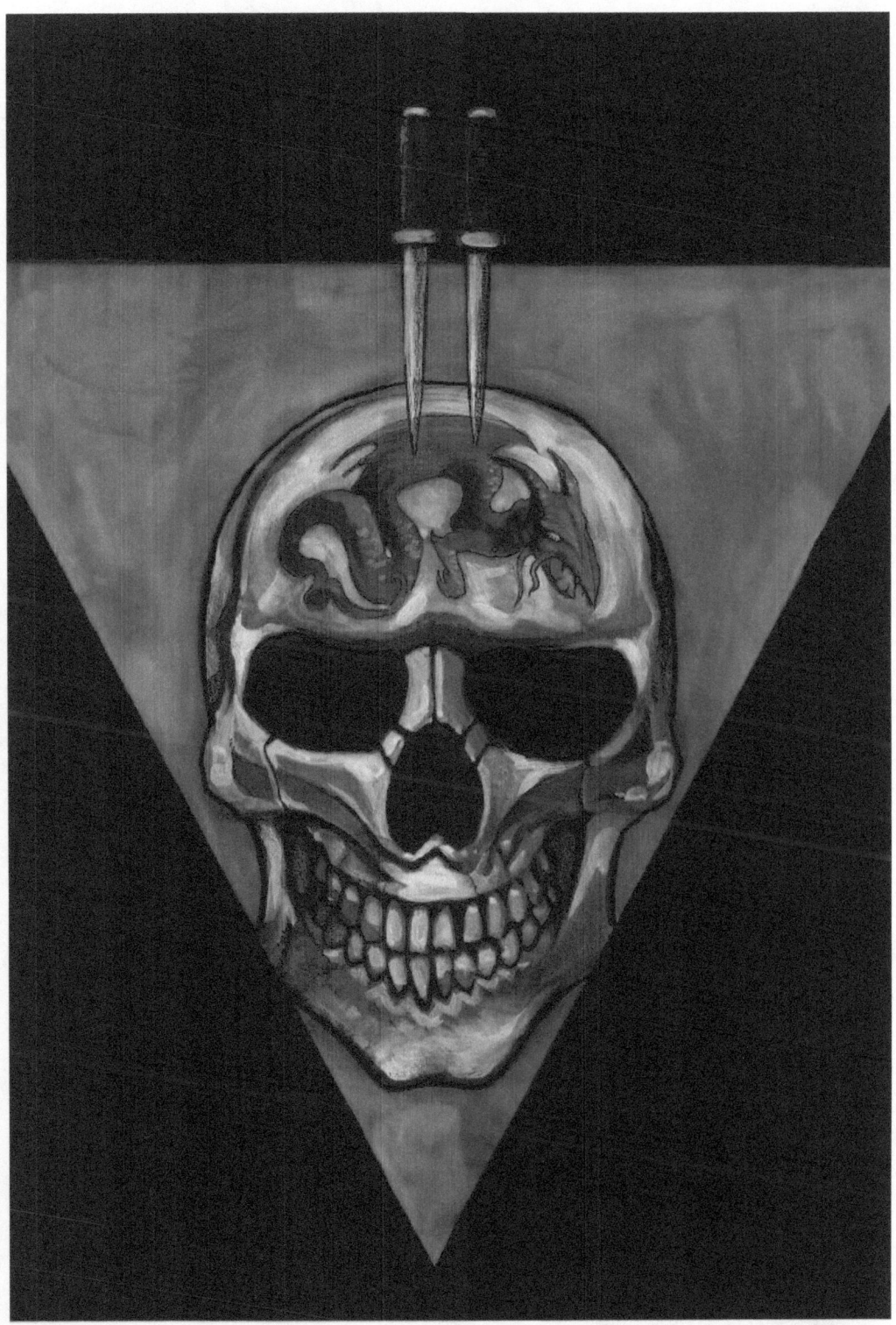

Mark Randolph Watters

The Ghosts of Benevolence

38

"SIMMONS, TAKE MISTER HAWTHORNE'S
jacket and bring us both a co'cola, a colander of boiled
shrimp, and a steamy loaf of sourdough bread. And fig
preserves. Don't forget the burgundy, Simmons. You're
always forgettin' the burgundy. Make it that bottle of 1976
Domaine de la Romanee Conti. *Damn* good stuff, even if I
do have a hard time pronouncin' it. Oh, an' Simmons, we
do *not* want to be disturbed."

"Yes, sir," Simmons replied, draping Lance's jacket
over his forearm.

Clinton Simmons, ever the loyal servant and confidant,
had been in the employ of Earl Bentley Devereaux, III
going on fifty years. His lack of most of the markers of
advancing age belied his seventy-five years. Chestnut-
brown hair, bronzed skin, original teeth—all a glistening
white—detailed a muscular, arrow-straight build of six feet,
five inches.

Lance smiled uncomfortably, Simmons' unblinking
eyes of coal-black staring into his. Lance turned his glance
upward toward the ceiling.

While no master of fine spirits, Lance presumed any
spirit that conjured a sense of opulence as readily as

Mark Randolph Watters

'Domaine de la Romanee Conti' must have a value complementary of the financial condition of its owner.

Earl Bentley Devereaux, the Third, removed his white Panama hat, hanging it neatly upon the yellowed ivory hook of a bronze hat rack just inside the front door. Devereaux's jaw line angled a sharp ninety degrees from its hinge, just as Lance had remembered it.

A lean, fit man, Devereaux displayed no signs of age-deposited crescents of fat or the curtains of listless skin that typically befell ordinary men. His concave cheeks clung snugly over high bones. He swept back his white, hat-flattened hair with a single stroke, strands of it angling back onto his forehead. He sighed and settled into a high-back wicker chair. Lance followed his lead.

"Thank you, Mr. Devereaux. I—"

"Earl."

"Sir?"

"It's *Earl*; not Mister Devereaux. For now, anyway. Besides, 'Earl' is quicker to say, don't you agree?"

"Why, yes … yes, I do agree … Earl. You know of Mr. Barrett King, of Standard Paper Industries of Georgia?"

Devereaux reached for his mahogany box of hand-rolled cigars but gave no response.

"Well, he is … that is, I report directly to him," Lance continued, "and he has asked me to approach *you* with an offer for the tract of land you've indicated a desire to sell; I believe it is twenty-five thousand acres?"

Lance placed his briefcase on the marble-topped coffee table and opened it.

"I have here from Mr. King a letter of understanding and a prelim—"

"Cicadas?" Devereaux offered, lifting a porcelain bowl.

"Sir?"

The Ghosts of Benevolence

"Cicadas. Maybe you know them as tree crickets? Roasted this morning. All the crunch of peanuts without the allergies. Go ahead. *Damn* good, these little bastards!"

"No ... no thank you, sir." Lance cleared his throat. "Just ate."

"Figured as much." Devereaux shoved two into his mouth, the crunch sounding more like fried shrimp than peanuts. "Ain't for sale."

Lance paused to digest Devereaux's unexpected words.

"*Ain't* for—" Lance repeated, catching himself and clearing his throat. "*Not* for sale?"

"Not to *Yankees*, it ain't. But I may make an exception in your case. You a *natural born* Yankee, *transplanted*? You sound like an *Ohio* Yankee. Or maybe you're one of them Yankee *wannabe's*?" Devereaux swallowed and grinned as he planted the cigar between his stained teeth. Toying with Lance, Devereaux knew full well he had tapped into a phony persona.

"I'm ... uh ... *southern*, sir, born and raised. Right *here*, as a matter of fact."

"What's the offer, Mister Hawthorne?" Devereaux asked, chewing on his cigar. He bent down and scratched a match across the soul of his shoe. The match's erupting flame consumed the cigar's tip. Devereaux drew rapid puffs to quicken the burn. Lance felt the Devereaux-King connection grow stronger.

Simmons returned with the colas and a decanter of Romanee Conti, boiled shrimp and cocktail sauce, and sourdough bread, its toasted aroma overtaking the cigar's.

"*Preserves*, Simmons! You're always *forgettin'* the fig preserves!" Devereaux shouted.

"I have them here, sir," Simmons calmly announced, unscrewing the jar's lid.

"So you do. Good man, Simmons. Look here, Mr. Hawthorne," offered Devereaux, pointing to an antique secretary. "I got me some *sillabub* in a bowl. Maybe you'd prefer *that* to fig preserves, though these *are* the best figs *you'll* ever eat. Made with Old Jack, this sillabub, not that wine stuff, and curdled with just enough cream to give your pancreas a jump. Even got me some *liquid* sillabub in that decanter yonder, except it ain't got as much of the cream. Just Old Jack's all, and a touch of cayenne. *Liquid fire* is what they ought to call it!"

"Thanks," replied Lance. "The preserves are fine and … I'll just stay with the coke and Romanee."

"Hmph! I ain't met an Atlanta boy yet that'd drink creamless sillabub and cayenne, much less one who knew what the hell the stuff *was*!" said Devereaux, shaking his head and laughing. "Fact is, I don't believe there's a soul north of Macon anymore who was even *born* in Georgia and remains *true* to the South. They're all … what's the word … *yankeefied*. You a *Georgia* boy?"

"I live in Raventon, sir, seventy miles northwest of Atlanta."

"Raventon; Atlanta," Devereaux huffed. "It's all the same place—*north* of Macon."

"Born and raised in Benevolence, like I said, Mr. Dev … Earl."

"In *Benevolence*? Now I *know* you're crappin' on my parade! No Benevolence soul carries *that* accent. Hawthorne … Hawthorne," Devereaux repeated, eyes closed, trying to place the familiar surname with the faces of his past. "Well, if you *say* so.

"Now, what's this here *offer* you spoke of? Wait. Before you give me *any* offer, let me tell you a thing or two about the land. It *ain't* twenty thousand acres. It's more like twenty-*five* thousand acres, an' you'll either take it *all* or you'll take *none*. There's prime timber on that land. Water, too. Lots of both. Water's the one thing most folks ain't got these days. It's got a river borderin' one side and a creek on the other that cuts clean through the property and flows straight to the river. Full of trout, that creek is.

The Ghosts of Benevolence

"Earl, sir, I think I *mentioned* it being twenty-five thousand acres, didn't—"

"Don't interrupt me! I *hate* it when folks interrupt me," Devereaux said, shaking his head, taking another roasted cicada into his mouth and a puff on his cigar. "What was I sayin'? Oh, yes. Now, I happen to know King is more than just a company man lookin' to pull the strings of his bosses' attention. I think Mr. King, more'n most folks, appreciates the value of a good stick of pinewood. And, he knows I'm gettin' on up in years and am lookin' to rid myself of my burdensome tax base. That's his leverage.

"I got *me* some *leverage*, too. It's called Consolidated, and it's somethin' y'all need to think about. They ain't going to just walk away, let y'all north Georgia papermakers come waltzin' in and take what they consider to be *their* resources. No sirree, bob! They been cuttin' trees off my land for fifty years, growin' 'em back and doin' it all over again, again and again. But, I'm sure your offer reflects a lot of thinkin'—thinkin' that'll help me forget all about Consolidated, if you get my meanin'."

Devereaux lifted a crystal glass of liquid sillabub to his lips, slurped, and swallowed. "Come *at* me, boy! I'm *waitin'*. Whatchu got for me?"

Lance paused. Taken off stride by the avarice of the ambience and the bluntness of his host, Lance sifted the papers in his briefcase, like a child fumbling before reciting a half-memorized poem, not sure how, or if, to proceed. All his rehearsing failed him at this crucial point. Then he remembered Barrett's instruction.

"Uh … How does eight hundred and fifty dollars per acre sound?"

FFFTTFTFTF!

Devereaux's mouthful of Sillabub drenched the coffee table, splattering onto Lance's briefcase.

Mark Randolph Watters

"Have you taken *leave* of your *senses,* boy? What it *sounds* like is a hornfull of *sour notes!* You're going to have to do a *lot* better than that, boy. Say, about *four thousand dollars* better is what I'm talkin' about!"

"I thought you'd say that, sir. In fact, I *knew* you'd say that, only I hadn't counted on your having a mouthful of drink. Give me credit for trying."

"I'll do nothing of the sort! Only Yankees and *idiots* make such offers, even when they know such offers are nothing more than a waste of my valuable time. Forty-eight hundred dollars, sir. No, no, make that a nice round *five thousand* dollars per acre. I just wasted the equivalent of two hundred dollars per acre on the sillabub, fixins, and Romanee."

"Mr. Devereaux, sir, that land isn't worth that kind of money. Consolidated's top price is no better than eight hundred per acre."

"That's just timber rights. I'm selling all or nothing, remember? Five thousand per, final offer."

"Might I ask you about the most interesting series of billboards I could not help but see along the highway, the skull in a red triangle, the dragon, and those intimidating swords? What's "The Kingdom" and 'Damocles'? Twelve hundred dollars."

"Glad you found it … intimidating. That's exactly my intent. Wide open country down here, Mr. Hawthorne. Can't have vagrants and drifters thinking their uninvited paths can pass unnoticed through … the Kingdom. Anyway, Damocles is the name of my company, a manufacturer of agricultural treatments and machinery. Four thousand dollars."

"Not a chance. Damocles? Now I understand the swords. Farm machinery; interesting. I suppose what I saw out back was a sampling of your company's equipment at work? Thirteen hundred."

The Ghosts of Benevolence

"Mine, indeed. Best cotton pickers and corn harvesters in the industry. You will eat supper with me tonight, won't you?" insisted Devereaux. "I ain't going lower than three thousand."

"Well, I really—"

"Good. We eat at six."

"Well, then," Lance said, glancing at his watch. "Looking forward to it, sir. Fifteen hundred, and I won't go a penny higher."

"Then consider yourself lucky, sir, to get a free meal. Simmons, see our guest to the door."

"But, Mr. Dev—"

"Six o'clock, Mr. Hawthorne. Please be prompt. You may tour the grounds if you wish. Afternoon, sir," Devereaux said as he turned and exited through the parlor door. Lance stood silent. A half minute later, Devereaux returned.

"You believe in money, Mr. Hawthorne?" Devereaux asked, eyes squinted as he pushed his dormant cigar into the ashtray, crushing its tip.

"Money? Yes ... oh, yes, I *do* believe in money, Mr. Devereaux," Lance replied. "Is there a reason you ask?"

"Glad to hear it. Me, too. Someone once said—and I paraphrase—'the religion of money is the only one with no unbelievers.' You and I *are* believers, Mister Hawthorne. After all, it *is* how we keep the score, right, Mr. Hawthorne?"

"Indeed it is, Mr. Dever . . . *Earl*."

Devereaux smiled, scratched to life another match and held it to a new cigar. "Money comes to us at the *strangest* times, in the *most unexpected* ways, Mr. Hawthorne," he said, sucking the cigar and blowing a gray cloud toward the ceiling, "but it's still how we keep the score that matters. Whether it's an inheritance or a bonus check or a promotion or even a ... well, a FedEx package; it all comes down to how we *keep the score*. Reconsider the three thousand, Mr. Hawthorne. We'll talk again at supper."

Devereaux chuckled and nodded smugly, like a lawyer who knows the answers to his questions before asking them.

"See you at six, Mr. Hawthorne."

"Earl?" said Lance as Devereaux turned to leave. "It's *Lance*."

Devereaux stared at Lance.

"So it is," he said, walking away, wisps of smoke curling over his head. "So it is."

"I'll see myself out, Simmons," Lance said. "Thank you."

Lance wanted a consummation of the deal without closing it over dinner, but he saw no wisdom in refusing Devereaux's invitation. He might deem such as an insult to his honor, challenging Lance to a duel of pistols, or worse, a sword fight. Lance smiled at the absurdity, the utter juxtaposition, of these images of Southern gallantry. Then he remembered the skull topped by swords inside the inverted triangle. His smile vanished, expectations now wide open.

39

EVERYTHING LANCE SAW CONFIRMED his suspicions about Devereaux. He had amassed an empire, rebuilt an aristocracy, buoyed by a culture of fear and the fortune left him by his father. Work remained in order to bring fruit to the negotiations for the land deal, but Devereaux had uttered one word that stopped Lance in mid-thought.

'FedEx'.

Why, Lance thought, *would he use that specific example in his rambling oratory on money? Make that two words. He also mentioned 'promotion'. He and Barrett are more than mere industry acquaintances.*

Simmons accompanied Lance on his slow stroll through the parlor. Lance pretended to admire the hanging artwork and bronze sculptures.

"Pity to waste such good food and beverage as you have prepared for us," Lance said to Simmons. "Think I'll just make me a fig preserve biscuit or two and pour me a bit more of that Romanee Conti stuff. If that's okay with you, Simmons."

"If you need anything, sir, I'll be close by. Just give a wave of your hand; you'll be seen, and I'll see to you," Simmons instructed.

"Simmons."

"Yes, sir?"

"You eat cicadas?"

Simmons grinned. "I only gather them, sir, for Mr. Devereaux's pleasure. I prefer fried scorpions. If you need anything, sir."

Lance's eyes widened as he nodded. He fingered the decanter of burgundy, taking in the cool of the glass. He turned and in an instant found himself alone inside this sinister structure of elegance. He felt suddenly as a germ on a specimen glass, under the magnifying lens of a microscope, his every move studied. The antiques and French-inspired décor; tapestries sweeping the length and breadth of walls; the fourteen-foot ceilings of relief-carved cherubs and gods touching the tips of humanity's reach; oil paintings and yellowed daguerreotypes of ancestors, each hanging, staring, like guardians—like cameras.

Fried scorpions?

On the far wall, above the fireplace, hung a collection of several dozen Civil War-era muskets, bayonets affixed to each, hammers cocked, ready.

All of these yester-world antiques, displayed with utmost care and respect, ushered Lance back into an era of pomp and chivalry, of honor and tradition, of valor and violence.

Lance sipped some burgundy and nibbled his figs-filled biscuit, sticky crumbs falling to the floor. He saw through the windowpanes clusters of live oaks, their limbs wretchedly bent by time, as if pleading with their master for a moment's relief, instead lavished with clothing of moss hiding their pain.

Lance glanced back, half expecting to see Simmons, even Devereaux himself. He stepped out the front door

The Ghosts of Benevolence

onto the porch. Pockets of gnats, invisible until upon him, filled the air, each finding an orifice on his body. Nothing but gnats could spoil this outdoor opulence or distract his attention with more effect.

He pressed his glass to his cheek and absorbed its condensation, serendipity drowning a few of the trapped pests. The cool droplets of water gave some relief to the crescendo of afternoon heat. In spite of growing up here, Lance found it amazing that humans still chose to remain here. He knew well the toil of working these fields in the height of summer's heat, but he could not imagine the torment of slaves who once labored here.

He sipped the last few drops of burgundy and searched the porch for an obvious place, a tray, a table, anything, to set his glass. Finding none, he set the glass on the plank floor of the porch, next to one of the columns, and wondered how long it might take to attract notice.

Let's see just how scrutinized I am, thought Lance.

A glare off the window of his Mercedes, punching him squarely in his eyes, reminded him of the box in the backseat. Glancing over his left shoulder, toward the porch, Lance unlocked the car's doors. He noticed the absence of the empty glass. The glass, at least, was scrutinized.

Lance recalled Barrett's warning to leave the box unopened, a warning he no longer felt compelled to heed. With compulsive disregard of likely detection, he reached into his pocket and took out his Swiss Army knife, the same knife he had once managed to smuggle, on a dare, through the security of Hartsfield-Jackson International Airport. Such days of innocent crimes often possessed his memories.

He opened the door and crawled into the backseat, closing the door behind him. He felt a level of privacy from the tinted windows.

Mark Randolph Watters

Slicing the tape, Lance pushed back the flaps and found a sealed, letter-sized envelope. Pocketing the envelope, Lance pushed aside a layer of packing peanuts, uncovering a desktop computer and keyboard sitting snugly in Styrofoam fittings and plastic bags.

"*Looks* like hardware. This has got to be the heaviest personal computer since cathode ray tubes," Lance whispered. "And there's not even a flat screen in the box! If this is intended for *me*, I'm giving it to Heather instead. Way too heavy to be a desktop. A server maybe. If I can just pull this thing up ..."

Lance struggled to wrangle the computer from the confinement of its box and the restraints of backseat space. Managing to maneuver the machine halfway free, out tumbled onto his forearm a brick-sized packet.

"Ow! *Damn!*" Lance lifted the packet. "Well, well, what have we here?"

Its shape and hardened feel, covered with tight plastic wrapping, reminded Lance of similar sized bricks of freeze-dried coffee. He turned the computer on its side, revealing three neatly arrayed stacks inside the guts-emptied case, perhaps fifteen bricks of the white substance. The packet that had fallen out was marked "2 kilos".

"Cocaine? Sure ain't sugar for my coffee!" He stared at the neatly arrayed packets. "That Ruben fellow was shipping *cocaine* back to *Barrett*. And *I* was their courier. The FedEx package is Barrett's payment for it, but to whom? Ruben? Wonder what's Devereaux's role? The *envelope*, please."

Lance pulled the folded envelope from his pocket and ripped open an edge. Scrawled in blue cursive, its legibility diminished by the smear of coffee stains, the words answered a wealth of questions:

'Barrett, enclosed is the final shipment the Afghan H you ordered, per our agreement. Look forward to working with you as your operations expand. You and

The Ghosts of Benevolence

Carl are wise to be partnering with Dev. The success of the skull and sword as a distributor of agricultural insecticides has made his operations the envy of cartels everywhere. You will profit mutually from your contacts. Thanks for including me, and I hope we can continue doing business.

*   'B. Rubin.*

*   'P.S. – Good luck on funding that "land deal" with D. SPIG's board will never know what hit them. At least not until it's too late. B.R.'*

"Holy *drug lords!* Devereaux and Barrett! Carl, too? Damocles! Drug-running, under the guise of insecticides. Pretty darn clever!" whispered Lance, folding the note and tucking it into his back pocket.

"This explains a lot of things, including the *countless* boxes received from Global Technical Solutions. It also explains the *absence* of computer equipment as well. Just as I suspected from my perusal of a *few* of Global's invoices.

"My guess is that Barrett is *trafficking the heroin* to offsite locations, maybe directly to the street or for resale to distributors.

"Meanwhile, he's *stealing* company funds by redirecting payments somewhere, to an account he's set up perhaps. Wouldn't surprise me if he's been processing the payments himself, from the comfort of his overstated office." Lance sighed, wiping sweat from his forehead. "Need to call Heather."

Lance pulled out his cell phone, pressing her number. "Answer, sweetheart! Heather? Lance. Don't talk; listen! Do you recall processing any of Global's invoices?"

"Not I. Brenda handles that vendor, I think. You okay?"

"So far, so good."

"Let me check with her."

Lance clamped the phone between his shoulder and ear and waited for Heather. He closed the box and, folding forward a backseat, shoved the box into the trunk, mindful of any approach of grounds personnel or Devereaux himself.

"Lance?"

"Here."

"She hasn't paid *any* Global invoices, not for several months. Neither has anyone else. I hope you've accrued their billings."

"You're telling me that payments to Global do *not* show up in the payables system?"

"A few, here and there, going back a few years, those that Brenda *did* process. Nothing amounting to much since '08."

"Heather, *someone's* paying those invoices; you gave me two boxes *filled* with them, remember? Did we issue checks or EFTs?"

"EFTs are handled by management, Lance."

"I know, but can you query that system?"

"Never had reason to. Let me check the payables menu options."

Lance heard Heather's frantic clicking on her keyboard. "Darn thing's so *slow!*" she shouted. "Lance, you have *got* to get me a new PC!"

"Working on it. First thing, when I get back. I Promise."

"Promises, promises. I'm holding you to it, Hawthorne! Okay, *got* it. Let's see ... all ... EFTs. Every payment."

"To *whom?*"

"First Federal Credit Union, upstate New York."

"*Upstate New York?* We don't have accounts ... What's the name on the account?"

"Global Technical Solutions, B. King, custodian."

"Gotta go, Heather. Thanks. I'll call you later."

The Ghosts of Benevolence

"What's going on, Lance? *Tell* me!"

"*Later*, I said. I Promise."

"Promises, promises."

Lance smiled as he ended the call. The last person he wanted caught up in this was Heather. Loyal and smart, Heather played by the rules, an attribute now liable to be to her detriment in the emerging game.

The afternoon waned, but the heat did not. The faint rumble of a thunder, its storm clouds bubbling yellow-orange on the western horizon, tumbled on the air like square wheels.

"*Somebody's* getting rain," observed Lance, echoing an observation he had earlier made.

A golf cart pulled alongside Lance as he rested under the shade of a magnolia. Masked by a soft smile of acknowledgment, he considered his options as he sniffed magnolia flowers.

"Sir," said Simmons, "dinner is now served. I am your ride to the house."

"Thank you, Simmons." Lance climbed in back, and the cart rolled forward with a slight jolt. "Say, Simmons …"

"Yes, sir?"

Lance paused, not sure probing into Simmons's relationship with his employer was an avenue prudent for pursuit.

"Never mind," Lance said. "I … answered my own question."

"Very well, sir."

Lance turned his gaze toward the setting sun, spears of light exploding from the edges of billowing gray thunderheads. He gave a slight smile to Simmons's use of the noun, 'house', as reference to Devereaux's mansion. *If Devereaux's is a 'house', then Vanderbilt's is a summer cottage.*

Mark Randolph Watters

The cart stopped at the front of the mansion, near the curling steps. Lance stepped out.

"Thank you, Simmons," Lance said, extending his closed palm, a twenty inside.

Simmons acknowledged the gesture by ignoring it. "Follow me, sir," he said.

"Hope you like your chicken Southern-fried and your ham honey-baked, Mister Hawthorne!" Devereaux shouted from the end of the breezeway, which extended two hundred feet to the back patio.

A choir of cicadas sprang to life, as if on cue, their song filtering through raised floor-to-ceiling windows.

Simmons escorted Lance to the dining room, its space graced with furnishings rivaling those of the parlor. Two place settings of bone china trimmed in 24-karat gold adorned the twenty-foot oval cherry table. Engraved Asa Blanchard silverware flanked each plate; carved ivory rings secured linen napkins; a silver bowl filled with a bluish liquid and topped with pink camellias complemented the formality.

Lance assumed correctly that the place setting at the head of the table must belong to his host.

Simmons pulled out Lance's chair slightly, indicating the appropriate time had arrived for seating. Recordings of Mantovani's Orchestra supplied musical ambience. The rich strings of 'Yesterday' swept from wall to wall as Devereaux entered the dining room.

"Evenin', sir," Devereaux announced, taking his seat. "Good tune, 'Yesterday'. Don't you agree, Mister Hawthorne? Don't write 'em like that no more."

"No, sir, they don't," Lance agreed, sitting.

"Hope you don't mind Mantovani's Orchestra while we eat, chat. Sets a *civilized* mood, I think, and keeps out the … riffraff." Devereaux's eyes drifted toward Simmons. "Anyway, I believe you are in for the treat of your *life*

The Ghosts of Benevolence

tonight, Lance. Simmons has prepared a feast fit for a …
king."

Lance noticed. *Or for a kingdom.*

Simmons returned with silver trays of food atop a
polished copper and silver catering cart, serving first long-
stemmed crystal cups filled with wafer cuts of strawberries
and peach wedges. Next came fried chicken breasts stuffed
with cornbread-and-mozzarella dressing; baked honey-
glazed ham, garnished with parsley sprigs and apple rings;
whole new potatoes, boiled, bathed in hand-churned butter
and sprinkled with chives; sweet corn on the cob; golden-
brown biscuits fluffed three inches tall; and cups of
steaming Argentine coffee.

"I think I've died and gone to Southern heaven, Mr.
Devereaux," Lance said, smiling. "I think I've not seen,
nor smelled, so *glorious* a meal."

"Interesting choice of words, 'died', Mr. Hawthorne.
Nor have you *tasted* so glorious a meal, Mr. Hawthorne."
Devereaux clapped twice. "*Tomatoes*, Simmons, peeled
and sliced!"

"On their way, sir."

"Ha, ha. Simmons can be a bit forgetful sometimes,
though he means well. Been with me fifty years, give or
take. Suppose he's due some mistakes. So, how was your
stroll around campus?"

"Campus? Oh, just as glorious, sir."

"Please. Call me Earl. I insist."

"Pardon me, sir … Earl. Old habits, you know."

"Indeed. Manners and respect are rare commodities
these days. Your mama taught you well. Pour yourself
some sweet tea," Devereaux said, pointing to a carafe.
"Brewed right here. You know, as opposed to those
sinister gallon jugs you can get at any grocery store. Tastes
of plastic, that tea. Probably brewed in Bangor, exported
south."

"Yes, I believe I will. Thank you, Earl."

Mark Randolph Watters

"Pleasure's mine," Devereaux said, taking the carafe after Lance and pouring the amber liquid into his own glass. "So, back to your afternoon stroll. Anything … interesting?"

"Astounding is a better word, I think," Lance said, taking a sip of water and choosing his words with care. "Landscape and vegetation are unequalled; your home unrivaled; and the things one can *learn* here without relying on a *computer*—unbelievable. Truly mindboggling. I must say, Earl, you have quite the kingdom here. A *toast*, sir. To you … to Damocles … to *scorekeeping*."

"Hear, hear! And to *you*, my boy."

Devereaux drank, then bellowed a laugh, plunging a fork-stabbed whole potato into his mouth, followed by a bite of biscuit.

"Never much liked computers, anyhow," Devereaux said, crumbs of biscuit spraying forth onto the polished cherrywood. "Just as soon *strip 'em out* and *stuff* 'em with trinkets, coins, such things as that; make 'em *useful*."

"Indeed."

Lance sipped his tea, his eyes never once leaving his host's.

The Ghosts of Benevolence

40

NOT ONE FOR TABLE etiquette, Devereaux let loose a series of belches during the meal, a hint of their pungency lingering throughout.

"You must … forgive me, sir." Devereaux pleaded, dabbing the corners of his mouth with his satin napkin. "Learned the art of the belch from a sixth-grade friend who had the throat of a toad frog."

Lance lifted his coffee cup to his lips, suppressing an urge to issue a sixth-grader's laugh.

"My mama taught me manners, too, bless her soul," Devereaux continued, "but rich food does this to me. And, well … it *is* my table."

"Indeed, your table, sir. Apologies not necessary. You should hear me in *my* home."

"I hope to one day have that opportunity, Lance. Pass the taters, please."

"Here you are. So, are you unmovable?"

"Unmovable, sir? In what regard?"

"Three thousand?"

"That was then. Perhaps not *unmovable*, dependin' on the direction. I believe it now *four*, Lance. But the roots do run deep. Is thirteen hundred the best you can do?"

"Is four thousand the best *you* can do?"

Devereaux did not answer Lance. "Simmons!"

"Yes, sir?"

"More coffee. And the tomatoes?"

"There, sir, in front of your plate," Simmons replied, pointing. "Coffee coming."

"Ah, yes, so they are. Thank you, Simmons. And I believe we are ready for some peach cobbler, topped with vanilla ice cream, that bean-specked stuff, not that sissy French vanilla crap."

"Very good, sir. Right away."

"Good man, that Simmons," Devereaux said. "They should *all* be so loyal. Did you see that?"

"See what, sir?"

Devereaux paused, his eyes moving side to side. "Never mind. Damn floaters again. Look like squirrels running across the room. Need to get these old eyes checked. As I was sayin', thirty-five hundred."

"At least you're moving in my direction."

Devereaux laughed. "This way, my boy," he said pointing Lance toward the Smoking Room and high-back leather chairs that flanked a white and gray marble mantle.

"Sit, please. Cigar?"

"Don't mind if I do," Lance replied, taking one from the silver box. "You roll and cut your own?"

"Indeed I do. Can't get Cuban *cigars*, per se, so I just smuggle in their *tobacco*." Devereaux paused, hoping for a reaction. "It's a *joke*, Lance."

"So it is," Lance replied. "I knew that."

"Yes, well …"

Devereaux cleared his throat, making way to regale his guest with one of his after-dinner tales. He brought his cigar to his lips.

The Ghosts of Benevolence

"Did I ever tell you about my brother Lewis?" Devereaux asked, moistening the cigar's end, a gleam of pride in his eyes. "Folks 'round here called him Bubba. *Looked* like a Bubba, too."

"Don't believe you did, sir."

"Why, Lewis, he was the talk of Benevolence back in '46. You may know of him, though he was *considerably* older than you, I suspect."

An antique mirror rose eight feet above the mantle to a hand-chiseled marble cornice. Cedar and oak logs crackled in the fireplace, spitting upward sparks and embers and creating the comfort of security and warmth, offsetting the chill of the low setting of Devereaux's twenty-first-century central air. The fire thus altogether seemed fitting, despite the oppressive summer atmosphere just beyond the walls.

Simmons returned with the coffee, as well as L'Esprit de Courvoisier cognac, vintage 1802, in anticipation of Devereaux's requesting it. Lance took note, raising his eyebrows as Simmons poured the drink. Devereaux took his glass, swirled the liquid, sniffed it, discerned its essence, his eyes fixed upon Lance.

The men sipped, each exchanging snippets of their families' histories and tidbits of their pasts, mostly embellished 'fish stories'.

"Anyhow, back to Lewis. He just got home from Berlin, back in '46. You know, from the occupation, and did he *ever* get a welcome from the homefolks! He strutted around this county showin' off his Medal of Honor and silver stars—two of them star bastards—and a purple heart he earned at Normandy. That ol' boy would saunter into Prather's—heh, heh—and you'd think he just parted the bloody *Red Sea*. People'd step aside, like he was some god or somethin'. Can you imagine *anybody* from this backwater dump doin' *anything* worth half a crap in this world, much less a goddam *Medal of Honor*? *Two* of 'em!"

"I thought it was two silver stars."

Mark Randolph Watters

Devereaux drew fast on his cigar, eyes squinted, and ignored the correction. "Hell, now that I think about it, I s'pose I would have showed 'em off, too!" Devereaux spit flecks of tobacco to the floor.

"Shot in the shoulder and the calf, clean through both. He always said to me, 'They got me *high* an' they got me *low* but not in the *middle* where it counts.' Heh, heh, heh. A great man, that Lewis; sense o' humor to beat all. Yes, sir, a *great* man, Bubba."

Devereaux paused, fixing his eyes upon the wall of Civil War muskets, his rows of Springfields in particular.

"Died two years ago. What the Germans started, blood clots finished, I reckon. Scar tissue built up over the years. Bubba never liked doctors; refused checkups as he got older. Blood flow got sort of constricted in his legs, I reckon. Got to where the man could hardly take a step. Clots formed, broke away … a frontal assault straight to his heart. Killed him as quickly as if a German bullet had hit him there. His only consolation, I suppose, was that he was able to fend off that assault longer'n most folks."

Devereaux's smile diminished as his gaze upon the muskets tightened. He cleared his throat and took a sip of cognac, followed by a puff on his cigar.

"Any of your folks serve in the war after the war to end all wars?" Devereaux asked.

"Well, I think—that is, I mean … World War Two? I don't think so. I don't *think* they did. I had a brother in Nam. Killed during Tet. Daddy never talked much about that," Lance said, in a now-that-I-think-about-it way. "What …. what did Lewis do to earn his Medal of Honor?" asked Lance.

"Well, like I said, he was shot in the shoulder and the calf. Of course, a bunch of our boys got hit worse. But what made Lewis's so special was how he came to get shot, an' what he done afterwards.

The Ghosts of Benevolence

"They'd just landed on Normandy, Omaha Beach, in the Dog Green sector. The Germans were blastin' 'em to hell and back, pickin' 'em off like tin cans with their damned 42s, before many of that first wave could even get off their goddam Higgins. As Lewis told it, it was like wadin' into a damned firin' squad, like Pickett at Gettysburg or Grant at Cold Harbor."

"Or Burnside at Fredericksburg," Lance added.

Devereaux paused, lowering his cigar.

"You makin' *fun* of me, boy?"

"Sir? No, sir." Lance shifted his body. "Not one bit, sir. Please forgive my interruption. I wanted only to contribute my own understanding of what you were describing."

"What do *you* know about the War Between the States?"

"I love to *read*, sir, particularly the history of the Civ—the War Between the States. Fredericksburg just seemed to fit the discussion, of assaults into firing squads. I do apologize for any unintended offense."

"Accepted." Devereaux refilled his glass. "Anyway, as I was sayin', he managed to make it across that beach. *How* he was able to do that he *swore* was *God's* purview. Behind him about thirty feet, back in the middle of that god-forsaken beach, he saw a company of men scatter in the air like bowlin' pins. Mortar shell, he said it was. Three of 'em wounded, the rest dead. He dropped his rifle and ran back, under fire, to render aid. One by one, he dragged them boys off the beach, to the relative safety of a seawall. He made it clean with the first one, but while draggin' the second boy, he caught a bullet in the calf, which, as you might imagine, made it all that more difficult for Lewis to move *himself*, much less the burden of another body. He said it was sheer fear that carried him and the second boy out of harm's way. Then, he hobbled back for the third boy. I always believed it was the shock of blood loss that made him go back for number three. Anyway, that's when he got it in the shoulder.

"What's amazin' is that he told the medic to go find somebody *hurt*—like he *wasn't*—and he fought the rest of the day on that beachhead with only the comfort of morphine. He recovered in France and rejoined his outfit two months before the Bulge. Fought in that sombitch, too … *unscathed*. He was a *miracle* man, that Lewis."

"An amazing man, indeed, your brother," said Lance. "A toast to Lewis, to his bravery."

The two raised their glasses.

"To your brother as well, my boy," Devereaux whispered in rare acknowledgement.

Devereaux reached for another cigar. The haze of smoke drifted through the air, like the stench of battle.

Lance fingered the bulge around his glass, thinking not of how to match stories with Earl Devereaux, but instead how to consummate the pending land deal. Lance wanted to pull a miracle of his own. He had choices, now that circumstances had changed; choices with dilemmas, choices to manage, with skills he had yet to discover. Cognac swirled as Lance turned his glass in a circular motion. He felt the fleeting air of opulence, of superiority. He soaked up the splendor, untouchable inside this bubble of aristocracy.

"Ever held a Springfield?"

"Sir?"

"A Springfield. You ever held one, shot one?"

"Got one at home, actually, but I've never *shot* one. Bet they kick like a mule!"

"Nine point two pounds of metal mule shoe, boy. Soldiers thought the gun shot backwards, into their shoulders, but they got used to the kick pretty fast." Devereaux gazed upon his prized antiques. "These guns were passed down to me. *Proud* to have 'em. Most of 'em

The Ghosts of Benevolence

picked up from dead Yankees, some captured outright. Yes, sir. *Mighty* proud to have 'em."

The evening was spent posturing, though Lance hardly realized the extent to which Devereaux gave him scrutiny. Lance closed his eyes for a moment and imagined this, *all* this, were his. He took a long draw on his cigar, circled his lips and released the smoke in a slow stream toward the ceiling. Devereaux measured his prey, as would a spider an insect.

"Here you go, son. Take another cigar, for later."

"Thank you, sir. Don't mind if I do."

"I'm sure you *don't*. Five thousand dollars, Mister Hawthorne," Devereaux blurted, sipping his cognac. The tide of the conversation had turned.

"*What?* Five thous—why, that's ... that's ... *too* generous of you, Mister Devereaux," Lance replied, stuffing the cigar into his shirt pocket, his sarcasm suggesting Devereaux's offer was lump-sum, for the entire twenty-five thousand acres. "You must take *at least six*. But you'll have to throw in an unopened box of cigars and a bottle of the Romanee stuff, too."

"Per *acre*, sir," Devereaux clarified, sensing Lance's coating of disrespect. "And *six* it shall be! Per acre." Pausing, Devereaux furrowed his singular brow, which stretched above his eyes like a caterpillar across tree bark. He bent forward, his metallic-blue eyes searing a hole in Lance's.

"Why, Mister Hawthorne, I'm surprised at you. A man of your intelligence and business acumen. Do you really think I'd let go of prime southern timberland for a mere *twenty-four cents* on the acre? Of course you don't. You were only *kiddin'* me!"

Wow. He calculated twenty-four cents on the acre before I hardly took my next breath!

Mark Randolph Watters

"I did not come into possession of all you see here by way of stupidity or government handouts ... or the disrespect of strangers."

Lance felt the blood rush to his skin and a prickly sweat break out from forehead to foot. Sarcasm had not been his smartest play.

Cigar smoke meandered and rotated above the men like sludge down a river current. The stench deepened.

Devereaux continued, "I agree, Mr. Hawthorne, the price is a might generous—for *you*. But I'll get over it."

"But, Mr. Devereaux, Barrett King won't pay—"

"He'll *pay*," Devereaux interrupted, grimacing in pain and leaning to his left. "*Shit!* Excuse my language, sir, but I had surgery some years back. Got me a brand new *kidney*," Devereaux disclosed, touching his lower left back. "Liked to never found one, but, with a little ... *help* ... I found two actually, but only one any good. Rascal still ain't *never* worked as advertised. *Ummpph!* Must have been a *yankee* kidney. Keeps givin' me the *bayonet*!

"Anyway, don't you think for a minute he *won't* pay; he'll *pay* all right, and his SPIG directors will *approve* the purchase."

Devereaux bent over and picked up the Benevolence Connoisseur.

"Read this," he said, handing Lance the newspaper.

Lance took a look at the paper and immediately recognized the story.

"I've seen this. So?"

"So, Mr. Hawthorne, surely even *you* recognize what a politically correct society we live in these days. Show these damned environmentalists a flatwood salamander in wetlands during a period of extreme drought—such as we're experiencing now—and they'll declare an environmental *emergency,* the likes of which we've *never seen*, that is until the *next* environmental emergency.

The Ghosts of Benevolence

"Their hearts'll *bleed* all over it," Devereaux whined, hands clasped, head tilted, spewing his own brand of sarcasm, "and they'll *insist* we must be *enlightened* to the plight of the helpless flatwood salamander, to all species non-human, for that matter, even if the *true* detriment falls upon those humans who rely on the land and water for their very *lives*, for their very *livin'*."

Devereaux plucked a Springfield musket off the wall, turning it, admiring it. He pulled back the hammer, clicking it to full cock, taking casual aim in Lance's direction, at Lance himself.

"Effective killin' range of a thousand yards, boy."

He shoved the ramrod in and out of the barrel, following the cadence of his words. "This government wants to *take* our water and our land, just like they took our—"

Catching his words, he stopped and cleared his throat. He carefully replaced the musket on its wall hold.

"How do you think I was able to get them to divert all that river water to *my* land, these twenty-five thousand acres? Hmmm? Yeah, I got some *political clout*, maybe, but even Earl Bentley Devereaux the Third's got to have a rhyme and reason for diverting *public* resources. Introduce a little ol' lizard—an' *voila!* —the government and them environmentalist yahoos come runnin' out of the woodwork, like hordes of pine beetles. They'll *eat* out of your hands, listenin' to your every word, like such was Gospel. Besides, I got *too much invested* in my farm and my company to let it dry up and blow away like some goddam sagebrush.

"Now, no mistakin', there's good timber on all that land, a regular *canopy* of trees, valuable trees, from oak to hickory to pine to pecan. Mister King *wants* those trees, yes sir, he *does*, and he needs the *guarantee of water* that goes with 'em, too. But, you know what? He wants the *cover* of the *canopy* even more.

291

Mark Randolph Watters

"He'll pay, oh, I'd say … one hundred and twenty-five million greenbacks for those twenty-five thousand acres, Mister Hawthorne. *Gladly*, he'd pay it. What do you think SPIG would have to pay for that kind of land in *North* Georgia, Mister Hawthorne, assuming such acreage became available? Anything within a hundred miles of Atlanta is prime *commercial* property, these days. We're talkin' twenty, twenty-five thousand dollars per acre, *minimum*, just for *rural* acreage. Developers are posturin' for better times, which, in time will come.

"Sure, the economy's tough *now*, but it won't be so *forever*, and the potential *windfalls* will *still* be there. Landowners *know* that. Not to mention King'll do anything to dissuade those Alabama papermakers from gettin' their grubby paws on that same patch of woods in *their* backyard. If King's nothin' else, he's competitive. He's got *enough* trouble from *South Georgia* papermakers. Oh, he'll pay, all right.

"Besides, Barrett's a man of vision. He knows good … shall we say, *cropland* … when he sees it. It's a damn *bargain*, sir, five thousand dollars per acre! And King *knows* it. He may not have told *you*, but he knows it. You *ought* to know it."

Lance expected Devereaux's stubbornness. In spite of the serendipity of 1802 cognac and Devereaux's unexpected hospitality, Lance held his ace, his faded photographic witness to long-latent events forever attached to Devereaux's lifelong interests. His promotion no longer in play, Lance focused on other options to augment to his *own* cash windfall waiting in his suit bag.

The Ghosts of Benevolence

41

"MR. DEVEREAUX, I'LL NEED to call Barrett and let him know your terms. I'm sure he'll be willing to negotiate with—"

"They ain't going to *be* any negotiating, Mister Hawthorne. The price is firm and *non*-negotiable. Either he wants it, or he don't. If he *don't* accept my offer *now*, you can tell him the price will most assuredly go *up*, not down. I *will* sell this land; the only question is to *whom*. You tell him that, Mister Hawthorne. Right now, sir, I'm goin' to bed. This old kidney's givin' me *fits*."

Devereaux turned and suffocated the waning ember of his cigar. He placed his glass on the lamp table, and, bracing on the arms of the leather wingback chair, pushed up.

"Unhhh!" Devereaux grimaced, electric pain stabbing his lower back. "That ol' ball of fire rises awfully early around here, Mister Lance Hawthorne, an' I got a whole field of corn, about a hundred acres' worth, I need to get off the stalks tomorrow. Matter of fact, I can think of *twenty-five thousand acres* that'd be *perfect* for corn. Ethanol's in high demand these days, pays pretty well, so I hear.

Mark Randolph Watters

"Right now, I need to go pull these daggers out of my back. Go ahead, now," Devereaux said with a wave. "You call King. I can *assure* you he *will* see this whole thing *my* way. Good night, Mister Hawthorne.

"Oh, one more thing I b'lieve you might find interestin' to know about this house, these whole grounds for that matter. The place is, in a word ... haunted."

"*Haunted?*"

"Indeed. Let me tell you a little story. Not that I believe in spooks, mind you, but perhaps there is a nugget of *wisdom* you can glean from this little episode.

"Seems the original owner of this property, a Percy Wyndham, had an unfortunate midnight encounter with his wife's lover, the plantation's overseer. Belvedere was his name.

"Story goes that Belvedere lured him to that pecan grove out yonder by making sounds Wyndham himself believed to be the spirits of Indians. With good reason, too. Native American habitat, these grounds, many a grave plundered over the years. I've taken a few skulls and pots myself.

"Anyway, poor Wyndham! Belvedere gave Wyndham's throat a single slash with a Bowie knife. Stood *laughing* while Wyndham pulled and tugged at his neck in full panic, desperately trying to stop the life draining from the wound like grain from a silo. Belvedere just watched ol' Wyndham die. Wasn't a *damn* thing Wyndham could do. Except *bleed*. And bleed he did, 'til he could bleed no more.

"Instead of diggin' a seven-by-three grave—the sort you and I understand—Belvedere buried him *standing up* in a hole occupied a few days prior by a pecan tree stump he had removed. Wyndham had demanded its removal time and again, and then only by Belvedere himself, a chore Belvedere believed was *beneath* him, no pun intended. Maybe the indignity of Wyndham's demands is

The Ghosts of Benevolence

what made the overseer snap. More likely Belvedere and Wyndham's wife just wanted the poor bastard out of their way.

"Anyhow, a patch of blue hyacinths now occupies the spot of that pecan stump hole, of old man Wyndham's grave. Story goes that Wyndham walks these grounds at midnight in search of his murderer, sheddin' hyacinth petals in his wake.

"Moral is, fascinating to think of what an *underling* might do to his boss if pushed hard enough," Devereaux said, his voice trailing off as he walked away. "Of Simmons to me; of you to King."

Devereaux sighed and turned facing Lance. "I've kept you too long, Mister Hawthorne. I'm sure you can find your way out. Come back in the morning prepared to deal." Devereaux stopped with a purposeful pause. "Or don't come back. Give Mr. King my regards."

Lance remembered the Wyndham story from childhood and the many nights he spent searching these very grounds for the ghost of Benevolence.

He watched Devereaux exit the room. Then Lance exited the house, Simmons nowhere to be seen. He reached into his jacket pocket, retrieved his cell phone and pecked the digits of King's office phone, forgetting the single-digit access he had programmed into the phone. Disregarding the cameras and other electronic security equipment that sat scattered about the property like aluminum cans on a roadside, he continued with the call. The likelihood of surveillance, for a moment, escaped Lance's care.

King always worked late. Lance once wondered whether King had any life beyond his work. He wondered no more. Once upon a time Lance believed Barrett to be a wholly dedicated company professional, a blue-chip executive glistening white from the incandescent glow of industry-wide respect. Barrett had now revealed his self-serving colors of money and power. Lance didn't care for the power, necessarily, but the money—the irresistibility of the *money* held Lance like metal to a magnet.

Barrett answered after the third ring.

"King here!" he growled.

The Ghosts of Benevolence

42

"BARRETT. LANCE HERE."

"Lance! Lance, my boy!" Barrett answered. "Everything okay? I suppose by now you've met with Devereaux. I bet he took to you like pigs to slop."

"Barrett, I'm fine, but this land deal of yours is tanking!"

"Tanking? What in God's name are you talking about now? What's his price? You got the twenty-five hundred per, right?"

"Barrett, Mr. Devereaux doesn't *want* twenty-five hundred per acre."

"No?" King replied. "Good, then. You managed to keep the price down."

"He wants *five grand* per acre, Barrett. One hundred and twenty-five million dollars. Says you'll *gladly* pay his price for this *cropland*. What does he mean by *that*, Barrett, by 'cropland'?" Lance pushed his curiosity. "Says you want your *canopy*, Barrett, even more than the timber itself, as if SPIG were purchasing the land for … well, for *you*. Of course, that's not true, right, Barrett? I mean, this land-purchase is a SPIG *strategy* to increase our low-cost timber assets while minimizing our competition's access to the same, right, Barrett?

"I get the impression from Mr. Devereaux that this whole deal is laden with, oh, I don't know, *malfeasance* perhaps? Certainly not, but what are you *not telling* me, man?"

"Look, Lance, the deal's *legit*," Barrett lied. "Why *wouldn't* it be?"

Lance rolled his eyes. *Why, indeed.*

"But a *hundred twenty-five million*?" Barrett asked.

"I thought you said the board had *blessed* spending that amount, Barrett."

"They have. They *have*. But, how do you think *that'd* look on the *balance sheet*? While our *board* may be stupid, our shareholders are *not*. The memory of SPIG ditching its timberland is far too fresh in the minds of most of our stockholders. Now we're going to drop a hundred and twenty-five million dollars to *replenish* those assets on the books? They'll conclude SPIG's management is *nuts*, that it doesn't know its butt from a stump in the ground! And they'd be *right*."

"Barrett, SPIG's cash position is sound, whether or not we purchase Dev's land. And the balance sheet won't change. It's just an asset conversion."

"How the balance sheet *looks* will change. They'll see the forest *and all its trees!*"

"We can put together a dog-and-pony PowerPoint show, throw all sorts of financial projections at people and show how our profits will *soar* thanks to some good ol' American foresight and vision. Think of the credit you'll get, Barrett, not that you *need* more of what you already have plenty of."

"Even if we take this off-balance-sheet, Lance, we'd at least have to *footnote* a deal of this magnitude, telling shareholders we paid five thousand per acre for five hundred dollar land. That'd raise far more questions than

The Ghosts of Benevolence

I'm prepared to address, not to mention possibly sending shareholders bailing and SPIG's share price into a tailspin. The economy's damn tenuous enough as it is! You *got* to get that old man to come down on the price, Lance. You *do* want that promotion, don't you? You *do*—"

"Barrett, calm down. I can get the price down. I can convince him to sell it for less, probably a *lot less*. One thing troubles me though. Actually more than one, but let's start with this. Devereaux has used his considerable old-boy influence to persuade the State to divert millions of gallons of river water to the acreage in question. South Georgia is in the midst of its worst drought on record, Barrett, and a rich plantation owner gets the *lion's share* of the water? How do you suppose he managed *that* trick? Whatever you have in mind for that land is going to need a *consistent* supply of water. Seems to me Devereaux is pulling the water strings down here by dangling the flatwood salamander, a *wetlands* creature, in their faces.

"Now, I wouldn't know a flatwood salamander from an insurance gecko, but I do know *this* much. No Environmental Protection Agency worth its meddling salt is going to turn down the opportunity to *obstruct* economic progress in the name of species preservation. Does the species have to actually *exist*? One would *think* so, but in this case, probably not. Government has a history of slamming the paper industry with the strictest interpretations of environmental rules, anyway, so I doubt the *confirmation* of the existence of a flatwood salamander on the land in question held much priority in the minds of officials.

"But, once the State and the EPA get wind of any timber harvesting—if you get my drift—they're going to come snooping. And you've *got* to harvest *some* of that timber *somehow*, or else even our own comatose board's going to start asking questions about the *relentless high cost* of our wood, in *spite* of all the timberland we purchased from Devereaux, in *spite* of our continuing struggles to maintain mill-site inventories of wood for chipping and chips for making paper."

Lance paused a few seconds to catch his breath and to allow Barrett to squeeze in a word or two. King said nothing, anxious to hear more of what Lance might know.

Lance continued.

"I'm not much of a betting man, Barrett, except perhaps when it comes to my *career* and a *poker game*. But I'd bet my *promotion* Devereaux's got you by the short ones. My guess is he ain't *got* a flatwood salamander, *never did*. But he *does* have lots of *wetlands* here, Barrett, on *these twenty-five thousand acres*. More than that, what he *does* have is *political pull*. If Dev *says* there are flatwood salamanders splashing around in those dry-as-dust wetlands, then, by God, they're as good as *there*.

"The abundant presence of water—*irrigation* water, Barrett—is like gold in them thar hills and *jacks up* the value of the land. Any board of directors can accept such a high valuation, right? Any board can see the *long view* of eventual raw material cost reduction, given the sheer volume and availability of that raw material, right? That is, of course, as long as that same board doesn't have to deal with an EPA that *all but restricts SPIG's access to* and *use of* their *own* land. In which case, you can kiss availability—and low-cost wood—bye-bye.

"So, what happens after the land ownership changes hands to SPIG, and the need for the *appearance of propriety* forces *you*, Barrett, to somehow *harvest* some of that EPA-protected timber? Enter the EPA.

"What happens when you *can't* produce a flatwood salamander, the species of record, when the government comes a-knocking? And they will come a-knockin', Barrett, probably sooner than later, I can guarantee you. My guess is SPIG'll *lose the water*, water so desperately needed by farmers and timber harvesters ... by you and

The Ghosts of Benevolence

Devereaux. They'll turn it back to the Chagoochee faster than Elliot Ness splintered a whiskey barrel.

"And, Barrett, if this drought *continues*—and all weather models forecast it to continue well into 2017— your *trees* will likely be infested with the pine beetle, just like *everywhere else* in South Georgia. Your vaunted investment of company capital—brown, dead, and in *ruins*. Your reputation as a corporate visionary, a legend—*ruined*. Just a matter of time, Barrett.

"By the way, you'll lose that *canopy* of yours, too. Question of the day, Barrett; why such an interest in a *canopy*? Got that term from Devereaux."

Barrett's silence was conspicuous, telling, as stiff as ice.

"Oh, and *here's* something you'll *really* like! Almost got *killed* this morning, Barrett. Yes, sir, there I was at Global, delivering that package and picking up that box for return to you, when the next thing I know I'm being ushered into the back of the store. Two men came in, Barrett, and decided *they* wanted that pretty FedEx package I'd given Ruben and the box Ruben had given me to deliver to you. Long story short, Ruben bought the proverbial farm, unfortunately. Your two goons are *still out there*, Barrett. But *I* have the FedEx package, and you know what I *found* inside it? Well, why waste words; you already *know*! Got the box, too, Barrett. *Funny* the stuff they can use to build a computer these days. Why, if I didn't know better, I'd swear the computer was filled with some sort of confectionary sugar. Works better than circuits and silicon, so I assume.

"We're not talking scarce raw materials or corporate assets or promotions or balance sheets or even shareholder value here, are we Barrett? That's window dressing for the *real* game. No, Barrett, we're talking about money and orders of magnitude. The kind of money that causes men to salivate like starving dogs at a cookout. The kind of money, Barrett, that pushes a man beyond the brink of decency and sanity and clarity of thought. The FedEx money is *my* down payment, thank you very much."

Silence still.

"Don't you want to get a word in edgewise, Barrett? This is probably not one of your best cigar moments. I've got a ... how shall I say this ... an *ace* up my sleeve. There goes that darned *card analogy* again. Gets a bit clichéd, doesn't it?

"Use me to our mutual advantage, Barrett. I'll run the paperwork by Devereaux, accept his counteroffer, get his signature and document all the reasons the real estate market supports Devereaux's asking price, all the reasons owning timberland, in lieu of leasing it, makes better sense nowadays. I'll even make ours a convincing argument, financially speaking.

"In other words, Barrett, I'll make you *look good*, a task, might I add, that's *damn worth* my cut. The deal will have all the earmarks of a legitimate transaction. The board will have its documentation needed to satisfy their idle curiosity, maybe even survive an audit or two. I'll even back off approaching the EPA.

"I don't need you to tell me what you're *really* going to use this land for, Barrett. I've got a good idea, but enough said about that. I don't want to know who's involved, though I *do* know Carl's in it up to his eyebrows. I just want *my* slice of this *outstanding pie* you've baked, and I'll forever be out of your hair. In fact, the *less* I know, the better. Why don't you give that promotion to ... Carl? Nah, better keep him where he'll do you the most good and cover the most sins."

"What do you *want*, Hawthorne?" Barrett demanded.

"Didn't I just *explain* that to you, Barrett? And the industry worships *you*? Okay, here's the deal. I'll get for the company—for *you*—that land for three thousand per acre. Tell the board you expect to spend only one hundred

The Ghosts of Benevolence

million dollars of the hundred twenty-five they've already authorized, or *four thousand* per acre. I'm guessing you've already primed their pump for five thousand per acre, right? Devereaux insists he wants the five grand per acre, and I'm guessing you and he have had … 'conversations' … on the matter of setting the price—a price I'm betting the board has been made aware of."

"Cut the *guesses*, and just *spill* it!" King shouted.

"So, the board approves the hundred million, thinking they've saved the company twenty-five million. Spend a *hundred*, save *twenty-five*. *Now* I'm beginning to see just how easy management is. Lesson learned, Barrett.

"Better still, everybody sleeps well. *You* come out smelling like a *rose*, Barrett. You saved the company a *whopping* twenty-five million dollars. *Congratulations!*

"You then wire Devereaux the hundred million. Here's where it gets good, Barrett. I want twenty-five million of that wire. The remaining seventy- five translates into three thousand dollars per acre. See how *tidy* that is, Barrett?

"You're *insane*, man!" Barrett screamed.

"No more than you, my friend."

"Devereaux will *never* agree to three thousand dollars per acre, and even if he did, what makes you so smug in believing you can take twenty-five *cents*, never mind twenty-five million dollars?"

"Oh, I think he *will* agree, Barrett. Look, you're the one who 'insisted' I get Devereaux to come down on his asking price. While I didn't *exactly* do that, why not let the *company* share *some* of the good fortune while we're at it? Unless it's just selfish *greed* you're after here, Barrett. Nah, couldn't be that.

"Besides, there's a little … *incident*, if you will … from Devereaux's sordid past that's about to become, shall we say, *problematic* for Mr. Earl Bentley Devereaux the Third. I think he'll come around to seeing this deal my way and will only be *too glad* to sell the land for three grand per acre. Hell, if I were a betting man, I'd bet I could convince him to *give* me the land, for *nothing*. Either he *bites*, or I *will* bury him."

"He'll bury *you*, you *stupid*—He'll *kill* you, man, unless I beat him to it! You have *no idea* what you've gotten yourself into, you little freakin'—He'll blow your ass away and use your bones in his fertilizer."

"He won't have the *chance*, Barrett. And neither will you. I've got *every* angle worked out."

"*Every* angle, do you? He has *angles* for which there are no theorems, no proofs, no geometry. How do you intend to pull off this scheme of yours?"

"The twenty-five million, Barrett ... it's going to come from *you*."

"*Me!* Now I *know* you're insane. How do you suppose *I'll* give you twenty-five million dollars? For a brief minute, Lance, you had me worried, but *now*—"

"Look, I know about your *slush fund*, Barrett. The little stash of cash you've been skimming from the company for the past several years. Does First Federal Credit Union, upstate New York, strike a chord? It took some time to figure it all out, but figure it out I did. I spent many an hour after work and very early each morning combing the numerous transactions made with the likes of one Global Technical Solutions. Lord knows what other vendors are involved. And you thought I was wholly devoted to the *company*, didn't you, all those before-and-after-hours of sacrifice spent at my desk. I guess in a way, I was. Turns out, you were bleeding the company slowly, Barrett ... but surely.

"True, ours is a company whose understanding and appreciation of its employees and their work—not to mention the basics of internal controls—could fit on a pinhead, with room to spare. You zoned in on SPIG's administrative weaknesses quite well, Barrett, like a

The Ghosts of Benevolence

buzzard circling road kill. You managed to gain the audience—and the confidence—of corporate senior management and our esteemed Directors. My hat's off to you for that feat alone. With management's and the Board's attention, you next acquired their blessing and unquestioning authority to execute 'agreements' with information systems companies. These companies supplied hardware upgrades, replacements, technical services, most all of it fictitious. Except for the income stream it generated, most it flowing to you. Noble gesture, Barrett, very noble indeed, making us think you were taking the company into the twenty-first century. Your care for your fellow worker is *touching*.

"It's no mystery that many of our employees are still crawling along with ten-year-old boxes. I know *I* certainly never got *my* replacement PC you promised those many moons ago. A few key managers and a couple of squeaky whiners got their upgrades, of course, just enough to keep the boat sailing smoothly, right Barrett?

"Sad, really, in a way. Some of your work was, in a word, *sloppy*, Barrett. Plain sloppy. One might characterize it as *amateurish*. But you're no *amateur*, Barrett, no, not *you*. I think you simply were blinded by the glow of your own ego. As a measure of balance, you have remarkably low opinions of the abilities and talents of your people.

"To wit—I just *love* that phrase, 'to wit'! Sounds so much like 'twit'. Anyway, I noticed during some unrelated documentation reviews—you know, the sort we do in preparation for the *outside auditors*?—different ship-to addresses on Global Tech invoices for hardware purchases. Naturally that aroused my curiosity. So, being the hound I am, I tracked down a few of those addresses, Barrett. I'm a *nosy* little prick, aren't I? Call it an undying fetish to … *audit*.

Mark Randolph Watters

"Speaking of which, since when did Carl's *garage* become one of our receiving warehouses? You shouldn't have left those invoices so *available* for review, Barrett, especially after *you* had processed them for payment. Sloppy, I tell you. Shame, shame. A smart man like you should have made arrangements with the vendors to ship the hardware to your bogus addresses but indicate *our mill's ship-to* on the invoices. That, and the total absence of physical receiving reports, is going to cost you *years* of unfettered pilfering, Barrett, pilfering which our inept audit department would have overlooked indefinitely. You know what else, Barrett? No *purchase orders*! What *were* you thinking? You of all people should know that interrupted, incomplete paper trails, even the digital sort, raise flags. *Very* sloppy, Barrett.

"Anyway, after an extensive reconciliation of new hardware onsite versus hardware purchased in just the past three years, all with your signature of approval, I determined that you had purchased, with the company's funds, over *thirty million dollars* of computer hardware and software, only a tenth of which exists on our *books*—but not onsite. But the thirty-plus million? Now *that* exists, tucked away under your quaint mattresses.

"I had suspected for quite some time that our board had become lax in its demand for accountability of expenditures of capital funds. I hadn't been asked for an analysis of return on investment for *any* capital project for over a *year*, Barrett. I was beginning to feel *unwanted*.

"But, even after having now revealed my knowledge of this to you, I say *screw* the company! If they choose to be *comatose*, why should *we* care? So, here's the deal, Barrett. I want the twenty-five million dollars, all hundreds, unmarked and untraceable, sealed in a black Hefty yard bag—or yard *bags*—waiting in my office day after tomorrow."

"What are you—"

The Ghosts of Benevolence

"*Ha!* Just kidding. *Too* amateurish. Do this instead. I'll get my offshore account number to you in a couple of days—never mind how—and you can *wire* the money to me, just like you and Dev wire money to each other's accounts. I just *love* this sort of intrigue, don't you? Makes me feel like I'm in a Tom Cruise movie.

"Tell the staff I've resigned in pursuit of a better opportunity. Oh, and Barrett, *forget* my new computer. I'll drop a few grand for a new one later.

"If it makes you feel any better, make arrangements with Devereaux to forward you the money to make up for what you're going to pay me from your *stash*; that is, if you have the nerve to *make* such a demand of Devereaux. Or, take it out of the hundred million up front, before you wire Dev his payment for the land. But, then, Devereaux's going to want to know why he's being *shorted* twenty-five million dollars. Yes, that *is* a problem, I must admit. I'm confident you'll figure it out, Barrett.

"If you have problems following through, just know that I have copies of everything, Barrett. *Everything.* Do I have to spell this part out for you, not that I haven't already?

"By the way, I'm guessing that you made the Board aware I was sent on this 'official' business trip to execute the contract for the land, to test my worthiness for a promotion. And, what exactly *is* VP of Finance and Corporate Analysis, anyway? Seems to me I've already fulfilled the 'Corporate Analysis' part and am crossing the 't's on the Finance part. Guess I was qualified for the job after all. Oh, well. Not really an issue, now, is it?

"Whew! I'm quite a talker, but this is getting to be fun! You and Devereaux had *no* intention of my coming home alive, did you, Barrett? I'm guessing I was an *intended target* of the Global robbery, along with Ruben, but now Devereaux is going to have to do that little piece of the dirty work himself. Sounds like Dev not only wanted

Global's cut of your drug sales, he also wanted his cocaine shipment back."

"*Heroin*, you idiot!"

"That's *right*! Heroin. Thanks for the clarification. Maybe Devereaux wants *you* out of the picture, too, Barrett."

Stunned by the extent of detail in Lance's revelation, Barrett asked, "What do you *have* on Devereaux? What about his past is so … *problematic* for him?"

"I know it was a long time ago, but do you recall the hubbub with the 1965 church bombing down here, the one that killed a several African-Americans?"

"I recall a church exploding, if that's what you mean. So what?"

"I happen to know conclusively, *conclusively,* Barrett, that Devereaux was one of the principals."

"Principal *what*? They blamed that explosion on a *gas leak*! That church had a propane tank sitting next to it."

"The case went cold, Barrett, but rest assured, it *wasn't* a gas leak. I've got my hands on some pieces of evidence that'll just about get his ass tarred, feathered, and fried. It will at least re-open the investigation, something I don't think you two want to happen. I've got the *hook* in this fish, Barrett, and I intend to *reel it in*." Lance tapped his jacket pocket.

"Evidence? What sort of *evidence*?"

"That's all you need to know, Barrett. Fact is, I've told you too much. But know this. If you want that land without the Board knowing *your* game, you're going to have to play *my* game. And I don't think you want to call my bluff on this. I got my poker face on, Barrett. See you day after tomorrow. Oh, I wouldn't mention our little discussion to anyone if I were you."

Lance pressed the 'end' button on his cell phone and released all the air from his lungs. He had set the wheels churning.

The Ghosts of Benevolence

Frantic, Barrett King punched the buttons on his cell phone. He called Carl.

Mark Randolph Watters

43

JESSICA LAY ON HER side, as her doctor had advised, enduring a semi-conscious sleep. Coupled with Lance's absence, nights morphed into black, unmovable masses of infinity. Jessica punched four feather-stuffed pillows supporting her back and head. She may as well have been punching boulders.

Awake again, she sighed and lifted her left hand, turning with the mindless staccato of a wall clock the pages of Maternity Today. She had not heard from Lance since his arrival at the Lights Out Inn on Wednesday.

Her anxiety mounted.

The house emitted a morgue-like quietness, an occasional groan or pop coming from somewhere deep within the settling of the house.

Just as Jessica resumed her doze, the phone rang, yanking her attention from its abyss. The abrupt breach of silence and reflexive jerking of her arms sent the magazine leaping from her hand. Gerri kicked in response.

Maybe it's Lance, she hoped, disorientation guiding her hand toward the phone.

10:22 p.m.

"Hello? *Lance?*"

Mark Randolph Watters

"It's me, babe."

"Thank *God*! Lance, where have you *been*? I expected your call this morning. Are you *okay*? I've had a *bad feeling* about this whole trip all day long! I think you—"

"Jess, *Jess!* Hold on. Calm down and *listen*. You've *got* to listen to me. Never mind how I am; just *listen*!"

Jessica swallowed, wiping away the swell of tears.

"Okay."

"Jess, we—you, me, and the girls—are about to hit the biggest of the big time!"

"Biggest—?"

"*Shut up!* Just *listen*!"

Jessica's semi-consciousness evaporated like fog in the desert. "Don't you *tell me* to shut up, Lance Hawthorne!"

"Jessica, if you'd just—"

"I am *not* your *yard dog*, and I will *not* be spoken to in such manner, not by *you*, not by *anyone*! Are we *clear*?"

"I'm—I'm sorry, Jess, I didn't *mean*—I'm sorry," Lance repeated, the magic words lackluster to Jessica's ears. He swallowed and took a breath. "Let me start again. I'm about to *slam the door* on this land deal with Devereaux, probably tomorrow morning. But there are some ... some *things* you've *got to know*. You might want to sit down."

"Lance, I'm *lying* down, on the *bed*. Don't make me *sit*."

"Remember the photo I took with me, the one you *insisted* I leave at home for this trip? Well, that forty-six-year-old photo, my dear bride, is about to be redeemed. Jackson Willoughby, eat your heart out!"

"Who's *Jackson Willoughby*, and what do you mean 'redeemed'?

"Brace yourself, babe. That *photo*, that little faded square of *Polaroid serendipity* you said was no more than a

The Ghosts of Benevolence

death wish waiting to happen ... well, my sweet ... are you sitting down?"

"Lance, I'm *pregnant*, remember? And it's practically the middle of another *endless* night. I'm *lying* down, so get to the point."

"Oh, right. Well, that photo, it's worth a cool *twenty ... five ... million ... dollars*!" Lance paused for the expected avalanche of joy.

"Say that again. Did you say twenty-five ... *million* ... dollars, Lance? Have you and that photo, along with a few drinks, won some other-dimensional contest, like perhaps 'What's Your Life Worth?'"

"You might say that, wife of mine!"

"I just *did*! Lance, what's going on here? Are you *drunk*? When are you coming *home*?"

"Soon, babe, *soon*. Meanwhile, it ain't going to be *easy* money. Twenty-five million never *is*. Call it one of my newly acquired ... how did you put it ... Yankee ways. Devereaux doesn't know yet what's about to *hit* him. But when he finds out, all kinds of you-know-what's going to hit the fan and *scatter* to the four winds."

"Lance, don't tell me Devereaux knows about that damned photo!"

"Not yet, he doesn't. That's the one sour note in this sweet, twenty-five million dollar song, but I'll *deal* with it. I know what I'm *doing*, Jess. Now, there's *another* copy of that photo, Jess ... no, *two* copies. One's a JPEG stored in the computer in the 'Bucket List' folder. The file name is 'Black Death'—appropriate, huh? The other copy I printed and laminated last March. It's in our safe deposit box. Those copies, Jess, are our *insurance policies* against Devereaux ... and Barrett King."

"*Barrett*?"

"Indeed Barrett. I learned today that Barrett is driving the acquisition of Devereaux's land, and he's using certain weak-minded members of SPIG's trusting senior management to steamroll—and bankroll—the deal. It's a long story, Jess, a *very* long story, but Barrett has the board *wrapped* around his pious finger. Always has.

"Barrett is embezzling company funds, trafficking heroin, and is in bed with Devereaux, has been for years."

"How did you find out—"

"Never *mind* that, Jess! Please, no questions. I've got evidence, lots of it. Unless he cooperates, he and his goons *will* go down. I haven't told him everything I have, but he knows very well the jig is up. Believe me, he *knows*! I have evidence in the trunk of the car, too, but I won't have the time to drive home and put it in a safe place; I'll have to deal with it here for now.

"I think King's smart enough to know he's *got* to meet my demands. He'll huff and puff, but … he'll go along," Lance said in an effort to reassure Jessica. Instead, skepticism laced each word as his confidence eroded.

"Lance? *Lance!* Do you *hear* yourself? What's come *over* you? If I could reach through this phone and *slap* some sense into you, I *would*. Do you realize for a minute the *danger* you've put me in—and *Ginibeth* and *Jerri*? God, Lance, they'll *kill* us! What were you *thinking*? This isn't a *Disney ride*, Lance. This is *real*! They *will* come and … kill *us*! You, too! You've got—"

"Jess, Jess, *Jess*! Yes … there *are* risks, I *admit*. But we're talking twenty-five *freakin'* million dollars here. Don't you *understand*? That's more than enough to do whatever the *hell* we want to do for the rest of our *miserable*—" Lance stopped to collect his composure. "For the rest of our lives," he said softly. "We can *buy* new identities, Jess. We'll be long gone before *anybody's* able to put the pieces together. They'll be too busy sorting out *Barrett's* shenanigans to worry about *me*. And … if I leave 'em a little *Devereaux bone* to chew on … well, they just might forget all about me."

The Ghosts of Benevolence

"Lance, you don't have *any* of that money yet! You're talking like it's *in the bank*, and all we have to do is withdraw it. What makes you think these people are going to just lie down and hand you twenty million dollars?"

"Twenty-*five* million dollars," Lance said.

"*Whatever!* This is money they consider *theirs*, no matter *how* ill-gotten, and you're going to take it from right under their *noses*, using a faded, forty-seven-year-old Polaroid?"

"Don't forget the inimitable Lance Hawthorne charm, charisma, and powers of persuasion."

"Oh, yeah, of course. How could I forget *that?*" Jessica replied. "Besides, it's not *your* money to take, Lance, or have you forgotten *basic* right from wrong? No matter how *screwed* you perceive yourself to be by SPIG, you *can't* justify this. *You're* no better than a *petty thief* ... times twenty-five million! This isn't the swiping of another kid's *Twinkie*, Lance! How do you know Devereaux won't *shoot you on the spot* tomorrow, just as you present that photo, or take you out to some remote dirt-road site, shoot you and leave you for the vultures and ants?

"Unless, of course, King's people get you *first*! Or get *us* first!" Jessica shouted, realizing the imminence of the danger. "Lance, I've got to get Gini out of here! Barrett *does know* where we live, you know. *Now! You've* got to get out of *there*! You've—"

Lance paced the front lawn, phone lowered to his side, for the moment tuning out Jessica's frantic, sensible concerns. He noticed, but paid little attention to, the rhythmic flicker of a red light adjacent to one of the magnolia trees veiled by the black of a moonless night.

"Jessica, *wait*, listen to me! These people, Devereaux and King, are *not* going to risk losing their empires, or *future* earnings, for a paltry twenty-five million. This is *chump* change to these people."

Mark Randolph Watters

"If twenty-five million dollars is *chump* change to them, Lance, *God knows* how deep and organized their operations really are."

"I'm just a *gnat* in their ear. They'll *pay* it. Trust me, I *know* these people, and I know what I'm doing. Look, I've got to go, but if it'll make you feel better—"

"Make me feel *better*! Ain't *nothin'* you can say to me now, Lance, that's going to make me *feel better*!"

"—take Ginibeth and go somewhere, *anywhere*."

"Any *suggestions*, Einstein?"

"A *hotel* maybe. I don't know, but *lay low* for a few days."

"If we *live*, we'll be laying low for the rest of our lives."

"Take your cell phone. I'll be in touch. Call me if you suspect *anything*. Wish me luck. Twenty-five *million*, babe. Don't forget that. I love you."

"*Love* me? Lance? *Lance!*"

Jessica dropped the phone and rushed frantically into Ginibeth's room.

Lance put his cell phone in his pocket, gave quick glances left and right, and trotted to the Mercedes. He started the car and pulled away, again noticing the flashing dots of red lights, this time scattered across the property. He tried focusing on the location but could see nothing, then remembered the ubiquitous cameras. Shrugging, he accelerated, preoccupied with tomorrow's presentation, tomorrow's ultimatum.

The Ghosts of Benevolence

44

SOON, THE CLAUSTROPHOBIA OF darkness snatched Lance's attention. A night void of sound and civilization beyond the borders of the Kingdom, except for the occasional flicker of light from a far-off kitchen or the bedroom of a distant farmhouse, gave stark contrast to the boiling cacophony of thoughts churning in Lance's brain.

Lance wondered about the lives of these rural folks, the hardships of living from crop to withering crop; the uncertainties that haunted these have-nots; the unfairness of random events; the nightmares of dreams unfulfilled; the search for meaning in a wilderness of apathy; the hopelessness of regression; the abject disparity between Devereaux's kingdom, his unmitigated lavishness, and the peasants who surrounded it.

Lance believed his endeavor noble, that despite the illegality of his deeds and the immorality of the means, relieving Devereaux and King of millions of dollars had become, in Lance's rationalization, a symbolic gesture, heroic even, made on behalf of the poor of Sutter County. That none of the residents might benefit directly from the booty was beside the broader point.

Mark Randolph Watters

But the rationale was short-lived. Lance felt suddenly awash in midnight loneliness. He found a pullover and parked. He got out of the car and remembered the hand-rolled cigar given him by Devereaux. Twirling it in his fingers and giving it a hearty sniff, Lance lit the cigar. Other than burnt toast, he hadn't smoked anything in a dozen years, maybe more, until today. The 'imported' Cuban tobacco coursed through his mouth and lungs as if welcoming him home. Lance tilted his head upward, releasing the smoke, and noticed the velvety blur of the spine of the Milky Way arced across the silence of infinity, like a line separating reason from insanity.

Or, perhaps, a line in the sand.

He thought of Gwen Summers. The touch of her hands and the remnant of the scent of her hair gripped Lance, like the power of Aphrodite. Forgetting the Milky Way, Lance recalled her invitation and retrieved the paper on which Gwen had written her phone number.

He unfolded the paper and stared at the number. Glancing at his watch, he determined it early enough still to make one short call. *After all, she's home alone, right?*

He punched the number.

"Hello?" Gwen answered with the breath of a whisper.

"Gwen? Gwen, it's—"

"Lance!" Gwen finished, as if expecting his call.

"Did I wake you? I'm sorry. I'll—"

"It's *okay*, Lance, really, it *is*. I went to bed early tonight, well, earlier than usual. How are *you*?"

"Fine, Gwen. I just thought … we might chat awhile; that is, if you feel … if you *want* to."

"If I *want* to? You *know* I want to, Lance. What I *feel* like doing … well, I *can't do* right now 'cause … you're not *here*," Gwen whispered. Lance felt the seduction dripping, like the bite of an overripe peach.

"Yeah, I'd … like a little of that, too, Gwen."

"A little of *what*, Lance?" she teased.

The Ghosts of Benevolence

"A little of … what I mean is—"

"How'd you like to come on over and … *inspect* my new furniture. Got it today. I need a man's opinion, and you *know* I'm going to want you to *move* it around. Dining room suite; some patio chairs; sofa and … love seat. But I think this *bed,* darn it all, is a little too … well, '*stiff*' best describes it, I think. You know how mattresses are. And I'm going to need some *help* … working out the lumps."

Lance cleared his throat, took a long puff, and steered the conversation away from his carnal instincts.

"Gwen, I need … I *really* ought to get some sleep, but I wanted to say 'hello' to you once more. I'm … heading home tomorrow, but it was *great* … seeing you this afternoon."

"Marriage can be *such* an … *inhibitive* thing," Gwen lamented. "But it doesn't *have* to be, Lance. Take the ring off. Turn over the pictures. You'll never feel the guilt. I'll make *sure* of that. We're *adults*, Lance. We can handle this."

Lance paused under the weight of temptation.

"Gwen … you're wrong. I'd … I *would* feel the guilt," Lance replied. "And, it *would* be more than I could handle."

Silence.

Lance heard only the hooting of a distant owl.

"Hello? Gwen?"

Maybe the call's been dropped.

Lance tapped the digits of her number, feeling compelled to hear her voice one last time.

Beep, beep, beep. *"The number you have reached is no longer in service …"*

"No longer in service? Strange." Lance stared at his phone. An owl hooted. "Just as well."

Lance released the sigh of relief, of temptation half-conquered. He dropped his cigar and smashed it with the toe of his shoe, relieved he had not relented.

Mark Randolph Watters

45

THE SUN, RED AND fog-blurred, arose over the rolling fields of Devereaux's plantation. Lance pulled to a stop in front of the mansion. Taking a deep breath, he swept a comb across his hair, adjusted his paisley suspenders and stepped toward the front door. Lance hated suspenders, from the day Sara made them to hold up his beltless Sunday school pants, to the Christmas that Jess gave him *three* pairs. He wore them today in remembrance of Jessica. Or was it his attempt to turn his obsession with Gwen into a loathing?

He knocked, once more straightened the suspenders, and checked his shoes for blades of grass. Lance fidgeted and tugged on his shirt collar, sweat welling up on his forehead. He awaited Devereaux.

This is it. This is the day, finally, that I've waited for all these decades. Today, I get paid!

The double door squeaked open.

"Good mornin', Mr. Hawthorne," Devereaux greeted. "I trust you received a night's worth of *satisfactory* sleep?"

"Indeed I did, Mr. Devereaux. Or, is it still ... Earl? No matter, really. I think you'll find I'm ready to do business."

Mark Randolph Watters

"Good, good! Have you taken your breakfast?"

"No, as a matter of fact, I haven't, but—"

"Come in, *come in*," Devereaux urged as he stepped aside to allow Lance passage. "Man's got to *eat!* I reckon you'll appreciate takin' more of Simmons's fine South Georgia cookin'."

Devereaux directed Lance to a table sprawled with China dinnerware, filled with mixtures of scrambled eggs and pigs brains; plates of salt-cured bacon, fried to the perfect crispness; steaming biscuits; honey and mayhaw jelly; strawberries jubilee; carafes of hazelnut coffee and pitchers of hand-squeezed orange juice. The aromas alone would have directed Lance well enough.

"Pour yourself some coffee, my boy. Hell, pour yourself some *champagne,* if you've a mind to."

Lance returned the courtesy of a smile as the two men made their way to the buffet. The room's octagonal walls supported a fourteen-foot ceiling. A 24-prong brass-and-crystal chandelier, inserts filled with lighted candles, hung over a Shaker table covered with an ivory-white tablecloth and a centerpiece blend of African Sunset Phlox and wild blue indigo.

Floor-to-ceiling windows, scarlet and ivory satin curtains open, covered five sides of the octagon, providing a panoramic view of the gardens and fields. Lance watched the distant harvesters crawling in opposite directions, like bugs, the machines' sedative hums and clouds of translucent dust lifting in their wakes. Workers scurried about the grounds on golf carts. The kingdom's day was well underway.

"Help yourself, now," encouraged Devereaux.

Lance filled his plate with generous portions of each offering. He sprinkled his coffee with cream and sugar and spread freshly churned butter and mayhaw jelly across steaming biscuits. This was the sort of breakfast he remembered his mama making. The aromas of the coffee

The Ghosts of Benevolence

and bacon blended in the air like soul mates, offering the comfort of a threadbare teddy bear. The moist scrambled eggs and brains were a delicacy unknown to Jessica and untried by Lance since boyhood. Closing his eyes to preclude the intrusion of any distraction and to garner the full effect of this work of culinary art, he sipped first the coffee.

Devereaux asked dryly, "So ... what'd you decide? King accept my askin' price, or what, because I *know* you talked to him?"

Lance swallowed the scalding liquid and returned the cup to its saucer.

"Yes sir, I did, and no sir, he did not."

Devereaux poured coffee into his saucer, raised it to his lips and slurped, never taking his steely steam-veiled eyes off Lance.

"A-a-ah-h-h!" Devereaux blurted with a shake of his head, a reaction to the shock of the coffee's heat. "*Damn*, that's good! Now, sir, what do you *mean*? He don't want the land after all?"

"Oh, no, sir, he wants the land all right, and he'll buy it. In fact, he's willing to pay you four thousand per acre. That's a nice round sum of one hundred million certified, untraceable U.S Federal Reserve notes. What's more—"

"What that *is*, sir, is *negotiation* and an *unacceptable* price reduction of twenty percent," Devereaux interrupted. "My *original* offer just went *up* twenty percent, to *six thousand* per acre. Your *insistence* on negotiating has cost you a ... *nice round sum* ... of twenty-five million dollars, Mr. Hawthorne."

"No, Mister Devereaux. I think you'll accept my ... *our* terms," Lance replied, lifting the cup to his lips. "Needs more sugar. Pass the sugar, please? Oh, Sim-m-mons ..."

Devereaux, unaccustomed to insolence from any quarter, and *never* in the midst of doling out bountiful hospitality, reached under the table and returned a nine millimeter Glock 26. Devereaux pointed the handgun squarely at Lance's forehead. Lance recoiled.

"Sir, I have in this handgun—I like to call her Flossy— *one* hollow point bullet with *your* name on it. I'll give you *one minute*, first to *apologize* and then to *explain* yourself. Flossy's been achin' to serve up some of her acclaimed Southern fried lead."

Shaken by the surprise of facing the business end of a dark barrel, Lance quickly regained composure.

"Barrett's talked to you, hasn't he, Mr. Devereaux?" Lance asked, taking another sip of coffee. "It's simple, really, and if you'll put the gun down, I'll explain it all to your satisfaction."

"I'll give you *three minutes*," Devereaux snarled, "not a *second* more."

"Won't need *that* long, but thank you for your patience."

"Surly you must know, Mister Hawthorne, the specifics of this deal are *already consummated.* Two minutes, fifty seconds. Your presence here is merely a dotting of the 'I's and a crossing of the 'T's, as it were, to make the record of the transaction above-board in the eyes of an anachronistic board of directors who believe more in the honor of eye-to-eye *handshakes* rather than the legalities of fine print."

"No surprise, Mr. Devereaux," Lance said, bringing his napkin to his lips. "I suspected as much."

"Then, suspect *this*. King's *already* got the legal paper in his hands; we don't *need* you anymore, Mister Hawthorne. Remember your little *cell phone call* you made last night to Barrett?"

Lance's attention piqued. He had *not* suspected this. Then he recalled noticing the flashing red dots of light scattered about the night-darkened property.

The Ghosts of Benevolence

"Bet you were surprised to find such a *clear signal* all the way out here in no man's land, no cell tower in sight. That phone call is all the record the board needs to prove you were down here finalizing the deal with me. A call on *your* cell phone, from Benevolence, to the office of Barrett King."

Lance cleared his throat and fingered the handle of his cup. "Refill?" he asked.

"Help yourself, while you can." Devereaux kept the pistol aimed at Lance. "You have two minutes."

"What … what would you say if I asked you to remember a *certain July night* in the summer of 1965? How silly of me—of *course,* you remember!   The church service? The explosion? And what an *explosion* it was! Sure got *my* attention. And thus you surely must also recall the flash of light in the bushes along Pumpkin creek."

"You're going to have to give me more information than *that*, Mr. Hawthorne," Devereaux chuckled. "1965 was a long time ago, and seeing as there were *thousands* of lightning bugs along Pumpkin Creek on any given summer evenin', well … any *particular* flash of light you got in mind? Seems I *do* recall a church blowin' up, now that you mention it. Tragic thing, it was, that propane gas leak. Besides, what's *that* got to do with *this*?"

Lance chuckled, setting his coffee cup on a window sill. "Don't worry," Lance said, seeing Devereaux's furrowed brow. "This is why you have Simmons, right? This, and Southern cooking.

"Okay, how about this," Lance continued. "Three men, a dark cotton field along Pumpkin Creek, and thirteen dead black people."

Devereaux closed his eyes and pretended to sort through forty-six years of memory.

"You must be talkin' about—what was the name— Thankful Baptist Church. Barrett told me y'all discussed it."

"Thankful*ness*, and that I am, sir, and that we did."

"Only *thirteen*? I could have *sworn* there were at least a couple dozen. What about it?"

"I was *there*, Mr. Devereaux. And darned if *you* weren't, too."

Devereaux fingered the trigger of the Glock, then released the safety.

"I was nowhere *near* that church that night." Devereaux's words drawled from his mouth with the deliberation of cold motor oil. "I resent your accusation, sir. I ought to put this bullet in your brain right this minute. You can't prove one damn thing, Hawthorne."

"Can't I? You'd be surprised what a ten-year-old keeps … and remembers. A flash in the woods following the bombing? I think you remember. The, chasing a couple of boys down the Pumpkin Creek bank through all those thorns and honeysuckles and blackberry bushes, dusk casting our forms as silhouettes?"

Devereaux squinted as if staring at the midday sun.

"Me and a friend of mine just happened to be there that night, Mr. Devereaux. We'd been hunting arrowheads along Pumpkin Creek all afternoon and were making our way home. Found some *doozies*, too, I might add, all of them from *your* fields, by the way. I appreciate that! Still have them, too, but I don't reckon I'll be giving them back. You might be pleased to learn there was this one particular point, a *Clovis,* I do believe, about five inches long, if memory serves, *perfectly* chipped, a real beauty, fluted perfectly on both sides halfway to the tip, made from pink sugar quartz. You had some valuable artifacts in those fields of yours; *still do*, I'm sure. But you don't *really* want to hear about *that* now, do you? Maybe another time?" Lance said, toying with Devereaux.

"Anyway, we heard all the *commotion* in Kelsey's Field above the creek." Lance paused to study Devereaux's expression, mounting dread sweeping across his creviced

The Ghosts of Benevolence

face like the torrents of a thunderstorm. "I'll cut to the chase, Mr. Devereaux. We saw what you and your boys did to that church, saw every last evil bit of it. We not only *saw* it, but—and you're gonna *love* this—we *photographed* it. Yep. Took your ever-lovin' *mug*! Sometimes, Mr. Devereaux, you just have to *laugh* at the twists life takes. I suppose this is one of those twists. Ain't it a hoot you had *witnesses*, and in the middle of freakin' *nowhere*! When you think about it, it *is* pretty funny, ironic even. I mean, who'd a-*thunk* it? Two ten-year-olds in Kelsey's Field past dark, toting a new-fangled *Polaroid*, of all things, and there y'all are.

"I remember how Jackson—you remember the Willoughby boy, don't you—anyway, Jackson was as poor as ditch weeds; his family couldn't afford *anything*, much less a *Polaroid camera*. *None* of us could! What Jackson lacked in monetary wealth, he more than made up for in athletic skills. He could *flat throw* a knuckleball, sure enough, whenever he could *borrow* a ball to throw, that is. Ah, but in stepped *fate*.

"That camera just so happened to be *first prize* at the *hog-calling contest* at the Sutter County fair. First prizes in prior years had never been more valuable than maybe a bushel of squash of a couple of Miss Whitney's apple pies. But that year, the prize was a spankin' new Polaroid camera. Everybody wanted it, Jackson more than anybody.

"Jackson always could call a pig better than most *pigs* could call a pig. And he really wanted that camera. He didn't want squash or pies; he had those most everyday anyway. But a *camera* …

"Used to call him 'pig boy'. Not that he was *fat*, you understand. He was as skinny as a blade of grass. He *just knew* how to talk to pigs; a gift, I reckon.

"Ain't it *funny*, Mister Devereaux, how the most insignificant, *teeniest, tiniest, trivialest* little things can come back to *haunt* a person, and after all these years? If there had been no county fair, then there'd been no pig-calling contest; if no contest, then no prize; no prize, no camera; no camera, no Jackson bringing it along to photograph artifacts; no Jackson ... well, you get my point.

"I warned him not to do it, that if he *did* do it, we'd be *toast*. Almost *were*, too. There you three men stood, including you, all in camouflage, you on the back of a horse, drinking and laughing and looking *directly* at us; only you didn't *know* you were looking at us, because we were obscured by the little dots of light dancing in your eyes from the flash of that Polaroid. I shudder *still* to think how *close* your machete came to cutting me in half."

Lance reached into his jacket pocket. Devereaux extended his arm, and the Glock, into Lance's face.

"Hold on, now! I'm not armed. Color's faded a bit, but man, oh man, your mugs in that picture are as *clear* today as the crystal in your curios. All of you are holding flaming torches and beer bottles, laughing, and carrying on like it was New Year's Eve. You can even see the burning aftermath in the background, like it was some macabre celebratory bonfire. Take a look."

Lance handed the photo to Devereaux, who analyzed it for several minutes.

"That ain't no *church burning* in the background!" Devereaux shouted. "Could be *anything*; clearing out brush for plowin'; *anything*."

"Only it isn't just *anything*, Earl. Take a closer look at the upper-right corner of the photo. If I'm not mistaken— and I'm not—that's *your deer stand*, your big D painted on its sideboards, the *only stand* you owned and the one you *trumpeted* to the Benevolence Connoisseur that you would be mounting in Tucker's Field opposite Thankfulness Baptist Church. That Connoisseur sure gave you lots of attention. And I quote, 'Ain't never seen so many deer in one field.' I got the article. Want to read it?

The Ghosts of Benevolence

"There's more, as if this weren't enough. See that yellow, the gleam right … there?" Lance asked, pointing to Devereaux's smiling mouth in the photo. "I do believe that yellow matches the same side of your mouth today, your three gold-capped teeth? Yes, sir, I am a *firm* believer in *that* match.

"And you might as well know. I know who your *two friends* were, too. Enter fate again; they're *still alive*, Earl, like *you*, and I just bet *one of them* will be *more* than willing to cut a deal for immunity. So, all in all, I'd say that's *some damning photo*, wouldn't you, Mr. Devereaux?"

Devereaux pressed the barrel to Lance's forehead.

"Wait, Mr. Devereaux! This is *not* what you want to do, *believe* me!"

"Why not? I haven't the least concern for your scrawny carcass."

"Because, s-sir," Lance stuttered, "this *isn't* the only copy; in fact, it's not even the original."

Devereaux wadded the photo and shoved it into his pocket.

"What do you want, Hawthorne? King said you was startin' to ask questions, *smart* questions, gettin' your nose in places it didn't belong. I suppose even *he* underestimated your tenacity."

Devereaux slid his other hand under the lamp table next to his chair and pushed a button emitting a silent signal to somewhere.

"You *better* tell me where the original and the other copies are, boy, or heads *will* roll, starting *right* now."

Mark Randolph Watters

46

MORNING BROKE, OFFERING LITTLE relief. Jessica had spent the night wide awake sitting in Ginibeth's room, expecting at any moment the home invasion she feared. In her lap rested Lance's unloaded Beretta. Dropping the pistol into her robe pocket, she strained to maintain a quickened mobility as she tossed essentials into a suitcase.

"Gini," Jessica said, softly jostling her arm. "Get up, sweetie."

Ginibeth issued a resistant moan as she grabbed her pillow and, with a twist, rolled over.

Jessica flipped the light switch.

"*Now*, Ginibeth," Jessica urged. "We haven't time to waste. Put on your clothes, sweetie. I have them laid out for you at the end of your bed. We're going on a trip."

"Mommy, what's ... what's *wrong*?" Ginibeth asked, rubbing sleep from her eyes, struggling to adjust to the bedroom light.

"Can't explain now, sweetie. Trust mommy. Just do it."

"But I'm still slee—"

"*Hurry*, Gini! No time to argue."

Mark Randolph Watters

Ginibeth pulled on a pair of Phantom jeans and a red and green plaid shirt given to her by Barrett King for her birthday last month.

"Let's go."

"What's going on, Mommy? What's the rush? Is Daddy home yet? What time is it? Is the house on fire?"

Jessica glanced at her watch.

8:18.

She ignored the questions spilling from Ginibeth's mouth and focused on getting out of the house.

"Ready, Gini?"

"I'm coming, Mommy," Ginibeth replied, navigating the right-angled staircase, her stuffed lamb in tow.

Jessica snatched the car keys from the hook in the kitchen wall and swept Ginibeth into her arms in one simultaneous motion. Jessica scrambled for the garage, when, from the foyer came the sound of knocking at the door.

"Daddy!" Ginibeth shouted.

Jessica's eyes widened with terror. She fixed her stare in the direction of the knocking. Ginibeth slid gradually from her mother's arms to the floor.

"It's not Daddy, sweetie," Jessica said, her voice fading as her mind raced. "Get ... go get in the car, Ginibeth," Jessica directed, her heart racing.

"Jess? *Jessica?*"

"Barrett!"

"Jess, it's Barrett King. Come to the door, please. I need ... I need to tell you something about ... about Lance!"

"Gini, wait in the car, please. Mommy will be right there."

Jessica hustled to the bedroom and opened the closet. She reached for the top shelf, shoving aside stacks of clothing, which showered helter-skelter around and on top of her.

The Ghosts of Benevolence

"The box. Where's the damn *box*?"

A few hand sweeps later, Jessica located in the shelf's corner a mahogany box Lance had made and adorned with crude hand-carvings of daisies and butterflies, painted a rainbow of colors and given to Jessica on their tenth wedding anniversary. She raised the lid on the unlocked box. She gasped.

"Wh—Where *is* it?"

"Jessica! We need to talk. I know you're here! Please open the door!"

Jessica turned to exit the closet and felt a thump against her thigh. Then she remembered. She reached into her robe pocket and lifted out the Beretta. She grabbed a box of nine millimeter short rounds from Lance's underwear drawer and dashed for the garage.

Jessica had long chastised Lance for owning a handgun and had insisted he get rid of it. Now thankful for his disobedience, Jessica kissed the barrel.

"Jessica! Look, I *know* you're awake! I see the *lights,* and I saw your *shadow* move down the hall. We got to talk! Lance … Lance is in some trouble! Open the door!" Barrett shouted. Fed up with the charade, he shouted louder, "Open the *damn door*!"

Forewarned, Jessica knew better than to comply. She hurried to the car and buckled Ginibeth into the backseat. She did not bother buckling her own belt.

Jessica punched with her left hand the garage door control button, while starting the car with her right.

"Open, damn it!"

"Mommy!"

"It's okay, sweetie. Mommy just got a little frustrated." The garage door began its indifferent ascent. "Remember how frustrated you got when the flour wouldn't pour from the bag? That's how I feel now. Tough to play your game when the flour's stuck in the bag, right, sweetie?"

333

Mark Randolph Watters

"Unh, hunh!"

Jessica exchanged glances between the rear-view and side-view mirrors. Overwhelmed with impatience, she ripped the car's transmission stick into reverse. She crushed the accelerator. The car lurched backwards, tires churning, squealing, and crashed into the still-rising garage door, peeling it upward like a banana and slicing away the left side-view mirror against the garage wall. Jessica yanked the steering wheel left, gunned the accelerator, and destroyed a patch of junipers as she bounced off the driveway and onto the road. She did not look back to see Barrett at the front door, or whether he or anyone else might be pursuing her.

"Let her go, Carl," Barrett advised as he watched the SUV fishtail around a curve. "What we really want now is any evidence Lance may have that can be used against us, against Devereaux. I talked to Dev this morning. The man was frantic, spitting his words like chips from a sawmill. He mentioned some photograph Lance had of him, copies of it, rather, that was taken of Dev years ago. Not sure exactly what *that* might look like, but Dev said it was a Polaroid photo of three men, at night. Knowing Lance like I do, it's scanned into some computer file or lying under a mattress; in a wall safe; maybe all of the above. I've already purged the files on his office computer. Let's get inside this house."

47

"HOW ARE WE GETTING in, Barrett, without raising suspicions?" Carl asked.

"Fair question. But if that SUV of hers didn't raise some flags, nothing will. See anyone outside?"

Carl scanned the homes and yards in view. "No, not a soul."

"I don't think she took time to set the alarm. Be right back."

Barrett walked to his car, looking further to see if the commotion of Jessica's exit had stirred the neighbors' notice. He lifted the trunk lid and took from it a brown backpack and returned to Carl.

"Follow me. We could *bludgeon* the knob and *force* our way in, I suppose," Barrett said, searching the exterior for the least conspicuous point of entry, "but I think now it might be best if we do all we can to cover our tracks and not draw attention. Let's check around back. Plenty of foliage back there."

Carl scanned the exterior of the house as if he were girl-watching, eyes roving up and down. "How do you know the alarm is not armed?"

Mark Randolph Watters

"This is the safest neighborhood in town, Carl, or so Lance believes. The lots are large; the entrances are gated; Lance never figured he'd *need* security, I suppose. Told me himself he wasn't going to spring for thirty dollars a month for monitoring. Cheap little bastard. I told him he was an idiot. He was even stupid enough to share his gate code with me. Besides, Jess was in too big a hurry to set it."

King unzipped the backpack and set it on the ground.

"Put these on," King said, handing Carl items pulled from the backpack.

"Gloves, goggles, a *gardener's* mask? What *for*, Barrett?"

"Hard hat, too. Just do it, and follow me."

The pair walked to the back of the house. Barrett pretended to jot notes on a clipboard, the added prop of the hard hat giving the impression of a building inspector, perhaps a property assessor or an exterminator, to anyone watching.

"Okay, this looks good."

King took from the pack a plastic bottle filled with fluid. He removed the screw-on cap, replacing it with a spray mechanism.

"We're going to get inside using a *spray bottle* and gloves?" Carl asked.

"Such an astute observer, Carl!"

"So how's the plastic bottle getting us inside? Some magic potion, is it?"

"Right again, Carl."

"You're going to break this window, Barrett, with this *bottle*?" Carl asked, twisting its sprayer. "Isn't forced entry what you wanted to avoid?"

"Only the *appearance* of forced entry, Carl. *Don't* open it!" Barrett placed the clipboard on the ground. "Hand me the bottle. Now, listen *carefully*. Inside this container is *hydrofluoric acid*. Don't breathe its fumes.

The Ghosts of Benevolence

The liquid can *kill* you on contact; at the very least burn you severely. Its absorption into your skin can cause death by cardiac arrest in a matter of *minutes*."

"*Damn*, Barrett! *Conspicuous* forced entry's looking better all the time. Why don't we just *break* the freakin' *window*?"

"Broken glass is messy, Carl, especially when it's found with *messy blood* all over it. Ever heard of DNA?"

"So how's ... how is this *hydro*-stuff going to get us inside?"

"Watch and learn, my friend. Watch and learn."

"Gladly," he replied, adjusting his goggles and mask and stepping back.

Barrett squeezed the sprayer slowly, forcing the gradual spread of acid droplets onto the surface of the windowpane. He repeated the process, wetting the glass thoroughly, until the reaction weakened the pane's surface enough for King to pull the remaining glass out.

"Voila! Sort of makes one feel like a mad scientist, doesn't it, Carl?"

"Look at *that*! I wouldn't have *believed* it if I hadn't *seen* it."

"The glory of science, my friend."

Barrett reached his gloved hand through the hole, unlatched the window lock, and raised the window. Both climbed through, behind the cover of a holly bush, closing the window behind them.

Lance had discovered and accumulated a damning trail of paper, thanks to the diligence of Heather. This evidence had to be in Lance's house, Barrett believed, having not considered looking under his nose in Lance's office. Even that would have been fruitless, since Heather had had the foresight to remove the boxes of invoices from Lance's office to her home.

Methodically, the men searched, mindful to look behind every wall picture and mirror for safes or other modes of containment. Barrett and Carl combed the house from attic trunks to dresser underwear, careful to do so with gloved hands, replacing each moved object in its original position.

"Find anything, Carl?"

"Just doughnuts. Want one? Krispy Kremes."

"Let's get the hard drives out of those two PCs," Barrett directed.

The drives removed, Barrett replaced different drives inside the computers.

"Devereaux's people will take care of Lance," Barrett assured Carl. "Jessica will have a hard time proving we were here tonight, at least for a while. She's not a computer hawk, and she doesn't know we came into her house, not yet anyway. And by the time the police add two and two, we'll be yachting in the Caribbean and trafficking H and weed from Columbia to Seattle. Say 'hello' to my little cartel."

"*Cartel!*"

"No need to *worry*, Carl."

Carl's eyes revealed a growing realization that he had crossed the line.

"What is it, Carl? *Lighten up*, man. Things are going to be *fine!*"

Barrett paused a moment to articulate his reasoning and to assuage Carl's concerns.

"Look, man, there's no *real* war on drugs going on in this country; just the *illusion* of one. The drug war is nothing more than another political tool to exploit the voters, to make the masses *believe* the government gives a tootie-frootie. Politicians care about two things ... no, *three* things ... power, money, and *more* power. The way I see it, if *they* can obtain money and power with the wave of a hand, *why shouldn't we?*

"We don't have anything to worry about, Carl," Barrett declared, as the two walked to the car as if nothing had

The Ghosts of Benevolence

happened. "Dev and I have … well, let's just say we have *friends* in high places. We're *covered*, my friend!"

"What's stopping your friends from whistling, Barrett?"

"Think about it, Carl. And when you think you've figured it out, lift your eyebrows."

Barrett turned and stared at Carl.

"You've got to think long-term, Carl. You've had a nice career at SPIG, but it's time to move on, to greener pastures. A politician's most important job is getting *re-elected*, and given the short-term, sound bite mentality of our culture, it's better for said politicians to trim the branches than to cut down the tree. Those politicians will go after some of our *expendable* operations, the ones we've set up for bait, the low-hanging fruit. But, *we* are the tree. Don't forget that, Carl.

"Now, get on the phone to Devereaux and tell him we've got Lance's computer files. If Lance Hawthorne is as thorough as I think he is, this photo has been scanned and is somewhere on these hard drives."

King reached inside the backpack and removed one last object, a rectangular pane of glass.

"You really do think of everything, don't you, Barrett?"

"*Somebody* has to. Ah, perfect fit."

Mark Randolph Watters

48

HINGES ON AN ANCIENT door leading into the breakfast room cackled with torment, the pitch rising and falling, like the damned begging for mercy.

Lance and Devereaux turned facing the door.

Maybe there is something to the legend of the Wyndham murder, thought Lance.

A light-skinned mountain of an African-American ambled through the entrance. Lance froze, as if face to face with Judgment. The man's waistline formed a vertex of an inverted equilateral triangle, the base of which crossed shoulder to shoulder on his six-foot-six body. His tee shirt stretched taut across his granite-like chest, giving definition to its chisel. That it did not rip with each lift of his arms defied explanation. His stride, fluid and athletic, exhibited none of the awkwardness of a body builder. Chain-link tattoos circled his biceps and neck, and when he flexed his arms, the links stretched to cartoonish proportions. The man was a chain unto himself, not a weak link apparent. He stood a few feet inside the room, arms crossed, still as a robot, staring, awaiting instructions.

Once Lance's shock subsided, something about this superman triggered neurons in Lance's brain, all of which screamed their warnings. Square jaws flanked his white mustache. The man's brown-gray eyes seemed to sear holes, like lasers, into Lance. Devereaux faced Lance and gestured to the man with a twist of his hand.

"Please close the door, Bama."

"Bama?" Lance mouthed, his lips parted with surprise at the sound of the name. *"The* Bama?"

The man wore a black Stetson hat, tilted forward. A familiar plume of feathers adorned the hat's front.

This is definitely the Belle's Diner guy. Gwen's friend is not only a mountain ... he's a Devereaux goon!

"Mr. Hawthorne, I take great pleasure to introduce you to my assistant, one Mr. Al 'Bama' Jenkins. Bama, Mr. Lance Hawthorne. Bama is, shall we say, my *special-projects* man. If I have a project that needs a special ... *touch* ... well, Bama's the man.

"Now, Bama, it seems that Mr. Hawthorne here, a man native to *this very town* but a man considerably lackin' in basic business *sense*, not to mention *manners*, is in possession of a few pictures—*photographs*, it seems—that have for me a ... *sentimental* attachment. Seems also that Mr. Hawthorne is not so willin' to *part* with those photographs or even to let me know where all the *copies* might be found.

"I've asked nicely, I believe, as any Southern gentleman ought to ask, to receive these photographs. I've gone so far as make Mr. Hawthorne what I *believe* to be a most *generous* offer for those photographs. For *God's sake*, I'm offering the man his *life*, something one might think, with good reason, to be *beyond price*, certainly of higher value than a couple of faded old photographs.

"But, *alas*, it seems Mr. Hawthorne either does not *recognize* or does not *respect* the *value* of my offer. I think perhaps *both*, Bama." Devereaux poured coffee into his saucer. "Coffee, boys? Good an' hot. No? Anyway, Bama, might I impose upon you to offer your skills of

342

The Ghosts of Benevolence

persuasion, to perhaps *convince* our guest that a change of mind is in his best interests?"

"Be delighted, Mr. Devereaux," replied Bama in a voice as deep as a Kentucky cave.

"I'm a-thankin' you, Bama. Now, Mr. Hawthorne, I await your response."

With that, Devereaux rose and hobbled towards the door. He stopped and sipped from his saucer.

"*SSSHHLLLPPP!* Quite good, *indeed.* I *must* replenish my supply. Simmons, make a note of it, please."

"Right away, sir," Simmons replied.

"Now, Mr. Hawthorne, just so you're aware, you have about a *minute* to decide whether this little extortion scheme of yours is worth the infliction of roughly fifteen minutes of *extreme* personal discomfort. And I *do mean* extreme in its *strictest* context, followed by your premature *demise*, something I believe, when all's said and done, you *will* welcome."

Devereaux pulled the doorknob, then stopped and turned towards Lance.

"Come to think of it, it really don't matter *what* your decision is. Bama's going kill you *anyway*, after first a bit of *fun*, that is. How long's it been, Bama?"

"A week."

"His fun, Mr. Hawthorne, not yours. He's *all yours*, Bama." Devereaux said, laughing, sprinkled with intermittent coughing. "Damn kidney!"

"Mr. Devereaux!" Lance shouted, arms extended. "Hey, if you want *six thousand* per acre, who am *I* to argue *or* refuse? That's the beauty of free enterprise! Demand meets supply ... meets Bama. *Let's talk deal!*"

"Mr. Hawthorne, sir, if I wanted six *million* dollars per acre for that land, I could likely get it. It ain't the money, not anymore. It's those photographs you claim to have. Or, *had.* You might be interested to know that Barrett has confiscated your personal computer files, you know, the computers in your *home*, not to mention the files on your office PC. Those he destroyed. We believe you were smart enough to create backup files. Why else would you flash the *original photo* like some street pimp flaunts his gold?"

My home compu—Jessica! Ginibeth.

Instantly, a freefall of realization flushed through his being. For the first time in his adult memory, a desperate caring for lives other than his own pierced Lance's conscience.

"What have you *done* with my *family*?" Lance screamed.

"I don't think you need to spend what little time you have left worrying too much about *that*, Mister Hawthorne. The disposition of your family is the *least* of your worries, I should think. You see, in a few minutes none of that's going to matter."

"You depraved piece of *crap!* You cold, freaking *son of a bitch*!" Lance shouted, lunging at Devereaux, saliva spewing from his fury.

Bama intervened, sending Lance fast to the floor with a right cross. Shaken, Lance squirmed onto his knees as he spit blood from his mouth. His plan unraveling, he remembered the lone print he had stashed away in a safe deposit box.

"There *are* … other prints, Dev … Earl," Lance spat between breaths, blood filling his mouth and dripping to Devereaux's maple floor.

"Well, now, maybe there *are* and maybe there *ain't*," Devereaux replied.

"Are you willing … willing to *risk* that?" Lance asked, wiping blood from his chin.

"Risk *what*? Risk somebody turnin' us in? Heh, heh. Boy, you *are* naïve. You actually think I give a royal shit about that photograph? I'm going to kill you *anyhow*, whether you got other copies or not. Hell, you might have

The Ghosts of Benevolence

one copy, a *thousand* copies … or no copies. Don't *matter*. What matters is you ain't going be around to *identify* the subjects in that picture. I don't think there's anything else worth discussing, Mr. Hawthorne. Now, if you'll excuse me, I'll—"

"There's *another* witness," Lance reminded Devereaux, playing one of his few remaining cards.

Devereaux stopped.

"To the bombing," Lance added.

"Gas leak!"

"Okay, gas leak. But, there *is* another witness, one you've not counted on."

"Of course, you must be referring to Jackson what's-his-name, the … *pig boy* with a Polaroid."

"Yes. Willoughby. And he knows that if anything … *anything* … should happen to me, he goes straight to the police. He—"

"Hawthorne!" Devereaux screamed. "Mister Hawthorne, you are *wastin'* your breath. I *ain't* buyin' it. If we for a *moment* suspect that Jackson possesses the *gumption* to approach the police, we will simply *take him out*, like a coyote on a field mouse … or a sausage factory on a pig. He's all yours, Bama. Do be careful with my maple floors," Devereaux said, glancing at the blood already spilled, closing the door behind him.

Mark Randolph Watters

The Ghosts of Benevolence

49

BAMA REACHED INTO HIS jeans pocket and pulled out a set of diamond-crusted brass knuckles gleaming like freshly stamped pennies. He slid them onto his right-hand fingers. Simmons dissuaded any attempt to flee, pressing the barrel of a pistol against Lance's temple.

"I won't be needin' you now, Simmons," grumbled Bama.

"Yes, sir." Simmons pocketed the pistol and departed.

Bama grabbed Lance by the throat and thrust him against the wall, lifting him several inches off the floor. He pressed his right knee into Lance's groin. Bama drew back his fist. Thinking fast amid his effort to breath, Lance appealed to Bama's materialistic side.

"Bama, what do you say … aaaah … to a couple of *million* bucks … aaaaa … hard cash?"

Bama paused, releasing his grip. "What the hell you mean by *that*?"

"What I mean is, don't knock me into the next life, and I *promise* you a payoff of *five million* tax-free dollars, cash on the barrel head." Lance wiped away rivulets of blood streaming still from Bama's earlier assault. "How much does Devereaux pay you? Couple a grand a week? I'll bet it's *nowhere near* the kind of money I can get into your hands. And simply for letting somebody *live*. But if you *kill* me … the money dies, too."

"You ain't *got* no five million dollars." Bama's grip tightened.

"How do you know I *don't*? I got photos of Devereaux, don't I? I got five million dollars, too!" Lance coughed. "That is, I *will*."

"Just as I thought—"

"Let me *explain*. Just … *let* me explain. What do you have to lose?"

Bama withdrew his fist and again loosened his grip on Lance's throat.

"You got *thirty seconds*."

"It'll … it will take a bit *longer* than thirty seconds to explain the details. You'll just have to *trust* me, Bama. Day after *tomorrow*, I'll have my hands on enough cash to send *both of us* our separate ways. I can split it with you. You won't have to do Devereaux's dirty work for him, *ever* again. Think of it as *blood money*, man, because that's *exactly* what it is. *Think* about that. This is payment for what *Devereaux* did to *your people* over half a century ago, probably even to your *own blood family*."

Lance scanned Bama's eyes, hoping some of his words had hit home. Bama stared, unblinking, like a snake.

"Think of the five million as payment for what he's *always* done to your people, for how *little* he thinks of your people, of *you*. Sure, he pays you well, but he *uses* you, man. Probably laughs himself to sleep every night. Consider it reparations, payback … *justice*.

"Keep on being Devereaux's and King's *mule*, their runner, and it's going to get you *killed*, probably sooner than later. Do you think for a minute they'd put *their* asses in slings for *you*? They'll be sitting back in their air-conditioned suites zipping bills through cash counters, while you're running gauntlets and neutralizing enemies …

The Ghosts of Benevolence

pulling their weeds. Is that what you *really* want, Bama, when you can *rid* yourself of that risk and be financially free, all within a *couple of days*?

"King's not going to risk his interests going up in smoke, either. I've given Devereaux and King my price for silence. They'll *pay* it, *believe* me, but *only* if I'm out of here, *alive.* And if I'm out of here alive, *you* get paid.

"I need to shut up, give you a chance to think," Lance said, taking a sigh, wondering if these were his last moments on Earth. He glanced at the wall mirror, getting his first view of the damage done by Bama's brass fist.

"Unh, you sure loosened *those* three," Lance observed, grimacing as he poked the affected teeth. He held his breath awaiting Bama's reaction.

Bama didn't blink, nor did he seem impressed. His expression seemed icy as ever. Then, just as Lance started a silent, unfamiliar appeal to his Maker, Bama's fists unfurled and the brass knuckles fell to the floor.

CLUNKKK.

Relieved, Lance managed a smile and sighed, asking, "Does ... does this mean we have a *deal*, Bama?"

"All this means is I'm givin' you more than thirty seconds."

"That's all I ask."

"How much more depends on *you.* It means I'm gonna be your *bodyguard*, your *shadow*, for the next little while, Mr. Hawthorne."

"Of *course.* Makes sense."

"If I'm not five million dollars richer ... cash in hand ... by 10:15 a.m. day after tomorrow, I'll snap your neck like a matchstick, and I won't care who sees it."

"Completely understandable."

"Shut up, Hawthorne. I may just rip your tongue out first, to stop your yappin'."

"Sorry."

Mark Randolph Watters

"Then I'll take your body back to Devereaux's place, cut you up in small pieces, and bury you in a stump hole, next to Wyndham. You *run* from me between now and day after tomorrow and I *will* come after you. And it won't be a matter of *if* I catch you. It might take me the rest of my life, but I *will* find you. Am I clear?"

Bama shackled Lance's neck against the wall with the embrace of his thumb and forefinger. "I said, am ... I ... *clear?*"

Bama's breath, a cesspool of rotted teeth, tobacco, and liquor, slammed into Lance's nostrils like a bloodless left hook.

"Crystal," Lance confirmed. "Thank you for your trust."

"You ain't got my *trust*, Hawthorne. What you got is two extra days to live. If you *deliver* your promise, we'll shake hands and forget we ever met. You fail me and ... well, *don't* fail me."

"How do I know you won't take the five million and *then* ... kill me?"

"You *don't* know, do you? I guess you'll have to trust *me*."

"So, how do we ...get out of this current situation? Devereaux expects you to exit that door with my dead body."

"True, and if I thought he'd be waitin' on the other side of that door, you'd have a little problem. But that don't mean there ain't folks millin' around out there who have a *good idea* of what's goin' on in *here*. They're Devereaux's eyes and ears."

"I have a *bad* feeling about this, and I'm not talking about my aching *teeth*."

"I'm going to have to hit you again, Hawthorne. Draw more blood, make it look like I beat you to death. A nose shot ought to do it. Noses are always good bleeders."

"Mine's no exception."

The Ghosts of Benevolence

"You already got a good start all over your shirt and face. I'll try not to do too much damage. Can't make no promises."

"I *hate* nose shots!"

"You got to do your part. I'll carry you out, as if to dispose of your body. They'll see the blood. He won't question my work, never has. In fact, as far as he's concerned, the less he sees of you, the better. When Devereaux gives me a ... project ... he washes his hands. Besides, I've never failed him ... up to now. Which is all the more reason you'd better not fail *me*, or I'll be on you like a spider on a fly."

"Can't you just ... *carry* me out? I can fake death like a Georgia possum."

"Got to make it look right. I don't want *nobody* even *thinkin'* about questioning my work."

Lance sighed. "Okay, Bama. Do I get a last smoke, one of Devereaux's cigars?" Lance grinned and closed his eyes, lips tightened, realizing the tangle of his web. His mind filled with rushing memories of his mama's death under the crushing weight of the iron-rimmed wagon wheel. Bama's brass-knuckled knuckles offered little difference. "Go ahead."

Bama fitted the brass knuckles and with lightning speed, Bama gave Lance a jab and an uppercut. Lance went down like a sack of lead balls, blood pouring from his nose and mouth, as promised. Bama surveyed the damage and determined a shiner and more cuts would eliminate all doubt.

He pulled the unconscious Lance by the shirt collar and punched the bone under his left eye. Blood spilled from the cut. Satisfied with his handiwork, Bama tossed Lance over his shoulder and walked out of the room, leaving a trail of red on the maple planks.

Mark Randolph Watters

His trust in Bama's skill evident, Devereaux had left the grounds to patrol his kingdom, to smoke his cigars, to drink his sillabub, to wallow in his leisure and his luxury.

Bama strutted from the house, Lance draped over his shoulder. Blood covered his shirt and pants, spilling from Lance like a leaky hose. Farm employees who witnessed Bama's removal of Lance glanced from the curiosity of their peripheral, and almost as quickly resumed their duties. No one dared ask Bama the question already answered.

50

BAMA REACHED HIS BLACK Dodge Ram and dropped Lance limply to the ground. Though very much alive, to any distant onlooker, he was as dead as the dark side of the moon. Bama pulled back the tarp covering the pickup's bed. He lifted Lance, deposited him in the truck's bed and replaced the tarp. Bama retrieved a walkie-talkie from the glove box.

"Bama to Damocles. Come in, Damocles."

"Go ahead, Bama," Devereaux answered, lifting the coffee pot to pour a cup.

"It's done, sir. I'm disposin' of the body. The usual place, sir?"

"Indeed. Good work, Bama. I knew I could count on you. Did he suffer any?"

"Oh, yeah. Let's just say even his wife wouldn't recognize him."

"Heh, heh, heh! We ought to drop his worthless body on her doorstep, just to see her reaction." Devereaux dropped three cubes of sugar into his cup and stirred. "Only trouble is, she ain't going be around much longer herself. Pity, really. Okay, Bama, I'll see you on the flip. Oh, now that I think about it, instead of the usual place, take him down to the holler, chop him up and shove his pieces in one of them pecan stump holes that need fillin'. Ol' man Wyndham's lookin' for a *soul* mate, I reckon. Cover it up real good, pour in some cement, to keep the smell in. Won't really matter anyhow. That orchard's so far away from anything, ain't nobody ever gonna find him."

Devereaux paused to relish the thought that Lance's burial would also bury forever Devereaux's involvement in the 1965 church bombing murders.

"One more thing, Bama."

"Yes, sir?"

"After you dispose of the body, take his car an' get rid of it, too. I suggest takin' it over to Dothan or down to Panama City an' have one of our choppers paint it and alter the VIN. Or, take it down to the river, one o' them backwater spots, an' dump it there. I don't really care *how* you do it; just don't leave a trace of that car."

Devereaux gazed at the mid-morning sky, eyes empty and cold from a lifetime of hatred, murder, and greed.

"*Nobody* screws with Earl Bentley Devereaux, the Third," he boasted. "Nobody."

Just then, Simmons entered the kitchen, returning a butcher knife to its drawer. He saw Devereaux sipping coffee, his back turned. Hand on the knife drawer, he eyed the glistening sharpness of the knife's blade. Other thoughts instantly gripped Simmons imagination. He turned his gaze toward Devereaux's back and gripped the knife's handle tighter. *How easy this would be*, though Simmons. *And it ain't like he don't deserve it, the bastard.* Opportunities such as this seldom presented so glaringly, but such opportunities would have to wait.

"Coffee, Simmons!" Devereaux barked, detecting his presence.

"I'm on it, sir," Bama lied. "I'll get rid of the car."

The Ghosts of Benevolence

Tossing the walkie-talkie to the passenger-side floorboard, Bama promptly ignored Devereaux's instructions. He sat still, arms extended and hands gripping the wheel. He had not yet plunged into the depths of no return, but he stood teetering on its precipice. Bama considered killing Lance here and now. But he thought about Devereaux's closing comment just seconds ago, considering those words a personal challenge.

With a growl, the whipping fishtails of the powerful pickup spewed sand and rocks in its wake. Bama steered the truck onto a side road suitable only for one-way traffic and four-wheel drives. The road, long ago used to transport harvested trees, cut several miles through the cavernous pine forest and eventually to U.S. Twenty-seven.

Jolts of wheels striking holes shook Lance to a hazed consciousness. He lifted the tarp to get a bead on their location. The green blur of pines and a blue sky splotched with puffs of clouds dominated his limited view. He knew that Bama had performed well. The bleeding had stopped, but Lance felt the gummy coagulation of blood clutching his skin. Pain throbbed in his skull, sending him into the merciful bliss of semi-consciousness.

Lance's dreamlike thoughts conjured scenes of long drives he and Jessica once took, once upon a happier time, in the autumn of the year, along the winding kinks of mountain roads, through forests pristine.

Jess and Lance stopped at roadside produce stands, rickety put-togethers upright out of a sheer force of will more than the durability of careful construction, and browsed the triangular-stacked jars of wild clover honey, jams, ciders, souvenirs and such. The wafting drift of sweet hickory smoke from fires under black cauldrons of boiling peanuts grabbed wallet and purse as effectively as pick-pockets, much to the delight of peddlers and patrons alike.

Mark Randolph Watters

They took in the air's crisp embrace. They held hands clammy with love and scanned the gray overcast for signs of snow. They explored side roads of side roads and visited churches that, until that moment, never existed, sneaking unnoticed into back pews and joining in the singing.

They spread blankets on grass cooled by the evening dew, meadows overlooking vistas of cloud-kissed mountaintops flush with the golds and ambers of mid-autumn, lines of cabin smoke coursing skyward from chimneys dotting the vastness of the Appalachian wilderness. They nibbled at tomatoes and cheese between thick slices of sourdough bread and drank bottled water. Hawks hovered overhead on rising currents of blue air.

They inspected shops filled with the art and craft of mountain artisans. They marveled at the juxtaposition of the emotion of art and the practicality of function. They bought five-cent cups of coffee, more for warming hands numb with cold than for consumption. They walked the streets of touristy-yet-cozy mountain communities and peered at wares behind shop windows and on occasion took home a hand-stitched quilt, a turned-wood vase or perhaps a few antique marbles once flipped by the thumbs of mountain boys.

These days defined the early years of their marriage, a sort of unbridled youthfulness filled with the hope of innocence, exuberance for a future untainted and unbounded by the dictates of experience. Lance had grown to understand the priceless treasures of his memories, moments unique in their utter scarcity. Indeed, Lance had grown.

He remembered the God before whom they vowed their lives as one. Their words, then, flowed freely from their hearts, written by their hands, and spoken with their mouths. These were *not* the sterile promises of the cerebellum, rote words recited void of conviction, vows

The Ghosts of Benevolence

that otherwise might bounce off ears like cans tied to bumpers bounced off pavements.

Now God had brought Lance back to Benevolence, to the familiar dusty red roads of Sutter County, removed from the haven of the hills, away from the seduction of money and materialism. He laid beaten and bent in the bed of a pickup truck, his mind too groggy to make sense of anything anymore, surrounded by the tribulations of his enemies, comforted only by the treasures of his memories.

Lance thought of Horace Candler and chuckled. *"God just wants our faith, not our flawlessness."*

Still, the passing years, like the winds of erosion, had rubbed away the smooth of Lance's faith, until only the pitted rough remained. Doubt and indifference filled his dustbins of faith. Lance felt God as a presence past tense, like moments that drift away, inexorably farther, never again to be recaptured.

God, like home, *was*.

Lance touched his bruises and cuts and felt the sticky saturation of blood in his shirt.

"Oowww!" he moaned. "That bastard beat the *crap* out of me! Least I'm still living."

Lance cradled his head in the palms of his hands.

"I—I have to call Jess," he muttered, unaware of the transpirations back home. Lance waited through four rings before the answering machine activated.

"Jess? Jess, it's Lance!" he whispered through the whoosh of truck-blown air. "If you're there—oh, God," he said, awareness trickling in, "they've *taken* her! Gini! Pick up, honey. Lance, you *idiot!*" he shouted, realizing if Jessica wasn't home, neither was his daughter.

Bama glimpsed into his rearview mirror and noticed Lance's head tilted toward his left shoulder, a black object wedged in between. Suspecting Lance's betrayal, Bama swerved the truck to a skidding halt. Lance slammed against the right side of the truck.

"Who the hell *you* talkin' to?" shouted Bama through the sliding glass panel that separated the cab from the bed, the glare of sunlight reflecting off his gold-capped teeth.

"*Nobody!*" Lance replied, slipping the cell phone into his pocket and from Bama's view, hoping to distract Bama's attention from the device.

"That is ... just got a call from the office. Heather ... my assistant ... says she has the payables files ready for the ... for the *audit*." Bama just stared, oblivious to payables and audits.

"It's *nothing*, man!" Lance insisted. "Here. Want to call her back to confirm? Go ahead, *call* her. She'll *tell* you." Lance played his two-of-a-kind bluff against a full house.

Brows furrowed and Bama's snake eyes slanted as he stared at Lance.

The Ghosts of Benevolence

"How you gonna *get* that five million, anyway?" he demanded to know.

"Like I said, Bama, they'll *pay* it. It's complicated, but you'll have to be patient. It *will* happen, just a couple more days. Five million untainted dollars will buy a lot of tatts and pickups."

"Don't be makin' fun of my tatts. Or my trucks. Might have to open up some cuts."

"Not making fun of *anything*, believe me. Just saying that five million dollars is worth two days."

Lance's promise of rainbow gold deterred Bama for now.

"Where … where are we anyway?" Lance asked, scouring the scraggly monotony of pines for familiar sights. "Man, you sure gave me your Mike Tyson special!" Lance declared, touching his nose and eye.

Bama remained stoic as a stone. "Loggin' roads. We're a couple of miles from the highway. If you need to take a piss, do it now, 'cause I ain't stoppin' till I get to Raventon and get my money."

Groans coming at every move, Lance climbed out of the truck.

"Okay, thanks. Just need to stretch. I'm fine, I think. Piss-wise, that is; just a little dizzy's all. So, let's go get that money!" Lance said with contrived confidence.

"Ride up front. I want to keep an eye on you."

Lance reached for the passenger door handle. Bama wrapped his vise-like fingers around Lance's forearm, staring into Lance's eyes like a hungry wolf. Lance froze.

"*You* drive. That way, I can watch you better. Oh, and you better not be lyin' to me, boy. I'll tear your beating heart out through your mouth if you're lyin' to me about the money."

Lance felt like a tightrope walker crossing Niagara Falls. One mistake, one look down …

The Ghosts of Benevolence

"When things get tough," Sara often said, "never look *down* and never give *up*. Look only ahead."

He gathered his nerves, which lay quivering in heaps like the last breaths of roadkill.

"Let's go get that money, Bama," Lance said with a gulp, as he gestured an uppercut with his clenched right fist.

The two made it over the precipice of Devereaux's kingdom onto U.S. Twenty-seven. Lance pondered the possibilities of his next move. No doubt Bama would not hesitate to kill him and take his body back to Devereaux's for disposal. The empty five-million-dollar promise threaded Lance to any chance of life beyond day after tomorrow. No more honeysuckles and blackberries to hide in; no more cover of darkness; no more Belle Diner debates with harmless old men; no more clutter of boxes in which to hunker down; no Aunt Pearl to buffer the blows; no more reliance on a charmed life. The two-day delay, Lance knew, accomplished little more than to delay the truth of Bama's full promise.

Lance must act. Now, before he was acted upon, before they arrived at the Raventon mill of Standard Paper Industries of Georgia. Lance had to find a way—and the guts—to dispose of Bama somewhere in route. Escape was improbable. Lance knew somehow he would have to kill Bama. Such a move, he knew, was rife with risk and would require pure speed, like the strike of a rattler, without a smidgeon of hesitancy. Else, all would be lost.

All of Lance's what-ifs crowded his mind like children around an empty ice-cream truck. The miles melted behind them and neither spoke a word to the other. The truck's air conditioning had malfunctioned, and the evening's wet air rushing through the opened windows did little to offer relief.

Lance spilled sweat like a high-noon sheriff. On occasion, he glanced over at Bama, relaxed but wide

Mark Randolph Watters

awake. The ride mesmerized. Scenery repeated itself like cartoon backdrops. Intermittent groves of pecan trees and row after endless row of cotton, white oceans, consumed the earth for miles on either side of the highway. He inspected with careful, subtle glances the area within the perimeter of an arm's length, the nooks, pockets, and floorboards of the truck's cab.

Then, something caught Lance's eye, down in the door pocket below his left arm. An object glimmered metallic and long, a screwdriver perhaps, or pliers.

The Ghosts of Benevolence

51

IF I CAN DISTRACT HIM for a few seconds, just a few seconds, maybe I can get my hand on that screwdriver.

Lance shuffled in his mind a few scenarios, each more outlandish than the last. It was either the improbable success of an act of absurdity, or the certainty of death, either now or two days from now. Lance noticed Bama not wearing his seatbelt.

"State Patrol's really looking out for folks not buckled up," Lance said.

"Shut up and drive."

"We're asking for trouble if they pull us over, so—"

"I said *shut up*! I don't care about the freakin' State Patrol. You sound just like a *woman* I know."

Lance smiled, knowing of Bama's woman.

"Got any smokes?" Lance asked.

"*What?*" Bama fired back.

"Cigarettes. Got any? I just need *one* to help me stay awake. You slugged me pretty hard back there; took a lot out of me." Lance didn't smoke anymore, except for Devereaux's cigars, but he prayed Bama did.

Bama gave Lance a piercing gaze and reached to retrieve a half-empty pack of Marlboros folded inside his tee-shirt sleeve. Lance inched his left hand down into the door's pocket. Touching the screwdriver, he curled his fingers quietly around its handle. Lance's heart hammered with anticipation as his left hand twitched upward. He stiffened, sensing too little room to navigate the screwdriver vertically. Bama would have noticed.

Like a fly oblivious to the spider's parlor, Bama dug a cigarette from the crinkled pack and handed it to Lance.

"Only got three left; don't be askin' for another."

"Thanks. Won't need another."

Lance took the cigarette to his mouth.

"Can you light it for me?"

"*Damn*, man! Ain't you never done this *before*, drive and smoke?" Bama rattled off a rash of curses.

"I … I don't have a match," Lance explained, "and my lighter's in my car back at Devereaux's. I don't see a lighter … here," Lance said, pointing to the empty hole where the Ram's lighter belonged, "so … I appreciate it."

Bama scraped a match across his bent matchbook, most of its contents spent. The match failed to light on the first attempt. Bama tried again. Lance fixed his grip upon the screwdriver, springing the trap.

Bama held the lighted match, one hand shielding the flame from the air rushing in, ready to light the cigarette. Lance let the cigarette fall to his lap, which distracted Bama's focus. Like the spider upon its fly, Lance struck. Screwdriver in hand, Lance pivoted his body right, sweeping his left arm over the steering wheel. In the same instant, he crushed the brakes to take advantage of inertia. The screwdriver found its mark, sinking into the center of Bama's chest, just above the sternum, into his heart, like a laser beam through ice.

Bama's eyes widened with shock. Fingers extended, the still-burning match fell, extinguishing as it settled onto Bama's left leg. The screwdriver penetrated to its handle, a full six inches of blade inside Bama's chest. Gasping in

The Ghosts of Benevolence

disbelief, he turned his head to Lance, then down toward the point of entry.

"You won't be needing this," Lance said, as he seized the gun from Bama's lap. "Or this." Lance plucked the Stetson off Bama's head, placing it on his own.

Disarmed and dispatched, Bama could do nothing but die. And die he did. Blood trickled forth from his mouth as he collapsed forward, his head resting against the dash and facing Lance.

Lance winced at the sight of the once-mighty Bama. *That could have been me*, he thought. *Thank God!*

A blood-red glow spread over the western horizon. Cloud shadows drifted across the arc of a lifeless full moon peeking above the eastern horizon. The truck's tires whined against the asphalt. Lance felt the flow of life's balance wash over his soul too long void of it. He turned onto road after road, driving without aim for hours, his speeding thoughts crashing into each other. Free of Bama's death grip and away from Devereaux's Kingdom, Lance exalted in his victories.

"My *God*. I *did* it! No more Bama!" Lance gasped as realization of the blessings hit him, pearls of sweat crawling down his cheeks and forehead.

Even in the face of this improbable turn of events, the evidence of which sat crumpled in the passenger seat, Lance pinched himself, as if to awaken himself from the grips of a nightmare. Just last week, Lance Hawthorne was little more than a risk-averse numbers cruncher feeling the pangs of a post-midlife crisis. He was prepared, though not content, to ride out the mediocrity of his American Dream. He possessed a well-paying, dead-end career; a seven-figure house complete with the requisite manicured lawn; flat-screened computers and HDTVs; a luxury SUV; a Mercedes sedan; a country club membership; annual passes to Augusta National; high-speed Internet access, even a personal web site. He slept with a trophy wife he had taken

Mark Randolph Watters

for granted; he sent Christmas cards to high-profile acquaintances, people that in private, he despised; night after night, he tucked in a four-year-old girl whom he all but ignored but otherwise flaunted when it served him; he had a baby on the way. What more could anyone want?

Lance Hawthorne was a man tormented, haunted, by the demons and angels of his memories, each side forcing him to decide between the ignominy of surrender or the courage of commitment. In a span of forty-eight hours, his life of ennui took a turn for the bizarre. Lance recalled the aces-and-eights hand, the so-called "dead man's hand." It seemed ages ago, as if an entirely new life had emerged in its aftermath.

"AAAAAHHH!"

Bama twitched, sending Lance into a scream of panic. The body finished its collapse, sinking to the floorboard. A body needing disposal, Lance considered his options. He could dump it in some remote area, a plentiful commodity at the moment. He thought better of that idea.

Then a thought struck him. "I've got nothing to hide," Lance reasoned. "If this ain't self-defense, nothing is."

Twilight danced with the sway of oak and pecan leaves, like a celebration of apparitions. Lance pointed the truck northwest. He knew Barrett and Devereaux believed him dead. Lance had twice escaped death in as many days. Now he had the advantage of the deception of nonexistence.

"So ... Devereaux and King believe I'm dead," Lance observed, pondering the possibilities. "Who was it that said ... what was it ... the news of my death has been greatly exaggerated?"

Lance smiled.

The Ghosts of Benevolence

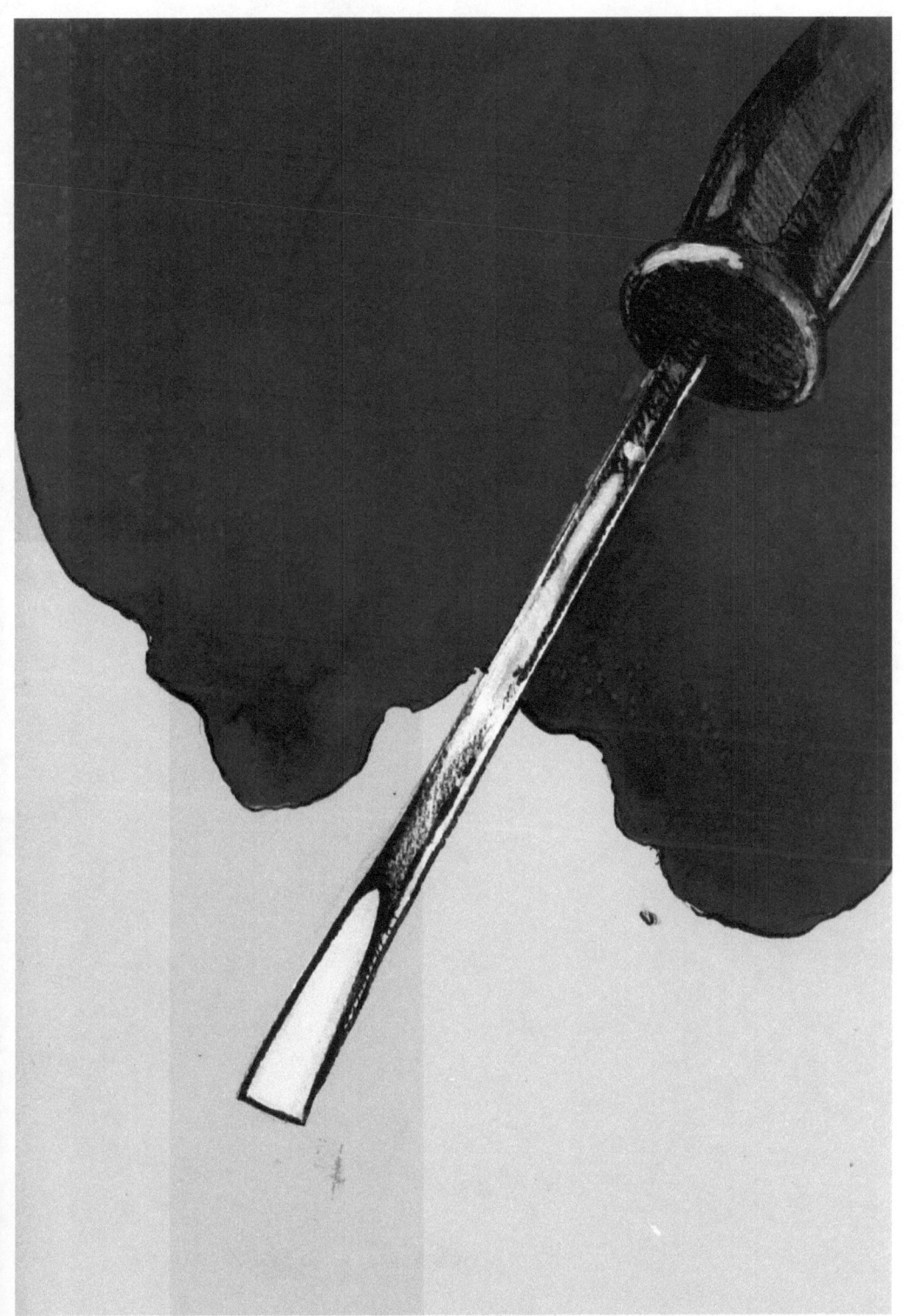

Mark Randolph Watters

52

DEVEREAUX SCRAMBLED ACROSS HIS living room to answer his cell phone.

"Always puttin' this damn thing in places it ought not be," he muttered under his breath. "Where's Simmons when I need him? Devereaux here!"

"Earl, it's Barrett. Well? Do I need to ask it?"

"Ask what!"

"Did you take care of *Hawthorne*? Is he enjoying his celestial dirt nap?"

"Oh, him. Deader'n a snail in a bucket of salt, my boy," Devereaux revealed, looking out the kitchen window for Bama, whom he realized had not reported back. "My man, Bama, made sure of that. What about them computers of his? Anything interestin' on 'em?"

"You bet! We found the picture. It was in a folder named 'Black Death.' How appropriate."

"Never you mind that. Did you get *rid* of it?"

"You can rest assured that file no longer exists, Mr. Devereaux."

"What did you do with his computers?"

"Nothing to worry about. Took their hard drives and replaced them with new ones. Lance's wife rushed away so fast she practically tore down her garage. Not sure *why* she was in such a hurry." King snickered.

"She see y'all?"

"Don't know. Could have, maybe. I did call out her name a few times, trying to get her to the door. So what?"

"So *what!* Are you an idiot?"

"What do you mean?"

"Did it ever occur to you she and Lance talked last night? No doubt he told her everything, which explains her rush to get away from you! What about fingerprints?"

"We didn't just fall off a pulpwood truck, Mr. Devereaux. We wore gloves, to protect us from the hydrofluoric acid we used to dissolve a window pane, not to mention prevention of fingerprints."

"Which window?"

"In the back, a basement window. It's pretty much hidden by a holly bush and some azaleas."

"How many panes?"

"Just the one, enough to reach inside, unlatch the lock."

"Anybody see you?"

"No one that knows us, if anyone at all. We were wearing garden masks, for ventilation; hard hats, too. We searched that house from top to bottom, front to back, side to side. We didn't change the position of any objects; didn't leave a streak in the dust; hell, we didn't even piss in his toilets, though I sure needed to."

"I hope you boys got alibis."

"Indeed we do. I had a ten-o'clock scheduled with Carl, to go over the upcoming audit. My alibi is his alibi. Even reserved the conference room. Locked it, too. You know, to preserve the privacy of such an important meeting."

The Ghosts of Benevolence

"Okay, I guess." Devereaux paused. "Sounds pretty good, Barrett. Yeah, pretty damn good indeed. But, won't Lance's wife realize stuff 's missing on her computer?"

"Well, she might in time, but I doubt it. So what if she does? According to Lance, Jessica knows diddly about computers, won't go near 'em. It's my opinion she won't realize their value to us, not until someone suggests it to her, anyway. Even if she does happen to discover that files are missing, it'll be far too late to matter.

"Mr. Devereaux, Jessica Hawthorne cannot prove we were there; she might *say* we were there, but she can't *prove* anyone was in her house. We left no physical evidence. Yes, a pane's replaced, but she'll never know the original's missing."

"What did y'all do with the glass?"

"Most of it dissolved. Took the remaining pieces with us, what few were left. Even cleaned up residual hydrofluoric acid. There was no bludgeoned entry; we left no fingerprints. Her husband's missing, and she panicked. The police will take her account, do their investigation, and write her off as a loon."

"Here's somethin' I bet y'all didn't think of. Did you—"

"Yep, we re-latched the window, exited through the door to the garage."

"Good, good. But, did you—"

"Re-paned the window, too, just as I said."

"You boys are *real* pros. What happens when she reports Lance as a missin' person and starts droppin' names. He's *dead*, remember? When he don't show up, the police *will* investigate. No telling *what* she knows and what she'll *say*. All she has to do is squeal an' I'll have me a parlor full of feds."

"Thought about that one, too. The authorities will need probable cause to conduct any searches. I think after Jess soils her reputation trying to convince the police *we* broke into her home—never mind that her home was broken into *at all*—she'll have an even harder time making them believe Lance is a missing person. Lance and Jessica have been having tons of personal problems. He spends more time at the office than home.

"But I don't believe it'll come to that, Mr. Devereaux. We've—"

"Could be," Devereaux interrupted.

"Yeah, it's unfortunate that she was able to elude us," admitted King. "Could've killed two birds with one visit. My runner has trailed Jessica Hawthorne and her daughter to a Hampton Inn off the interstate. We're monitoring her every move, as well as her cell calls. We even know her room number. Her room phone has been disabled. Once she leaves the hotel, my people will intercept them and—"

"Why wait until she *leaves* the hotel? Just *bust* into her room, grab 'em, and be *done* with it!" Devereaux said.

"—neutralize them," Barrett finished. "Mr. Devereaux, we need to do this as seamlessly as possible. We need stealth, not stupidity. For one thing, she's not going to answer the door for any reason, no matter how harmless it appears. Second, if we go in there and take her by force, we risk four scenarios, three of which are bad. We could get out of the room clean, but we'd likely have to fight our way through police or hotel security or both. I'm a gambler, but I don't like *those* odds. Why do you think we were so careful at her house?"

"How do you know she didn't alert the hotel clerk when she checked in?"

"Well … actually, we don't know for sure that she *didn't*, but we haven't noticed any unusual activity around the hotel. That's another reason still to keep our distance and observe her next move before we commit," reasoned King. "Besides, she's not going to risk getting her kid hurt. And she's pregnant, too. She might not know much about computers, but it's my hunch she's smart enough to avoid

The Ghosts of Benevolence

provoking a confrontation between the cops and us. My guess is she'll continue to try to reach Lance somehow."

"Can you *scramble* cell phone calls?" Devereaux asked.

"As far as we can tell, she has not used her cell phone, not yet. Personally, I doubt she *has* her cell phone; else she would have used it. She fled her home in such a panic; I'm sure that taking a cell phone was the last thing on her mind. Nevertheless, the signals of any calls she attempts from her cell phone will be intercepted immediately and scrambled."

"Incoming calls, too?"

"Lance is dead, remember?" King said.

"Okay. Good," Devereaux said, shades of doubt lingering. "Don't know how you've managed all this cloak-and-dagger junk, but very good. Welcome aboard, Mr. King. I can see I have chosen well. It is fortuitous for us that the members of your board are as complacent as you are clever and attentive. What's the ceiling of your spending authorization?"

"One hundred and twenty-five million dollars. Cost of ongoing operations, they conceded, when they considered the scarcity of this sort of real estate and raw material in our neck of the woods.

"The funds are ready to be wired to our Brussels account, Mr. Devereaux. We've got a man in First American Bank up here ready to initiate this end of the transaction. Once that wire is complete, all digital and paper records of transactions with First American will be purged. Carl and I will catch up to you tomorrow after our meeting with the board."

Mark Randolph Watters

53

LANCE FELT A STRANGE urge to initiate a conversation with Bama's corpse. Rendered harmless by death, Bama's presence seemed more like that of a hitchhiker, a silent soul eager to dispense with idle chatter. Instead, Lance punched the autodial button for Jessica on his cell phone. The late evening drifted into the depths of night.

Jessica remained in her hotel room with Ginibeth, afraid to risk being seen. Both were hungry, especially Gini. Punching "0" on the room phone, Jessica placed a call to the desk clerk.

"Bonk-Bonk-Bonk," repeated the sound.

She tried again.

"Bonk-Bonk-Bonk."

Same sound.

Again.

"Bonk-Bonk-Bonk."

She reached inside the pocket of her robe and took out her cell phone retrieved from her car's glove box. She punched the hotel's number.

"Bonk-Bonk-Bonk."

Jessica gasped with terror, realizing this was no coincidence. The icy sensation of dread gushed over her, like a weakened elk stalked by wolves.

"What's wrong, Mommy? I'm hungry. Can't we go get something to eat *now*?" Ginibeth whined.

"In a while, sweetie, I promise. Everything's fine."

Jessica pulled closed the window curtains.

"But why are we here, Mommy? Where's Daddy? It's time for a story."

"In a while. Daddy will be here in a while to read to you. Here. Drink this," she said, handing Ginibeth a sippy cup of apple juice. Jessica stared at the doorknob, hand on her Beretta planted in her robe pocket, expecting at any moment having to fend off attackers.

Another agonizing hour passed. Jessica paced the floor, one hand on her stomach and the other on her hip, stopping every few seconds to peek out the curtain. Ginibeth clutched a triceratops plush toy and watched DVDs. Soon, Gini slept.

The cell phone beeped. Jessica squeezed her moist palms, as if wringing water out of a washcloth, and stared at the phone, afraid the caller might be Barrett. The phone beeped several times. She was not familiar with the number showing onscreen, or any number for that matter, paying no attention to such details.

"Phone, mommy!" Ginibeth said, wakened by the sound.

"Maybe it's Lance," she mouthed in silence, frustrated she had not programmed Lance's number into her phone, "but, what if it's Barrett?"

"Aren't you going to answer the phone, mommy?"

"Y-yes, sweetie. I'll ... answer it."

Jessica picked up the phone, turning it over and over. Each beep seemed to pulse louder than the last.

"Mom-m-m-y!"

Jessica pushed the 'Accept' button.

The Ghosts of Benevolence

"H-hello?" she mumbled.

"Jess? *Jess!* It's *me*, La—"

"Lance! My God, Lance, *where are you*? Are you all right? I've been worried *sick* about you!"

"I'm okay *now*, babe. I'll fill you in later. How are you feeling? How're my girls? Wh—where are you?"

"Gini and I are at the Hampton Inn off Fantasy Drive. God, Lance, Barrett tried to *break* into the house! Gini and I got out of there, but I think they've followed us here. I've—I've tried calling the police from the room phone *and* my cell phone, but I keep getting sounds, like busy signals. On *both* phones. Can *they* be doing that, Lance?"

"Yeah, they can scramble your outgoing calls. But, don't worry about this call. They can't mess with your incoming signals."

"Do you think you can get out of there, *tonight*?"

"I don't know, Lance. Gini's hungry. She needs to eat, but I'm so *scared*!" Jessica whispered, her hands cupped around the phone trying to avoid further alarm to Ginibeth.

"Listen, Jess! Wait until around midnight, and slip out the hotel's side door. Do not, I repeat, do *not* attempt to go to your car. That's where they'll be watching and waiting. Walk to the LaQuinta and call a cab. Have the cabbie take you to the Raventon police. Explain to them *everything* you know, just as I've explained it to you, and wait for me to call you. Got it?"

"I got it. But how am I going to slip out the side door when I'm afraid to *open my room door*? Why not wait until light?"

"As dangerous as this seems, Jess, you need the cover of darkness. They *want* you to try to get to your car. They're *hoping* that you'll leave through the main lobby, amid what you perceive to be the safety of people milling about. That's where I believe their focus will be.

"Another thing, a *good* thing. Both Barrett and Devereaux believe I'm dead. I had a little ... *run-in* with one of Devereaux's men today. That's another long story I'll share with you over ice cream and The Adventures of Winnie the Pooh. Anyway, Devereaux thinks his man took me out, but, fortunately, *Thank God*, he did not. Quite the opposite, really. Right, ol' boy?" Lance shouted to Bama.

"Jess, I'm going to pay Barrett and Carl a visit tomorrow. At the office. Barrett's got a board meeting ten o'clock tomorrow morning, to close the funding approval for Devereaux's twenty-five thousand acres and to secure approval for the transfer of funds. He's going to give them a—"

"What are you driving, Lance?" Jessica interrupted.

"What? Oh, I'm ... I'm driving a beat up pickup truck, one of Devereaux's. That's part of the long story."

"Where's the Mercedes?"

"At Devereaux's. I'll get that car back, Jess, but it'll take a few days. Anyway, Barrett's going to give the board a little dog-and-pony tap dance to explain the competitive advantage the company will gain from this acquisition as well as the financial fruits that will accrue over the years, blah, blah, blah. He'll throw 'em the numbers, like chunks of meat to greedy sharks, and they'll gobble every morsel in blissful ignorance. That's when I'll make my entrance."

"Your ... *entrance*? How will you know when to enter?"

"The walls to that conference room are like paper. I'll be standing outside the closed door. I'll know when the time is right. Barrett thinks I'm *dead*, Jess. No better time to take him and Carl down. *Somebody's* got to awaken our moribund directors.

"Jess, I've managed to cheat death twice in two days. I've had some time to reflect on some things. Yes, I *wanted* to cash in on this deal, babe, which is why I took the photograph."

The Ghosts of Benevolence

"I *told*—"

"I *know* you told me so, and I should have listened. I wanted to be the leech on their legs and score the big one, for *us*, Jess. I realize what I've done was wrong-headed. I knew it *then*. I've *always* known it. But this whole thing had slapped me silly for a long time, like the smells of a hot apple pie cooling on the sill of an open window. I just *had to have* me a slice, Jess. I believe now that I've been given some of that pie, only not quite how I had expected.

"All my life I've chased material things, Jess. You know that. But what could be more materialistic, more precious to own, than one's living body, one's life? One's family. We don't need the fancy house, or the country club, or the luxury cars. What we need is each other. And our children. A tolerant, wise old gentleman down here helped point that out to me over coffee and rubbery eggs."

"Learning the values of minimalism, I see," Jessica observed, smiling. "Another part of the *long story*, I presume?"

"Yep, the good part. The *long-view* part."

"Lance, I'm scared. *Really* scared."

"I know, Jess. Me, too. I've put you in this position, and I am *so sorry*! *Hang* in there just a bit longer. Before I forget, tell the police about the photo of the church bombers; they can find the original, as well as the remaining copies of the photograph, in our safe deposit box. Also, I've got reams of evidence against Barrett and Carl tucked away in a special place even Barrett would never consider looking—the *cabinets* under his bookshelf in his *own* office. He *never* opens those cabinets. He thinks those cabinets are full of old general ledgers and other decades-old reports. Now you know what I've been doing these late nights. Ask the police to meet me at the office at 10:00 in the morning, Jess, armed with backup and warrants. They *won't* want to miss the show."

"I hope you know what you're doing, Lance."

"I do now, Jess. I do now. Please be careful tonight, and stay away from your car. Give the girls a great big hug for me."

Jessica was not fond of the idea of walking from the Hampton to the LaQuinta, a distance of several hundred yards. She pressed her right ear against the room door and listened. Sounds of chattering adults vibrated through the door, fading as they passed down the hallway. Several children thundered down the corridor, stealing a heartbeat or two from Jessica. She waited for silence, then reached for the door handle, pushing it down slowly. She touched a finger to her lips, giving Ginibeth the signal for absolute silence. Inching the door toward her, she pursed her lips and peeked out the narrow space.

Left.

Nobody.

Then right.

Nobody.

Spying a courtesy phone a few feet away, near the elevator, she motioned for Ginibeth to stay in the room. Just as she picked up the phone, the elevator doors opened. A man, a woman, and two children stepped out and walked past. Jessica stood as still as the wall, the phone tucked in her palms, against her robe. As the four passed, the man turned and stared. Jessica returned a slight smile of courtesy, placing the phone to her ear. She pressed '0' and requested the clerk send a cab to meet her at the building's eastside exit door in fifteen minutes. She was not going to wait until midnight.

The Ghosts of Benevolence

54

LANCE DROVE THROUGH THE night, the speedometer rarely exceeding fifty, plenty of time and space to put behind him before the climax of the day to come. At some point during the meandering drive, he stopped along a remote strip of wood-lined roadway and pulled Bama's body into the bed of the pickup. He covered the body with the same tarp used earlier by Bama to cover Lance.

He touched tenderly the wounds inflicted by Bama and marveled he had emerged the victor over so physical a foe. He peeled away strips and pieces of semi-dried blood, sticky, clinging, like tape. He spat on his hands and rubbed the saliva across his face. More blood came off. The pain of his cuts and bruised flesh amplified with each heartbeat, as if the spirit of Bama had invaded his bloodstream to continue the beating. Lance chuckled at having advised Horace Candler of his need to bathe and at Candler's clever retort regarding Lance's need for a cleansing. Indeed, the redemption had begun.

The drive was relaxed, despite the tumult of the events preceding it. Lance's arm hung out the window. He allowed the whims of the wind to flap his hand back and forth. The rush of cool air sailed through his hair. Lance laughed at the thought that his adversaries believed him dead. Death, indeed, exacted its own freedom.

"So, *this* is the afterlife," he observed, grinning.

His grin blossomed into a full-fledged smile as he watched power poles zip past, their thick wires curving downward and up, forming their own smiles. He began humming "Moonlight Serenade", a favorite of his mama's and Aunt Pearl's.

Nighttime stretches of featureless roads, for Lance little more than ribbons of reminiscence, once more took his mind adrift, back to the Benevolence that, like a mother clinging to her grownup son, held fast. As much as he had resisted the notion of going home, home had now tugged at him to stay. His memories anchored him to Benevolence, like permanent moorings in the harbors of his mind, tying him irresistibly to his soul.

Just as the monotony of the ride set in, Lance felt the shiver of bumps down his neck, as if fingertips were coursing lightly over the hairs, like a cold breeze on sweat. His was the only vehicle in the blackness for miles, and it contained a dead body, a fact sure to squirm under the skin of the firmest pragmatist. The chill turned to dread, an anxiety like one feels in the abyss of darkness, wondering if there might be a spider crawling up the bedspread.

True, he was free of the clutches of Bama and Earl Bentley Devereaux, the Third. But Lance was uneasy, a sense of paranoia enveloping him. Maybe it was the thought of Bama's body in the bed of the truck. Maybe it was the dead of night or the empty continuum of featureless geography. Maybe it was uncertainty of the pending confrontation with Barrett. Maybe it was a combination of all these things.

Or, maybe it was the guilt he felt having taken a life. Again. Ah, again, the taking of a life.

The Ghosts of Benevolence

The sign read: "Picnic area one mile". He needed a leg-stretch and one of Bama's bent cigarettes. He slowed the truck and pulled off the road to a picnic table. The memory of his mama's death again throttled his mind like the pounding of a rock concert. He got out of the truck and adjusted the tarp, careful not to get a view of the body. Lance stared at the starry night and lit the cigarette, sucking into his lungs its poison.

"Thought you'd given up those cancer sticks," a soft voice said.

"What?" Lance asked, startled. "Who's there?"

"Just me, my son."

Lance turned slowly, afraid and anxious to face his companion.

"It's your life, son, but those things *will* kill you. I miss you, yes, but there's no hurry, you know."

"Ma—*mama?*"

"Hi, Lance."

"But you're—you've been dead for … for—"

"I know, years."

"Are you a …"

"No time for such talk, Lance. Those answers will become clear enough in due time. There's something else I think you should know."

Lance looked around in disbelief, half-expecting one of Devereaux's cronies to complete the macabre surprise by slashing his throat.

"Lance, you've lived a lot of years wondering, believing, that you were responsible for my death. I thought that with time you might see the events more clearly or at least get beyond your sense of guilt."

"But I *did* kill you, mama. I remember those horses, *pasture* horses. I was *a teenager*, mama, strong enough to control their jumps. Only I didn't. The reins, they … I couldn't control *them* either. God knows I tried! God knows … why didn't I get some help from *God*, mama?

Was God mad at me for holding on so long to that Polaroid of the bombing?"

"You didn't kill me, Lance. Nobody killed me; it was an accident. But if you must assign guilt, look to *me*, not yourself and certainly not God."

"You?"

"I suggested your daddy put blinders on the horses, to calm them. But I didn't *insist* upon it, knowing those horses hadn't tasted a bridle in years. I told Peyton not to take the bullwhip, not to give it to you that day, not until he had finished it, but I didn't *insist* upon it. He was stubborn, your daddy. But he loved you, too, Lance. Just didn't know how to show it, I guess, not through words, anyway. He relied on the skills of his craftsmanship to do his talking, and, well, denying you the bullwhip, after you had discovered it, just didn't seem right to him. Losing Becca … then me … was too much for his shield of pride to withstand. He had his weaknesses, Lance. But he loved you."

"But all you wanted was time to finish the pickles. He could have given you that. Sweetgum Hollow would *always* be there."

"Times were hard back then, Lance. Any moment available to spend away from those times, like our times at the Hollow, was like gold in our pockets.

"You've conquered a lifetime of challenges in just a couple of days, Lance. Go home, make things right, and then move on. Other challenges await you, and you must be strong, for Gini's sake."

V-V-V-R-R-R-O-O-O-M-M-M-M

A pulpwood truck rushed past, shaking Lance, shaking the pickup, ripping up the tarp covering Bama. Lance covered his face and eyes from the storm of debris swirling all around him.

"And Jerri, too, right, Mama?" Lance asked, wiping dirt from his eyes.

The Ghosts of Benevolence

No answer.

"Mama?"

Lance opened his eyes. He saw nothing but darkness and heard only the waning drone of the pulpwood truck.

"Mama?"

The empty, opened eyes of Bama stared toward the stars. Lance quickly replaced the tarp and scrambled back into the truck, starting it and spinning his wheels out of the picnic area and onto the highway.

Dawn, at last, broke through the shield of Lance's memories. He rubbed his eyes like a schoolboy erasing a blackboard. Sunlight bled over the eastern horizon painting the wisps of cirrus clouds purple and pink.

Lance avoided the downtown connector through Atlanta, and with it the sludge of slow traffic. He had neither the time nor the patience to maneuver through the tangle of cars. He turned his gaze eastward and saw in the distance the neo-classic towers of a twenty-first century city silhouetted against the rising sun.

Let's see Sherman take that, he thought, thankful to be back near his neck of the unhurried woods.

A great place to visit, Lance surmised, watching the glimmer of glass and steel and the dash of a frenzied populace, but it could never be home, not in his post-Devereaux world. Too crowded, too congested, too sprawling, too fast. And Lance? Too old.

Lance lamented how the lure, the tentacles, the temptations of the big city had wrapped their sensual grip around small towns like Benevolence, rendering innocence as a refugee without a home.

Sara reminded him tonight in a moment of stillness that the loss of innocence, the loss of precious life, was not an end-all. Lance felt a wisp of peace for the first time in his adult life.

Mark Randolph Watters

The Ghosts of Benevolence

55

LANCE STEERED THE PICKUP onto a Waffle House parking lot a couple of miles from his office. Exhausted, he leaned back in the seat of the truck, sighed, and wiped sweat from his forehead. The constant presented by a Waffle House gave familiar comfort. Lance thought about a waffle and some scrambled eggs, bacon perhaps, the cravings of comfort food, but determined his stomach was in no condition to consume any rotgut that was not served from Belle's Diner, regardless of the restaurants' obvious similarities. Not now. Butterflies were slinging the mother of all break dances in the pit of his belly.

Besides, he thought with a laugh, *my luck, Horace Candler walks in and takes a seat at my booth!*

The chain of pending events replayed like an endless loop. Meet with authorities outside the building; interrupt the board meeting; give reasons for the interruption; produce Ruben's letter found in the heroin shipment; disclose the evidence of fraud and theft by Barrett and Carl; mention the church-bombing photograph and Earl Bentley Devereaux and his links to Barrett King; bask in the subsequent glory. Sounded simple enough. All that was missing was a laptop, PowerPoint, and some Krispy Kremes. Again, the curse of what-ifs surfaced.

What if Jess hadn't made it to the police? What if Barrett and/or Carl spot me before Jess and the police arrive? What if Barrett had, indeed, discovered the evidence stashed in his office cabinets?

9:50 a.m.

Time to go to work. He had the element of surprise.

Lance stroked the calluses on his hands but refrained from pulling off the dead skin. Even dead skin deserved another chance.

The Ghosts of Benevolence

56

"OUR BENCHMARKING STUDIES SHOW
clearly our reality in the twenty-first century world of
papermaking. Our mill, *this* mill, is a *high-cost-low-
producer* mill, not the opposite we *must* become, what our
competition *has* become."

Barrett barked his opening remarks to the Board of
Directors and senior corporate management.

"We can point the fingers of blame to several obvious
culprits—weak management; strong unions; and
ineffective, costly maintenance, to name a few.

"But blame is for losers and gets us nowhere. I want
us to focus today on our most important raw material and
the only reason we exist—*wood,* and its procurement."

Barrett enjoyed his bask in the limelight. Always had.
He knew he had the Board right where he wanted them,
like stroking the bellies of old lap dogs.

"As you are aware, the radius of our wood basket has
contracted, not expanded. For a paper mill reliant on virgin
pine timber—how's that for an understatement?—a

shrinking source of supply does not bode well for a vibrant future.

"Please direct your attention to the two graphics. The graphic on the left shows our reach of accessible pulpwood as of 1985. The coffers then were full, even expanding. Long-term wood supply was not an issue. The graphic on the right, however, depicts *today's* available supply and how that supply has trended downward over the past fifteen years. Not a pretty picture. Our Forest Group has done a remarkable job managing renewal timber on company-owned land. It's the leased land, the owned land, and other potential sources that have diminished at almost exponential rates. Gentlemen, we are *losing* control. The market is controlling us, not vice versa.

"Expansion of Atlanta and emerging metro areas and retirement communities in north Georgia along the I-75 and Georgia 400 corridors, as well as the rezoning of rural woodlands for residential and commercial use, have all but eliminated our ability to compete for these resources. Our rising cost of wood reflects that.

"In short, selling mere timber rights is *out of the question* for most landowners who can now command far more dollars per acre. Acquiring this land *outright* is simply too damn expensive for us. Would *you* sell to a paper mill a tract of land for twenty-five hundred per acre when developers will give you a hundred and fifty *thousand* per acre? Of course not.

"If this mill is to remain viable for *long-term* operations—and I'm sure you'll agree our recent capital outlay of four hundred and fifty million dollars commits our focus to the long-term—then I submit to you that the acquisition of timberlands outside our traditional radius, in addition to constructing remote chip mills to process this new capacity, is our *only* reasonable option.

"We *are capable* of competing with other paper companies for resources in an economically distraught

The Ghosts of Benevolence

South Georgia, despite our distance from those resources. The cost of freighting wood two hundred and fifty miles is more expensive certainly than our current freight costs. But there are means—competitive means—available to us, rail and truck, for cost-effective shipment of wood to this mill, whether is log form or chipped.

"The alternative—doing nothing—is far costlier, to the mill, to its employees, to the communities in which we live, and to our futures. In the final analysis, going after South Georgia pulpwood will not only ensure this mill can remain productive long-term, it will also severely strain our competition. Raw material cost and supply, gentlemen, is what we're about now.

"And, consider this. Perhaps by invading the raw material sources of our competitors, we will realize the serendipity of increasing their *already-growing* idle capacity, thus generating upward price movement for *our paper*. Think about it."

Barrett was on a roll. He scanned the room and saw the elders of management exchanging words of acumen, nodding, like the gods of Olympus. He had the board eating out of his hand.

"I propose we move ahead with the purchase of this twenty-five thousand acre tract of woodlands down in Sutter County, Georgia. The outlay of one hundred and twenty-five million dollars is well within our fifteen-year projections for wood cost and, given we will own this land and can manage it, we will more than meet our long-term need for wood procurement. Gentlemen, I say to you, carpe diem! *Seize the day!*"

Lance found a place to park the truck. He looked around for signs of Jessica and the police. He found none.

"God, where *are* they?"

Lance turned the rearview mirror and reviewed his damaged face, pushing down renegade twigs of his hair using his fingers and saliva.

"This is definitely a face for radio," Lance observed, caressing the knoll under his left eye and fiddling with loosened teeth.

Lance turned to look in the truck's bed, Bama's abode, and, after a moment of reflection, blurted, "You're a *deader* man than I am, Gunga Din!"

10:42.

Lance determined that he had better make his move now, despite the absence of police support, or lose the opportunity. *The Board must know of the fraud under their noses.* Lance believed he had been given a chance, divinely granted or not, to do something right in this world, something noble and unselfish for a change. He stepped out of the truck and tugged the tarp to make certain it held securely. Still no sign of Jessica. Disheveled and unshaven, he tucked in his shirttail as he approached the mill's Administration building.

Lance had no choice but to navigate his way past Carl's office to the conference room. Hopeful Carl had been invited to the meeting, he strolled with hands in pockets past Carl's open door.

"Lance!"

Lance stopped dead in his tracks.

"You're ... *alive*!" She looked him over. "My God, you're alive! Pummeled, but alive. Barrett said you'd—"

"Heather! No time to explain. Is Barrett in his meeting with the Board?"

"Yes. But—"

"Thanks. We'll talk later, over lunch."

"Salad Palace, I presume?"

"Where else?"

"How about Tombstone Steak House? They have salads there, too. *You* graze; *I'll* eat."

"Tombstone it is. We'll *both* eat. By the way ... you done good, kid!" Both smiled.

The Ghosts of Benevolence

Lance rounded the corner, colliding with a man exiting the men's washroom. The force of the impact scattered the man's armful of papers across the carpet. He uttered a few expletives and bent to retrieve the papers. Lance stooped to help.

"Lance?"

"Hello ... *Carl*," Lance replied, his heart skipping a beat or two.

"Lance ... you're ... you're *back*. I ... um ... *heard* you got the land for us. Great work, guy. Guess this means the promotion's *yours*!" Carl said, as he cleared his throat, unsure of what Lance knew but certainly not expecting him to be alive. The two men stared at each other for an eternal moment.

"I know *everything*, Carl," Lance revealed. "I know the game of collusion you and Barrett are playing. I know about the drug-running partnership you two have with Devereaux, and I know you and Barrett have absconded at least thirty million dollars of company funds and computer equipment, and the meter's running."

"Lance, what ... what are you *talking* about?" Carl asked, the attempt to feign obvious in his tone. "We ..."

"Save it, Carl. You and innocence clash like plaid and stripes."

Cornered, Carl asked, "What ... what are you going to do, Lance?"

"Do? Well, first I'm going to crash a certain Board meeting and introduce myself to some of top management. It's about time they knew just what a *damn good job* I do around here. Then I'm going to save this company from making a one hundred and twenty-five million dollar mistake.

"I know there's no way King and Devereaux are going to allow those twenty-five thousand acres of land to be clear-cut for pulpwood. Why, that would destroy their *canopy* of cover from air surveillance, crucial trees needed to avoid detection of certain ... *cash crops*. That's why Devereaux convinced the State's EPD of the existence of flatwood salamanders down there. How he managed to avoid a confirmation study, I'll never know. I suppose he's got some *highly-paid* friends in the Environmental Protection Division.

"The State's not going to allow SPIG to harvest timber—*any* timber—off land occupied by so much wetlands, flatwood salamander or not. This land deal is a one hundred and twenty-five million dollar boondoggle for the company and a windfall for you three, who, my guess is, have secured living arrangements offshore and out of sight.

"This was going to be your last hurrah before bailing. I always thought you were a little 'out there', Carl, but to stoop to this level? I mean, not even *I* was *this* greedy."

Carl shifted subtly between Lance and the conference room. Busy employees passed by, ignorant of the powder keg, its fuse sizzling.

"Tell you what, Lance," Carl said. "You can get in on this, too. I'll see you get five million dollars, cash, *right now*, if you'll walk away. Just take the money and *walk away*. You can quit your job and move your family anywhere you want. *Five million dollars*, Lance. Think of the life you can live with *that* kind of money. No more late nights at the office; no more thankless weekends crunching numbers. Well, Lance, what do you say to that? Good offer, eh?"

Lance rolled his eyes and gazed with a tilting smile on his face. He thought of the similar delaying tactic he'd used on Bama. His disdain for Carl surged in his soul like a belch of indigested pizza.

"You've got *five million cash* on you, Carl? Right *now?* Wow, *that* I'd like to see. Yesterday I might have taken your offer, Carl, but I've had some time to think about things, to think about my family, to think about *me*.

The Ghosts of Benevolence

Too many people, *innocent* people, have died to pave the way for the sort of greed you're offering me so casually. And if you bought me now, surely more would die, myself and my family included. A matter of time, Carl. Like you, your money's *no good*. Out of my way, Carl."

Lance stepped forward. Carl moved to block.

"I can't ... I can't *do* that, Lance," he whispered. "You *know* I can't do that. Take the money now, or—"

"Or ... *what*, Carl? Are you going to kill me *here*, and *really* blow your cover while your man, Barrett, is in the middle of the greatest con act of his career? After Barrett's dog-and-pony and the Board's final blessing, he will wire funds to temporary accounts you've set up. How am I doing so far, Carl? God knows what country the money'll end up in before you and Barrett are paid; maybe you've already *been* paid. I'm sure your plans are well-laid. You can't afford to drop the ball now, Carl.

"You're *this* close," Lance said, holding his two index fingers a half inch apart. "Too bad that's a *light year* away from success."

Lance shoved Carl aside and raced for the conference room. Carl ran to his office.

Mark Randolph Watters

The Ghosts of Benevolence

57

LANCE OPENED THE DOOR, interrupting Barrett's presentation in mid-slideshow. Heads turned.

"Somethin' we can … do for you?" one of the Board members asked.

"This man's a *fraud*!" Lance replied, pointing to King.

"What *is* this? Who *are* you?" shouted a bald man in a charcoal suit seated at the head of the oval mahogany table. Barrett stood aghast, wearing a slight smile of surprise, unable to speak.

"Mr. Aycock, my name is Lance Hawthorne. I work here—or rather *worked* here—under the dubious tutelage of Mr. Barrett King. I've labored long and hard under his acclaimed-but-mythical leadership—learned a lot, I must admit—and, well, I figured the time had come to demonstrate to you the fruits my focus and work have borne. Now, before you call security, hear me out."

"Who is this man, Barrett?"

"I don't … that is—"

"Sir, Barrett might have some difficulty answering your questions because, you see, Barrett believes I am *dead*. Meanwhile, maybe it's better that I first answer some questions about *Barrett*. Of course, you've not asked those questions yet, so let me help you.

"First question. Who has skimmed *thirty-plus million dollars* of company funds over the past ten years? Anyone care to guess? Give up? Your Barrett King, standing right *there*. Take a bow, Barrett. You can sign autographs later.

"Next question. Who was just *minutes away* from making off with *one hundred and twenty-five million* company dollars, and with *your* blessings? Again, Mr. King, stand up and let these fine people acknowledge you. Oh ... you're *already* standing.

"Third—and it's with hesitation, and a bit of fear, frankly, that I say the following—Earl Devereaux's land, these twenty-five thousand acres, is ground zero for a marijuana-growing and heroin-trafficking operation run by none other than ... Barrett King and Carl Forsch, the audit guy, whom I expect to join the party any minute. Barrett, give a wave of your divine hand; let the people see."

Everyone stared alternately at Lance and Barrett.

Barrett stood stone-like and whispered something inaudible, his voice sucked out of him by the shock.

"Oh, before I forget, Mr. Aycock, you'll want to read this," Lance said, pulling from his back pocket the note he found in the shipment of heroin from Billy Ruben to King. He tossed the folded document onto the table. "Darn thing speaks boldly for itself.

"You know, Barrett, *now* I understand something Devereaux told me during our meeting. He'd just finished sharing with me a little after-dinner ghost story about his mansion, formerly the old Wyndham place. Then he said something to this effect: 'amazing what an *underling* might do to his boss if ... pushed hard enough.' Pushed me too hard, Barrett."

"Lance!" shouted Jessica, breathing fast, one hand on the apex of her stomach bump. Two police officers, guns drawn, followed her.

The Ghosts of Benevolence

Lance exhaled at the sight and smiled. "Better late than never, babe."

"You—you're supposed to be—" Barrett said, catching up.

"Not quite as dead as you thought, am I, Barrett?" Lance interrupted. "Don't look so surprised. Stranger things have happened, you know. If cats can do it, why can't I?"

Lance leaned against the wall, full of confidence.

"Just think, Barrett, if you had given me a promotion *last* year, the one I *deserved*, you might have carried out your scheme to perfection, and a long time would have passed before anyone would have been the wiser. But, then, the converse of that pesky *Peter Principle* bit you in the butt, Barrett."

Peter Principle? King and members of the Board gazed at Lance as if he were delving into the inner workings of the second law of thermodynamics.

"You remember, Barrett, that great principle of business that says people are promoted to their level of incompetence. Well, seems the longer I was *not* promoted, Barrett, the more *competent* I became. Check the contents of the cabinets in your office for further confirmation."

At that moment, Carl shoved the door open with his fist, revealing a handgun, pointed at Lance.

Mark Randolph Watters

The Ghosts of Benevolence

58

AN OFFICER PULLED HIS weapon. Carl hooked Jessica with his forearm around her neck, jerking her as a shield to his chest, and fired his gun at the officer. The bullet smashed into the officer's skull above the right eyebrow, killing him. The second officer froze, his hand inches above his holstered weapon. Carl turned to face Lance standing a dozen feet away.

"Maybe you cheated death twice, Lance, but the third time won't be your charm. Barrett, I've already notified the bank with instructions to wire the money. It's done. *Sit down*, cop, unless you want to join your colleague and Hawthorne. Don't any of *you* bother to leave your seats.

"Now, Lance, this won't hurt a bit … or at least not long."

Carl raised his pistol to a point level with Lance's forehead. He placed his thumb on the pistol's hammer and pulled it back.

Cl-click.

Jessica squirmed with desperation but could not break Carl's grip. Directors twitched erect in their seats, bracing for the inevitable.

Mark Randolph Watters

"Lance! Lance, she's ... *coming!* She's coming *now!* Oh, God, *help* me. God, my baby's coming!"

"Jess!" Lance shouted. "Carl, for God's sake, man, put down the gun. What, man, you—you gonna kill us *all?* Look around you. How do you think you and Barrett are going to pull this off? My wife's having a *baby*, Carl. Put the gun down," Lance pleaded, conscious of the need for calm. "Put the gun—"

"*Shut up*, Hawthorne! I don't give a crap about you; you think I give a rip about your *wife,* even less for the unborn? Hell, she's young enough to be your *daughter.* Can't have much of a brain in her head to have married *you.* Barrett, let's *move!* She's our ticket out of here, and ... *what the* ... what the *hell!*"

Carl looked down, distracted by a stream of warm liquid flowing over his knees and shins. Jessica's amniotic sac had broken. His surprise caused him to release his hold on Jessica—just long enough to present a singular target. The window was now or never. A shot exploded.

Everyone hit the floor. Except Lance and Carl. Jessica ran to Lance's arms.

Carl looked down to his chest, his eyes fixed on the red blotch in the middle of his baby-blue tie and starched white shirt. Gasping, he touched his shirt and felt its stickiness as the spill of blood, crimson and warm, spread unstoppable. He looked up, breathless, eyes wide with shock. As he collapsed, his lungs expelling their last breath, he managed to squeeze the trigger on his raised pistol.

The bullet slammed into Jessica's upper chest, sending her sprawling to the floor.

"Jessica!" Lance screamed.

Carl crumpled to the floor, dead. Behind him rushed in three agents of the Drug Enforcement Agency and three police officers.

Lance bent over Jessica, conscious but pouring blood. "My God, *Jess!*"

The Ghosts of Benevolence

"Shhhh, Lance," Jessica said, gasping.

Lance ripped open Jessica's buttoned dress, desperate to undo this one terrible instant.

"I never ... noticed this until now, Lance," whispered Jessica, her trembling fingers clutching for, and missing, Lance's shirt.

"What, Jess?" Lance asked, keeping a conversational tone as he pressed his palm against the hole. "What haven't you ... you noticed until now?"

"How blue your eyes are."

"My eyes?" Lance asked, taking a towel someone handed him and pressing her wound. Jessica's eyes narrowed.

"Blue ... blue as cornflowers. Know what else?"

"What, my precious ... another towel, please. Somebody get the *damn paramedics*!"

"On their way, Lance."

"Take a 'u' and ... and place it between the two s's ... and you have ... 'Jesus'. Neat, hunh?"

Jessica's chest heaved.

"Hang in there, Jess. Help is coming!"

"Lance?"

Lance held her hand and lowered his head, turning his ear close to her mouth.

"Save the baby," she whispered. "Save Jerri."

Jessica Hawthorne issued her last breath, her eyes open, pupils dilated. Her lips seemed to curve into the slightest semblance of a smile, Lance accepting it as such. He caressed her forehead with his bloodied palm, pushing her hair from her face.

Paramedics performed a C-section, there on the floor of SPIG's conference room.

After several anxious minutes, Lance, Heather, and several others gathered in the conference room, heard the wails of a crying infant, just as they had fervently prayed they would hear.

Mark Randolph Watters

Lance took out his wallet, opened it and removed four cards he had stashed deep within one of its pockets several days earlier. Two aces, two eights. He stood over Carl's blood-soaked body.

"I think these belong to you, Forsch," he said, letting go. The cards scattered onto Carl's chest, the only card landing face up being the ace of spades.

Later that evening, at the hospital, a nurse approached Lance.

"Sir?" she asked. Lance, face in hands, did not look up. "The baby's doing just fine. What's the child's name, sir?"

"Je—," he started, pausing.

"Yes, sir?" the nurse asked again, pen poised to take it down.

"Jessi. Her name's Jessi."

"J-e-s-s-e?"

"J-e-s-s-*i*."

"Got it. Beautiful name, sir. Want to see her?"

59

THE PLANTATION BELONGING TO Earl Bentley Devereaux, the Third, sold a few years later under the oversight of the Federal government, commanding a portly three hundred million dollars at auction.

The working plantation became the last of such with antebellum roots in Sutter County. The mansion was converted to a bed and breakfast, and its acreage of woodlands and fields sculpted into grand walking gardens. Its vistas of fields and streams cowered to the whims and privilege of wealthy sportsmen.

Earl Bentley Deveraux, the Third was never found. Some speculated, per clues left by a paper trail, he made his escape to Central America, perhaps Brazil. He had ties everywhere. A Damocles flag and staff was found stabbed in the ground of the pecan grove behind the mansion, adjacent to the Wyndham burial. The flag remains. Some places just aren't meant to be disturbed.

Lance searched the Sutter County public archives and property tax records but found no mention of the one-armed old man, Horace Candler, whom Lance credited with providing him pivotal direction at a personal crossroads. No person admitted having heard of the man. Perhaps the

old man was a creation of Lance's tortured conscience.
Perhaps he was the embodiment of Aunt Pearl's spirit. For
Lance, Candler was real, and that's all that mattered.
Horace Candler was the beginning of Lance's exorcism, the
cure for his haunting.

The Ghosts of Benevolence

60

EIGHT YEARS HAD PASSED since Jessica's murder. During this period, Lance received a half-million dollar reward from Standard Paper Industries of Georgia and another hundred thousand dollars from the State of Georgia, both amounts donated to establish endowed scholarships in Jessica's name. Lance did not remarry, nor did he return to his position with SPIG, opting instead to work from home as a free-lance writer and on several book offers that had showered his way.

He raised Ginibeth and Jessi, homeschooling them, never missing a Sunday in church. The family lived well, without want, in Raventon, surrounded by friends and admirers.

Still, despite having cast aside his considerable burden for Sara's death, an orb of guilt he lugged upon the shoulders, like Atlas, he replaced it with a new sphere of guilt, that of Jessica's death. He could not shake the fact that, despite his best intentions, he had brought Jessica and Jessi into the crosshairs of harm's way, of Death's way.

One night, well past another sleepless midnight, Lance heard the sweet music of little-girl-giggling coming from Jessi's room. He went to investigate.

"Okay, sweetie," he said, a side of his smiling face pressed against her closed door, "getting late. Let's turn off the Nook. You have a multiplication test bright and early."

No reply. Believing the silence meant she had received the message, Lance returned to his writing. A few minutes later, he heard another sound of giggling, the pitch higher, more animated.

Frustration growing, he huffed down the hall and opened Jessi's door.

"Young lady, I thought I—"

"She says it's okay, Daddy," Jessi said, her elbows propped on her knees.

"What?" Thinking perhaps Jessi was dreaming, Lance approached her bed and sat. He kissed Jessi's forehead, gently pressing her cheek against his chest. "Who says *what's* okay, sweetie?"

Jessi lifted her head and stared straight into her daddy's eyes. "Mommy says. She said to tell Daddy to stop feeling guilty, that nothing's his fault." Jessi fidgeted with a plush toy stegosaurus. "So, I'm *telling* you."

Lance stared at Jessi, looking back at him with a smile touched by the glow of moonbeams filtered through the window blinds. Lance had never told Jessi the details of her Mom's murder.

"She said that, Daddy. She was right here, and she said that."

Lance sat silent, gazing deeper into his daughter's eyes.

"Don't you believe me?"

Lance took Jessi into his arms and hugged her.

"You *saw* her, sweetie? *Here?*"

"I did. She was beautiful, Daddy," Jessi observed, picking up a framed photograph of her mom. "Do I look like her?"

Lance embraced Jessi, gently kissing her forehead. "You *do*, my sweet girl. Just like her."

The Ghosts of Benevolence

Jessi smiled, hugging her daddy with all her strength. Lance wiped away a droplet nestled in the well of his eyelid.

"Daddy?"

"Yes, sweetheart?"

"Have you met our new neighbor?"

"Not yet. Saw him directing his movers as they unloaded the truck. Looks really old."

"Was he alone?"

"I think so. I talked to him today."

"Did you? Is he nice?"

"Seems to be. Kind of quiet, but he smiles a lot. He even offered me some fig preserves, on sourdough bread."

"That was nice of him. Did you eat—"

Lance froze.

"Did you say ... *fig* preserves, sourdough—"

"I wasn't hungry, but I thanked him. Bread smelled *good*. I saw the smoke rising."

"*Steam* rising. Did he ... did he tell you his name, sweetie?"

"Something like ... Simone, Persimmon, something like that." Jessi cuddled her steggie. "I'm sleepy, Daddy."

Lance's gaze turned from Jessi to the window blinds. A harmless coincidence or another ghost of Benevolence?

"Daddy?"

"Yes, precious?"

"She was here, talking to me. Sat right here, beside me." Jessi pointed to the slight depression in the blanket. "You *do* believe me, don't you? That she was here."

Lance looked straight into Jessi's eyes.

"I believe you, sweetie," he said, hugging her, his eyes upon the window blinds, his mind on their new neighbor. "Indeed, I *do* believe."

Mark Randolph Watters